I0675522

# Little Girl Lost

Jane Blythe

Copyright © 2015 Jane Blythe

All rights reserved.

No part of this publication may be reproduced, transmitted, downloaded, distributed, reverse engineered or stored in or introduced into any information storage and retrieval system, in any form or by any means, including photocopying and recording, whether electronic or mechanical, now known or hereinafter invented without permission in writing from the publisher.

All characters and events in this publication, other than those clearly in the public domain, are fictitious and any resemblance to real persons, living or dead, is purely coincidental.

Bear Spots Publications
Melbourne Australia

bearspotspublications@gmail.com

ISBN: 0992418046
ISBN-13: 978-0-9924180-4-5

Cover designed by QDesigns

*Also by Jane Blythe*

Detective Parker Bell Series

A SECRET TO THE GRAVE
WINTER WONDERLAND
DEAD OR ALIVE

# SEPTEMBER 4<sup>TH</sup>

2:11 P.M.

The room was small, dark and dirty.

Windowless too, Cassandra Stanton thought dismally as she stared at the rough concrete wall. If only she could see the sky, then everything would be better. She and Olivia had loved lying on their backs on the warm, sweet-smelling grass, and gazing up at the clouds sailing effortlessly across the huge expanse of summer sky, they would take turns finding shapes in the soft, fluffy wisps.

It had been the middle of August when he had taken them, she didn't know what the date was now. It seemed like they had been holed up in this horrible place forever. By now the weather must be getting colder, although it was always unpleasantly hot down here. The sky would be slowly turning a lighter, watery blue, which would soon melt into grey, the endless grey of winter.

Across the tiny cell, Olivia moaned in her sleep and Cassandra went to her, dropping to the floor to sit cross-legged beside her sleeping sister. Despite the fact that there was only fourteen months between the girls, Cassie had always relished the role of big sister. She looked out for Olivia, took the blame when they got in trouble, and bossed her around like crazy.

Everyone said the two girls looked like identical copies of one another, and smaller versions of their mother. All three had thick, shiny auburn hair, hazel eyes, white skin that always burnt in the summer, and a smattering of freckles across their nose.

Reaching out to her baby sister, she was taken aback by the grimy, tear-streaked face, the matted stringy hair, the skin that seemed to have melted into the bone. Olivia had lost so much weight. Both girls were tall for their age, once again taking after their mother, and fit from hours of playing sports, basketball for Olivia, tennis for Cassie. Now after days, weeks, maybe months of next to nothing to eat her sister looked like a skeleton.

Cassie knew that she looked no better.

Gently tracing the scar on Olivia's cheek, an injury from a day long ago where she had dared her sister to see who could climb the highest in the old oak tree outside their bedroom window. It was a competition that Cassie had been sure she would win, but Olivia had put up a fight, following her from limb to limb, never giving up, willing to do anything to prove that she could be just like the big sister she idolized. At eight, it had been the first time Cassie had realized just what a responsibility it was to be a big sister. The thought had scared her at first, but over time she had come to relish the opportunity to help guide her sister, had worked hard to be a good example, and now . . . now . . . now she was letting Olivia down.

Withdrawing her hand, she accidentally bumped her sister's shoulder. Olivia's eyes snapped open, her head whipped up.

"Shh," Cassie whispered, stroking Olivia's dirty hair, "it's only me. I didn't mean to wake you."

Slowly Olivia's ragged breaths became more even and she gave Cassie a thin smile. "I was dreaming."

"Yeah?" Cassie returned her sister's smile with the brightest one she could muster. "What about?"

"We were flying," Olivia's face was faraway, stuck firmly in the only place left where there was any joy. "Really flying, Cass, not in a plane but just soaring through the sky. And the sun was rising, the whole world was pink and gold," a genuine smile lighting her face, the first since that fateful afternoon when they had been taken.

Sunsets and sunrises had fascinated Olivia since she was a toddler. They used to wake early on summer vacations, sneak outside and watch as the sun slowly rose over the world. The sky would turn whiter and whiter, then slowly it would turn pink, the pink would deepen to red then all of a sudden the sun would be there and the whole sky would be flaming with the light from the big golden ball.

Tears pricking at the back of her eyes Cassie stood quickly, with her back to her sister, she couldn't let Olivia see her cry. She was supposed to be the big one, the strong one, she was supposed to be the one to come up with a way out of here.

"We're never going home are we?" Olivia asked suddenly.

Turning to look her sister in the eye, she owed her that much, the utter hopelessness she saw there scared her more than anything else, and her tears began to fall.

\* \* \* \* \*

3:26 P.M.

"What are you doing?" Parker Bell laughed, keeping one eye on the road as he turned to look at her.

Shrugging, "I hate music, you only put the radio on to bother me," Tessa shot back, forcing her lips to curve into smile but knowing it wouldn't make it to her eyes.

"How can you drive without music?" he asked, golden caramel colored eyes wide in mock-surprise. "And how on earth is it possible to hate music?"

Once again she shrugged, absently this time, her eyes leaving his to resume her study of the deserted country road, really more of a dirt track, twisting her thin hands together tightly in her lap. They were deep in the woods, usually Tessa loved being surrounded by tall trees, the wind whispering softly, birds chattering, but today she was on edge. It was too quiet, too deserted, anyone could be lurking around out there, watching unseen from the shadows.

Growing serious, "there's no one out there, Tess," Parker said softly. Reaching out a hand to clasp hers and gently releasing the death grip she held them in, murmuring, "you'll dislocate them."

Tessa said nothing, keeping her face turned to the window so that her husband couldn't see the tears that threatened to spill down her cheeks and biting her lip to keep from crying. Unwanted memories and fears, over fifteen years invested in keeping them carefully buried, brought back by Lachlan Mountain Junior and aggravated by her birthday four days ago. Not just her birthday but Ellie's too.

Usually on Ellie's birthday, she visited her grave, not the memorial plaque in the local cemetery, but the place where Ellie's body had been hastily buried after her murder. She alone knew the location of this place. This year however she hadn't made it there, hadn't been able to face it on her own, but neither had she been able to face telling anyone, even Parker, where Ellie's body was buried.

Besides Parker had insisted that the two of them take this trip together, to celebrate her birthday he'd said. She had begged and pleaded with Parker to postpone the holiday for a few weeks, but he had insisted. In the end Tessa had given in because revealing the reason why she did not want to go away at this particular time of year would invite a truckload of questions from her police detective husband whose answers she was not prepared to give. Not now, not ever.

"Tessa?" she blinked as Parker shook her gently.

"What?" Obviously she had missed whatever he had been saying to her.

"You okay?" he was watching her closely, brow creased with concern. After everything that had happened Parker had a tendency to treat her like a china doll, as though she might break into a million pieces if he said or did the wrong thing.

"I'm fine. What did you say?" she offered as bright a smile as she could muster.

Tugging on one of her white-blonde ringlets, "it's okay to be scared, Tessa. After what he did to us you're entitled to . . ."

"I'm fine," she interrupted, turning to give him a firm smile, a smile that told him this line of questioning was closed.

"Tess . . ." he began again.

"Parker," she warned, "I told you, I am fine, end of conversation," and with that she pulled her hands away and turned to stare silently out the car window.

"Talk to me, Tessa," he pushed gently. Endearingly undeterred by her constant refusals to talk about the events that had almost led to his death three months earlier.

A twinge of guilt poked at her. Parker had been very patient with her the last few months, ever since their encounter with Lachlan Mountain. Been patient with her when she couldn't stand to be on her own. When she'd moved out of their house because she couldn't face being there anymore. When she couldn't bear to leave the mansion where they were now living because she was too scared to go outside.

Sighing, she spoke quickly, letting the words tumble out before she lost her nerve, "Ellie's birthday."

A little confused, "what?"

"Ellie and I had the same birthday," she explained.

Shock and dismay mingling together on his face. "Tessa, I'm sorry. Why didn't you tell me?"

"You would have asked questions I didn't want to answer, and . . ." her voice trailed off as she once again studied their surroundings, looking for any signs that someone was following them.

"And . . ." Parker prodded gently.

Reluctantly, "and I keep expecting him to pop up. He always leaves me something on Ellie's birthday."

Fear flashed across Parker's face and she knew he was remembering the night he had rushed inside her burning cottage and saved her life. At the time he had assumed that the attempt on her life was related to the serial killer who was stalking her. However he now understood that the fire was related to Ellie's murder, and lived in constant fear that this person would come back and finish the job he started.

This was the *him* that she was referring to.

"If he comes back . . ." Parker began fiercely, eyes flashing with panic and anger. "I won't let him hurt you again."

Offering a weak smile, she reached out and smoothed his thick black hair, "I know, but I'm not afraid of him."

Amber eyes studying her, Parker couldn't understand why she wouldn't just tell him who it was that made the attempt on her life so he could just arrest the guy and it would all be over. She understood why he thought that way, he was a cop, but things were not as simple as Parker wanted them to be.

Lapsing once again into silence, each lost in their own thoughts, then Parker announced cheerfully, determined to lift her spirits, "almost there. You are not going to believe this place," he beamed, "it's magical. Mattie and I absolutely loved coming here when we were kids."

"I'm sorry, Parker, I know you were only trying to help," she whispered, stretching over to let her fingertips brush lightly across his cheek. She knew that while lately she had been clinging to him physically she had been pushing him away emotionally. "I'm sorry I've been such a mess lately, I'm sorry I've been pulling away from you, but I'm so scared, I can't lose you . . ."

"Shh, it's alright. I'm not going anywhere," he said softly, catching her fingers and bringing them to his lips to press a gentle kiss.

He'd said those words to her at least a thousand times in the last three months, a thousand more in the two years they had known each other. "Every time I think of you lying in that hospital bed I just get so scared, but I'm not being fair to you, you were the one who was abducted, who almost died . . ."

"Hey, hey," he soothed, stroking her forehead. "After

everything you've been through, after everything Lachlan did to *you*, you're entitled to be scared, we both are, but all I want, all I need is you."

Staring into one another's eyes everything else seemed to fade away . . .

Catching a glimpse of something in her peripheral vision, "Parker, look out."

A deer stood in the middle of the road, just a couple of yards in front of them. Parker swerved wildly but the tyres were unable to find traction in the dirt and rocks, and the car went spinning out of control heading straight towards a steep decline, crashing into one tree after another.

Someone was screaming. Tessa wasn't sure whether it was herself or Parker.

Parker was stomping on the breaks, trying desperately to slow their careening path through the thick forest but the car picked up speed as it went, seemingly undaunted by the trees it bounced off on it's way down.

Thrown about inside the car as it flew down the hill, kept in place only by her seatbelt. Fire shot through her body as it was slammed against the side of the car. Their descent seemed to move in slow motion, it felt like they had been rolling forever, though it couldn't have been more than a couple of seconds.

On and on and on . . .

Then it stopped.

Neck snapping with the sudden halt.

Head pounding.

Then nothing.

\* \* \* \* \*

3:31 P.M.

Alone. Tired. Scared.

Clara Meyers wanted to give up.

Almost did.

But then she decided there was nothing else to do but keep on walking.

Someone would find her eventually. They had to. Right? But she'd been walking forever and hadn't seen a single living soul.

Surely she'd meet someone if she just kept going.

"This is hopeless," she said aloud to break the oppressive stillness. No map, no directions, no idea of where she was or where she was going. "I may as well be walking in circles."

Exhausted, Clara stopped and leaned against a huge, round tree trunk. Sinking to the ground, she scratched absently at the blood drops on her bare arms, dismayed to see that it splattered the front of her long white nightgown. The same thing she had been wearing when the man had taken her many months ago.

She wasn't sure how long she'd been kept in that awful house but so many girls had come and gone that Clara was sure it had been at least a couple of months. Maybe longer.

Maybe she'd been gone so long that her parents had stopped looking for her.

Maybe they'd gotten too caught up in their impending divorce to think about her. The last few weeks before she'd been taken had been awful. The screaming fights, her father leaving, the insults and threats they made to one another each time her dad came to pick her up.

Tears threatening, Clara blinked them back determinedly and pushed to her feet. Her parents would never give up on her she was sure of that, however much they hated each other right now they both still loved her. And after everything that she had gone through to escape she was not going to rest until she got safely back home.

Taking a deep breath, Clara resumed walking.

* * * * *

3:42 P.M.

Ringing.

Something was ringing.

At first he thought it was a phone.

Why doesn't someone answer it he thought dismally.

Slowly he realized that it wasn't a phone that was ringing but his head.

Blinking open eyes that felt as though they were weighed down with rocks, Parker moaned as the sudden light shot straight through his head like a flaming arrow.

Confused at first, he couldn't remember where he was or what had happened. Then it all came back in a rush, the deer, losing control of the car, the mad descent down the hill, the crash.

"Tess?" he called hopefully, part of his still numb brain reminding him that if Tessa was conscious she would have said something by now.

Gingerly moving each part of his body, starting with his toes and working his way up. Every minuscule movement sent fresh waves of pain coursing through his limbs. Hand moving to touch the epicenter of pain in his head, his fingers coming away sticky with blood. Completing his self-examination Parker decided the wound to his head was only superficial, and that he wasn't seriously injured. Ignoring the pounding in his head, he forced his eyes back open to turn his attention to Tessa.

His wife was slumped in her seat, held in place only by her seatbelt. Her skin was deathly pale and blood streaked the side of her face. His heart stopped, she looked . . . he couldn't say the word, instead he stretched a trembling hand towards Tessa and pressed his fingertips to her neck.

Dizzy with relief as he felt her pulse fluttering weakly beneath his fingers. She was alive, although by the looks of things she was in bad shape.

"Honey, can you hear me?" he called.

Expecting no answer and getting none.

"Hang on, baby," he murmured, stroking her cheek. "I'll get us out of here."

Struggling to unbuckle his seatbelt when he realized that the car was swaying backwards and forwards like a swing in the breeze. Peering out past the cracked front windscreen, at first he couldn't believe what his eyes were seeing. In front of the car was nothing. Just empty air. The car was teetering on the edge of a cliff, balanced precariously against a huge, gnarled old tree.

Managing to cling to calm by planning his next move in his head to keep focused. Getting himself and Tessa out was his number one priority. Next he needed to call for help, feeling in his jeans pocket for his cell phone, wiggling it out he saw it had been crushed in the crash and no longer turned on, it was useless, hopefully Tessa's phone had fared better.

Painfully aware that any movement could send the car, Tessa and himself tumbling down to the rocky bottom of the cliff, Parker carefully pushed against the car door. Easing the door open he cautiously climbed from the swaying car. From the outside he could see that the SUV had been crushed and twisted beyond recognition. Its front wheels were hanging over the edge, the one on the passenger side caught in the roots of the tree, the other resting on nothing at all.

Against his better judgment, Parker made his way tentatively to the edge of the cliff, leaning over to peer down the sheer drop. Rocky ledges jutted out sporadically, the odd spindly tree that had attempted to take root on the near vertical slope stood out amongst the rocks and tufts of dead grass.

Crossing to the rear of the dented and half mangled car, Parker yanked open the back and pulled out his first aid kit, the picnic dinner he'd packed, some bottled water and a blanket. Dropping the things a short distance from the teetering car, Parker's stomach dropped as a gust of wind left the vehicle wobbling precariously. The sky that had been a clear, bright blue when they set out was now thick with angry grey clouds. A storm was brewing. Another squall of wind barreled the car, sending it's nose tipping dangerously down towards the fifty-foot drop.

He had to get Tessa out now.

Falling to his knees beside the passenger side door, which had been wedged shut by the impact with the tree, what he saw both appalled him and filled him with dread. The collision had caused one of the branches to pierce a hole through the twisted metal door, it's end wedged firmly into Tessa's thigh.

The window, designed to crack but not break, was partly open, but not far enough for him to reach inside. Searching the ground at his feet, looking for something, anything, to use to smash the glass . . .

"Parker?"

The voice was so faint at first he wasn't sure it was anything more than the whispering of the trees.

"Parker?" she mumbled again.

"Tessa, honey, I'm right here." Hands pressed against the broken glass, aching with the need to take his wife in his arms and hold her, stroke her, touch her.

"I hurt," her voice slurring.

"I know, baby, hang on, I'm coming." Parker picked up a short stick, but paused, worried that the impact would shower his wife with shattered glass shards. "Cover your face, Tess," he commanded gently.

She made a feeble attempt to lift her arm but didn't have enough strength and it dropped limply back to her side.

Carefully as he could, Parker struck the window again and again until he was able to knock out the remaining slivers with his hand. Leaning carefully inside, trying not to add his weight to the already top heavy car, he took Tessa's face in his hands, angling it towards him. "Tess, look at me." She didn't move. "Tess, sweetheart, I need you to open your eyes for me." When she still didn't answer he shook her gently, "Tessa, can you hear me?"

"Mmm," she moaned softly.

"Tessa," panic making his voice sharper than he intended. "Open your eyes now," he ordered.

Blinking open eyes that were dazed with pain, she struggled to focus on him. "What happened?"

Frowning slightly, post-traumatic amnesia was a potential sign of a concussion. "We crashed the car, you don't remember?"

Eyes sliding closed, Tessa shook her head.

"Tess, I need you to stay with me, okay? Come on, honey."

Forcing her eyes back open she focused with difficulty, her pupils dilated.

Smiling encouragingly, "where do you hurt?"

"Everywhere," she whispered.

Tessa's breathing was heavy and strained as though each intake of air sent pain rippling through her body. Most likely she'd cracked some ribs, hopefully she hadn't broken any. A broken rib could puncture a lung and he couldn't deal with a punctured lung out here with no medical equipment.

"What about your neck?"

Considering this for a moment, "it's okay."

"Can you wiggle your fingers and toes?"

Tentatively she moved them and nodded.

Thankfully, so far Tessa had been too woozy to notice the blood that streaked her face and clothes. Tessa was terrified of blood, the sight of it was likely to send her tripping over the edge and right now he needed her as calm as possible.

"My head hurts," she groaned weakly, eyes fighting to remain open.

"Come on, Tess, stay with me just a little while longer," he encouraged, forcing a smile to his lips. "It's alright, baby," he soothed. Eyes straying down to the tree limb protruding from her leg, her glazed eyes followed his, growing wide and panicked as she saw what he was looking at.

Breath coming in painful gasps, her whole body trembling. "Get it out, Parker," she shrieked, hands reaching to pull at the branch that pierced her flesh.

Catching them before she had a chance to yank it out, they both froze as the SUV swayed. Tessa's eyes darted to glance out the window, then back to his, understanding dawned.

"I have to pull it out," he told her, tracing his thumbs along her cheekbones hoping to calm her a little.

"It'll bleed," she whimpered.

"I know, baby, but if I don't then this car is going to go over the edge with you in it," his heart beating so loudly he was surprised she couldn't hear it.

"How deep does it go?" her voice wobbling.

"I don't know," he answered honestly.

"To the bone?"

Battling against his own panic, if the end of the branch had reached the bone then Tessa was at a high risk of infection. Choking the words out past the lump in his throat, "maybe."

Her eyes fluttered closed and Parker thought she had passed out once more. Almost wished she had since it would make things so much easier, but then she whispered, "do it."

Hesitating, almost unable to bring himself to pull it out, to inflict pain on the woman he loved.

"Parker," Tessa's trembling hand ran softly through his hair, tears spilling silently down her cheeks. "I know it's going to hurt, just do it."

Clutching at straws, "where's your cell phone? I can call for help, wait for the paramedics," he was rambling and he knew it, putting off doing what had to be done for as long as possible.

The SUV lurched again, front tipping further forward so that the car was almost vertical.

Tessa's eyes bored into his, begging him to save her.

Without a second thought he braced one hand on Tessa's leg, the other gripped the branch. Tessa clenched her eyes closed, and he looked away, unable to look at her face. Taking a deep breath, he clenched his own eyes shut and counted to three.

One, two, three pull.

He almost wished that she had screamed in agony, the pitiful whimper she gave made him feel physically ill.

Forcing open the door, he crushed Tessa against his chest, wrapping his arms tightly around her and clinging to her as though she might disappear at any second. She lay slumped against him, breathing ragged, unmoving, her energy spent.

Reluctantly pulling away, Parker eased Tessa back against the seat, she didn't so much as flinch. Checking the wound on her thigh he saw that it was bleeding profusely, but there was no time to retrieve his first aid kit and dress it, right now he had to get her out. Undoing her seatbelt, he held her in place with one hand while he reached with the other to grab her purple leather bag. Then easing an arm under her knees, his other behind her back, he slowly and carefully maneuvered her out of the car. When he had her clear he swung her quickly up into his arms, ignoring with an effort her small moan of pain, and ran a safe distance from the SUV before dropping to his knees.

Gently laying Tessa down on the ground, he was pulling out a thick bandage when he heard a loud crack behind him. Turning just in time to see the car, and the tree that had been holding it in place, plummet from view.

A second crack sliced through the air as a bolt of lightening lit up the sky. Thunder rumbled in the distance and the heavens opened sending a torrent of rain pounding down.

* * * * *

3:45 P.M.

"She's gone."

Irritated, letting out a small puff of air and rolling his eyes, he'd been looking forward to a quiet afternoon. Settled in his den, book in hand, glass of wine on the table beside him, an array of delicious pastries prepared by his personal chef awaiting consumption. It wasn't often that he planned for some down time, and inevitably whenever he did take some time for himself something went wrong.

Looking up at the man with open loathing. "Who?"

Agitated he flexed his hands, "one of the girls."

John Doe sighed long-sufferingly and made no attempt to hide his displeasure.

John Doe. That was who he was, who he had become anyway. It was what everybody called him. He was the man with no name. There was only one person on the face of the planet who knew his real name. Of course, those from his past knew who he was, he had just been gone so long they didn't know that he still existed. His previous life was nothing but a distant blur, as though he were looking at it through a thick fog.

To look at John Doe he was unexceptional, of average height, thinning chestnut hair that was streaked with silver, crinkly laugh lines around bright brown eyes. Reasonably fit for his age, he was in his early sixties, but starting to go a little doughy in the middle. He looked, so he'd been told, like an English gentleman, and many a person had underestimated his ability to defend himself, to their own detriment of course. He was a black belt in karate, trained in hand-to-hand combat, and a near perfect shot.

Some would say that he was a powerful man, and he supposed that was true. He was rich, a mixture of old money, new money, and dirty money. Yet he knew all too well that power was subjective, he held the lives of others in the palm of his hand, yet the one thing he wanted he could never have.

Eyeing the man in front of him, his second in command, Dino Rollino, he felt a wave of hatred towards him, for everything he represented. Dino was short, only five foot seven, with a smooth shiny head, not shaved but naturally bald. Too large muscles

15

bulged beneath his tight-fitting black t-shirt, compensation for his short stature, and tattoos criss-crossed his arm. He was repulsive John Doe thought, but a necessary evil in his business. "Which one?" he enquired wearily, it had been a long day.

"The quiet one . . . with the black hair," Dino added, noting his boss' blank expression.

Taking a moment to place the girl, flipping through his mind's catalogue, finally settling on the correct face. "Clara Meyers."

Dino nodded, "what do you want me to do?"

Disbelief at Dino's stupidity, he wondered how someone who had been involved in this business for as long as he had could have no common sense. Dino had grown up in this line of work, unlike himself who became involved not because he wanted to but because he had to. There had never been a choice. He had turned his back on his life; on everyone he had ever known because this was his only option.

Leveling Dino Rollino with a frosty glare, "find her."

\* \* \* \* \*

3:48 P.M.

"You still with me?"

Parker's insistent voice cut through the fog that was threatening to engulf her once again. It kept pulsing up and down, ebbing at her like waves on the beach, creeping up at your toes then receding, only to come back again moments later. The backwards and forwardsing made her feel nauseous.

"Tessa? You still with me?" he repeated patiently, but even in her dazed state she could hear the fear creeping into his voice.

"Yeah," it was all she could manage, given the circumstances.

"Stay with me, okay?" Repeating when she didn't answer, "okay?"

"Okay," she returned softly, closing her eyes.

Rain was drumming down outside, thunder purred in the distance like a contented cat, she was wet and cold and numb. After the storm started Parker had gathered her into his arms and searched for a dry place to wait for help. Finding a small alcove in the rocks he had settled them inside. He'd stripped off her soaking wet clothes, jeans and a lavender colored light woolen sweater, both of which had been streaked with blood, and wrapped her in a blanket that he had somehow managed to keep mostly dry.

Now he knelt beside her, cleaning and dressing the deep wound in her thigh.

She hardly felt it though. It was like she had been anaesthetized. All that was left was a dull, distant throbbing that crept up and down her body.

A whiteness was washing over her, not blackness like in other times when she had passed out, but a soft, velvety white. Like being wrapped in a big, fluffy cloud. It was comforting and warm and . . .

"Tessa," voice sharp, hand slapping lightly at her face.

Forcing her eyes back open, because she knew that was what Parker wanted, to meet terrified amber eyes staring down at her, they softened when he saw her awake.

Cupping her face in his hands, "hey, you passed out on me again. I need you to stay awake, I think you have a concussion. Tell me if anything hurts," he instructed, his hands started methodically making their way over every inch of her body, checking for other injuries. Each touch sent fresh waves of pain radiating throughout every inch of her battered body but when Parker's hands reached her stomach, she shrunk away as a flame of fire exploded inside her.

Parker stopped, peering down at her, face creased with worry, "it hurts there?"

Nodding, eyes clenched shut against the pain, she tried to breathe through it but that only worsened the pressure in her chest. After a moment, Parker resumed his quest, finding nothing else that sent shock waves, just dull beads of pain.

Focusing her gooey mind with difficulty, "did you call yet?"

"No," letting go of her he reached for her bag, "I wanted to patch you up first," he gave her one of his goofy grins, albeit a half-hearted one and she smiled back just as half-heartedly. Rifling through her bag he found her phone and pulled it out, squeezing her hand, "I'll be right back."

Moving a short distance away, deeper into the small cave to block out as much of the storm's noise as he could, he dialed.

"Wyatt? It's Parker. Hey, can you hear me? You're breaking up . . ."

Tessa tuned out his voice and tried to take a breath that didn't make it feel as though a rock was pressing down on her chest. Since Parker had broken the stillness that washed over her earlier the pounding in her head had come back with a vengeance. Lifting a hand to press to the wound when another hand wrapped itself tightly around her wrist stopping her before she could find the source of the pain.

"Don't."

Blinking, Parker's face came into view. His worried face.

"Is Skylar coming?" Tessa allowed a moment of hope to flood through her but it was quickly dampened when she saw the look in her husband's eyes.

"I don't know."

Confused, "what do you mean you don't know?"

Wiping at her head with a damp cloth he'd gotten from somewhere, cleaning away the blood. "It was a bad connection, I don't know if he heard me. I tried dialing again but got no reception." Parker's tone was short, clipped, she could see him planning his next move in his head. "If there's no one here by morning, we'll make our way back to the road."

"We?" she echoed, eyes drifting to her injured leg, then wishing they hadn't as she saw the bright red blood staining the white bandage.

Parker took her face in his hands and made her look at him, "I'll carry you," jaw set determinedly.

Overwhelming tiredness washing over her in waves, no longer gentle ripples but roaring tidal waves. "It's too far," voice fading even to her own ears.

"Now is not the time to be stubborn."

She flinched at the anger that seemed to reverberate through the claustrophobic space.

Face softening instantly, Parker pulled her towards him. "You're shaking," he whispered, keeping one arm around her as he wrapped the blanket tighter, settling her against his chest. "Talk to me," he murmured against her hair.

"About what?"

"Anything," he pressed her head against his shoulder and stroked her hair.

Mind searching for something to talk about, Tessa knew Parker wanted to keep her talking to keep her awake. The only thing she could settle on was Ellie. Not the way she had been the last time they had been together but the way she was the day they met.

Beginning at the beginning, "it was my first day of school, the first time I met her . . ."

"Met who?"

"Ellie."

"Tessa," Parker warned, pulling her back so he could see her properly.

Tessa knew that he was worried that talking about her murdered friend would upset her. Well not just upset her but send her plunging over the edge, upon which she had been teetering precariously for months now, into a full-blown emotional breakdown. Usually she never talked about Ellie, didn't even like to think about her old friend because it filled her with a horrible sickening guilt. But right now she thought that nothing could make this day any worse.

Ignoring Parker's fears, and her own, she continued haltingly, the memory as vivid as though she were reliving the events at this very second. "I wandered off . . . I was bored, the teacher was talking about learning to write our names . . . I already knew how to write and read . . ." she had an IQ of 178 and had begun reading as a toddler.

Aware as she spoke of Parker's hands rubbing her arms and back, trying to keep her warm, but she was only vaguely aware that she was shaking.

Resuming her story, "I snuck outside . . . found a nest that had been abandoned . . . there were three eggs inside . . . they were so small . . . I was trying to think up a way to keep them warm . . . so they wouldn't die, when suddenly she was there . . ."

"Tessa, maybe we should talk about something else," Parker interrupted, wiping away tears she hadn't known were falling.

She hardly heard him, "a teacher found us out there. Asked why we weren't in class . . . he was angry . . . he yelled at us . . . I tried to explain but he wouldn't listen and I kept wondering why Ellie didn't just tell him that she was just going to the bathroom and happened to find me . . . he gave us time out at lunch time . . . even then Ellie never said anything . . . we did the punishment together and after that we were friends forever."

For a long moment neither of them spoke, then Parker asked quietly, "what happened to them? The eggs?"

"They hatched." Suddenly she didn't want to think about this anymore, she just wanted to sleep.

"Did you keep them?"

Shaking her head dully, "I tried to look after them but they wouldn't eat, I tried everything, but they died. I should have known then . . . it was an omen . . . they were the first thing I ever loved that died . . . I was only five . . ."

And then she was sobbing, huge wracking sobs that sent bolts of fire shooting through her aching body. Parker was holding her, trying to calm her down, but she couldn't hear what he was saying, the pounding in her ears drowned out everything else. She couldn't breathe, she was going to die, right here in this cave, in the middle of no-where, and right now she welcomed death.

* * * * *

4:01 P.M.

"Tessa, baby, calm down," Parker laid her gently down on the cold dirt floor, cradling her head in his palm. "Come on, sweetheart, breathe, breathe for me, honey." He'd known that talking about Eleanor was a bad idea, he should have stopped her right away, before it came to this.

Slowly her sobs eased to a trickle. Her breathing sharp, shallow gasps, face paler than pale, the purple bruise on her forehead standing out in stark contrast, her eyes clouded with pain and shock. It grew quiet inside their small cave, the storm outside had eased, the thunder and lightening were gone as quickly as they'd come, nothing but a light mist remained.

Stroking Tessa's hair back from her face. "Shh," he soothed. "Everything's going to be okay."

She opened her mouth to speak but he jumped in before she could, "don't try to talk, just rest, concentrate on your breathing."

Tessa was still shivering, and he was worried that she might be in shock, possibly hypovolemic shock from loss of blood, the deep wound to her leg was still oozing blood, seeping through the thick bandage he'd wrapped around it. He was also concerned about internal bleeding, a blue and black line crossed her abdomen from the seatbelt. He thought it was just bruised but he couldn't be sure that she hadn't ruptured something.

Looking down at his wife, as her chest rose and fell unevenly with each harsh breath, she'd been falling apart on him these last couple of months. Tessa had just turned twenty-seven and had

21

never dealt with any of the traumatic experiences of her past. She hadn't dealt with being abducted and seeing her friend murdered when she was eleven. She hadn't dealt with being sexually abused as a teenager or anything else related to Dylan Riley. Nor had she dealt with Cordelia and her actions.

A breakdown had been inevitable, he'd seen it coming, known it was only a matter of time, but that didn't mean it was any easier to watch. Ever since Lachlan had disrupted their lives she had been clingy, nearly falling into a panic attack whenever she was alone. She'd also become quiet and withdrawn, pulling away from everyone, even him, *especially* him.

Parker understood why Tessa was distancing herself from the people she cared about. When they had first met it had taken him months to convince her to put her trust in him. He had promised her that unlike everyone else she had ever loved he would never leave her, but then he had. Not only had he been taken from her, but all their friends and family had been willing to believe that he had walked out on his life, Tessa had been more hurt by their betrayal than he had.

Beginning to play with her round blonde curls, determined to do whatever was necessary to get his wife back on track.

Beneath his touch Tessa began to stir. Dazed eyes struggled open, holding him in an unfocused stare. "Where are we?" Tessa murmured. "What happened?"

Keeping a reassuring smile on his face as he brought her hand to his lips and pressed a kiss to it. "We crashed our car, honey," he reminded her gently.

She attempted to sit up but he held her in place with a hand firmly on her shoulder. "Don't try to move, you've already lost a lot of blood, you need to stay still and rest. I called Wyatt, he should be on his way here by now." Parker desperately hoped that was true. Tessa needed a hospital, he was probably injured too, although not seriously, and concern for his wife had pushed everything else, even his own pain, from his mind.

"Parker, I hear something," she whispered.

Focusing instantly, there was no way it could be Wyatt. Even if Wyatt has been able to hear all of their phone conversation, and left immediately, his friend could not have gotten here this quickly. Hearing nothing he was about to turn his attention back to Tessa when he noticed the faint rustling of leaves. It could be just the wind but it might also be someone who could help them.

"Stay here," he instructed, not sure Tessa could move even if she wanted to. Jumping to his feet Parker hurried to the cave's entrance, trying to locate the direction where the sound was coming from. Seeing nothing, his hand strayed automatically to his waistband, fingering his gun, they were pretty far away from any houses and there shouldn't be anyone out here. Even if there was it didn't mean that he and Tessa were in any danger he told himself. Still his hand didn't move. Tessa's paranoia had definitely started to rub off on him.

Examining the woods carefully in the dimming light of pre-dusk, Parker was about to give up and return to Tessa, deciding it was nothing more than an animal, when he caught sight of a small shadow. A few yards away a little girl appeared from the trees. She looked to be about ten, was dressed in a nightgown, was dripping wet and looked exhausted almost to the point of collapse. Instincts kicking in he took a step towards the child. "Hello?" he called.

Jumping like a frightened mouse when she heard his voice, the girl turned to look at him, eyes growing wide in terror. Hands held up placatingly, he took another step towards her and noticed that the front of her nightdress was spotted with something dark.

Blood.

"Honey, are you hurt?" Moving quickly towards her now but halting when she cowered away from him. "It's okay, I'm a police officer, my name's Parker, everything's okay now."

Expecting her to come to him when she heard he was a police officer, but the little girl remained where she was, big brown eyes radiating fear.

"Sweetheart, can you tell me your name?"

The child said nothing, and Parker felt an uneasy sense of déjà vu spark through him. When Tessa was a child, she and her friend Eleanor had vanished one Friday afternoon. Tessa was found two days later, wandering alone in the woods, covered in blood. She didn't speak a word for four months. Eleanor was never seen again.

Taking another tentative step forwards. "I'm not here to hurt you."

The girl shrank further away and once again he stopped, gazing helplessly at the child, unsure how to proceed. Wyatt, his partner and best friend, was the one who was good with kids, had two of his own, a ten-year-old son and a daughter who had turned six a couple of months ago, and always took the lead whenever they interviewed a child.

Suddenly, the girl's eyes darted to look at something behind him, following her gaze he saw Tessa. She was standing with one thin hand clinging to a tree trunk to keep herself upright, the other clutching the blanket around her shoulders.

Holding up a hand to stop him when he started towards her, she never took her eyes off the girl. The child held her gaze then shot Parker a quick look asking a silent question that Tessa seemed to sense. "He didn't hurt me, our car crashed," Tessa told the little girl.

Tessa possessed an amazing ability to read others and an unnatural zeal to help those around her no matter what the cost to herself. And right now Tessa looked like she might collapse at any second. Struggling to fight the urge to run to her, Parker was holding back only because he didn't want to do anything that might startle the child.

"It's okay," Tessa somehow managed to make her voice sound strong and reassuring. "We can help you if you let us."

The girl studied her, twirling strands of her black hair around her finger as she decided whether to trust them. Slowly she took a step towards Tessa, then shot him a wary glance. Parker held his breath and tried to look as nonthreatening as it was possible for a six-foot tall man to look to a child. Then she hurried the rest of the way to Tessa, making sure to stay well clear of him, and threw herself into Tessa's arms.

Tessa swayed, and for a second he thought she was about to pass out, her face had changed from white to an unearthly grey, but she managed to hold on. Keeping one arm on the tree she wrapped the other around the girl, the blanket tumbling to the ground behind her leaving her thin, bruised body exposed to the elements.

"It's okay, it's okay," she whispered to the child as she rubbed soothing circles on her back.

Parker crossed to them and asked Tessa his own silent question when she raised her eyes to meet his. She nodded that she was okay, but looked like she might topple over if she got caught in a gentle breeze.

Kneeling down so that he was eye to eye with the little girl, he gently extricated her from Tessa's grasp. "Will you let us help you?"

Looking to Tessa who smiled encouragingly, the girl nodded shyly.

Tucking her hair behind her ear, Parker too smiled at the child, but before he could say anything, Tessa lost her fight with consciousness, her eyes rolled back and her legs gave out. He caught her before she hit the ground.

# SEPTEMBER 5<sup>TH</sup>

6:12 A.M.

It was just beginning to get light.

A wasted night.

Dino had spent the whole night trudging through the woods, in the rain and thunderstorm, worried that he might get struck by lightening, or by a falling tree.

He was wet, cold and frustrated.

John Doe hadn't offered to help of course. Just dolled out orders, then sat back and enjoyed the stormy evening in luxury from his warm, comfortable, cozy mansion.

Dino hated John Doe. Hated him with a passion, hated him more than anyone else on the planet, well almost anyone. There was one other person he hated as much as he loathed his boss, one person who had taken from him all he had. That person's time was limited. He would make her pay.

Sighing irritably as his arm bumped a tree branch laden with water, sending it showering down upon him. Anger got the better of him, he'd just dried off after the last time that had happened, and he rammed his fist into the tree trunk. Yelping at the pain that rocketed up his arm he cursed his own stupidity. Dino was all too aware of his own lack of intelligence, reminded by John Doe on a daily basis, it was why he would never make it to the top in his business.

Unlike his brother Jake.

If Jake had lived, he would have been running things by now, and the brothers would be living in the lap of luxury, rather than with whatever John Doe deemed sufficient. Not that Dino lacked for any material want, his boss made sure that his underlings were happy, but neither was he swimming in cash as he had always longed to be.

Sighing once again, he was about to give up when he noticed skid marks and battered trees before him. Following the trail of destruction to the edge of a cliff, where a gaping hole and some broken roots remained. Peering carefully over the edge he could just make out the shape of a huge black SUV down below, some unsuspecting driver had obviously been caught in the storm.

Wondering if the passengers had made it out alive before the car sailed off the edge, his question was answered a few feet away. On the ground were footprints. One set, large, that of a tall male, the treads were heavy, indicating that he had been carrying someone. A second passenger. Dino may not be smart but he was an excellent tracker, not that it was a skill that was particularly helpful.

There was no sign that help had arrived, no other tyre treads, if the car's occupants had been caught in the storm and with one of them injured, they were no doubt still nearby. If Clara came this way then their paths might have crossed. He wasn't worried about what the girl may have said, she knew enough to keep her mouth shut. If he could find them he would convince them Clara was his mentally ill daughter who had wandered off. Then he would simply reclaim the child and return. John Doe did not like unnecessary killing, but if it were up to him, Dino would merely shoot the unlucky people who had stumbled into a world they did not understand. However, his livelihood depended on pleasing John Doe, so, for now at least, he would do as he was told.

Following the trail a little way through the woods he knew immediately where they would be holed up, waiting for rescue. Not far from where he stood was a small cave, only a few yards deep but enough to offer protection from the storm and to keep them warm and dry. Now that he knew where he was going he made his way as silently as possible, he always like to have the upper hand and thought it best to scope out the situation before he was seen. For all he knew they had not stumbled upon Clara in which case he would simply slip past and carry on with his search.

Approaching the cave he slowed, angling himself so that he was mostly hidden behind a tall tree he studied the cave carefully. Inside lay three motionless figures, one a tall dark-haired male, the second a smaller blonde woman, and the third was the object of his search, young Clara Meyers.

Preparing to move in and collect the child so he could return to the warmth of the mansion, take a shower, maybe go downstairs and visit with one of the girls, when suddenly he froze.

It couldn't be . . . and yet it was.

It was her.

Backtracking quickly so that once again he was hidden from view he considered his options, knowing even as he did exactly what he planned to do. There was no way he could let her go. It was a sign. It had been years since he had been this close to her, and every fiber of his body tingled delightfully with anticipation.

Tessa Micah deserved exactly what was coming to her.

Before he even registered what he was doing, Dino's hand was slipping into his waistband, retrieving his gun and taking aim. This was not how he would have like to exact his revenge. He had dreamed of something a little more personal than a bullet to the head, but at least it would be done and she would be dead.

Taking aim, he lifted the pistol and was about to fire when sirens sounded in the distance and a chopper soared overhead.

Knowing he had no choice but to leave immediately, a gunshot would only bring the police in quicker, their own guns drawn. Smiling to himself as he snuck away, he had found her, and now that he had seen her again after all those years, he realized that nothing was going to get in the way of his revenge.

Not the police, not John Doe, no one.

He was going to see Tessa dead if it was the last thing he ever did.

* * * * *

6:20 A.M.

Awakened by a presence, Parker gently eased Tessa's head from where it rested against his shoulder so that it lay against the floor. She did not stir. Her face was white, twin circles of red staining her cheeks, breath coming in rapid, shallow gasps, placing the back of his hand on her forehead her skin felt hot and sweaty. She was still shivering, and when he pressed his fingertips to her wrist to take her pulse he found it weak and thready. A quick check of her leg, which he had elevated by placing a rock underneath her knee, showed that blood had once again soaked through the bandage.

After Tessa had collapsed in his arms the previous evening, he had cleaned the wound, the edges of which were already red and enflamed, thoroughly to try to ward off infection for as long as he could, then changed the dressing, and wrapped her back in the blanket.

Then he had spent at least half an hour trying to coax the little girl inside. It had taken the reassurances of a semi-conscious Tessa to at last convince her to enter the cave. He had tried to check the girl for possible causes of the blood that splattered her clothes but she wouldn't let him near her. Eventually deciding that she didn't move as though she were injured he let her be. Exhausted, he had settled his wife in his arms, and with the girl lying on Tessa's other side since she refused to come too close to him, they had all fallen asleep.

Remembering what had awakened him, Parker pushed wearily to his knees, his body stiff and sore from the accident and a night spent on the cold dirt floor of the cave. Surveying their surroundings from the cave's opening, he saw nothing out of the ordinary and was about to return to Tessa and the girl when he heard a siren wailing in the distance.

Help.

Somehow, Wyatt had been able to ascertain enough from their earlier phone conversation to send out a search party.

Quickly checking behind him, neither Tessa nor the girl had stirred, so leaving them he hurried in the direction of the whirling sirens. He hadn't travelled more than a couple of yards when he heard someone calling his name. It was Wyatt.

"Wyatt, over here," he yelled back.

Within moments, his partner appeared from the tree line, and Parker almost collapsed in relief. Friends for over twenty years, ever since ten-year-old Parker and his twin sister Mattie had been adopted by the Bell's, the next-door neighbors of Skylar Wyatt's family. Fifteen-year-old Wyatt, had quickly become an angry and withdrawn little Parker's best friend and role model, despite the five year age difference. Wyatt was the brother that Parker never had, and the two had been partners now for almost five years.

Wyatt was at his side in seconds, panic written all over his face. "We found the car. I thought . . . I didn't know if you . . . are you okay?"

"I'm fine, but Tess isn't."

Grabbing his radio, "I found them," Wyatt spoke into it. "We need paramedics now." Turning his attention back to Parker, "where is she?" Wyatt loved Tessa like a little sister and was devastated by the distance that had developed between them ever since Lachlan Mountain.

"This way," he began to lead Wyatt back to the cave.

Once inside Wyatt paused as he noted the girl, now awake and sitting with her knees pulled up against her chest, chin resting on them, one small hand tightly clutching Tessa's limp one.

"We found her in the woods, or rather she found us," he summarized in answer to Wyatt's unspoken question. "She hasn't said a word since we found her, covered in blood," he emphasized hoping Wyatt would pick up on the significance of that. Then to the girl, "it's okay, this is Wyatt, he's a policeman too. He's here to help Tessa, he's not going to hurt you."

The child said nothing, just studied them with her big brown eyes, but she made no move to shrink away from them as they both dropped down at Tessa's side.

Progress.

Wyatt's fingers moved quickly to Tessa's neck, and then just as he himself had done yesterday, his partner began to check the rest of her for injuries.

"The wound to her leg won't stop bleeding," he explained to Wyatt. "And it's infected. How far away are the paramedics?" glancing out the cave's entrance, Parker wanted Tessa in the hospital now, before her condition got any worse.

"They'll be here any second," Wyatt soothed, continuing his examination of Tessa.

She winced as he pressed her stomach, eyes popping open. "Skylar?" she asked, surprise tinting her weak voice. "What are you doing here?"

Tessa was the only person, bar his mother, that Wyatt allowed to call him by his given name. The last of five of boys his mother had been sure during her pregnancy that she would be having a girl. When Wyatt was born, another boy, she had decided to stick with the name she had chosen. As a child Wyatt had associated his name with his mother's disappointment over his gender, and around adolescence had ditched it, and started calling himself by his surname.

"Rescuing you," Wyatt answered, tugging on one of her sweat damped ringlets and smiling down at her reassuringly. "Just hang in there, you're gonna be fine, medics'll be here any second."

Nodding, "where's Parker?"

"Right here," taking her hand in his, fingering the delicate gold chain encircling her wrist, her name engraved in cursive script on the small bar. He'd given it to her for her birthday, just four days ago. "I'm not going anywhere."

Exhaustion had her eyes sliding closed again. Wyatt shook her gently, "hey, goldilocks, stay with me, let me see those big blue eyes of yours."

Offering up a faint smile, she forced her eyes back open for Wyatt, who retrieved a bottle of water from his jacket and then spread the jacket over Tessa. Her eyes were glittering brightly with fever, she was running a high temperature.

Pressing his hand to her forehead. "She's burning up," Parker caught the panic in his voice.

"I got her, Parker, try to relax," Wyatt reassured him, opening the bottle of water he poured some on a handkerchief and laid it over Tessa's forehead.

"I can't relax," he snapped. "You said the paramedics were only seconds away, so where are . . .?"

Then the room was suddenly alive, paramedics and police officers flooding inside, bustling about as they took control of the situation. Parker was gently pushed aside as medics knelt beside Tessa and started treating her. It felt good to relinquish control of Tessa's wellbeing to professionals. For a minute no one bothered himself or the girl, their attention focused on the most critical patient.

"Sir, why don't we move over here and I'll check you out."

Blinking a face came into focus before him. Pushing away the well meaning hands of the paramedic. "I'm fine," he murmured, gaze fixed firmly on Tessa as another medic inserted a needle into the back of her hand and started an IV.

Following his gaze the young female medic smiled understandingly. "She's in good hands, the best thing you can do for her right now is let us make sure you're okay."

Studying the EMT, Parker saw a determined look in her black eyes and relented. Nodding his assent he allowed the young woman to take his blood pressure, check his pulse, shine a light in his eyes, and examine the bump on the side of his head. When she finished, he looked up at her, "told you I was fine."

She nodded back noncommittally, "you're a little dehydrated," she told him.

Shrugging, attention returning to Tessa. He winced as he watched one of the medics tilt back her head, and with the aid of a laryngoscope slide an endotracheal tube down her throat, then begin to bag her, making her chest rise and fall more easily. "Is that really necessary? She was breathing on her own."

"We need her stable to airlift to hospital," the medic explained.

"You're airlifting her?" he repeated, surprised.

". . . blood pressure's plummeting again . . ." one of the medic's treating Tessa announced, her words making his own blood pressure spike in a panic.

"I'm going with her."

"Detective Bell, that's not really . . ."

Ignoring her, Parker hurried to Tessa's side as they lifted her onto a stretcher and started carrying her towards a small clearing where the helicopter was just landing. Catching up to them, "I'm riding with her," he announced.

One of the medics turned, gave him a once over and nodded his assent.

Aware of someone trotting along behind him Parker turned to see the girl following him, a police officer hot on her heels. One look at the little girl's terrified expression and he announced, "the girl comes too."

"She's not injured," the officer who'd obviously been assigned to stick like glue to the child protested. "We'll take her to the local hospital . . ."

Cutting the officer off, "we don't know who she is, where she came from, or what happened to her, and so far Tessa is the only person she'll let come near her."

"Once we get her somewhere safe, she'll probably open up. If not we can run her picture through missing person's," the officer shot back.

Bending over to meet the girl's eye, "honey, do you want to go with this lady, or with me and Tessa?"

Her eyes darted from him to the middle-aged police officer and back to him again, and he read the answer there. Holding out his hand, she hesitated for barely a second then reached out and took it. Lifting the kid into his arms, he took off at a jog and arrived at the helicopter just as they were loading Tessa inside. Passing up the girl, he paused and turned to Wyatt, who had remained by Tessa's side, unsure how to thank his friend for being there for him when he needed it. "Wyatt, I . . . ."

"You're welcome," Wyatt cut in with a grin. "Now go, I'll meet you at the hospital."

Sliding the door shut behind him, Wyatt waved then hurried off to his car to make the long journey to the hospital. Now that it was over, they were found and Tessa was going to be okay, Parker felt drained. Resting his head against the glass window of the chopper, it was several minutes before he realized that the little girl had climbed into his lap and fallen asleep.

\* \* \* \* \*

6:20 P.M.

Clara sat alone in a hospital room.

Pale pictures of safari animals dotted the wall, more animals covered the hospital gown she'd been given to wear. The curtains were drawn across the windows that looked not to the outside but back into the hospital. A TV hung from the wall, she could have watched it but she didn't feel like it, she was used to sitting alone in the silence. And so she lay in the bed, under the scratchy pink blanket, and waited, for what she wasn't quite sure.

They had taken her clothes, not that she minded since she'd been wearing them for the past two and a half months. She'd read the date on her chart, the one hanging from the end of the bed, it said today was September 5th. The man had taken her on July 2nd.

She couldn't believe she had been gone that long. That no one had rescued her. That she had gotten away on her own.

She was still a little surprised at her own reaction to being found.

When she had heard him, Parker, calling her, and she saw him standing there it was like she had been paralyzed. It had occurred to her that she didn't know who she could trust. If her time in that place had taught her anything it was that monsters come from all walks of life.

Clara had been about to run back into the safety of the woods, she had stopped only when she'd seen the woman. Tessa. Looking at her Clara had known instantly that this was someone she could trust. For some reason that she couldn't fathom, Tessa understood, she knew.

But then they'd come, and they'd taken Tessa away. Put a tube down her throat to help her breathe, stuck needles in her, and she'd been so scared that Tessa might die, that she'd be all alone again.

Unable to go forwards and unable to go backwards.

She hadn't told them her name, hadn't said a word to anyone, but it wouldn't take them long to figure it out. Then her parents would come and she didn't know if she could face them. But she couldn't go back either. She knew what Dino would do to her. He'd never touched her before but she'd heard stories from the other girls. They weren't supposed to talk to one another but during the day the cell doors were often left open and sometimes they crept into another room to whisper together.

It was during one of those times that she'd heard all about *the room*. The one at the end of the corridor, she'd never been inside but she knew what happened in there. If Dino found her he'd take her back, take her into the room, and she would never be seen again.

Wiping at the tears that trickled down her face. No, that wouldn't happen. She would never go back there, Dino would never find her, Tessa wouldn't let him. Tessa and her husband Parker would protect her.

When she had awakened this morning in the small cave and found Parker gone and Tessa unconscious, she had been terrified, worried that Dino had come and killed Parker. But then he had returned with his friend. Wyatt had bright green eyes, calm and soothing eyes, and he had been so gentle with Tessa. Clara had begun to feel that everything would work out but then the place had been filled with a swarm of police officers and paramedics. It had been overwhelming. She'd wanted to stay with Tessa, but the medics had gently pushed her away. And then they were taking Tessa away and she hadn't known what else to do so she'd pushed past the female police officer who'd sat beside her and followed.

Clara wasn't quite decided yet if she could trust Parker or not. But Tessa did. So when she'd been forced to choose between the other officer and Parker, she'd chosen Parker. The soft and panicked way he'd looked at Tessa on the helicopter, had been the deciding factor, so she'd climbed into his lap and fallen asleep.

Since they'd arrived at the hospital she hadn't seen him. In the commotion of unloading the helicopter and being whisked down to the ER Clara had hoped he would stay with her, but he'd had eyes only for Tessa. He had been consumed with worry for her. Refused to leave her side while the doctors worked on her, then stayed with her when they'd taken her up to surgery.

He hadn't even stopped to tell her goodbye before he left.

Doctors and nurses had buzzed around her like bees around a flower. They all had kind faces but they all melded together until they looked like one giant image of *his* face.

Pronouncing her okay, although they said she was suffering from mel . . . no mal . . . malnutrition. The doctor had explained to her that meant that she hadn't been eating enough good food since she'd been gone. She had lost a lot of weight, she used to be a little chubby, but now she was so thin that the bones in her ribs stood out, and her joints were all knobbly.

The other police officer, Parker's partner, had come to see her briefly, sat with her and chatted away easily, seemingly not deterred by the fact that she didn't contribute to the conversations. However, he had quickly disappeared when he heard that Tessa was coming out of surgery. The nurses too had left her alone to sleep but she'd been afraid of bad dreams.

And so here she sat alone in a hospital room . . .

A gentle knock sounded on the door and she blinked in surprise. The only people who had entered the room so far had been nurses and the occasional doctor and none of them had ever knocked.

Slowly the door opened and a giant teddy bear popped through, a squeaky voice said, "hello, I'm looking for Clara Meyers."

So they knew her name.

Parker's face appeared above the teddy bear's, he shot her a warm but tired smile, and she wondered how much rest he had gotten since they arrived here. "That's your name right? Clara?"

There was no point in pretending otherwise so she nodded.

Crossing the room in a few short strides Parker sat beside her on the bed, set the teddy bear in her arms and held out his hand to shake hers, "nice to meet you, Clara."

Slipping her hand into his she let him shake it, then pulled it quickly back and twisted her hands tightly together in her lap. She wanted to ask if Tessa was okay but she couldn't make the words come out. It was like she had lost control of her own voice.

Smiling at her, "Tessa is going to be fine, the doctors patched her up and she's tough, she's resting now."

Letting out a breath she hadn't known she was holding as relief flooded through her veins.

"Your parents are on their way up," Parker told her.

Startled, Clara hadn't expected them so soon. She couldn't face them yet, she was about to tell, or gesture, to Parker not to let them in yet when the door swung open once again, this time revealing her mom and dad. They stood staring at her as though she were an apparition that might vanish if they blinked. Tears stood in both their eyes, it was the first time she had ever seen her big, strong father cry.

Then they were running at her, but they weren't her parents anymore, they morphed into Dino. If her parents had really been looking for her how could they not have found her? How could she have been gone two months without them finding her?

Unless they were in on it.

Unless they were working with Dino.

Letting out a strangled squawk, she dove beneath the thin covers of her hospital bed, clutching the teddy bear as though it were the only thing that could keep her safe.

Frozen, her parents stared at her in fearful disbelief. Her mother took an uncertain step towards her. "Sweetheart, it's me," voice faltering. "It's mommy."

Her mother said the word reverently as though it held magical powers and would make everything okay because her mommy was here now. Clara had aged too much in the last two months to believe that anymore.

Standing over her, hand hovering between them, unsure whether touching her daughter would make things worse. "Clara, baby," her mother continued. "We're here now, you're safe, no one's going to hurt you any more."

Staring at her mother's hand as though it were dripping poison, Clara scrunched away from it, almost falling off the other side of the bed.

Tears were flowing down her mother's cheeks now. "Baby, it's okay, I'm here, mommy will make everything better."

Her mother choked out a sob and then grabbed for her. It was too much. Leaping from the bed Clara scurried to the other side of the room, eyes flying to Parker, begging him to make them go away.

"Mr. and Mrs. Meyers, I think maybe you should go for now,"

he placed himself between Clara and her parents.

"No," her mother shrieked. "She's our baby, we only just got her back . . ."

"I know," Parker began placatingly. "She's your daughter and you love her. You want what's best for her."

Mother's head bobbled like a toy's.

Parker took a step towards her mom, took her hands in his, "right now Clara needs time, what is best for her is to get some rest."

Yanking herself free of Parker's grip, her mom came lunging towards her, but Clara cringed away from her mother, squashing herself into a corner of the room. Making herself as small as she could, just as she had done so many times before in the last two months. Parker wrapped an arm around her mom's waist and physically pulled her towards the door. Her mother trashed wildly like a fish when you pull it out of the water.

"Let go of me, I want my baby, I can help her, I just want to hold her."

Parker was trying to soothe her as he dragged her from the room, murmuring in her ear in a soft and gentle voice. Even after the door swung closed Clara could hear her mother screaming. Then she noticed her father. He'd been standing still and quiet the whole time her mother had been raving, tears trickling slowly down his face, brown eyes devastated. With a shock Clara realized that her dad too had lost weight over the last few months, he was thin, his hair was streaked with grey, face unshaven.

He came slowly and crouched in front of her, he opened his mouth but no words came out, then he smiled, "I love you, Clara."

Then he was gone.

Squeezing her eyes closed Clara tucked herself into a tight ball, and blocked out everything else. It was an ability she had perfected in the last few months. An ability that had saved her life and kept her sane in the time she'd been gone.

"Clara?"

Opening her eyes she saw Parker's face before her.

"You okay?"

She nodded. As okay as she could be she guessed.

"You need to rest."

Holding out a hand to her just as he had done at the helicopter, that time she'd hesitated for barely a second, this time there was no hesitation. Slipping her hand into his she allowed him to carry her to the bed and tuck her in as if she were a small baby. Then he sat beside her until she fell asleep.

\* \* \* \* \*

8:47 P.M.

Tessa lay asleep in a hospital bed. A plastic tube crossed her face and looped at each end over her ears, delivering oxygen through her nose to her lungs. Hooked to an ECG which measured each beat of her heart with a tiny beep, an IV continued to drip into the back of her hand delivering fluids and antibiotics.

She was alone in the room, Parker having gone to check on Clara Meyers, but Wyatt was just outside the door, talking on the phone to his wife. She looked like she was sleeping peacefully, but sometimes looks can be deceiving.

\* \* \* \* \*

*Sixteen Years Ago*
*Friday morning*

*"Come on, Ellie, don't be such a worrier," eleven-year-old Tessa rolled her eyes, then held up her face to drink in the warm late summer sun. Enjoying the way the sunbeams sprinkled down through the thick leaves of the towering trees, it made the forest look like a giant patchwork quilt.*

41

*"I don't know, Tess,"* Ellie glanced around nervously, she liked being involved in Tessa's crazy schemes but the girls had just started the sixth grade and she wasn't as smart as Tessa. Her parents were pressuring her to do better in school and the only way she could do that was by actually attending classes instead of Tessa's little trips.

But Tessa was off in her own little world, she never had to worry about grades, she was a genius. Today's fascination was carving, Tessa had decided that she was going to re-create a life-size circus out of figures she carved herself.

Skipping through the trees, dancing to a tune only she could hear, Tessa felt free as a bird. Most of the other kids in school were unhappy that the summer break was over, but Tessa didn't care, was glad for any excuse to be away from that awful house, and she didn't mind school, just used it as an opportunity to entertain herself. On the whole the teachers left her to do as she pleased. She was streaks ahead of her class, of the whole school, she could have graduated years ago, but had refused to be separated from Ellie.

*"Come on, Ellie,"* she sang. *"We need to find an area with trees that are all the same size."*

Sighing long-sufferingly, Ellie complied as she always did. The girls were so preoccupied with their search that the man stood and studied them for several minutes before they became aware of his presence.

Startled, it was Ellie who noticed the man first. *"Tess,"* she nudged her friend and gestured with her head.

Tessa stopped her search and looked up, surveying the situation with a glance and deeming it non-threatening. The mystery man was reasonably young, probably in his mid-twenties, he was tall, but not too tall, medium build, with very short black hair, and eyes so black she couldn't distinguish between the pupil and the iris. Dressed in a white t-shirt and jeans he reminded her of a slightly older version of her big brother, Daniel and his friends.

Behind the man stood a girl about the same age as herself and Ellie. Dressed as they were in a school uniform, but while theirs consisted of white school dresses with blue and gold stripes, navy blazers, and white straw hats, the other girl's uniform was a green, purple and navy plaid pinafore over a shirt, it was not a uniform from any school Tessa recognized. The girl's face *was sad, her black hair hung in two long braids down her back, her black eyes pleaded silently for help.*

*"My daughter and I are looking for our dog," the man announced, slinging an arm around the girl's shoulders.*

*"We haven't seen any dog around," Tessa told him, looking to Ellie for confirmation.*

*Disappointment flashing over his face, "you sure? It's just a little thing, only eight weeks old, a birthday present for Sarah, we only got it yesterday, we're on our way to visit Sarah's grandparents, it ran out of the car when we stopped."*

*Tessa loved animals, had been pestering her grandparents for months to let her get a puppy of her own. "What kind of dog is it?"*

*"A golden retriever," the man replied, hope flashing through his eyes at the thought of more helpers to find his daughter's lost puppy. A good father wanted to make his children happy, unlike Tessa's own father who had abandoned her and Daniel a year ago and never contacted them since. Hadn't even sent her a card for her birthday, September 1st had come and gone without a word.*

*"We can help," Tessa said immediately.*

*"Great," the man beamed at them, black eyes incandescent.*

*"I don't know, Tess," Ellie cast an anxious gaze in the direction of their school.*

*"We'll be right back," Tessa smiled apologetically at the man and his daughter and gestured for Ellie to follow her a short distance away. "What's wrong with you?" she demanded the second they were out of earshot. "Of course we have to help look for the puppy."*

*"We're supposed to be in class," Ellie moaned miserably. Looking at her friend, standing in the streaming sunlight, Tessa looked like some sort of carefree woodland creature, a pixie. Her enormous greeny-blue eyes glowed animatedly, the sun gleamed off her white-blond braids, round curls as the ends, making them shimmer like snow, to look at Tessa appeared to be no more than about eight. Tess was everything that Ellie wished to be, smart, pretty, confident, self-assured, the exact opposite of herself. While the girls looked similar Ellie's hair was a darker blond, wavy not curly, her eyes a*

muddy grey, there was nothing outstanding about her, she was like a movie star's body double.

"We don't even know him, he's a stranger," Ellie tried reasoning with her, but once Tessa got an idea in her head it was virtually impossible to get her to change her mind.

"Name's Jake," a voice called out to them.

"There you go," Tessa announced as though that solved all their problems. "He has a kid." Her frown softened into an engaging smile, one that lit up her whole face. "I'll help you study, we'll get your grades up, I promise. You shouldn't worry so much, everything will be okay. I promise," she added once more when she saw Ellie wasn't completely convinced.

Sighing, Ellie reluctantly nodded her consent and followed Tessa as she skipped back to the man and his daughter.

"What's your dog's name?" Tessa called out, then she froze.

From behind her Ellie couldn't see what had made Tessa stop so suddenly, and almost walked into the back of her. "Tess, what are you . . .?" she trailed off as she finally caught sight of what had captured Tessa's attention.

The man was no longer standing placidly beside his daughter. He now had the girl pressed against him, a knife held to her throat, his easy-going smile replaced by a cold glower.

"You're coming with me," the man said in such a way as though it were a for-gone conclusion.

Ellie wanted to run but her feet seemed to be concreted to the ground. She wanted to scream but her voice had disappeared.

Tessa however was glaring back at the man defiantly, her face set in a stubborn frown. "We are not going anywhere with you."

Moving quicker than light, Jake brought the handle of the knife down against the side of Tessa's head, sending her sprawling across the ground. Ellie wanted to move, to check that Tess was okay but she was still frozen in place. Looking across at Sarah she saw tears streaming down the girl's face, apologetic eyes seeking out hers, and Ellie understood that this man was not her father.

Wrapping a hand around Tessa's arm, Jake dragged her to her feet, but *she wiggled free, and boldly met his gaze. Hands on hips, pout on her lips, she stamped her foot, "I already told you we are not going to go with you. Come on, Ellie, Sarah." With that she turned her back on the man and started back towards the school, wiping at the blood that tricked down her cheek. Ellie wondered how Tessa could be so brave, and how she could be such a useless coward.*

*Jake sprung at her, face red with rage, knife held with the blade up this time, but Tessa dodged out of his way and shimmied quickly up a tree and out of reach. Instead of going after her, Jake lunged for Sarah and held the point of the knife in front of her eye. Squinting in the glare of the sun as he looked up at Tessa, "your choice," he said simply.*

*Legs dangling over the edge of a branch Tessa assessed the situation. "You don't need all of us," Tessa reasoned. "Let Ellie and Sarah go, you'll still have me."*

*Considering her, Jake gave an evil grin, "I don't think so, princess. Either you come down now or the girl loses an eye." When Tessa hesitated slightly he added, "then I move on to your friend."*

*Defeated Tessa slowly climbed back down, dropping the last couple of feet. "Fine, you win," Tessa said haughtily.*

*Laughing, "what's your name, princess?"*

*Tessa said nothing, making Jake laugh harder.*

*Moving the knife tip closer to Sarah's eye, the girl let out a terrified whimper. "Name?"*

*Letting out an irritated breath, as though she were the adult dealing with a recalcitrant child, "Tessa."*

*"Well, Tessa, I think you and I are going to have some fun together." With that, deciding to take no chances, Jake released Sarah and lifted Tessa off the ground pinning her arms to her side. Tessa started to scream but he clamped a hand over her mouth. She wiggled and squirmed but the man was bigger and stronger.*

*Without a word Jake began to walk through the woods, and without a choice Ellie and Sarah followed as he led them further and further from the school, from safety, from life as she knew it.*

\* \* \* \* \*

"Tessa, hey it's okay, you're in the hospital."

The voice murmured above her.

Still caught in her dream, the voice was Jake's.

Thrashing against his grip, trying desperately to get away. If only she could break free maybe she could re-write history, change the outcome of that fateful day.

"Baby, it's okay, everything's okay now."

Hands firmly gripped her shoulders, another set caught her forearms as she swung them wildly. Eyes popping open Jake's face loomed above her, and she screamed.

"Get a doctor."

Slowly Jake's image faded replaced by Parker's worried face, dim in the half-light of the hospital room. Behind her machines beeped insistently, protesting at the sudden spike in her pulse rate and blood pressure.

The room flooded with light and other faces appeared, hands touched her, voices jabbered incoherently.

A wave of warmth rushed through her as one of the nurses injected something into her IV.

"Shh, honey, it's okay. I'm right here. It's over now."

Parker's voice.

But he was wrong. It wasn't over it was only just beginning.

It was happening again.

# SEPTEMBER 6<sup>TH</sup>

9:11 A.M.

"You sure you're up to it?"

Parker looked up as Wyatt entered the room, a stack of papers in his arms.

"I'm fine," he whispered, casting a glance over at Tessa, who was asleep in the bed. "Just bruised."

Somehow he had managed to escape the accident with no serious injuries. Tessa however had three broken ribs, a concussion, and had undergone surgery on her leg to thoroughly clean out any dirt and debris left behind and to properly close the wound. For a while the doctors had been worried that the infection in her leg would spread to her blood but she seemed to be responding to the antibiotics. She had been sedated through most of the last twenty-four hours, he hadn't spoken more than a couple of words to her when she had awakened from a nightmare last night. Worried that she might injure herself further the doctors had administered another sedative and she had slept peacefully through the night.

"You brought them?" he asked, eyeing the folders his partner carried.

"Everything I could find that seemed to be even vaguely related," Wyatt answered.

Gesturing at the door, "let's talk out there, I don't want to disturb her, she needs all the rest she can get." Crossing to Tessa, Parker leaned against the bed's guardrail and brushed lovingly at the hair on her forehead. Long black lashes, the only hair anywhere on her body that was not white, fanned out across fair

47

skin, the white square bandage that covered the gash on her head the same shade as her face. Staring down at her peaceful face, a wave of tenderness towards her crashed over him as he realized how close he had come to losing her. Parker pressed a light kiss to her lips, before following Wyatt out the door.

"How's Clara this morning?" he asked once they were in the hall.

After Tessa's nightmare last night Wyatt had finally gone home to see his family and catch a few hours of sleep, before going into the station to look up and pull some files. Parker hadn't wanted to leave Tessa alone in case she woke screaming once again, so arriving at the hospital this morning Wyatt had stopped by to check on Clara.

"Still not saying anything," Wyatt told him. "And she still won't let her parents in the room."

Letting out a distressed breath as he led Wyatt down the corridor and into a small, sparsely furnished room that was supposed to be used by the family members of patients. However, the room was so dismal, with beige walls and carpet, and an assortment of mismatched chairs, that he had never yet seen anyone in it. Parker hoped that whatever Clara Meyers had been through she would be able to overcome. "She's gonna need them to get through this."

Nodding in agreement, Wyatt sat and laid out the files on a table that's four legs each seemed to be a different length so that it wobbled incessantly the moment you touched it. "Did you call Daniel?"

Parker winced. He had been avoiding calling Tessa's brother to inform him of the accident. "Not yet, I don't want to ruin his trip. Besides Tessa's doing better."

Raising an eyebrow to indicate he knew that was not the reason that he was delaying calling Daniel. "Are he and Matilda having a good time?" Wyatt asked.

"Yeah." Parker wasn't thrilled about the idea of his twin sister and Tessa's brother dating, but had accepted the fact that he didn't have a say in the matter, besides it wasn't worth losing Matilda over. If Daniel could make her happy then that was enough for him. Pushing everything else from his mind. "What did you find?" gesturing at the files and taking a seat on the opposite side of the table from Wyatt.

"Seven cases. All young girls between the ages of eight and twelve. All disappeared off the face of the planet, during the day, without a word. All went missing within the last year. In each case it was ruled that there was no chance of a custody kidnapping, the most common cause of disappearance with children, the parents were all happily married. There were no ransoms, no clues and no leads." Pausing, Wyatt shot his partner a careful look, "are you sure about this? We don't really have a lot to go on."

Skimming through the information, before asking incredulously, "how have these cases not been linked together already? *Seven* girls all go missing from the same state within a year. You said that family and acquaintance involvement had been ruled out?"

"Everyone appeared to check out."

"So someone's running around taking little girls and no one notices?"

"There's no evidence to suggest that there is any link in the cases," Wyatt reminded him patiently. "The girls all live in different parts of the state, they all have different backgrounds, races, they were all taken from different places and at different times of the day."

Meeting his partner's gaze evenly, "these cases are related, I'm positive. They're all related to Clara Meyers, and . . ." Parker paused reluctant to put his suspicions into words, "I think they're all related to Tessa's case."

Expecting to see surprise in Wyatt's emerald eyes instead he only saw wary apprehension. "I'm not saying you're wrong but you certainly don't have any proof."

49

"They all disappeared in broad daylight, just like Tessa and Eleanor. No family involvement, just like Tessa. There were no leads or persons of interest, just like Tessa. And Clara was found in the woods covered in blood that wasn't hers, just like Tessa."

"Sounds like it's just a coincidence. Tessa and Eleanor were abducted sixteen years ago, what are the chances that whoever took them is still out there doing the same thing?"

A familiar spike of fear sliced through him as he thought of the circumstances surrounding how he and Tessa met. He and Wyatt had been hunting a serial killer who abducted a young woman and left a list of clues pointing to nine other women he planned to kill. Discovering that Tessa Micah was one of the intended victims, they had only just managed to save her from being burned alive in her cottage. Assuming that the attempt on her life was related to their case, it wasn't until the killer was killed himself, that Tessa finally confessed that the man who tried to kill her in the fire was in fact related to her childhood friend Eleanor's murder.

"We know that he's still out there. Tessa used him to find me when Lachlan had abducted me."

"We *think* that Tessa used him," Wyatt corrected. "But there were no cases between Tessa and Eleanor's disappearance and a year ago. If it was the same guy then where was he during those sixteen years?" Wyatt asked reasonably.

"Maybe he got spooked when Tessa got away, left the area, operated somewhere else, then when he felt confident to return he came back."

"Okay, that's a possibility, but you're forgetting that we found the house. We know that Dylan Riley took Tessa to the place where Eleanor was killed. After everything that happened there, there is no way anyone would risk starting anything back up there," Wyatt rationalized.

"Then he probably found a new place to do his work. Another old house someplace remote where nobody would find his victims."

The look Wyatt gave him made him shiver. The two of them were more like brothers than friends, and Wyatt's look seemed to see right inside him. "Parker, I know you want the man who tried to kill Tessa caught, I hate that he's still out there too. And I know you're scared about what she bargained with to get you back. But all you have is theories, no evidence."

Before Parker had a chance to respond the open doorway was suddenly filled by a huge man, almost seven-foot tall and three hundred pounds, with a full brown beard, and a wild look in his eye. "Parker," he roared. "What sort of trouble have you gotten yourself into this time?"

Jacob Jacobsen, known to everyone as J.J., was in his mid-fifties, a father of four, and happily married to a beautiful musician named Linda for thirty-five years. He was also their boss.

"I'm fine, just banged up a bit," he winced as J.J. thumped him on the back with one of his giant hands.

"I came as soon as I heard." J.J. had been out of town visiting his daughter and son-in-law after a recent health scare with his youngest grandchild. Face growing serious, brown eyes full of genuine concern, J.J. had a wild and unpredictable temper. A terrifying force to any criminal unlucky enough to cross his path, but he cared about victims and his 'people' as he called the officers who worked under him. "How's Tessa?"

"Concussion, broken ribs, an injury to her leg, but she's going to be okay, she's sleeping," Parker told him.

Eyes straying to the stack of papers on the table, "what's all this then?"

Exchanging a glance with Wyatt, his partner raised a blonde eyebrow, agreeing that they may as well tell J.J. what they were thinking. "I think that the Clara Meyers case might be related to the abductions of these girls," waving a finger at the files, then added, "and to Tessa's case."

Surprise flickering quickly across this face, then he took a seat.

"Tell me why." J.J. was always prepared to listen to his people's theories, but if you couldn't back it up with evidence then he expected you to move on, something Parker wasn't sure he would be able to do.

* * * * *

9:56 A.M.

She was dreaming again.

Although this time the dream was pleasant. She and Ellie were playing, carefree, in the cold winter snow, running, throwing snowballs, building snowmen.

Tessa was dressed in a coat, gloves, scarf but she was still shivering.

Ellie didn't seem to notice the cold but Tessa couldn't stop shaking.

Then suddenly she began to grow warm.

Voices were whispering above her.

And then she was awake.

Blinking her eyes open, at first everything was fuzzy. Two ovals hovered above her, one black and one white, slowly taking the shape of faces.

Fingers pressed gently to her neck and someone called her name, but it was hard to hear through the rushing in her ears.

Then it was like someone snapped their fingers and everything came into focus. Casey Wyatt, Skylar's wife, and Maisy Wallace, a crime scene tech who often worked with Parker, were standing on either side of her bed.

"Hey, Tess," Maisy smiled down at her.

Casey, a doctor, continued to take her pulse. Tessa batted away her hands and frowned at her, "I'm fine, Casey."

Undaunted Casey simply picked up her wrist. "You were shaking," she commented mildly.

Tessa noticed that another blanket was covering her and assumed this was the reason she had suddenly grown warm in her dream. As much as she loved Casey, her best friend tended to fuss as much as Parker, more so than ever after Lachlan.

Tall and slender, Casey had been born in Sudan, orphaned as an infant, and adopted by an American family when she was fifteen months old. Skin as black as night, deep dark eyes as black as black could be, and corkscrew curls, tighter and smaller than Tessa's own ringlets, that Casey wore cut short. Originally a history teacher, after the death of her and Skylar's daughter, Casey had changed careers and was now a doctor.

Pulling a chair over to the bedside Maisy sat next to her, taking her hand, "we're really glad you're okay." Maisy was a year older than Tessa, with red hair and hazel eyes, she was bright, bubbly, and despite being new to the CSU, she was excellent at her job.

Attempting to recall the accident, and failing, "I don't even remember it," she murmured, frustrated, the lack of control over her own mind made her uncomfortable.

"Of course you don't." Casey lowered the guardrail and perched on the edge of the bed, holding the fingers of her other hand, carefully avoiding the needle in the back, and squeezed. "You have a concussion. The blow to your head wiped out your memory of before and after the crash as a defense mechanism."

Catching at a thread that half slipped away before she could properly grab hold. "There was a girl. In the woods." She looked from Casey to Maisy and back again and could tell from their faces that they were trying to hide something from her. "What?" she demanded. "Tell me."

"You lost a lot of blood, your body's battling infection, you're weak, you need to rest now," Casey told her.

Angry, ignoring the stabbing pain in her chest, Tessa pushed herself up. "Don't tell me what I need, I'm not one of your patients, Casey. Who is the girl?"

Neither of them spoke, just exchanged glances.

Throwing back the covers, "fine then, I'll go find out myself."
Both of them grabbed at her.

"Okay, okay," Maisy gave in first.

"You'll tell me?" Tessa asked.

"We'll tell you, just stay in bed." Casey pushed her back against the mattress and shot her a disapproving stare, "we're supposed to be keeping you calm."

Allowing Casey to settle her against the bed and rearrange the blankets, she didn't even protest this time when Casey checked her pulse. Maybe they were right. Maybe she did need to rest. The movement had sent pain rocketing up her leg and restarted a dull pounding in her head as though someone were using it as a drum. Closing her eyes and taking a moment to gather herself, she deliberately pushed the pain away, locking it up in one part of her brain and focusing the other.

"Go ahead," she told them, re-opening her eyes.

Hesitant, "maybe we should talk later, you don't look so good," Maisy told her, chewing her nails as she always did when she was nervous.

"I'm . . ."

"Fine," Casey interjected and huffed a mirthless chuckle.

Shrugging, then wincing as it made the pain in her chest worse, "I need to know."

Reluctantly Casey begun, "after the crash there was a storm, Parker carried you to a small cave that he found, you were in and out of consciousness. A couple of hours later he heard something outside. It was a little girl, a ten-year-old, wandering alone in the woods . . ." she trailed off.

Ears pricking, this was the reason her friends had been hesitant to tell her. "What?"

"She was covered in blood. It wasn't hers," the words tumbled out of Casey's mouth in a rush.

"Just like me."

Vision fading to black, Tessa remembered her nightmare. It

had been years since she had dreamed about Jake taking her and Ellie, usually her nightmares were of what happened later. The girl had been found just like she had after Ellie's murder, wandering in the woods covered in someone else's blood. Earlier, after her dream, but before the drugs took over, Parker had said something to her. He'd said that it was over, but he'd been wrong and she'd been right, this proved that it was starting all over again.

"Tessa? Honey? Maisy, get her doctor."

"No," making her voice work with an effort, something was coming back to her. "Clara, her name was Clara."

Maisy and Casey stared down at her with puzzled expressions. "How do you know that?" Maisy asked.

"She told me," not understanding their confusion.

"When?"

"In the woods, she whispered it to me. Why?"

"She hasn't spoken a word since you were all found. Wyatt found her name by running her picture through missing persons. She even freaked out when her parents came to get her. Why would she talk to you?"

"Because I know," hardly realizing she had answered, Tessa was already lost in thought.

\* \* \* \* \*

10:02 A.M.

"She got away?"

They were in the main dining room of the mansion, a room used by no one but John Doe and his guests. Or more accurately his clients. The walls of the room were painted burgundy and decorated with oil paintings, an enormous tapestry graced most of one wall. The huge mahogany table seated forty-two, although only the head of the table was set, each chair elaborately carved with dragons, John Doe was nothing if not ostentatious. The floor was centuries old floorboards that had been polished until they gleamed, and a huge fireplace, big enough for a half dozen people to stand inside, was behind his boss.

From his position flames framed John Doe, and Dino thought of the devil.

Today not even John Doe's disapproving glare could dampen his mood. Dino Rollino was on a high and nothing was going to bring him down, not even his boss' temper. "She was found by some couple who crashed their car. I was going to get her when the police showed up, thought it was best just to cut our losses and get out of there. Didn't want to risk getting caught and having to answer a truckload of questions."

John Doe studied him carefully, through brown eyes that were like a mirror, always reflecting never revealing, and for one excruciating second Dino thought that somehow John Doe knew. But then his boss shrugged with disinterest and returned to his breakfast. "She won't say anything."

Nodding in agreement, "she knows what will happen if she does."

"Maybe I'll beef up security around here, so we don't have a repeat performance of yesterday's escapades," John Doe gave him a pointed look.

"I'll get right on that sir," he muttered with mock sincerity.

"That will be all," John Doe commanded dismissively.

Turning to leave Dino had to bite his lip to keep from screaming an insult at his obnoxiously condescending boss.

"Oh and, Dino . . ."

Pausing, "yeah?"

Shooting him a withering stare, "try not to lose any more of them."

Then John Doe turned away. Dino was being dismissed.

Ignoring the urge to thump a fist straight through John Doe's smug face, Dino simply nodded and withdrew from the elegant room as quickly as possible.

Once back in his own tiny room at the end of one of the seemingly endless corridors, he kicked at the door, enjoying the crack of the wood. Not bothering to undress he threw himself down on the bed and closed his eyes, picturing every horrible thing he would do Tessa Micah.

He would make her wish she had never been born.

\* \* \* \* \*

10.10 A.M.

"How's she doing?" Parker asked as he met Casey and Maisy just leaving Tessa's hospital room.

"She's pretty shaken up," Maisy told him.

"And exhausted," Casey added.

"She remembered the girl and made us tell her about it, but she already knew her name," Maisy told him.

"How?"

"Apparently Clara told her in the woods," Casey explained.

"She spoke to Tessa? Did she say anything else?"

"I don't think so. Tess didn't say that she did, but after we told her about the girl she sort of zoned out," Casey cast a worried look at the door to Tessa's room.

"How is Clara?" Maisy asked.

He'd just left the girl's room, she was still refusing to speak, still refusing to see her parents, still lying curled up in bed with the teddy bear he'd given her. One of the hospital's shrinks had been in to see her but had no luck in convincing the girl to give up any of her secrets. "She's got a long road ahead of her," he told them, and they both nodded sympathetically.

"Wyatt said," Casey begun, "that you might have a lead. On who took Clara."

Nodding tentatively, "I'm on my way to talk to Tessa about it now."

Letting out a dismal sigh, "so you think this is related to what happened to her?" questioned Maisy.

"Maybe." Parker hoped desperately that they could put this behind them once and for all, for his sake as well as Tessa's.

Shaking her head, Casey frowned at him, "she's never talked about it before, what makes you think that she'll suddenly give up the secrets she's been keeping for sixteen years?"

"Because this time other children's lives might be at stake. We have six possible cases that might be related to this. Tessa loves kids, she loves helping others, she'll tell," he said with more confidence than he felt.

Doubtful, "I don't know, Parker. She was willing to keep the secret about Dylan Riley even if it killed her," Maisy reminded him. "Which it almost did."

"Yeah, but keeping that secret was saving people's lives, in this case telling the secret will save lives."

"Hey, lovely lady," said a voice behind them, Wyatt swept his wife into his arms and kissed her deeply.

"Awww," Maisy grinned at them. "You two are so cute."

Grinning back, "thank you," Wyatt took a bow.

Rolling his eyes at them, "you two are disgusting," Parker complained jokingly, there was no couple he admired more, barring his adoptive parents, than Wyatt and Casey.

Wyatt laughed then turned to his wife, "you off to work?"

"Yes, but I'll come by later to check up on Tess. Oh and the kids are sleeping over at my parents tonight, they're super excited."

"Ahh," Wyatt lifted his blonde brows high, "then we have the house to ourselves tonight."

Slapping him playfully on the arm, Casey gave him a quick peck on the cheek, "love you, but I have to go, I'm late."

"Love you too," Wyatt kissed her back.

"See ya, Parker, Maisy," Casey called over her shoulder as she hurried off to head back downstairs.

"I better go too," Maisy announced, checking her watch, "I'm on in less than half an hour. Bye boys, and, Parker," she looked up at him, her usually dancing hazel eyes serious, "go easy on her."

Watching as Maisy rounded the corner he sighed and put a hand to the door handle, letting it linger there, putting off for as long as possible what he knew was going to be an unpleasant conversation.

Biting the bullet, he entered.

Inside the room Tessa lay listlessly in the bed, her eyes open but staring blankly out the window, she didn't acknowledge their presence. "Tess?"

When she turned her head he saw tear tracks down her pale cheeks. "Sweetheart, what's wrong?" he asked, going to her and taking her hand.

"Nothing," she murmured softly. Catching sight of Wyatt, "hey, Skylar."

"Hey, goldilocks," Wyatt too crossed to her and gave her a soft kiss on the cheek. "You're looking better than last time I saw you."

Offering up a weak smile, "thanks."

Wanting, needing, to get straight to the point, "Tess, we need to talk to you about something."

She looked up at him with unnervingly serene blue eyes, but he'd seen in them the faintest tint of resignation. She knew what was coming.

"It's about Clara Meyers. Casey and Maisy told me that she told you her name when we were out in the woods." Parker was studying her closely as they spoke, all too aware of how good Tessa was at concealing her emotions.

"Yes."

"Did she tell you anything else?"

"No. At least I don't think so, the whole thing is a blur." Tessa's face betrayed nothing, but Parker sensed that she was being truthful.

Deciding it was time to push her, "it's kind of similar don't you think?"

"Similar to what?" she asked, the absolute epitome of innocence.

Patiently he explained, knowing full well she knew what he was talking about but willing to play her game for the moment. "The way she was found, wandering in the woods with blood on her clothes but no injuries." Parker paused to give her time to speak. She said nothing, just stared back at him calmly. "That's the way you were found after Eleanor was killed."

Tessa said nothing just continued to look him straight in the eye, making him feel as though they were two school children engaged in a staring contest.

When speaking with Tessa you had to be careful not to speculate. If you started down a track that was wrong Tessa would not correct you, she would simply say nothing and imply that you were right. It was a trick that had helped her many times in the past, so he must remember to stick to the facts.

"Clara isn't speaking to anyone. Whatever happened to her has her so scared that she won't even speak to her parents."

Tessa raised an eyebrow to say 'yeah so?'.

"Just like you. After you were found you didn't speak for four months." He didn't bother to add that she had spent several days sitting in a hospital room alone because the police couldn't identify her since her mother had not reported her missing. Had not even noticed that she was missing.

"You think the cases are related?" she phrased it as a question but it wasn't one.

"Yes I do."

"What happened to Ellie was sixteen years ago," she pointed out as though he hadn't already thought of that.

No mention of herself, that she too had been abducted. That was the way Tessa was, she thought more of others and how she could protect them than she did about herself and her own safety. It had almost cost her her life on more than one occasion. "We also think that your case and Clara's might be linked to six other cases of missing girls."

Gaze steady, she watched as he lay out six photos in front of her.

"This is Heather McCarthy she was eight when she was taken, almost a year ago. This is Carly Letcher, age twelve; she's been gone nine months. Ariyel Hannock, gone for seven months, she was nine. Judy Zammit is ten she's been gone six months. Libby Marks has been missing four months, taken a day after her eleventh birthday. These are sisters, Cassandra and Olivia Stanton, ages eleven and ten, they've been gone three weeks."

Giving her a moment to really look at the photos, her fingers traced each one as she studied them.

"All of these girls are missing, Tessa. All of them were taken from their homes or schools, or places where they ought to have been safe. I think that the same man who took you, who killed your friend, is the same man who took these girls." Taking her face and tilting it so that she was looking at him again. "I need you to tell me what happened to you and Eleanor."

Desperation flared in her eyes but then it was gone, replaced by a stubborn look he knew all too well. Pulling her head away, she gathered up the photos and handed them back. "It's very sad, Parker, what happened to them, but it is not in any way related to what happened to me. I'm sorry."

"Tessa," a twinge of anger lighting inside him, "Clara Meyers was gone for two months, these girls could still be alive. There might still be time to save them."

Guilt lingering in her eyes and this time she made no effort to hide it. "It's already too late."

Pouncing on her confession, "that sounds like an admission that you do know what's going on."

Suddenly she looked tired and worn out, "it can sound like

whatever you want, but I told you the cases aren't related."

"Please, Tess," he was begging and he knew it. Parker knew that Tessa always had reasons for the secrets that she kept but for the life of him he couldn't figure out whom she was protecting by keeping this secret. "Tessa, I know you. I know that you would do anything you had to in order to help someone in need. These children need help. Please help me help them."

"Don't, Parker," she whispered, looking up at him with the saddest eyes he had ever seen. "I'm tired and I'm in pain, I just want to rest now," she murmured, and with that she closed her eyes.

Heart softening as he gazed down at her, he loved her so much it was impossible for him to stay mad at her for long. He cupped her face in one hand, the other running gently through her hair, he'd let her rest for now, but once she was stronger he was going to get the answers he needed. "Okay, you sleep now, but we'll talk later. Tess?" waiting until her eyes opened to look at him, "I'm here for you. No matter what."

\* \* \* \* \*

11:17 P.M.

Tessa was still in shock after the news she had heard, her brain unable to process it all. She had thought he would stop. There was no reason for him to continue any more. She had made sure of that.

Slipping silently down the hospital halls, careful not to draw the attention of any of the nurses. Tessa's injured leg was protesting violently at being forced to walk but she pushed the pain away, had no time for it now, and continued through the empty halls. The physiotherapist had been by earlier and supervised her first steps, her leg was sore and stiff but usable.

Tessa had had to wait for hours until they had finally left her alone. This was the first opportunity she had had all day to sneak away. Parker had hovered around her most of the day, waiting for another opportunity to pepper her with questions about the missing girls. At her insistence he had eventually gone home to shower and grab a couple of hours sleep.

Checking to make sure nobody had spotted her, she eased open a door and crept inside, making her way straight to the bed. "I'm sorry, Clara," she murmured quietly. "I thought I'd stopped him."

Watching the sleeping girl, when she looked at her Tessa didn't see Clara but herself. There was no way she was going to let this girl make the same mistakes she had. She was not going to let him claim another victim.

Debating whether to reach out and wake the girl. She wanted the child to rest, but there was something she needed to know. Something that only Clara could tell her.

Placing a hand softly on Clara's shoulder she shook gently. The girl's eyes snapped open, she sat up, looking around her as though she suspected the bogeyman to suddenly jump from the shadows and grab her.

Taking the child's chin in her hand, she tilted her face so they were eye to eye. "It's okay, Clara, it's Tessa."

Calming when she saw who was there Clara smiled up at her.

Sitting on the bed beside her and holding the girl's hands, "you're okay?"

Clara nodded but said nothing, her eyes asking if she was okay.

"I'm fine. Tired and sore, but okay," Tessa assured her.

Smiling at her, Clara relaxed a little and held up a teddy bear.

"From Parker?" Tessa asked, remembering the teddy bear he had given her for her twenty-sixth birthday, the first one she had celebrated with Parker. It sat on her bed, soft and fluffy, it's fur the same caramel color as Parker's eyes, the ribbon around it's neck the same greeny-blue as her own eyes.

Tugging on her hand Clara frowned at her, eyes crinkling

around the edges as she silently asked what was wrong.

Tessa grew serious as she thought of what she had to tell the girl. "Parker tells me that you won't see your parents."

Clara glanced away, but Tessa took her face and turned it back.

"You know that I understand what you've been through, it's why you spoke to me in the woods, it's why you told me your name. You trust me, which is why I'm going to tell you this, I don't want to see you make the same mistakes that I made."

Clara met her gaze again and nodded, equally serious, and Tessa saw in her eyes a darkness too deep for the eyes of a child. Clara had seen the worst of human behavior and survived, there was no going back, she was a child no longer.

"When I was eleven my friend Ellie and I were abducted," she began. "Ellie was killed. I was gone for three days," she paused, even after all these years it was still hard to say the words aloud. "My mother didn't even know that I was gone. She suffered from depression and she was an alcoholic. She was never interested in me or my brother, just her painting. She would sit for hours painting anything and everything. My father left when I was ten and after that my mother got worse and we moved in with my father's parents. Emilie, my mother, started taking pills as well as drinking, she wouldn't even leave her room. When I was gone she never even noticed." Stopping to look at Clara, "can you say the same about your parents?"

Shaking her head reluctantly, Clara bit her lip and brushed away a stray tear.

"A year later, my mother had a psychotic break, she drugged me and tried to drown me in our bathtub. My brother Daniel found us, dragged me out, did CPR, called the police. Then he left. He's back now but my mother is in a psychiatric hospital, my father lives in France now, with his new family. He never came home through any of this, never even called to see if I was okay."

Tessa wasn't even aware that she was crying until Clara stretched up a hand and wiped away her tears. She hated when that happened, hated when her emotions took on a life of their own.

"Clara, you have two parents who love you, I had no one. You are going to get through this, your mom and dad will help you, don't push them away. Don't try to do this on your own. Take it from someone who tried. You do not want to end up like me, sad, scared, lonely, distrustful. Let them help you." Eyes searching Clara's for any sign that she was getting through, and saw a tiny spark of hope ignite.

"You don't have to talk yet if you're not ready. You can take your time, whatever you need, and you can call me any time, day or night if you do want to talk. The nightmares are never going to go completely away, neither is the fear that he may come back, but over time they will lessen, I promise you they will."

Settling Clara down against the bed, tucking the covers around her chin and placing the teddy bear in her arms. Tessa sat for a minute stroking her hair, a sudden maternal urge flooding through her and she thought of the baby she and Parker had lost a few months ago. Clara was starting to drift off to sleep and there was still something that she needed to know. Leaning over the girl she spoke in a whisper in case anyone was listening, "Clara, I need you to tell me something."

Clara looked up at her, snapping to attention.

"I need you to answer me with words. Can you do that?"

Nodding, eyes deadly serious.

"The man who took you he wasn't the one in charge was he?"

Clara shook her head.

"The place where you were kept, did you hear the name of the man who was in charge? Did anyone talk about him?"

Clara nodded her eyes glistening with unshed tears.

"He didn't have a proper name did he?"

Shaking her head again, a couple of tears tumbling out.

Tessa's heart was pounding painfully in her chest, her ribs shrieking in agony as her breathing quickened, the pain in her leg now so great that she couldn't box it away. She should leave it be. Go back to bed and rest. But she couldn't. She had to know. "What did they call him?"

Clara's terrified eyes penetrated her own and Tessa didn't think the girl could answer even if she wanted to.

"It's okay," Tessa patted Clara's hand comfortingly, "you don't have to tell me. You should rest now." She went to stand but Clara grabbed her hand and pulled her back down.

"John Doe," the girl whispered softly, voice trembling. "They called him John Doe."

Even though she had been positive that was the answer Clara would give, hearing it confirmed sent a mixture of unwanted feelings swirling around inside her so that she felt like a human washing machine.

"Tessa?"

Focusing with difficulty, "yes?" her voice sounded strange to her ears, as though it belonged to someone else.

"He hurt you too didn't he?"

# SEPTEMBER 7<sup>TH</sup>

6:27 A.M.

Someone picked up her wrist.

The feel of the hand on her arm roused her from sleep and she opened her heavy eyes to see a tall, brown haired, brown-eyed man standing beside the bed.

"What is it with doctors and taking pulses?" Tessa asked tiredly. "Don't you have anything better to do?"

"I was looking all over for you," Dr Eric Abbott rebuked mildly, not looking up from his watch.

It took her a moment to realize that she was not in her hospital room anymore. Clara's warm body was sleeping soundly beside her, and she remembered the nighttime rendezvous that had confirmed her worst nightmare. Thinking about what Clara had told her made her feel physically ill.

"How are you feeling?" Dr Abbott was watching her closely with that horribly probing stare that doctors liked to use.

Three months ago while she and Parker had been thrown into the middle of Lachlan Mountain's gauntlet of revenge, Eric Abbott and his wife Lila had been thrown into a nightmare of their own. The couple's five-year-old son, Joey, had been shot and killed by a deranged couple who thought that stealing the Abbott's baby daughter would bring their own dead daughter back to life. Luckily little Molly had been returned unharmed to her parents and Eric and Lila were working on putting their family back together.

Parker and Skylar had worked the Abbott's case and after things had settled down the six of them had caught up a couple of times. Tessa liked Lila, the woman's soulful brown eyes, her quiet strong presence, and the way that Lila never made her feel guilty for grieving the baby she had never even had the chance to hold while Lila grieved the son she had invested five years in loving and nurturing.

She liked Eric too of course, and thoughts of the doctor made her remember that he was currently hovering beside her. Tessa focused her gaze back on him and saw that his expression had shifted from a general concern to a deeper more concentrated worry.

When she tried to sit up, he placed his hands on her shoulders and held her down. "Just stay put for a moment," he ordered gently, producing a penlight and shining it in her eyes.

Tessa did stay put, but only because the pounding in her head had become so severe that for the moment it precluded any other action. Unfortunately, this wasn't her first concussion so she knew that she was going to be in for lots of killer headaches over the next few days.

"Let's get you back to your room," Eric announced.

"What about Clara?" she cast a glance at the sleeping girl. After everything Clara had been through she didn't want the child to be alone when she woke up.

"Her parents will be back soon and I'll make sure someone's keeping a close eye on her," Eric assured her as he slipped an arm behind her shoulders to help her sit up.

"I can do it myself," she protested.

"Uh huh," Eric nodded but made no attempt to remove his arm.

Tessa sighed, but as Eric helped her sit and then stand up, she was glad his strong, steadying arms were holding her upright. Her leg protested wildly at the sudden pressure and sent lightening bolts of pain right up her body to meet the scraping in her brain. The sudden onslaught of pain made her gasp, which of course set off the aching in her chest as her broken ribs objected to the deep breath.

"There we go," Eric murmured as he lowered her down into a wheelchair.

"You know I could have walked," she told him stubbornly a minute later once the pain had eased to a more manageable level.

"Of course you could have," Eric agreed.

Catching the smile in his voice, Tessa twisted her head back to glare up at him. "I really could have," she grumbled.

Eric just laughed and opened her hospital room door, pushing her inside and over to the bed. "Now are you going to be obstinate or can I help my favorite patient into bed?"

"I can manage," she stuck to her guns.

"I think what you meant to say," Eric knelt in front of her, "was yes, thank you for your help, Dr Abbott."

Scowling at him. "Fine," she relented, reluctantly allowing Eric to wrap an arm around her waist and help her stand. Once she was on her feet, she pushed away Eric's arms and tried to take a step on her own. That turned out not to be the best of ideas. Her wobbly legs buckled and she would have hit the ground if Eric hadn't caught her first. And with an exasperated huff, he swung her up off the floor and deposited her on the bed.

"You know you don't have to do everything yourself all the time, Tessa," he admonished as he tucked her under the blankets. "It's okay to let people help you sometimes."

"I thought it was your brother who was the psychiatrist," she frowned as she rested her aching head back against the pillows

"I guess he's rubbing off on me," Eric grinned, but the concern wasn't completely gone from his eyes. "How's your leg?"

"Sore and stiff."

"What about your head?"

"Sore and swimming."

"I'm gonna guess your ribs aren't doing any better."

"They feel like they really, really, really want me to stop breathing." It seemed like no inch of her body had been spared in the crash, she was bruised and achy all over.

"How have you been lately? It's been a couple of weeks since we talked."

Groaning, "why oh why did I have to end up with you as my doctor?" Tessa was positive it hadn't been a coincidence.

"Don't make that sound like a bad thing," Eric reproved. "We're friends, when I heard you were coming in of course I wanted to make sure you were okay. And you didn't answer my question, how have you been lately?"

Rolling her eyes, "I'm fine."

"You know no one ever believes you when you say that," Eric was studying her seriously now and perched on the edge of her bed. "Tessa," he began gently, "you lost your baby, Parker almost died, and that man was planning on kidnapping you and forcing you to be his wife and raise your baby together, it's really okay to be upset about that. Lila and I are still struggling too. Most nights Lila still wakes in a panic from nightmares, she can't go grocery shopping without a small army around her, she still can't bring herself to change a single thing in Joey's room. And me, I'm still using this place as an escape, I still get nervous whenever Lila and Molly go out, I still wake up in the morning and for one blissful second forget that Joey's gone. But we still have Molly and we still have each other, and we're working hard on getting our lives back. And you still have Parker," he reached for her hand and squeezed it tightly, "he really loves you and he's not going anywhere. You should have seen his face the other day when you were brought here. He was in a total panic, he couldn't think of anything besides you, he wouldn't leave your side, we actually had to pry him off you to take you to surgery."

Tessa knew that Parker loved her, and more than anything she really wanted to believe that nothing could tear them apart but . . . "I think psychiatry runs in your family," she told Eric with a weak smile, noting the tears that stood in his eyes and knowing tears were glistening in her own.

"I'm going to leave you my brother's number," Eric jotted it down on a bit of paper and set it on the table beside her bed. "I want you to really think about calling him."

She hated psychiatrists, always had, ever since that horrible man her grandparents had insisted she see after Ellie's murder had attempted to rape her. Still lately she'd been beginning to crack so much that she was losing her will to resist seeking help.

"Now try to get some rest," Eric patted her arm. "And no more disappearing on me," he warned, wagging his finger at her.

Alone once again Tessa cast a glance at the piece of paper with Charlie Abbott's phone number on it. Stretching a hand that shook, because she was in pain not because she was scared, she convinced herself, she took the paper, folded it up and tucked it under her pillow. Then since she knew it was only a matter of time before Parker or another of their friends turned up to check up on her, she closed her eyes, attempted to clear her mind, and let exhaustion take hold.

\* \* \* \* \*

1:06 P.M.

They both stood listening to the chiming of the doorbell.

Parker was on edge.

He was sure that Tessa knew more about Clara Meyers and the other missing girls than she was letting on and he also knew that his wife was apt to do something stupid in the name of helping others. Tessa had pestered him into leaving the hospital last night to go home and shower and sleep, he had returned to the hospital early this morning half expecting to find she had disappeared over night. Thankfully, she hadn't, and had been sleeping fitfully when he arrived.

After checking up on Tessa, he and Wyatt had spent the morning going through each of the missing girl's cases step by step and listing all the similarities and difference between them. Now they were waiting at the Meyers' front door, ready to interview Clara.

Overnight Tessa had apparently slipped into Clara's room and convinced the girl to trust her parents. Eric Abbott, a friend of theirs and a doctor at the hospital, had found them early this morning, both curled up asleep in the bed, the teddy bear he had given Clara between them. Eric had been the doctor who had treated Tessa in the ER when they'd first brought her in after the accident. Actually, it was the second time that Eric had treated Tessa in the emergency room in the last couple of months.

Concerned about her, Eric had called to give him a heads up as to what Tessa had been up to during the night. Parker was sure that Tessa had managed to get more out of the girl than the rest of them. Clara still wasn't talking but she had indicated that she wanted to see her parents, and a few hours ago she had agreed to go home with them.

As he and Wyatt waited for someone to answer the Meyers' front door Parker absently studied the house. It was nice, a grey two-storey weatherboard with mint green trim, the garden however had been badly neglected. The grass was long, weeds poked their heads up in the flowerbeds and somebody had kicked over the mailbox, which had subsequently been propped up on a large rock.

A shadowy figure appeared through the frosted glass door that swung open seconds later by an extremely tall, extremely thin man. Dressed in grey suit pants, white shirt and grey vest, he looked like a telephone pole.

"Mr. Meyers?" Wyatt asked.

"Yes?" the man's voice lifted up at the end of the word as though asking a question.

"My name is Detective Wyatt, this is my partner Detective Bell. We're working your daughter's case and we wondered if we might talk to you for a few minutes?"

The man studied them with somber brown eyes. "I remember you from the hospital?" he said to Parker. "You're the one who found Clara, you were there when we saw her for the first time?"

It seemed as though everything he said was a question not a statement. "Yes that was me," Parker confirmed. "Sorry about having to drag your wife from the room." He hoped that the family's perceived first impressions of him would not be of someone who kept them from their child.

Mr. Meyers shook his head, "no need to apologize. You were just doing what was best for my daughter?"

"May we come in?" Wyatt asked.

"Of course, of course," he stepped back to allow them entrance.

The first thing Parker saw as he entered the house, was a huge family portrait, taken the previous Christmas, just months before Clara disappeared. Noting the tight smiles on each face, he remembered that the Meyers had been separated, planning for a divorce when Clara was taken. Looking from the photo to the real life version he saw how much the trauma had aged Robert Meyers. In his early forties he looked closer to sixty, with a haggard face and grey hair, his tall body unnaturally thin, the bones in his hands clearly visible.

"This way?" Mr. Meyers led them through an arched doorway and into a comfortable living room. Two tan leather couches pointed at a wide-screen TV and a piano stood in the corner with a stack of music books piled on top.

"Clara plays the piano?" he asked.

Following his gaze, Meyers answered, "yes. Since she was three?"

Starting to find the man's constantly questioning voice a little irritating Parker was glad when Mrs. Meyers came bustling into the room. She froze when she saw him. "What is he doing here?" directing the question to her husband.

Jumping in before Mr. Meyers had a chance to answer, "we're

working your daughter's case, we came to talk to you. Mrs. Meyers, I am sorry about the other day. I was only trying to do what was in the best interest of your child."

Studying him, expression inscrutable. She was as short and round as her husband was tall and thin. Dressed in a bright red knitted sweater and grey shirt, her brown hair pulled back in a bun, cheeks tinted with pink, she reminded him of a robin. After a moment she relaxed and smiled, a warm smile that lit up her face, the smile of someone who had been utterly devoid of hope only to receive the one thing they wanted and thought they could never have. "Please sit down," she gestured to the couches, "can I get you anything to drink?"

"Coffee if it's not too much trouble," Wyatt answered as he took a seat.

"It's no trouble, how do you take it?"

Exchanging smiles, it was a running joke between himself and his partner, Wyatt only drank his coffee white, he only drank his black, and they were always trying to convince the other to swap.

"Black thank you, Mrs. Meyers," Wyatt told her.

"Yvonne," she corrected. "Detective Bell?"

"White, thanks."

She practically danced from the room, leaving her husband standing awkwardly in the doorway. Taking the opportunity to study the room more closely, Parker saw that across the walls photographs chronicled the family's history. From wedding, to the birth of their baby, buying the house when Clara was two, first day of school, birthday parties, Christmases, ballet concerts, piano recitals. From the smiles on their faces he guessed that things in the Meyers marriage had started going pear shaped about a year ago.

"Here we go," Yvonne sang as she pranced back into the room, cups of steaming coffee balanced precariously on a tray that she swung about with the confidence of someone who had done it many times before.

Handing out the cups, she ushered her husband into a chair, pushing a cup into his hands, then plopping down beside him. "What can we do for you, detectives?"

"We wanted to see whether we could get a bit of an idea about your background. We know you spoke to the police when Clara was first abducted, but we were hoping that time might have jogged your memory a little," Wyatt explained.

"Yes of course," Yvonne Meyers tried to make her face serious but was unable to keep the smile off it, she was like a little kid on Christmas morning. "We're just so thrilled to have Clara back unharmed that it's so hard to think about those horrible months. It's like they're nothing but a bad dream."

Feeling bad about bursting the woman's bubble, "but it wasn't a dream," Parker reminded her. "Clara was abducted and held prisoner for two months, and while she has been returned to you unharmed physically, emotionally is another story. We want to find the man who took her to prevent him from taking another little girl, and also to give Clara a sense of closure. Often victims of trauma find a certain sense of peace after the perpetrator is found and punished. It helps them to start to feel safe again."

Smile wavering a little, Parker knew that at the moment Yvonne Meyers was on cloud nine, the reality of just what her young daughter had been through had not yet begun to sink in. "What do you need?"

"What can you tell us about your relationship, with each other and with Clara," Wyatt asked gently.

Slipping her hand into her husband's before answering, it was clear she was the dominant one in their relationship. "We were having problems in our marriage, I guess we just got to that point when we were both in a rut. We were arguing all the time, loud screaming fights, Robert had left, we'd filed for divorce, and then Clara was . . . and then she was gone."

Voice faltering her husband put his hand on her knee and patted it reassuringly.

Seeming to draw strength from his touch Yvonne smiled at Robert and squeezed his hand. "At first we blamed each other, the fights got worse. And then we just . . . just realized that our baby might never be coming back and we couldn't lose each other as well. We put a stop to the divorce proceedings, came together, Robert moved back in and we waited for our daughter to come home."

"What about Clara, how did she react to your marital problems?"

"She was pretty upset, hated it when we fought. When her dad left she begged him for weeks to come home, blamed me for pushing him away," Yvonne's eyes glazed at the memory. "We were so focused on our anger at each other that we put Clara in the middle of things," regret tinting her voice. "Whenever Robert came to pick her up for their visits we made a point of fighting with one another."

"What happened the day Clara disappeared?"

Face blackening, "we ah . . . Robert was supposed to pick her up early," she would no longer meet their gaze. "Clara said she wasn't feeling well. It was a Friday, I didn't think she'd miss much in school, but I had to go to work . . ." she started to cry and her husband put an arm around her shoulders. "I thought she'd be okay, I called Robert, he was only ten minutes away, it was daytime, I never thought anything would happen . . ." she broke off as sobs wracked her body.

Burying her face in her husband's shoulder, he rocked her softly while she cried, rubbing soothing circles on her back and whispering, "it wasn't your fault."

"Yvonne?" Parker reached a hand across and laid it gently on her knee, "is there anyone you can think of that might want to hurt you or your family?"

Composing herself, she wiped at her eyes and shook her head, "no. We told the police when Clara disappeared, there was no one who would hate us enough to do that."

"Mr. Meyers?"

Shaking his head vigorously.

"What about anything suspicious in the days or weeks leading up to the abduction. Maybe phone calls where there was nobody on the other end, anyone hanging around your house or Clara's school."

"No there was nothing like that. Everything was completely normal and then she was just . . . gone," Yvonne Meyers said it like she still couldn't believe it had all happened.

"May we see Clara?" Wyatt asked.

Brightening as she thought of her daughter safely upstairs in her bedroom and not in the hands of some maniac. "It was the most amazing thing. This morning she just woke up and wanted to see us, the nurse said that she had a visitor last night. She said that it was the woman who was with you when you found Clara. Your wife?" directing her question to Parker.

Nodding, "Tessa."

"Whatever she said to Clara worked like magic." Then seeming to remember her manners, "is your wife okay? Tessa? We heard that you were in a car accident, that was how you found Clara."

"She's going to be fine, thanks," he gave her a warm smile.

She smiled back, "I'll take you to Clara's room," pushing to her feet she led them to the staircase. "I'm afraid Clara still isn't speaking, she hasn't even spoken a word to us," a momentary glitch in her mask of joyful serenity.

"That's okay, we won't spend long with her. But we would like to set up an appointment for her with one of the psychiatrists who works with us. If that's okay with you," he added.

Nodding uncertainly, "whatever you need to catch the man who took her." Stopping at a white door at the end of the hall, she knocked, "Clara?"

There was no answer and after waiting a few seconds Yvonne tentatively cracked the door open. "Honey, the police are here to see you."

Clara sat in an oversized armchair by the window. Her room looked like any typical tween, a mix of little girl and teenager. The room was filled with white furniture; a bed sat in-between the room's two windows, a bureau and bookcase against one wall, a desk and matching chair against another, the armchair and a lamp by one of the windows.

Recognition flashed through her eyes as she saw him and she gave a weak wave. Taking it as a positive sign, Parker entered the room and knelt in front of her. "Hi, Clara, do you remember my partner, Wyatt? He was the one who found us."

She glanced at Wyatt, gave him a once over and nodded.

"We wondered if you might be able to give us a description of the man who took you. You don't have to tell us, I can ask you some questions and you can just nod when I say something that's true."

She considered this and nodded her assent.

"Great, let's get started. Was the man tall?"

A shake.

Confirming, "he was short?"

A nod.

"You're doing great. Okay did he have brown hair?"

A shake.

"Okay what about blond hair?"

Another shake.

"Grey? White?"

More shakes.

Jumping in Wyatt asked, "was he bald?"

Clara nodded.

Smiling, "okay so he was short and bald. Was he skinny like your dad?"

A shake.

"Muscley like my partner here?" Wyatt joked.

Clara smiled weakly and nodded.

"What about his eyes, were they blue?"

A shake.

"Brown?"

A shake.

"Green?"

A shake.

"Black?"

A nod this time.

"Okay so he was a short, well-muscled, bald man with black eyes, is there anything else distinctive about him that you can think of?"

Clara thought for a minute and then her eyes lit up and she sprung out of her chair, hurrying to the desk and grabbing a pink spiral notebook. She scribbled something and tore off the paper, handing it to him.

"Tattoos? The man had a tattoo?" he asked. This was a real lead, if it was a distinctive one then it could lead them straight to him. "What was it of?"

Wiggling her hand in front of him, pointing to the paper, he handed it back and she jotted something else down.

"Gemini? Just the word? You're sure?"

Clara nodded firmly.

"You did wonderfully, sweetheart," her mother gushed, coming to wrap her in a hug.

"You sure did, kiddo," Wyatt grinned.

Clara flushed with pride.

Taking her by the shoulders Parker lent over so that they were eye to eye. "When Tessa came to see you last night did you say anything to her?"

Startled, the girl stared at him in surprise and Parker knew that he was right.

"What did you say?"

Clara looked at him but remained steadfastly silent.

Resisting the urge to shake the child he released her and turned to leave. "Thanks, Clara," he called over his shoulder, Wyatt following him to the door.

"I'll be back in a minute, Clara," her mother murmured, then she too followed them. As soon as the door closed she asked, "did that help you? Will you be able to get him now?"

"I hope so," Parker replied as they made their way down the stairs.

No one heard the girl, alone in her room, murmur quietly to herself, "I told her his name but she already knew."

\* \* \* \* \*

3:33 P.M.

"He wants to see you."

Dino looked up from his laptop to eyeball the man in front of him. Tim Stevens. Young, too good looking for his own good, new to the organization, and with an unbelievably squeaky voice.

"What about?"

"I don't know, sir," Tim had the irritating habit of always referring to everyone as sir.

"Well go and find out," resuming his game of solitaire.

"Sir, he uh, he said it was important," picking at the cuticles of his nails nervously as he spoke. "He said I was to come and get you and bring you over to the library."

Slamming the computer closed Dino kicked over the chair in frustration. "Fine. I suppose if he wants to see me I have no choice."

Apologetic Tim hovered in the doorway, "we should go."

Storming from his room he was further annoyed as Tim trailed along behind him. Whirling on the young man, "I don't need an escort."

Stumbling backwards, face bright red, "I uh . . . I uh . . ." Tim stuttered. "He said I should . . . should make sure you came straight there."

Fuming Dino realized that something had happened to cause John Doe to lose trust in him. If his boss lost faith in him then he could lose everything he had worked so hard to get. Growing up poor he had dreamed of the future he wanted, mansions, fancy cars, tailored clothes, everything he had never had. Now that he had them, he was not going to let them go.

Bursting through the library door, John Doe was on the phone and halted him with a raised hand. Annoyed at the easy way John Doe brushed others aside as though they were inconsequential. And then annoyed that it annoyed him, he could not afford to say or do anything to get John Doe offside.

Pacing around the room, Dino had been in it only a few times in the years he'd lived in the house, and it still impressed him. Two whole walls were filled, floor to ceiling, with old, leather-bound books. The far wall contained a huge picture window with a spectacular view of the gardens. A deer head and a bear head were mounted on either side of the window, trophies from John Doe's hunting days. The furniture in the room was old and stately, leather armchairs, a huge desk, elegantly carved side tables, stained glass lamps.

"You can leave us now, thank you, Tim," John Doe had finished his phone call and dismissed the young man who was only too eager to comply. "Drink, Dino?"

Exasperated by his boss' overly calm demeanor, he nodded and took a seat, watching as John Doe poured two glasses of brandy then carried them over and handed one to him.

John Doe took his time, sitting and swirling the rich amber liquid in his glass. He did this, Dino knew, to make sure that whoever he was about to speak with was well and truly on edge. Taking a long drink John Doe studied him, head cocked to the side, brown eyes magnified by his glasses, his expression unreadable. Dino knew there was nothing he could do but sit and wait to see what his boss had to tell him.

Eventually John Doe spoke, "stay away from her."

Frowning in confusion, "what?"

Raising a silvery eyebrow, "you heard me."

Understanding dawning slowly, "I don't know what you're talking about," he stammered lamely.

Face growing deadly serious, "Tessa Bell is off limits." Voice quietly menacing, "now and in the future. You will not lay a hand on her, is that understood?" For an older man he possessed a fierceness unlike anyone Dino knew, and he knew an awful lot of colorful characters.

Feeling his cheeks redden with anger, Dino hated being told what to do by anyone. He had waited long enough for his revenge, and all the while Tessa had been living a charmed, unpunished life. He desperately wanted her to pay for what she had done, but if he disobeyed a direct order from John Doe then he would most definitely end up dead, and it wouldn't be a quick death.

"Do you understand?" John Doe enunciated each word, clearly incensed that Dino had not immediately acquiesced. It was well known that John Doe hated him, despised might be a better word, he made no secret of his feelings. Dino didn't hold John Doe in high esteem either, but he was his boss and his livelihood depended on him. John Doe tolerated him because he was necessary. There were some things in this business that he couldn't do himself, and so Dino had a job.

"I . . . I . . ." he could hardly gets the words out past the lump of rage in his throat. "I understand."

Nodding, pleased, John Doe pasted a smile that was as threatening as his glare, on his face. "You may go," he announced crisply and returned to his drink.

Breathing deeply to control his fury Dino stalked across the room, pausing as he opened the door to cast a last look at his boss. John Doe was lounging in his leather recliner, head back, eyes closed, Jazz music filtering through the room. He had been in the business so long that he had become accustomed to getting his own way, at having his orders followed to the letter. No one knew much about his past, where he had come from, who he had been before, he had just appeared one day.

Slamming the door behind him, as loudly as he dared, Dino stormed through the mansion and back to his room, where he proceeded to trash the place. Fury, rage, anger, resentment, popping inside him as though he were a giant popcorn popper. Energy spent he slid down to the ground and propped his head up on his knees. Making a decision that could cost him everything.

He would have his revenge.

Tessa Micah Bell would pay for her sins.

All he had to do was make sure John Doe never found out.

He'd get some rest and then once it got dark he'd pay the little princess a visit.

* * * * *

7:20 P.M.

Dropping wearily down onto the bed in her room, Tessa let her bag drop to the floor, too weary to bother picking it up. Swinging her leg carefully up onto the mattress, wincing as it burned with pain, then piling the pillows on top of each other, she rested her head against them and closed her eyes.

Parker was going to be mad when he found out that she had checked herself out of the hospital against medical advice. Eric Abbott had already thrown a fit when she'd announced she was going home whether he liked it or not, and she was sure that he would have blabbed to Parker by now.

People had been in and out visiting her all afternoon, Casey had come by with the kids, Maisy had been back, Parker's boss J.J. had come to see her and so had Maisy's boss Marty Jenkins. Eventually she had asked one of the nurses to keep everyone out because she was tired, then once they had all gone she signed herself out and took a cab back to the mansion. Tessa hated hospitals, too many bad memories, and hadn't been able to face another second there. After her abduction she had sat in the hospital for two days before the police found out who she was, another four before her grandparents arrived to collect her.

Another headache reared its ugly head, and she lifted her hands and massaged her temples. She didn't want to think about Emilie but ever since she had told the story of her mother to Clara, she couldn't seem to get the woman out of her head. Emilie had never cared about her, never known how to deal with a child with a high IQ, never tried to foster Tessa's talents and interests. On the plus side, neither had she cared about Tessa's experiments and projects and the many notes sent home from the school as a result.

Suddenly cold, Tessa kicked off her shoes and slid under the covers, reaching for the teddy bear that Parker had given her, she hugged it close as she listened to the creaks and groans of the old house. She hated this house but ever since her and Parker's home had been invaded by hidden cameras she had been unable to face going back there, and for some reason she couldn't fathom had felt herself being drawn back here.

In the distance she could hear the phone ringing but she was too tired to bother with it, too tired to talk to anyone. Ignoring it, she reached for the bottle of sleeping pills Eric had prescribed to help her sleep. Against her better judgment, she almost never took medication, Tessa unscrewed the lid, tipped two pills into her hand and swallowed them quickly.

Settling back against the pillows and snuggling down under the quilt, she pulled it over her head. Tessa was asleep within seconds and never noticed the figure in black slipping through the back door.

* * * * *

7:40 P.M.

Slipping through the back door of the mansion that he knew almost as well as his own. It was just as he remembered it, although it had been many years since he had last been here.

Those first few years Dino had left Tessa an anonymous gift on her doorstep, every year on Eleanor's birthday. A reminder of what she had done. When she had gone away to college he had started mailing her a gift, keeping tabs on her movements, but having become more involved in the day to day operations of his work, he continued to mail gifts to her even after she returned to town.

He'd missed the feeling of being so close to her.

Creeping through the huge stone mansion he felt the familiar rush of resentment towards Tessa, who had everything and yet had taken from him the only thing he had. It took him a little while to locate her bedroom, she had apparently stopped using the one she had grown up in.

Standing in the doorway Dino took a moment just to stand back and enjoy, to soak it all in, to make it a night to remember. He was surprised that Tessa was still asleep in bed. She was a security nut, her cottage had been wired to the hilt. Stepping closer he saw the reason, a bottle of sleeping pills sat on the bedside table.

Standing over her he took hold of the quilt and pulled it back, he wanted to be able to see her face. She looked just the same as she always had, naturally white-blonde curls tumbling around her head, black lashes fanned out against pale skin, a smattering of freckles across her nose. She was as beautiful today as the first day he had seen her. She looked like an angel. Everyone thought she was so sweet, he alone knew what she was capable of.

"Hello Tessa," he murmured softly.

Reaching down to brush his hand across her cheek, she whimpered softly but didn't wake. Dino wondered whether she still had nightmares about what she had done. He hoped so.

Seeing her so helpless. So completely and utterly at his mercy. The power rush was exhilarating. He could kill her right here and now. Or he could take his time with her and have some fun first.

Overwhelming desire flooding through him, Dino was reaching for her before he even knew what he was doing. Running his hand slowly down under the covers and along the length of her body, then back up to her neck. Encircling it with one hand. Once again, she whimpered but didn't wake and he was almost compelled to do it right there and then. To take her and then kill her, end it all.

"Not yet, not yet," he muttered to himself withdrawing his hand.

He wanted her to suffer first.

Leaning over he kissed her, then retreated from the room, quickly finding the kitchen, one of the few rooms in the house he knew she used. Setting her gift on the table, he was particularly pleased with this year's present. Most years he had just sent her a book, usually one with a theme of revenge, but this year he had been especially inventive. He almost wished he could be here when she opened it, just to see the look on her face.

Reluctantly slipping back out the door, crossing the huge green lawn to his car, parked next to the remains of her old cottage. Remembering the night he had laid in wait, knocking her unconscious as she came through her front door, then tying her up and setting the place on fire. She had never seen his face but he knew that she knew it was him who had attacked her.

With a serial killer after Tessa it had seemed like a perfect opportunity to kill her without drawing suspicion upon himself. Unfortunately, Tessa had been saved and John Doe had found out about the fire. He had been beyond furious, ranting and raving at him for hours about the need to keep away from the police's radar, as though Dino were nothing but an idiot. He had been forced to promise to keep away from Tessa, and had taken the failed attempt on her life as a sign that it was not the right time to pursue his revenge.

Now he had a new sign.

Despite what John Doe thought, Dino Rollino was *not* as idiot and he did not believe in coincidences. Finding Tessa in the woods was a sign that now the time had come to do what he had been waiting sixteen years for. He would rid the world of Tessa Micah Bell and then when the time was right he would take his rightful position as leader of the organization.

\* \* \* \* \*

9:47 P.M.

Something was wrong.

Tessa knew it as soon as she awoke.

Someone had been in the room with her.

Sitting straight up she was rocked by a wave of dizziness mixed with nausea. Pressing her fingers to her eyes she waited until the sensation passed then tentatively stood up. The painkillers had worn off while she was asleep and the pain in her head, chest and leg had come back stronger than ever.

Glancing at the glowing clock beside her bed, she saw that she had been asleep for two hours. Plenty of time for him to sneak inside, he already knew where she lived.

Her bedroom door was closed, she had left it open when she had collapsed into bed a couple of hours ago. Hobbling down the hall, past closed doors, the house had close to one hundred rooms, but she used only a few, the rest sat empty and forgotten. He could be waiting for her behind one of them.

Shaking her head. "No, that's not his style," Tessa said aloud to try and calm herself. "If he was here he'd want me to know it."

Gripping the ornately carved banister as she made her way down the huge central staircase, each step more agonizing than the one before. Using the wall to help keep herself upright, she almost wished she had taken a pair of crutches from the hospital, and inched her way towards the kitchen.

Flicking on the light switch the first thing she saw was a brightly colored box, covered with balloons, a rainbow bow on the top.

Heart pounding so violently each beat sent ribbons of pain through her ribs, tentatively Tessa let go of the wall and dragged her bad leg over to the table. Reaching out a shaking hand towards the package, struggling to untie the bow with fingers that wouldn't stop trembling. Hands lingering on the lid, she had a bad feeling about whatever was inside.

Clenching her eyes shut she lifted off the lid, took as deep a breath as she could manage and tried to settle the churning in her stomach.

Opening her eyes, she leaned over the box and peered inside.

A scream echoed through the large empty house.

Not usually one to scream when she was scared, it took Tessa a moment to realize that the sound was coming from her own mouth.

She couldn't breath.

She was gasping for air.

Her throat felt like it was closing tighter and tighter with each intake of air getting smaller and smaller.

White dots started to dance in front of her eyes.

She swayed and grabbed hold of the back of one of the chairs to keep from falling.

What was in the box was disgusting and yet she couldn't seem to draw her eyes away.

Lowering herself to the floor as her head felt like it was about to explode.

Lying down she pressed her burning cheek to the cool tiles of the kitchen floor and tried to focus on her breathing. When it had slowed sufficiently she crawled to the living room closest to the kitchen and reached for the phone. Dialing Parker's cell phone number with hands that still quivered violently.

Waiting anxiously for him to answer, counting the rings.

"Tessa?"

"Parker," voice coming out in a trembling rush as she fought back tears. "He was here. In the house. While I was sleeping. He . . ."

"Honey, try to calm down, you sound like you can't breathe." Parker's voice was calm, soothing, but she could sense his underlying panic. "Tell me exactly what happened."

Struggling for calm, "he was in the house, in my room, while I was asleep . . ."

"Tessa, did he hurt you?" voice suddenly fierce with concern. "Are you okay?"

"I . . . I . . . I'm okay," she assured him. "Just a little shaken up."

"What's going on?" she could hear Skylar's faraway voice ask.

Parker's muffled voice replied, "someone was in the house with Tess."

"She okay?" Skylar asked.

"I think so."

"Parker?" she called, she wanted him focused on her right now.

"Yeah, I'm here. Okay, Wyatt and I are on our way," things rustled in the background. "Is he still there?"

"I don't think so. No, I'm sure he's gone."

"Alright, make sure the door's locked then stay in the living room with the phone, I'll let myself in when we get there. Hey," she could tell he was making an effort to be calm, "everything's gonna be alright. Okay?"

"Okay," she sniffed.

"Hold tight, we'll be there as quick as we can."

He was about to hang up but there was something else she needed to tell him. "Parker?"

"What is it, honey?"

"He, uh, he left me something." Swallowing back bile as she thought of the horrible gift he had left on her kitchen table.

"What? What did he leave you?" car doors slammed and the engine revved.

Hardly able to get the words out, "a . . . a spider."

"He left you a spider?" Parker repeated, clearly confused.

"A huge one. Its legs were all cut off and its abdomen was ripped open." Tessa couldn't fight it any longer, pain, exhaustion, fear all taking their toll, she started to cry. "It's what he wants to do to me," she sobbed quietly.

Through the phone she could hear the siren of Skylar's car start up it's high-pitched wail. "It's okay, shh, it's alright," Parker's reassuring voice murmured. "We're gonna be right there, okay?"

"Yeah," wiping away tears with the back of her hand.

"I love you, baby," Parker told her.

"Love you too," she whispered back. And then he was gone and she was all alone again, except for the horrible broken beast still in her kitchen.

Letting the phone drop to the floor Tessa crawled to the settee, heaved herself up onto it, ignored the protest of her leg as she curled into a ball, and lay there sobbing her heart out.

\* \* \* \* \*

10:03 P.M.

"Come on," Cassie urged the other girls. "If we all work together we can take them."

Fifteen faces stared blankly back at her, among them a couple she knew. Carly Letcher played in the same tennis competition as she did, and was one of the only girls that Cassie had trouble beating. Judy Zammit's cousin was on Olivia's basketball team, they'd met her one Christmas at a party.

In the weeks or months they had been here many of the girls had lost their spark. They spent their days sitting wearily staring with empty eyes into space, waiting for whatever John Doe had planned for them.

At first glance, John Doe seemed to be friendly, almost grandfatherly, and Cassie remembered the first time she had met him. She and Olivia had been here only a day or so when he had come down to the basement dungeons, and for a minute she had believed that he had come to rescue them. He had smiled at her and her sister, and spoken to them in a quiet, gentle voice, leading them down the hall and into the room.

Unlike the rest of the rooms, this one had bright, striped wallpaper covering the walls, a huge four-poster bed sat in the centre of the room, thick fluffy carpet on the floor. A video camera was set up against one wall, pointed at the bed, and Cassie had felt a sick feeling settle in her stomach.

Once the door was closed John Doe had told them to take off their clothes, Cassie had refused, but he sprung forward with surprising agility, grabbed Olivia, and twisted her arm up behind her back. Her little sister had shrieked in pain, John Doe had smiled at her as though they were discussing nothing more than the weather. It was an evil smile. Complying with his request she had stripped off her clothing, including her underwear, and stood, cheeks bright red with embarrassment as he examined every inch of her body.

They were in there for over an hour as he posed her this way and that way, taking photos every so often, then he'd dressed her in a variety of outfits, again taking photos sporadically. When he was done he had questioned her about her sexual experiences. Cassie had stared at him with shocked disbelief, and stammered that she was only eleven and had never had sex, it was something grown-ups did. He said nothing, merely raised an eyebrow and told her she could put her clothes back on. Then he sent her from the room, Olivia remained behind.

When her sister returned to their cell later that day, she was crying and shaking, and promptly threw up. Olivia wouldn't tell her what had gone on in the room, but Cassie had a sinking feeling that she already knew the answer.

John Doe could hold her prisoner. He could torture and torment her here in this dank, dark place, but he could not break her spirit. Cassandra Stanton was nothing if not determined, and so she faced the other girls, eyes sparkling with fire, and urged them to regain their own spirit and stand up to their captors.

"We can take them, together we can do it," she encouraged.

"There's too many," one girl, Candice, cut in dejectedly.

"We're too small and they're too big," another girl added dismally. Cassie thought her name was Francis, but she kept to herself and wouldn't speak with the others so no one was quite sure.

"But if we work together," Cassie fought back, frustrated at the way they had allowed themselves to be beaten down. "We can do it."

"Maybe we could," piped up a tiny voice. A small Asian girl stood up, she was new, been here only a day or so, she had not yet met John Doe.

Cassie grinned at her, "that's the spirit," she encouraged. "We may be smaller than them but we're smarter. We can wait until they come down the stairs, rush at them. There's usually only a couple of them, so if we break up into groups of five, one group can focus on each of the men and the third group can go up the stairs. I don't know what the house looks like but all we have to do is run for the . . ."

"Stop, stop, stop," a voice shrieked.

All faces in the cramped little room turned to look at Isabel Freeman. A frail redhead that had been here longer than any of them, her eyes wild, face as bright red as her hair.

"It's okay, Isabel," Cassie begun, but the other girl cut her off.

"We are never getting out of here. And if we do it won't be to go back to our lives. He'll never let that happen. We have no chance of getting past the guards, they'll kill us before they let us go. It's hopeless, completely . . ."

"Shh, he's coming," Olivia stuck her head in the door, she had been keeping watch in the corridor.

"John Doe?" Cassie asked.

"No. Dino," Olivia replied.

Every single girl in the room shivered. As bad as John Doe was, Dino was worse. They'd all heard the stories of what he had done, of what he was capable of.

Silence filled the room then Dino's muscled frame filled the doorway, his bald head shining in the half-light of the basement. "I hear someone in here's trying to stir up trouble," he smirked at them as his eyes roved the scared faces.

None of the girls spoke.

Eyes settling on Cassie, she wanted to shrink away from his gaze but remained firm. "Was it you, Cassandra?"

Trying to speak but her voice wouldn't work.

As Dino took a menacing step into the room, Isabel screeched, "it was her, it was Cassandra, she was the one trying to stir up trouble."

Shooting her a disbelieving frown, then looking up as Dino stood right in front of her, she could feel his breath puffing against her forehead. Meeting his gaze squarely she tried not to show the terror that was pulsing through her.

"Well, Cassandra, maybe it's time you and I spent a little time together, learn how this place works, who's in charge." Grabbing her by the hair, Dino yanked her down the hall towards the room. Kicking and squirming she tried desperately to get free, but Dino was bigger and stronger, and like the other girls had said, she just didn't stand a chance against him.

The last thing she saw before the door snapped closed were Olivia's stricken eyes.

* * * * *

11:00 P.M.

"You know there's no gas pedal on your side, right?"

His partner's voice cutting through the haze of panic that hung over his head like a cloud of fog, Parker turned to him, "what?"

Taking his eyes off the road to glance at Parker's legs.

Following Wyatt's eyes he saw that he had been subconsciously pressing his foot against the car's floor as though he could somehow make it go faster. "Sorry," he said sheepishly. They'd been caught in a traffic jam earlier. It already took close to forty-five minutes to get from the station to Tessa's estate, and so far they'd been on the road for over an hour.

He had been on edge since Eric had called to let him know that Tessa had checked herself out of the hospital. Parker had been worried that she'd push herself too far, end up hurting herself more, the thought that *he* would turn up had not even occurred to him.

Frustrated with himself, he should have gone with his first instinct, which was to drive straight home when Tessa hadn't answered his earlier phone call. The panic in Tessa's voice had scared him. She was already balancing precariously on the edge of a complete emotional breakdown. If the man who wanted her dead made a reappearance in her life now it could push her right over the edge . . .

"We're here," Wyatt announced as he turned the car into the long, tree-lined driveway.

As they pulled up in front of the enormous mansion, Parker was out of the car before Wyatt came to a complete stop. Pulling his key from his pocket as he ran for the front door, jiggling the key in the lock and swinging the door open.

"Tessa?"

There was no answer and his blood pressure jumped as he ran

through the halls to the living room, thinking of every conceivable crisis that might have occurred since he'd spoken to her on the phone.

Wyatt caught up to him. "Parker, wait," he whispered. "He could still be here."

"Tessa said he was gone."

"She's not a mind reader," Wyatt muttered under his breath.

Rolling his eyes at his partner, but he did slow as he approached the closed living room door. With their guns drawn, Wyatt slowly pushed the door open, it creaked loudly, the sound magnified in the silent house. The room was dark, a shadowy form lay on one of the couches, checking the room for any other presence, when they found none Parker switched on the light.

Tessa blinked at the bright light that filled the room and sat up slowly. Her eyes were red-rimmed but she seemed to be calmer than she had been earlier. Without a word Parker dropped his gun on a table, crossed to her and wrapped his arms around her, crushing her against his chest until she gently pushed him away.

Holding her at arms length, gripping her shoulders so tightly she winced and he loosened his grip a little. "Are you okay?"

Her bottom lip trembled for a moment but she controlled it and pulled her mask of calm firmly back into place. "I'm fine."

Crouching in front of her, hands on her knees, "tell me exactly what happened."

Taking a deep breath, Tessa fixed her eyes on a spot above his head and recounted everything that had happened since she checked herself out of the hospital. By the time she was finished she was shaking like a leaf. Grabbing one of the throw rugs from the adjacent settee he wrapped it around her and then stood behind her rubbing her shoulders.

Wyatt reappeared from the kitchen with a glass of water, which he handed to Tessa. Parker caught his eye, silently asking whether he had called Marty.

Taking a sip of the water before setting the glass on the floor beside her. "Did you see it?" Tessa questioned Wyatt.

"Yeah," Wyatt said apologetically. "Marty's on his way to get it, it'll be gone soon."

She shivered, "I was kinda hoping I imagined it," she murmured softly.

Exchanging glances above her head, Wyatt gave an almost imperceptible nod, and Parker sighed, he didn't want to add to Tessa's stress right now.

Dropping onto the couch beside her he put an arm around her shoulders. She looked at him, distracted, "what?"

"We spoke to Clara today," he began.

"How's she doing?" Tessa asked.

"About as well as can be expected," he answered. "She's home with her parents, we went to see her, had quite an interesting conversation."

Raising a questioning brow, Tessa waited for him to explain.

Complying, "she told us that she spoke to you." Watching her closely, "I mean actually *spoke* to you."

Tessa nodded but didn't say anything.

"What did she say to you?"

Pressing her lips into a stubborn line Tessa refused to respond.

"Does the name Dino Rollino mean anything to you?"

Not so much as a flinch to show she recognized the name.

"He came up in two of the missing girl's cases. He works as an electrician and had done some work in the neighborhood in the couple of weeks prior to the girls abductions," he expanded, watching her closely for any flickers of recognition.

Once again, Tessa just stared back at him with impeccably serene blue eyes. It was the first time in a long that Parker had seen his wife so much like her old self, apparently having something to focus her attention on had worked wonders. If there hadn't been children's lives at risk he would almost have relished the opportunity to attempt to wheedle out of Tessa the information that he needed, but right now time was of the essence. "Come on, Tessa, it's been sixteen years since Eleanor was killed," he coaxed. "Since you were abducted, it's time to finally tell someone what happened."

"I'm not going to play this game with you now," she announced calmly. "My head is pounding, my leg is burning and each breath I take makes my chest feel like it's about to explode." She stood, attempting to hide her grimace as she put weight on her leg but failing dismally.

"Tessa," he wheedled, "those kids could still be alive. Seven innocent little girls, that we know of, probably countless others that we don't." Aware that Tessa's face had clouded over and she was scowling at him. "You can help them if you just tell me what happened the weekend you and Eleanor were . . ."

"She needs to rest, Parker," Wyatt spoke up.

Parker had forgotten his partner was even in the room. Looking at Tessa as she shot Wyatt a grateful smile, he knew he ought to ease up on her, she did look like she was half dead on her feet, but he needed answers. He'd thought that he could deal with not knowing everything about that weekend but he realized now that he had to know. "Tessa, please," he begged, "please. I need to know what happened to you that weekend."

"I'm tired," her voice dropped to a whisper. "And I can't tell you what you want to hear." Tessa turned her back on him and took a couple of hobbling steps towards the door, Wyatt springing to her aid.

Fighting disappointment but not surprised, he hadn't really expected getting answers out of his wife to be an easy task. Reminding himself that Tessa had been just a child when she had been abducted and that whatever had happened to her that weekend had changed the course of her life forever. Brushing away his frustration, he went to Tessa's side and slipped an arm around her waist.

Shrugging off his touch, "I don't need your help, Parker."

Smiling at the reappearance of her ludicrously independent

streak, he lifted her up into his arms. "Don't be stubborn, you look terrible and you can barely stay upright."

Holding herself stiffly for a moment then sinking down into his arms, nestling her head against his shoulder.

"Come on, we both need a good night's sleep." Shooting Wyatt a grateful glance for intervening before he had a chance to make things worse and make Tessa even more determined to keep her secrets. Taking the stairs two at a time and criss-crossing down several corridors to the bedroom that Tessa had chosen when they'd moved in here three months ago. Setting his wife down on the rumpled bed and arranging the covers around her before pulling off his clothes and sliding in beside her.

Immediately Tessa snuggled against him, clearly still shaken up about her earlier visitor. He began to rub soothing circles on her back and within minutes she had drifted off. As he watched her sleep Parker knew that whether Tessa liked it or not, if they were going to have any chance at finding the missing girls then she was going to have to provide answers about the worst days of her life.

* * * * *

11:57 P.M.

Stretching out in bed Dino couldn't be happier with how things had gone tonight.

Yes, his body was still tingling frantically as he thought of everything that he could have done to Tessa tonight. He'd had to visit downstairs with one of the girls to work off his overflowing energy. But he had made the right choice. He wanted Tessa to suffer, so the longer he drew things out, made sure she knew he was out there, watching her, hunting her, the better.

It wasn't going to be an easy run though.

Dino was prepared for that.

Tessa had married a cop, a good cop, and one who always

managed to rush in and save her at the last second. Underestimating Detective Parker Bell had been the mistake of everyone else who had ever tried to take down Tessa. Dylan Riley, Cordelia Micah, Lachlan Mountain, they had all misjudged just what lengths Detective Bell would go to in order to save his wife's life. Dino himself had made that mistake once already. When he'd taken advantage of the fact that Dylan, the man responsible for bringing Tessa and Parker together, had been stalking Tessa, and tried to burn her alive, Detective Bell had rushed inside her burning cottage to save her even though at the time he'd only known her a few days.

Tessa had lived because Dino had underestimated Detective Bell. He would not make the same mistake this time.

Parker Bell wasn't the only obstacle between Tessa and himself. John Doe was there too. For some reason Dino couldn't fathom John Doe had made himself Tessa's protector, refusing to allow him to exact the revenge that was rightfully his. John Doe had even gone so far as to insist that they help Tessa a couple of months ago. His boss was probably enamored with her, she seemed to cast some sort of spell over men. Or maybe she had something on him, Dino had never known John Doe to go to such lengths for anyone else.

Whatever the case, Dino was not going to be deterred.

Detective Bell wasn't going to stop him.

John Doe wasn't going to stop him.

He had been waiting sixteen years, enough was enough, it was time to make Tessa pay for her actions.

# SEPTEMBER 8<sup>TH</sup>

8:18 A.M.

"I still don't really understand why we came back here."

Parker shot his partner an annoyed glare, he'd already explained to Wyatt why he wanted to come out here, several times in fact. "I told you," he snapped irritably, he'd had hardly any sleep last night and his body still ached from the accident. "This might be the only place where we can find some answers about the missing girls."

Eyeing him doubtfully, "we don't even know if the cases are connected yet, and we have a dozen active cases waiting for us. Besides CSU already went over this place with a fine tooth comb after Dylan Riley's games and found absolutely nothing, so what makes you think we're suddenly going to find some answers?"

"Because this is Tessa's life we're talking about," Parker replied as they turned into the driveway. "It's *my* life and I need answers."

As Wyatt pulled to a stop they both lapsed into silence, remembering the last time they had been out here. The Tudor mansion looked even more dilapidated than it had that night. The grass around it longer and wilder, the window through which a young woman had been thrown to her death still contained the remaining glass shards. This was the house where Eleanor Matthews had been killed, the place where sadistic Dylan Riley had brought Tessa for the finale of his master plan to force Tessa to run away with him.

"I have to know," Parker murmured again. "I have to know what happened to Tessa and Eleanor."

"How is Tessa this morning?" Wyatt asked as they climbed

from the car.

"To quote her she's 'fine'." A little snarl crept into his voice, he hated that saying of Tessa's, mostly because she only ever said it when things were far from fine. Tessa had been up when he'd left and seemed to be back to her old self. While that sounded like a good thing, she had been so close to actually dealing with some of the traumatic experiences from her past but now she was right back to insisting everything was fine.

Nodding his understanding as they entered the gloomy mansion. "This is your plan so what exactly do you want to get out of it?" Wyatt asked.

"I don't know," Parker shot back, frustrated, he wanted answers but he wasn't sure how to get them. "Let's do the basement, I don't remember looking at it last time, maybe something there will spark something."

"There is no basement," Wyatt reminded him, brushing frantically at a spider web on his sleeve, after last night they were all a little freaked out about spiders.

Brow crinkling in confusion, "yes there is."

"No, there's not."

"Yes, there is," he insisted, positive that he had heard Tessa mention a basement in the little she'd told him about that weekend. Heading for the kitchen, "Tessa said there was a basement so there's one here somewhere." Reaching the kitchen he began to feel the walls checking for anything that might open a hidden door. "If someone was using this place to hide kidnapped children then they'd need somewhere out of sight."

Still looking a little doubtful Wyatt joined him in his search and they worked in silence for close to ten minutes, until Wyatt, who was over by the back wall of the enormous decaying kitchen leant against the wall and a panel on the opposite wall sprung open. They both turned, surprised, and moved simultaneously to the narrow doorway, peering down into the dark basement.

"Is there a light switch?" Wyatt asked.

Running a hand up and down the wall just inside the opening, finding and flicking a switch which illuminating the rickety staircase,

"Told you there was a basement," Parker grinned.

Descending down the steps they found themselves in a large empty room. The concrete walls had been painted a pale lemon, the paint peeling off in huge chunks, the floor had been covered in a rough grey carpet. Opposite the stairs was a single door, it was half closed and contained several open padlocks.

"Looks like no one's been in here for years," Wyatt commented as he examined the cobwebs in the corners and ran a finger along the dusty walls.

"Dylan mustn't have used the basement when he was staying here," Parker crossed to the door and slowly swung it the rest of the way open to reveal a long corridor along which were two rows of closed doors. "More rooms down here," he called to Wyatt who followed him down the hallway, both of them opening the doors as they went. Behind each door was a tiny cell. No window, no furniture, no carpet, just a bare concrete room. Parker's stomach started to spin. "Child trafficking," he heard himself say. When his partner turned to face him, Wyatt's grim expression confirmed that was the conclusion he had come to as well.

Wiggling his phone out of his pocket, he dialed Marty Jenkins' direct number, jiggling nervously while he waited for the CSU tech to answer.

"Marty Jenkins."

"Hey, Marty, it's Parker, I need a favor."

"Sure, what's up?"

"I need you to come out to the mansion where Dylan Riley brought Tessa."

"Did something happen out there?"

"No."

Clearly confused, "we went over that place with a fine tooth comb after Dylan was killed."

"I think this place might be related to a string of missing girl cases," Parker explained.

"What case is that? I didn't hear that we had a serial abductor."

"Right now the cases aren't officially linked, but there's six so far that I think are related. Plus Clara Meyers and Tessa."

"You think this is related to Tessa's abduction when she was a child?"

"Yeah I do, but you know Tess, she's not talking. If I can get something concrete then I think I can get her to open up." Or maybe that was just wishful thinking on his part.

"I won't be able to get out there for a few days," Marty sounded apologetic.

"Marty . . ." he began to wheedle.

"I'm sorry, Parker," Marty cut in. "I'm swamped and this isn't an official case."

"It would be if I could just get some solid evidence."

Pausing for a moment, "has Tessa officially linked that house to her abduction?"

Exhaling loudly, "she's told me this is where Eleanor died, but no, not officially," Parker reluctantly had to admit.

"Then my hands are tied. Parker, I'll do it as soon as I can, I promise."

"Yeah, thanks, Marty," trying not to sound too dejected as he hung up. "What happened to Tessa that weekend Wyatt?" he mused as he slid his phone back into his pocket.

"Are you really sure you want to know the answer to that?" Wyatt asked. "It could change things forever. Are you ready for that?"

As he trailed his partner back up the stairs Parker wondered if he really was prepared to know exactly what Tessa went through when she was abducted.

\* \* \* \* \*

10:24 A.M.

All night Tessa had been unable to shake the feeling of spiders crawling over her. Even her dreams had been dotted with the horrible creatures. Shivering once again as she pictured the giant spider, it's stomach split open, the contents spilling out into the bright box.

It had been almost two years since she'd last seen Dino. The night he'd hit her over the head and tied her to a chair leaving her to die in a fire. The night that Parker had rushed inside her burning home, without a thought for his own safety, to rescue her.

Tessa wondered when he had changed his name. She'd known him as Dino Killinger but now he seemed to be going by Dino Rollino. Whatever his name he seemed to still hate her as passionately as he had all those years ago.

At least one good thing had come out of Dino's visit, it had given her something to focus on, something to pull her out of the black hole she'd been stuck in ever since Lachlan Mountain had entered their lives. When she had awakened this morning she'd known instantly that she was back to her old self. Parker had known it too, she could tell from the mildly irritated way he had studied her before rushing off on his 'secret' errand. It wasn't that Parker wanted to see her turn into a clingy, emotional mess, but he had been positive that it would force her to confront her past and finally deal with things she'd rather keep buried.

And his 'secret' errand wasn't much of a secret. Tessa knew he had taken Skylar back out to the house where Dylan Riley had died. He was right, it was the house where she and Ellie had been taken when they were abducted, but unfortunately for him he wouldn't find anything even remotely helpful there. John Doe would have made sure the place was completely cleaned out before moving on.

Wondering whether she should call her brother and let him

know about everything that had happened the last few days. She knew Parker hadn't called him or Daniel would have jumped straight on a plane and been home by now. Tessa kept telling herself that the reason she hadn't already called her big brother was because she didn't want to ruin his and Matilda's trip. But she knew the real reason was because she was still a little mad at him.

Daniel had walked out on her when she was twelve and he was eighteen, after their mother, Emilie, had tried to drown Tessa in the bathtub. He'd left because he believed it was the only way to keep her safe and when he'd returned to her life nine months ago the two of them had started to heal their relationship.

That had all changed three months ago when Parker had gone missing and they hadn't known what had happened to him. She had believed someone had hurt him, everyone else, including her brother, thought her husband had walked out on her. She had eventually found Parker, who'd been kidnapped by Lachlan Mountain, but in the process she had suffered a miscarriage, Parker had almost died and Skylar had shot Lachlan, who had survived and was currently awaiting trial. Tessa had been hurt by her brother's refusal to support her and a rift had risen between them again. Daniel had tried hard to fix things but Tessa wasn't quite ready to mend fences with her brother.

Reluctantly she slowed to accommodate her throbbing leg.

Going on a walk probably hadn't been the smartest move but she couldn't sit around the house doing nothing, and it was her usual morning routine to go for a run so she'd decided to stick to schedule.

As she slowed her pace she became aware of a presence behind her. It wasn't so much a noise, or a glimpse of anyone, but more of a feeling, a feeling of being watched. Dylan Riley may have been a scumbag but he had taught her well. Among other things one of his favorites was to always be aware of her surroundings and always be ready for an attack.

Increasing her speed slightly, ignoring the protesting arrows of pain in her leg, and veering off the path into the thick woods. When she'd gone a short way in, she ducked behind a tree, shimmied up a few branches, practically dragging her bad leg behind her, then pulled the tiny gun from her ankle holster and waited.

Trying to figure out who could be following her and why. It wouldn't be Dino, he wanted to kill her himself, but that didn't leave her with many other options. Within minutes she heard the unmistakable sound of approaching footsteps, two distinct sets, one male one female.

When they came into view she pointed her gun at them. "Who are you?" she demanded as they spun around to face her. "And why are you following me?"

* * * * *

*Sixteen Years Ago*
*Friday afternoon*

*"It'll be alright, Ellie, I'll find a way to get us out," Tessa soothed, squeezing Ellie's hand while with her other she absently twirled the curly ends of her braids. When the nanny did her hair like this it always reminded her of little Cindy Brady on that old show The Brady Bunch. Tessa loved that show, loved the way everyone loved and supported one another, that was what a family was supposed to be. Not like her own family. It had been a year since Patrick, her father, had walked out on them and they had moved in with her paternal grandparents. Tessa hated their horrible old mansion with all it's creaks and squeaks. Emilie barely came out of her room these days and it had probably been a month since Tessa had last seen her. At least she had Daniel, he would look after her, nothing bad could happen when he was around. Only he wasn't here now and she was terribly afraid that she had gotten herself and Ellie into some sort of trouble that she wouldn't be able to get them out of.*

*They'd been driving for hours, in circles if Tessa wasn't mistaken and she rarely was. Jake had been whistling merrily most of the time, the incessant chirping was really beginning to get on her nerves. The other little girl, Sarah, if that was really her name, had curled herself up in a ball and squeezed herself as tightly as possible up against the far door. Tessa had tried to comfort the girl but it had done no good. Neither had her reassurances done much to calm down Ellie, her best friend was still sobbing hysterically on her other side.*

*Trying to formulate a plan, Tessa was still mad as can be about what had happened. That man had no right to take her and Ellie against their will, or to hit her over the head, which was still pounding but she had boxed the pain away, there was no time for pain right now. Probably her best chance of escape was to make a run for it when Jake stopped the car next. The only problem with that was she would have to drag Ellie and Sarah along with her, and the possibility of that being successful was highly unlikely.*

*Jake pulled the car to a stop in front of an enormous Tudor mansion, surrounded by perfectly manicured gardens, scattered with huge trees and brightly colored flowers.*

*"Home sweet home, girls," he sung as he climbed out.*

*Before Tessa even had a chance to think of making her escape two men emerged from the building, heading straight for the car. One opened each of the backdoors, and grabbed Ellie and Sarah, neither girl put up a fight.*

*"You're all mine, princess," Jake grinned at her, his black eyes glittering as he reached inside the car.*

*Wiggling out of reach. "I'm not going anywhere with you," she pouted.*

*Her defiance only seemed to increase his enjoyment. "I think you're going to be my favorite yet," he declared managing to wrap a hand around her arm, and since he was bigger and stronger than her, pulled her from the car.*

*Thrashing wildly and screaming at the top of her lungs. Jake struggled to keep hold of her but managed to bring a hand to her mouth, trying to clamp it closed but she was too quick and sunk her teeth down into his flesh. Letting out a yelp which morphed into a giggle as he carried her through the front door. "You're a little spitfire."*

*Pinned against Jake's chest Tessa was powerless to get away as he followed the two other men through to the kitchen and down a narrow staircase to a small basement room. The walls were a bright yellow, the carpet an ugly grey, a single globe hanging from the ceiling providing the room's only light. A card table and some chairs were the only furniture in the room, one of the chairs was already occupied by a teenage boy who looked to be only a few years older than herself but younger than her seventeen-year-old brother Daniel.*

*The door on the other side of the room opened and a tall, skinny man stuck his head out. "Hey, welcome home, Sarah," he beamed at the girl, who shrunk away from him.*

*The men carrying Ellie and Sarah set the girls down but Jake kept a tight hold on her. "Keep an eye out for John Doe," he told the others.*

*One of them frowned at Jake, "you know you're not supposed to do that. John Doe doesn't like it."*

*Jake merely smiled, "then lets make sure he doesn't find out. Come along," he ordered Ellie, who obediently fell into step behind him as he went through the door into a long corridor.*

*As Jake carried her along the hallway Tessa could see that through each open door off the hallway was a tiny cell and in each tiny cell sat a huddled little girl. Finally, Jake stopped in front of one of the doors, opened it and gestured for Ellie to go inside, then following her in. Once inside he slammed the door closed and snipped the lock before finally setting her down on the floor. The second she was free Tessa launched herself at him, feet kicking, fists beating. Jake merely batted her away and pulled out a gun. "Either you calm down or I kill your friend," he warned.*

*Reluctantly she stopped, positive that Jake would be more than happy to shoot an eleven-year-old if it got him what he wanted.*

*"That's better," he nodded approvingly. "Now go lie down," he pointed to a dirty mattress on the floor.*

*When she didn't move he lifted the gun and aimed it at Ellie's head, her friend whimpered pitifully and Tessa moved to do as she'd been told. As Jake stood above her she knew what was coming and carefully blocked everything from her head, settling herself in a quiet, peaceful place where nothing bad could reach her.*

\* \* \* \* \*

11:19 A.M.

"If you'd just listen to what I'm saying then you'll see that there *is* a connection," Parker barked irritably.

"I'm not saying there's not a connection," J.J. replied as patiently as a preschool teacher. "I'm just saying we need more proof other than your gut feeling."

"And how am I going to get any proof," he retorted, "unless you let me investigate and *find* it."

Sighing, "what do you think, Wyatt?" J.J. demanded.

"I think," Wyatt weighed his words, "that there are some similarities."

"You see," Parker jumped in. "Even Wyatt thinks the cases are connected, it's not just me and wishful thinking."

Shooting him an annoyed frown before relenting. "Okay," J.J. nodded, "tell me exactly how and why you think these cases are related."

Trying to hide his relief, "okay, Heather McCarthy was the first girl to go missing, taken last October. She was eight years old, taken from a park where she was playing with her brothers, ages six and four, and her babysitter. Babysitter says she turned her back for a minute to get the youngest boy from the swing and when she turned back Heather was gone. Mom and dad are happily married, family members all checked out, friends and colleagues too, no ransom, no body, the girl just vanished."

"Two months later," Parker continued. "Carly Letcher disappears, she's twelve and is taken from her school. She asks to go to the bathroom in the middle of art class and never returns, at first they thought she might be cutting class but she never turned up. Once again, there were no leads and no suspects. Another break of two months and then nine-year-old Ariyel Hannock disappears from a shopping mall. Parents deceased, she was an only child and lived with her maternal grandparents, again nothing to go on. Judy Zammit vanished six months ago, she was ten, she was walking around the block to visit a friend and never made it there. Libby Marks disappeared the day after her eleventh birthday, she's been gone for four months, she too was taken from her school. And sisters Cassandra and Olivia Stanton have been missing for three weeks, ages eleven and ten respectively, the girls disappeared from a basketball game, went to the bathroom and never came back."

"In each case" Parker summarized, "families, friends, colleagues and neighbors were all ruled out. There were no ransom notes, no bodies were ever recovered, it's like each of these girls just stopped existing. No one reported seeing anything suspicious, and there were no witnesses in any of the abductions. The name Dino Rollino came up in two of the cases, he did electrical work in the neighborhoods of Ariyel Hannock and Judy Zammit in the weeks prior to the girl's disappearances, but nothing substantial turned up when Wyatt and I checked him out. Then we have Clara Meyers, a ten year old who was taken from her home, so far she hasn't given us any information about what happened to her in the months that she was missing, but she did give us a description of the man who took her. His description fits Dino Rollino," Parker announced triumphantly, they had only made the discovery half and hour ago and he was still buzzed about it.

"Now as we know Tessa and I found Clara in the woods, covered in blood but without any injuries, just like Tessa was found. So far Clara hasn't spoken a word to anyone other than Tessa but we don't know what the two of them talked about. Wyatt and I think that this may be a child trafficking ring, that they're kidnapping these girls, holding them until the police investigation runs into a dead end, and then selling them on. I think that we need to recheck the house where Tessa was taken when she was abducted."

"The house was already checked out," J.J. inserted.

"I know but we didn't know about the basement then," Parker reminded him.

"Tell me what we know about this Dino Rollino fellow."

"Thirty one years old, five foot seven, a hundred and eighty pounds, bald, black eyes, no criminal record but for a few speeding tickets, all paid. An only child, parents both deceased, he's not married and has no kids and no family so far as we could find. I spoke with his employer, said that Dino is reliable, been working there for ten years, no complaints about his work or his attitude from either customers or co-workers. Said he keeps to himself a bit, doesn't really hang around after work, but he's friendly enough with everyone." Realizing the man he was describing did not sound like someone who abducted little girls, Parker continued, "I know it doesn't sound like this guy is involved, but at the moment he's our only link."

"Okay," J.J. began slowly, drumming his massive fingertips on the desk. "Even if I buy the connection between the missing girls now, what does that have to do with Tessa? Why is it not just a coincidence that Clara Meyers and Tess were found in similar circumstances? I mean you just happen to crash your car in the area where a girl who was abducted sixteen years later by the same man who took Tessa is wandering around? Does that sound believable?"

"Not similar," Parker contradicted. "Identical circumstances. And how can you not think this is related? Okay I buy that it was pure luck that we happened to crash our car close to where Clara was, but just because it was unlikely doesn't mean it didn't happen. And then what, like three days later someone breaks into Tessa's house and leaves her that disgusting spider . . ."

"Marty, anything on the spider?" J.J. inserted, addressing the crime scene tech who had been sitting silently throughout the discussion.

"Theraphosa blondi," Marty answered, then elaborated upon seeing their confused expressions, "Goliath Birdeater. It's a part of the tarantula group and considered to be the second largest spider in the world after the giant huntsman. It's native to the northern South American rain forests, and can have up to an 11inch leg span and weigh up to 6 ounces."

"Anything more helpful than a lesson," J.J. shivered, he was not a spider fan.

"They're reasonably hard to acquire so that may be an avenue for identifying your guy," Marty smiled.

"Anything else?"

"Nothing forensically, he probably wore gloves while he cut it open and there were no hairs or fibers or fingerprints on or in the box."

Wyatt cleared his throat uncomfortably. "We may be overlooking some forensic evidence we already have."

Confused, "what?" From the look on his partner's face Parker was getting the feeling he wouldn't like where this was headed.

"Tessa's sexual assault kit," Wyatt answered softly.

Chest tightening. "What?" he repeated weakly.

"I'm sorry, Parker," Wyatt looked devastated. "But that's what we thought the moment we heard that Tessa had been abducted as a child. Little girl, goes missing, what are the chances whoever took her didn't do something to her. If we thought it, then the cops at the time must have thought it too, I'm sure a rape kit must have been done."

Struggling to breathe. He and Wyatt *had* thought rape when they'd first been told of eleven-year-old Tessa's abduction. But this was his wife they were talking about. She'd only been a child, just a little girl. Acknowledging out loud that this was a possibility was horrifying.

"We need to check the clothes she was wearing that night," Wyatt continued, his face pained, Parker knew how much he loved Tessa and that talking about this was torture for him as well. "She was eleven, if she'd just been . . ." his partner paused, swallowed audibly before continuing, "if she'd just been raped then some of the blood on her clothes would most likely be her own. Maybe we can get DNA from whoever did it, run it through our databases, we could get lucky. If not we can at least compare it to Clara Meyers, see if we get a match, that would conclusively prove a connection."

"I'm sorry," Parker stood on shaky legs he wasn't sure could carry his weight. "I can't do this. I can't deal with this."

"Parker, you said you wanted answers," Wyatt was looking him squarely in the eye. "We always knew this was a possibility. We always knew this was the most likely possibility. You said you could deal with whatever happened to Tessa."

Freezing at the door.

"She needs you to be able to deal with this," Wyatt added gently.

Hand on the doorknob but he didn't turn it.

"You haven't convinced me of a connection . . ." J.J. began quietly.

Whirling around to face his boss, "how can I not have . . .?" he interrupted, clinging to sanity with every ounce of strength he had. Wyatt was right. He wanted answers, said he could handle them. If Tessa was going to heal, then he needed to face facts, track down the man who hurt her and make him pay. He needed to remain calm, keep his wits about him, so he could get to the truth.

"If you'd let me finish, I was going to say you haven't convinced me of a connection *but* I'm also not convinced that the cases aren't connected. So we can take a look and see what comes up. Marty find out if a rape kit was done on Tessa," J.J.'s hands trembled as he fiddled with the notes on his desk. "If nothing else then track down the clothes she was wearing, test them, let me know immediately if you find anything."

"Yeah," Marty said softly. "I'm sorry, Parker, none of us wanted to truly admit this might have actually happened to her."

"Parker, Wyatt, go and speak with the Stanton family since

those were the girls who went missing last, see if they can give you anything. Then take the photo of this Dino Rollino to Clara Meyers and see if she can positively ID him. Once you've done that try Tessa again, see if you can get her to open up. But you do it carefully," J.J.'s eyes flashed with a fierce protectiveness. "That girl has already been through hell."

Before he had a chance to comment his cell began to trill, glancing at the caller ID he felt butterflies begin to flutter in his stomach. "Uh oh."

* * * * *

11:24 A.M.

"How dare you do that."

Parker cleared his throat uncomfortably, "do what?"

"How dare you have me followed," Tessa snapped, seething with rage. When the two people who had been following her out in the woods surrounding her estate had turned around she had recognized them as two of Parker's colleagues. After she'd put her gun away and they'd helped her down from the tree they had explained that Parker had insisted someone keep an eye on her after the previous night's occurrences.

"Calm down," Parker's voice soothed on the other end of the phone. "I did it to protect you. We both know that when it comes to your own safety you're completely irresponsible. While you were asleep last night a man was inside our home, watching you, leaving you mutilated animals as a gift. And we're not just talking about *a* man, but one who wants you dead. I knew you'd throw a tantrum if I insisted on staying with you so I did the only thing I could think of to keep you safe. You know if you would just take this seriously then . . ."

Not in the mood for a lecture. Not only had she been furious to find out that her husband had gone behind her back and had her followed, but on the walk back to the house her injured leg had given out and she had been forced to let Detective Baker carry her the rest of the way home. "I don't need anyone looking after me," she spoke tightly, struggling to reign in her temper. "I can look after myself."

"But you don't," Parker snapped back. "You don't avoid trouble you run straight for it."

About to retort that she'd learnt her lesson after leading herself and Ellie straight into Jake's web when she caught herself and grumbled instead, "that's a lie and we both know it."

"It's a lie is it?" Parker was getting himself worked up now. "You went running off on your own to confront Dylan Riley even though you knew he was unstable and wanted the two of you to spend your lives together. You ran off to confront your sister and almost died, and you took on Lachlan Mountain and ended up losing our baby . . ." he trailed off as he seemed to realize that he'd just mentioned the miscarriage.

In the three months since they'd lost their baby they'd talked about it only once. Tessa didn't like to think about the child, about how she hadn't even realized that she was attached to her baby until it was gone. Whenever she did think about it she was overwhelmed by guilt, that she hadn't loved and wanted the baby more while it was still alive. Now she lapsed into stony silence, angry that Parker would bring up the miscarriage when he knew how painful it was for her to talk about.

"Tessa, I'm sorry," her husband's voice had softened, losing its frustrated edge. "I'm sorry I mentioned the baby, but I'm not sorry that I asked someone to keep an eye on you. I love you and I'm prepared to take whatever steps necessary to keep you safe whether you like it or not. After everything we've been through I can't lose you," he paused allowing time for his words to sink in. "I won't lose you."

Feeling her anger beginning to weaken, she strengthened her resolve, if Dino was back, if it was happening again, then the only way she knew to get through it was to focus on her rage. "I sent Detective Baker and Detective Hank home," she announced instead, managing to keep a hold on her frustration. Tessa did feel a little bad for taking out her annoyance on the poor officers Parker had asked to watch her. It hadn't been their fault but she had ranted and raved at them, while they stood there patiently listening. They hadn't wanted to leave, but she had insisted and in the end had given them an ultimatum, either they left or she did, and they had reluctantly complied with her orders.

"Tessa," Parker uttered a weary sigh. "I just want to know that you're safe why is that such an awful thing?"

Taking pity on him, "it's not an awful thing, but why can't you just accept that I know what I'm doing, and that I can take care of myself. I'm not going to break," she told him quietly, "I just have my own way of dealing with things."

Instantly her husband's voice was back to annoyed, "that's the whole problem, you *don't* deal with things. I thought you were finally going to but after the accident you're right back where you were . . ."

Interrupting, "I'm not going to have that conversation with you again, I'm sick to death of it." Ready to end the conversation, "don't even *think* about sending anyone else over here to babysit me."

"Tessa . . ." Parker started.

Butting in, "Parker, I'm really tired, I'm going to take a nap." Relenting a little, "I'll see you later tonight," then ending the call before he had a chance to say more.

Tossing the phone onto the sofa, then trudging tiredly up the stairs. Bypassing the bedroom she and Parker had been using, the room where she was sure Dino had watched her as she slept, Tessa entered her childhood room. It was just as she had left it the day she left for college, she hadn't been inside it since. When her grandparents had died a few years later and left the estate to her she had avoided the mansion and stayed in one of the small cottages on the grounds.

Crossing the room, which while full of expensive furniture was mostly free from the personal touches that usually filled a teenage girl's bedroom. There were no posters, no photos of friends or boyfriends, no stacks of CD's, no stuffed animals, no piles of makeup on the bureau, no clutter, nothing to indicate anything about the person who used the room. Just the way Tessa liked it.

Reaching the closet, she pulled over her desk chair to stretch up and pull down a bag hidden away on the top shelf. Taking the bag with her, Tessa sat on her old bed and emptied the contents out onto the covers. After she had stared at it for several minutes she collected it up with a sigh and replaced it in its bag. Aware of the fact that the memories and feelings she had dedicated more than half her life to burying were inevitably about to come tumbling out.

\* \* \* \* \*

2:47 P.M.

"Do you know something?"

Looking into hazel eyes that after everything they had been through could still be so hopeful was heartbreaking. Parker shook his head, "nothing concrete, but we do have a new direction."

Sinking down onto the couch beside her husband Joy Stanton continued to meet his gaze. "So you still don't know what . . ." a momentary wobble in her emotions, "what happened to my girls?"

"No. I'm sorry." Parker hated visiting the families of victims. Hated the mixture of grief and hope and denial that swirled in their faces. Hated that it made him feel so powerless. Hated that he identified too closely with them. "But," he continued, "we think that there's a possibility that your daughter's disappearance may be related to the disappearance of another little girl, Clara

Meyers."

Head shooting up, "the girl from the news?" Ron Stanton sprung to life.

"She was missing for months right?" Mrs. Stanton confirmed, a surge of hope causing her to rise to her feet. "And she was found alive and unharmed."

"She was found alive," Parker agreed cautiously, not wanting to raise the parent's hopes to high.

"So our girls are still alive too," throwing her arms around her husband's neck.

"*Could* be alive," Wyatt corrected. "Right now we don't know that the two cases are related. And even if they are that doesn't mean that Cassandra and Olivia are still alive. Right now we don't know anything, we just want to go over a few things with you."

Not to be deterred the happy couple couldn't wipe the wide smiles from their faces as they sat side-by-side, hands clasped tightly together. Apparently the crisis of their missing children had strengthened their relationship. Losing a child usually either tore a couple apart or made them closer, the Stanton's seemed to have gone the path of the latter.

Parker thought of the baby he and Tessa had lost thanks to Lachlan Mountain, and only half regretted bringing it up with Tessa earlier. If it upset her and pushed her into confronting it then ultimately it was a good thing. He was still uncomfortable with the thought of Tessa out on the estate all alone, but he was more afraid of what she would do if he sent someone else out to keep an eye on her. Last time Tessa had felt pressured she had gone straight to the man who wanted her dead to get what she needed.

Taking a calming breath, and making a mental note to call Maisy and ask her to check up on Tessa, Parker knew he had to focus on the task at hand. "Can you tell us about the day that the girls went missing?" he asked the Stanton's.

Trembling visibly, her good mood evaporating as they asked

her to confront the worst day of her life, "we were at Livy's basketball game," Joy Stanton began slowly. "It was Saturday morning, Cassie didn't have tennis till later so she was there too. We were waiting for the game before ours to finish. They wanted to go to the bathroom, they'd done it dozens of times before," she eyed them defiantly as though daring them to disagree. "They never came back, I went looking for them but it was as though they had just vanished. I searched the whole place but they weren't there. Spoke to everyone but no one had seen them. No one had seen anything . . ." she trailed off clearly still baffled about how two kids could disappear and no one notice a thing.

Taking over the narrative, Mr. Stanton continued, "when we couldn't find them we called the police. They closed the stadium down, spoke with everyone there but no one remembered seeing the girls leave, or anyone suspicious hanging around."

"Was there anyone or anything suspicious that you remember in the weeks before Cassandra and Olivia went missing?" Parker queried.

"No," Mrs. Stanton moved quickly from baffled on to frustrated. "We already told the detectives when the girls disappeared, there was nothing suspicious. No phone calls or emails or people hanging around. Nothing. Everything was just the same. One day we were a normal happy family and the next our daughters were just gone. How can two children be gone for three weeks and you still don't have any leads? What did that other little girl say? Did she tell you where she was? Who took her? Did she tell you that she'd seen Cassie and Livy?"

"Does the name Dino Rollino mean anything to you?" Wyatt asked, ignoring her questions for the time being.

"No," Ron Stanton replied. "Is he the man who has our girls?"

"He's a person with potential information," Wyatt answered vaguely.

"Are you sure you've never met or heard of a Dino Rollino?" Parker pressed, certain that this man was involved in all the girl's disappearances.

Frustrated, "I already told you no," Mr. Stanton snapped. "We don't know . . ."

Joy Stanton gasped, all the color draining from her already strained face.

"Mrs. Stanton, do you remember Dino Rollino?"

"They kept asking if anyone suspicious had been hanging around our house or the basketball courts," she muttered, more to herself than any of them. "I never connected him to what happened."

"Did he do some work for you or one of your neighbors?" Parker asked.

"Do some work?" Ron Stanton's brow crinkled with confusement. "Who exactly is this Dino Rollino?"

"He's an electrician who did some work in the neighborhood's of two other girls who have gone missing in the last year," Wyatt filled him in.

"But we haven't had any electrical work done recently," Ron protested.

"My sister," Joy's eyes were darting frantically around the room. "It was at my sister's house, that's where I met him."

"Is there anything you remember about him?"

Shaking her head dismally, "I didn't pay any attention to him. I don't even know if I saw him. If it wasn't for his name, it rhymes, I wouldn't even have remembered him. He was there working, my sister was preparing for an overseas trip, her husband's mother is dying."

"Is your sister back home now?"

"No she's still there," Joy Stanton had begun wringing her hands in distress. "She wanted to come back of course when the girls . . . but I told her to stay. It's important for her daughter to spend time with her grandmother while she can."

"Your sister has a daughter?" Parker asked, wondering if perhaps the niece had been the initial target but when she went to spend time with her dying grandmother he had moved onto the Stanton girls instead.

"Yes, Nicole, she's nine."

"Were Cassandra and Olivia with you that day?"

"Yes . . ." the wheels in her head turning. "Wait, you think that the man who took my daughters was originally after my niece?"

"It's a possibility."

Rejoining the conversation, Ron's cheeks were red with anger, "so this Dino Rollino you think he's done this to other girls? Ripped them away from their families? If this man has been doing this for a year why haven't you found him and stopped him? And just what is he doing with our girls?"

"We weren't able to link the cases until finding Clara Meyers," Parker told him apologetically. Hoping to put off providing an answer on what they thought Dino Rollino was doing with the girls he abducted.

"That girl," Joy pestered. "Did she tell you what happened to her?"

"Clara hasn't spoken since she was found," Parker explained softly.

"But she wasn't hurt right?" the woman asked desperately.

"She was physically uninjured," Parker agreed, but refrained from reminding them of the emotional scars the child would have, and that their own girls would have if they were found alive.

"So you don't know where she was or what happened to her?" Mrs. Stanton having run a course of emotions now looked just plain exhausted.

"Not yet, but when she's ready she'll open up. We are going to do everything we can to try to get your daughters back," Parker assured them. "What can you tell us about Cassandra and Olivia?"

A dreamy look flitting over her face, "they're such sweet girls." Joy reached over and retrieved a photo of her and her daughters. The girls were little clones of their mother. All three had the same slightly crooked smile, the same crinkles around their hazel eyes when they smiled, the same wispy auburn hair framing a pale face with a scattering of freckles across the nose.

"The best of friends," she continued, "they did everything together. They're only fourteen months apart in age but Cassie adores being the big sister. She looks out for Liv, takes care of her. Sometimes I think Cassie is more mature than I am, the way she looks at life, the way she faces difficulties. Cassie's best friend is a paraplegic, when she was in kindergarten she came home one day in tears because the other children were teasing the little girl in the wheelchair, she thought it was so unfair. The next day she went back to school and from that day on the two girls were best friends."

"And Liv," Ron's face lighting as he spoke of his youngest daughter and he reached for the photo his wife was holding. "She's a character. Not quite as serious as her sister, she's a dreamer, always getting into trouble in school for daydreaming. And she's very creative, a brilliant drawer, spends hours painting," he pointed to a brightly colored rendering of a sun rising over a lake.

"Your ten-year-old daughter painted that?" Parker asked, amazed. The picture was truly amazing and looked like it had been done by someone at least twice Olivia Stanton's age.

Beaming with pride, "over the summer," Mr. Stanton told them. "She wants to be an artist when she grows up."

Thinking of Tessa, herself a brilliant artist and children's book author and illustrator, and once again Parker began to worry about his wife alone in that big empty house. Deciding they had all they were going to get out of the Stanton's he rose to his feet. "Thank you, Mr. and Mrs. Stanton, we'll let you know if anything develops."

As the couple followed him and Wyatt to the door Joy Stanton grabbed his hand, her eyes imploring, "my girls are strong, they can get through anything. When you find them they'll be okay."

* * * * *

9:03 P.M.

Olivia really hated not being able to see the sky. It was the worst thing about being here.

Crawling across the floor to sit next to her big sister, feeling safer there than anywhere else in this horrible little cell. Cassie had been quieter than usual ever since she had returned from the room with John Doe about a day ago. Olivia had been horrified when Dino had dragged Cassie towards the room. They all knew what happened in there, but just as he had closed the door John Doe had arrived. He'd sent all the girls to their rooms, retrieved Cassie and then given Dino a roaring lecture that seemed to drone on and on for hours.

At least something good had come of the whole incident. Tugging on her sister's arm, "Cass."

Blinking and looking over at her with glazed eyes. "What is it, Liv?" Cassie put on a reassuring big sister smile.

"I think I found a way out," she announced triumphantly.

Doubt written all Cassie's face, "that's nice, Livy."

Annoyed, sometimes Olivia hated being the little sister. Cassandra always treated her like such a little kid even though she was only fourteen months younger. "No really, Cass, I'm pretty sure I found a way out," she insisted.

Still wary, "what are you talking about?"

"Earlier, when Dino was dragging you to the room I saw something," she began to explain but something rattled at the locked door of their little cell and moments later it swung open.

"Evening, girls."

It was Dino and from the look on his face it meant bad news. Olivia wiggled a little closer to her sister.

"I think we were interrupted earlier." Crossing the room in one giant stride, he stretched out his arms and snapped a hand around each of their wrists, tugging both girls to their feet. "John Doe's out, so this time there's no one to save you."

Dragging them through the door and down the hall, into the dreaded room. She'd been in this room only once before. A day or so after they had gotten here. John Doe had taken their photos before sending Cassie back to their room, but he had kept her behind. Olivia knew that Cassie thought John Doe had hurt her but he hadn't. He had simply sat her down, given her the only decent meal she'd had here, and told her a sad story from his past.

As the door swung closed, Olivia, even at ten, knew that this time she and her sister were not going to be as lucky. This time it was going to be the end of their childhoods.

# SEPTEMBER 9<sup>TH</sup>

8:36 A.M.

"I don't know that I'll be any help."

"Well you can't make things worse," Parker told Elisabeth Bennett, a psychiatrist and criminal profiler they often used to help with various cases. At the moment the favor he needed from her was more personal. He and Wyatt were going to confront Tessa with what they thought they knew so far and Parker knew it wasn't going to go smoothly.

Arching a disbelieving brow. "I don't know about that. I didn't really help matters last time."

Three months ago when he had been missing and everyone had believed he had walked out on Tessa, Beth had tried to talk to her and help her come to terms with what had happened. Luckily for him, Tessa had refused to believe that he would leave her, if she had he would be dead right now. "She's going to freak out when we try to talk to her about what happened with Eleanor, it's a secret she's kept since she was eleven years old, we need the support."

"Parker, you know how she feels about psychiatrists," Beth reminded him. "I think having me there is only going to make things worse."

Tessa had had some bad experiences with psychiatrists in the past and didn't believe that they served any useful purpose in society, but his wife wasn't the only reason he wanted Beth there. "*I* need you there," he admitted. "I don't know what Tessa's going to tell me but I can make a pretty good guess and I don't know how to help her."

Softening, "I'll come with you." She paused and placed a hand on her stomach, "but Tess hating psychiatrists is not the only reason it may not help to have me there."

Beth had announced that she was pregnant just a couple of weeks before Tessa had and was now six months along, a month more than Tessa would have been. Since the miscarriage was such a sensitive topic Beth had been trying to avoid Tessa the last few months. "I thought we were finally making some progress, Beth, but now she's right back to the old Tessa, you know the one who's impulsive and self-destructive. The one who doesn't eat or sleep or take care of herself, the one who refuses to talk about things and just pretends that they never happened. I wish I knew how to snap her out of it."

"You can't, Parker," Beth reminded him gently. "Tessa is who she is because of everything that she's been through. And to be honest I'm almost as concerned about you as I am about Tessa. Are you really sure that you're ready to know what happened to Tess and to deal with things at her speed? You know this isn't going to be something where Tessa confesses all and then instantly becomes a different person. It's going to take time, lots of time, and it won't help things if you're pushing her to go at your pace."

While Beth was definitely a brilliant psychiatrist not all of her advice was based on theory, a lot of it came from personal experience. A few years ago Beth had been brutally attacked by a violent sociopath on a desperate quest to escape. The attack had left her fighting for her life after the man plunged a knife into her abdomen before slicing her face. Still bearing the physical scars, the light pink line traced its way across one of her cheeks, as well as the emotional scars. Despite the fact that she was beautiful, with smooth olive skin, big brown eyes and long dark hair that stretched most of the way down her back, the attack had left Beth very conscious about her appearance regardless of the loving reassurances of her husband.

"I know all of that, Beth," rubbing his hands over his tired face. "And I'm pretty sure I know what Tessa's going to tell us, we've always known, but now it just feels so real."

"It was always real, Parker," Beth said softly. "Now it's just time to face it."

"You guys ready?" Wyatt stuck his head through the door and jingled his car keys at them.

Beth raised an eyebrow at him, "are you, Parker? Are you ready?"

"I'm ready," he assured Beth confidently as he crossed to the door. "I love Tessa and there isn't anything she could tell me that could ever change that."

\* \* \* \* \*

9:43 A.M.

Pacing restlessly around the room. What she needed was something to clean. Tessa loved to clean when she was stressed, found it very therapeutic. But she'd already done the only rooms she and Parker were using in the enormous mansion and all the other rooms were just sitting empty.

Parker hadn't come home last night, not that she minded she was still mad at him for having her watched. However Maisy had come over to spend the night, and while her friend refused to admit it Tessa knew Maisy had been sent by Parker to keep an eye on her. Tessa hadn't minded the company but the whole time she had been distracted by trying to make a decision on whether or not she ought to ring *him*. John Doe. She wanted to know why he had started again, she'd thought she had put a stop to what he was doing, and she didn't understand why he had come back.

About to move on to one of the empty rooms and clean it anyway just to have something to do when she heard footsteps in the hallway and instantly knew what was coming. Positioning herself in the corner of the room farthest from the door, she kept her face impassive as the door swung open to reveal Parker, Skylar and Elisabeth Bennett.

"Hey, honey," Parker smiled and moved towards her, halting when she shot him an annoyed scowl.

"Hi, goldilocks." Skylar wasn't put off by her scowl and crossed the room to kiss her cheek.

"Hello, Tessa," Beth was nervously rubbing her swollen abdomen and Tessa was once again reminded of the child she had lost.

"What do you want?" she asked flatly, not in the mood for pleasantries.

Clearly anxious to get the ball rolling, "we're here to talk about what happened to you and Eleanor," Parker announced.

Frustrated she flopped down onto the couch, tucking her feet up underneath her and clenching her hands into fists so tightly she could feel her nails piercing the soft skin on the palms of her hands. "I don't know how many ways to say this. I am not going to talk about that weekend," dotting each word emphatically.

"We found the hidden basement," Parker told her softly, crouching in front of her and covering her hands with his, gently prying them open and blotting at the smudges of blood from the small crescent shaped cuts.

Refusing to let him see her shudder, Tessa held herself completely still.

"We found the little cells," her husband continued as she tried desperately to block out his words. "Twenty of them. Twenty little girls like you and Eleanor. It was a child trafficking ring wasn't it? They kidnapped the girls and kept them there until they had a buyer," he trailed off and watched her with nervous anticipation.

Blinking back tears, still clinging to the notion that she could keep the secret of what happened that weekend. "You think Ellie and I were abducted by child traffickers? Did you ever think that maybe Ellie just ran away?"

"You were found covered in her blood," Skylar reminded her gently.

"Fine," her voice growing louder. "But why does that mean she was murdered? Did you ever consider that maybe Ellie just fell? Or maybe she got hit by a car, or maybe there was an accident? Or maybe . . ." her voice dropped to a whisper, "maybe I killed her."

"Tess," Parker began.

Talking over him as she recalled the days after Ellie died, "the police asked me if I killed her. They said if it was an accident that I should just tell them and then they could make everything better."

Bristling, "how dare they imply you killed your best friend, you were only a child. What did you tell them?" Parker demanded

"Nothing. You know I didn't talk for months after Ellie died. Not to my grandparents or my brother, not to the police and not to any of the psychiatrists they sent me to," she added with a pointed glare in Beth's direction. It wasn't that Tessa disliked Elisabeth on a personal level she just didn't trust psychiatrists. "It didn't matter anyway, they were right, I did kill Ellie."

"What happened, Tessa?" Beth asked carefully.

Defeated she uttered a weary sigh and gave in. Maybe she had been naïve to think she could keep it a secret forever. "Ellie didn't want to go."

"Go where?"

It was like something took hold of her and answers started tumbling out left, right and centre. "With Jake. He was at our school with a little girl. Her name was Sarah. He told us that they'd lost their puppy and asked us to help them look for it. Ellie didn't want to go with him. She wanted to go back to class, she was scared she was going to get into trouble from her mom for failing. I told her everything would be okay. I promised her. She agreed because she trusted me. When we turned around Jake had a knife. He said he'd hurt Sarah if we didn't go with him. I told him no but he hit me. He put us in his car and we drove around for hours. At last we got to the house . . ."

"The one where Dylan Riley took you?" Parker interrupted.

Nodding, "there were other men there. They took us to the basement and . . ." she didn't want to tell them what had happened next.

"Did Jake hurt you, Tessa?" Parker asked with barely controlled rage.

Tessa didn't like to think about Jake, had tried so hard to block him from her mind.

"Did Jake rape you, Tess?" Parker repeated.

Meeting her husband's eye for the first time, "yes. Is that what you've been waiting to hear? Jake raped Ellie and me. Was it worth it? Was it worth bringing all of this up just so you could hear me say it?" Storming over to the window where she watched a butterfly flitting through the late summer sky. Remembering when she used to be so carefree, that had all changed after Ellie was killed.

Coming up behind her, close but not too close. "How did you get away?" Parker asked, his voice carefully calm. "You said there were a lot of men there, how did you get out?"

\* \* \* \* \*

*Sixteen Years Ago*
*Saturday evening*

*"Come on, Ellie, it's now or never."*

*"I'm scared," her friend whimpered.*

*Reaching over to smooth out a snaggled snarl in Ellie's wavy hair, both their braids had come mostly undone. "It'll be okay, El, I promise."*

*"You said that last time," Ellie complained dismally. "And look where we are."*

*Surveying their tiny cell, the bloodstained mattress on the floor from where Jake had . . . Tessa wasn't going to think about that now. Now she had to get them out of here. "Come on, Ellie, there's only two guards at night."*

*"How can you tell its night, we don't have any windows," Ellie whispered, dangerously close to tears again.*

*Tessa hadn't cried, wouldn't cry, not even when Jake had . . . Tears didn't help anything, you had to be strong if you were going to survive in life, even at eleven Tessa knew this. "It has to be night because that's when most of the men go away," she reasoned, not really sure if she was right, but it made no difference, night or day they had to get away while they had a chance. If they stayed here much longer Tessa had a horrible swirly feeling in her tummy that she knew what would happen. "Come on, El," grabbing her friend's hand she began to forcibly tug her to the door. Luckily their doors weren't usually locked and it swung quietly open as Tessa turned the knob.*

*Once in the corridor she glanced up and down. The sound of chatting voices emanated softly from the room at the end of the hall, other than that the place was deadly silent. Knocking on each of the cell doors as she went, and soon all seventeen girls were assembled in a small huddle in the hall.*

*"Come on," Tessa urged them. "Follow me."*

*"No," Sarah shook her head wildly, glancing down at the closed door. "They'll hear us. They said that if we were good, if we did what they said, they'd let us go home."*

*"They'll never let us go home," Tessa informed the other girls. "Don't you know what they're going to do to us?"*

*The blank faces that stared back at her confirmed that the girls did not know what was going to happen to them. "Come with me, I can get us all out of here, then we can go home, but we have to go now."*

*"We should do what they said. Jake promised we could go home if we just did what they said," one of the other girls whispered.*

*"Jake's a liar, he's not going to let you go home."*

*"I want my mommy," another little girl began to sob.*

*"I can take you to your mommy but you have to come with me," the voices in the other room had stopped and Tessa knew it was now or never. "Come on."*

*"Don't listen to her," a redhead spoke up. "She's going to get us all killed."*

*There was no time to argue, the noises from the guards had ceased, so Tessa grabbed Ellie and began to drag her to the room at the other end to the hallway. The room where John Doe had taken her and Ellie just after they arrived, he had taken photos of them and examined their naked bodies. It was the room where Jake took the girls to entertain himself with when John Doe wasn't about. But Tessa had noticed something about the room, its dimensions didn't add up with the size it ought to be if the entire basement complex took up the same space as the house, and under one of the walls she had noticed the faintest line of light. Now she headed straight for that place, fiddling quickly with the wall until it sprung open revealing a narrow passageway.*

*Pulling Ellie along behind her, she navigated her way through the secret tunnel. The walls were solidly packed dirt, the odd globe hung from the wall, not enough to properly light the way but enough to cast spooky shadows. With each step she kept expecting someone to jump out from one of the many twists and turns to drag them both back to the basement.*

*Tessa was pretty sure she knew what was going to happen to them if they remained here, they were going to be sold. Sold to some horrible man who would do to them what Jake had done, who might keep them locked in his own basement, or in a box under his bed, or in an attic.*

*For as long as she could remember Tessa had dreamed about living anywhere but at her home. She hated living in her grandparent's huge old house, hated her grandparents with their strict distant attitudes, hated the father she hadn't heard from in a year, hated her mother who was too wrapped up in herself to pay any attention to her kids. Tessa had always wished to be anywhere else, had thought nothing could be worse than being with her family, but she knew that if she didn't get away from here her life would become a real nightmare.*

*At last they came to a short flight of stairs, "come on, Ellie," she snapped at her friend who continued to sniffle loudly. "Tears aren't going to help us."*

*Tugging on Ellie's hand Tessa led her up the steps to a trapdoor, releasing her grip on her friend Tessa pressed against the square door, but it held fast.*

*Frustrated, she banged against it with her fists then pushed with all her might, but still it refused to budge. "You have to help me, El," she turned to Ellie who was standing like a statue, her face a blank mask of shock. "Come on." In slow motion Ellie placed her hands beside Tessa's and began to push. With a creak and a groan, little by little the trapdoor sprung open.*

*Climbing through, the girls found themselves in a stable. The trapdoor had been covered in a thick layer of hay, which now stuck to their clothes and hair. Brushing off herself and then Ellie, Tessa closed the door and spread the hay back out across it.*

*"Almost there," she encouraged Ellie, as she reached once more for her friend's hand and tugged her towards the door. The docile grey horse in the stall next to theirs watched them with sleepy eyes and leaned it's head down to whoosh at the top of their heads. Making their way outside the girls both breathed in the fresh air, the late afternoon sun's rays casting long shadows across the huge grassy field.*

*Everything was going smoothly, they were going to make it, they were going to be free, they were going to get home. Tessa let out a sigh of relief, and let herself relax until . . .*

*"Going somewhere, princess?"*

\* \* \* \* \*

10:28 A.M.

"Wait, Eleanor was with you when you escaped?" Skylar asked, confused.

Tessa hardly heard him, "they wouldn't come with me," she said softly thinking of all those girls she had left behind.

"There was nothing you could do, honey," Parker consoled, placing a hand on her shoulder.

Shrugging away from him, "they were only children, how could Jake do that to them? How could those men do that? I should have done more. I should have tried harder to get them to come with me. I did try, but they wouldn't come. They thought if they did what Jake said then they would be able to go home. I tried to tell them that would never happen but they wouldn't listen. They kept telling me that Jake had promised. I left them behind. Children, just little girls, and I left them behind. I knew what was going to happen to them and still I left them behind. I was a coward, I should have done more to get them to leave with me . . ."

Parker took hold of her shoulders and spun her around to face him, gripping her so tightly she couldn't help wincing. "Listen to me," he commanded fiercely. "It was not your fault."

Tessa could see that Parker was struggling to keep his cool, fury crackled beneath his tightly controlled calm exterior. "They were just children, Parker. Innocent little children." She had never forgiven herself for leaving those helpless girls behind.

"So were you. You were only eleven . . ."

"But I knew what was going to happen," she wasn't going to have anyone defend her actions. "And I left them. I was a coward."

"If you had of stayed no one would ever have seen you again," Beth reminded her gently.

"What could you have done, Tess?" Skylar reasoned. "You were only a kid, there was no way you could have dragged all those girls with you by force. You tried to convince them to leave and they wouldn't, there was nothing more you could have done."

Not about to be placated, "we all know what happened to those girls. I could have done something to stop it and I didn't."

"So they were child traffickers?" Parker confirmed.

Bobbing her head up and down in agreement.

Her husband stared at her so intently that she couldn't help squirming. At last he asked softly, "other than Jake did anyone else . . .?"

"No," resuming staring out the window. "The men weren't allowed to touch the girls."

"But Jake?"

"Jake was a wild card, he did whatever he wanted."

"Sweetheart, I'm so sorry." Parker tried to take her in his arms but she pushed him away, she didn't want to be touched right now.

"Why? It wasn't your fault. It was mine. I was the one who fell for Jake's lie. I'm the one who got myself and Ellie into that mess in the first place." After finally talking about these events after sixteen years Tessa felt empty. She felt like she'd just lost the last piece of Ellie, like keeping the secret was like keeping a part of Ellie alive.

"How did Eleanor die?" Skylar asked again.

It had been bad enough telling them about the first part of that weekend but she couldn't face telling them what had happened next. "I'm really tired now and my leg hurts." That wasn't a lie, she hadn't taken any painkillers since the previous day and her leg was throbbing now. "I just want to rest."

Attempting to pass Parker but he wrapped a hand around her wrist and held her in place. "Is Jake the man who tried to kill you in the fire? Is he the one you went to for help to try to find me when I was missing?"

"I'm really tired, Parker," she tried to pull free, but Parker tightened his grip, practically crushing the bones in her wrist. "You're hurting me."

"Is Jake the man who was in this house the other night?" he demanded.

Hesitating, her brain kept yelling at her to stop talking, but it was as though someone had wound her up and now that she had started recounting the events of that weekend she couldn't stop. "Parker . . ."

"Tessa, please." The turbulent mess of shock and pity and guilt on his face, as though he should have done something to prevent all of this from happening even though they hadn't known each other at the time, pressed her into answering.

"No."

Visibly relieved he loosened his grip on her wrist but didn't release her. "How did Eleanor die?"

"He killed her."

"Jake?"

"Yeah," she answered in a small voice, knowing that if her husband pushed just a little more then the whole story would come tumbling out.

"How?"

Shaking as she pictured her friend's face seconds before she died. Once again she tried to pull free from Parker's grip, this time he let her go. "Jake snapped her neck."

They all stared at her open mouthed.

"But the blood?" Skylar stammered.

"It wasn't Ellie's blood," she whispered. "It was Jake's."

\* \* \* \* \*

*Sixteen Years Ago*
*Saturday evening*

*"We're leaving," Tessa announced defiantly.*

*"Are you now?" Jake smiled down at her with his malevolent smile.*

*Releasing her hold on Ellie to plant her hands on her hips. "We don't have to do what you want," she declared, stomping her foot and pouting, the way she got her own way at home.*

*"Actually, princess, you do," Jake reached for her but she dodged away.*

*"If you don't let us go I'll tell John Doe what you did to me and Ellie," she threatened.*

*Momentarily thrown, then he threw back his head and laughed. "You are an absolute card, I think I'm going to keep you for myself."*

*"I know what you're doing here, I know what you're going to do with all of those girls," Tessa told him.*

*"Do you now?" he asked with an amused smirk.*

*"Yes I do, and you're not going to get away with it," she declared forcefully*

*even though inside she felt her bravado begin to slip away, she was tired and scared and in pain, but desperately she clung to her outrage.*

*"How exactly do you plan on stopping me?"*

*"I'm going to go to the police and tell them exactly what you did to us and all those other kids. They're going to come here and find them and you're going to go to jail for the rest of your life."*

*Laughing again, "you and I are going to have some serious fun together," Jake beamed.*

*Throwing him a filthy look. "I'm leaving now."*

*Tessa was about to reach for her best friend, who had stood silently like a frightened mouse during the whole exchange, when Jake sprung forward and clamped an arm across Ellie's neck, pinning her against him. "You're not going anywhere," Jake challenged.*

*Torn, unsure what was her best option. Tessa knew she couldn't outmuscle Jake, he was too big, too strong. She could call for help but that would only end in the two of them being dragged back to that dungeon. Looking into Ellie's huge blue eyes, so large in her pale, terrified face, tears streaming down her cheeks, silently pleading for help, Tessa knew she had to do something.*

*"Let her go," she begged.*

*"I don't think so," Jake smirked.*

*Bargaining with the only thing she had to offer. "You said you wanted me, then have me, just let Ellie go."*

*"Come here," he commanded, a horrible glittering lust in his black eyes, his shaved head shining in the last of the sunlight. When she didn't comply quickly enough Jake tightened his grip on Ellie's neck.*

*Startled Ellie let out a shrill scream and began to thrash wildly, fighting for her life. Springing into action Tessa leapt at Jake, beating her fists, kicking her feet, snapping her teeth, trying frantically to get him to release his hold on Ellie. With an irritated sigh he swatted her away as though she were no more significant than a fly, and then with the coldest eyes Tessa had ever seen, he snapped Ellie's neck. The sound seemed to echo inside her head, as Ellie's body dropped to the ground when Jake released her.*

*For what seemed like forever neither of them moved. Tessa too stunned to move, Jake's breathing heavy with longing. As he took a step towards her*

*Tessa did the only thing she could think of, or rather the only thing her shocked brain could do. Her fingers curled around the small carving knife she had been going to be use to create her circus. When Jake was within striking distance she flung out her hand, the knife plunging into his groin, connecting with his femoral artery.*

*Blood spurted out everywhere, drenching both her and Jake as he staggered backwards, eyes open wide with surprise. Tessa watched with equally wide eyes as he fell to the grassy ground beside Ellie.*

*Kneeling beside her best friend, "Ellie?" she called, unable to look away from Ellie's blank, empty eyes. "Come on, Ellie, you can't leave me," but even as she spoke the words Tessa knew that her best friend was gone.*

*Jake had killed Ellie and she had killed Jake. She was a murderer.*

\* \* \* \* \*

11:07 A.M.

"I should have listened to her," Tessa was mumbling tonelessly, her vacant eyes staring at something only she could see, clearly in shock after reliving these events. "I should have done what Ellie wanted and then none of if would have happened. She didn't want to skip school in the first place, she didn't want to help Jake, she didn't want to try and escape . . . it should have been me who died instead of Ellie."

Pressing a finger to her lips to silence her, "Tessa, it should *not* have been you who died," Parker told her firmly. He was still a little shocked and a lot concerned that it had been so easy to get answers out of Tessa. Perhaps he had underestimated the emotional toll of what she had been through lately.

Her gaze focusing slowly on him, "I shouldn't have believed him. I shouldn't have fallen for Jake's trick. Only he had a little girl with him. I didn't think anyone with a child could do anything to hurt kids. I was stupid, I was naïve, and Ellie is dead because of me," she said flatly. "So many people are dead because of me."

Struggling to remain calm as he thought of the terrified little girl who had been forced to take a life to protect her own. "It was self defense, honey, you were *eleven*. He kidnapped you, raped you and murdered your best friend." Needing to ask because they needed everything they could get on these men, "Tessa, honey." Waiting until her eyes slowly rose to meet his. "Did they do a rape kit on you at the hospital after you were found?"

"What?" She shuddered so violently he wouldn't have been surprised if she'd shattered into a million pieces.

"You were a little girl, found alone, miles from anywhere, covered in blood, you were clearly traumatized, it must have occurred to them to do a rape kit on you. Did they?"

"No."

Already paler than he'd ever seen her, somehow the color seemed to drain further from her face, and she swayed unsteadily. Grabbing her and quickly dragging her to the nearest chair, Parker pushed her gently down into it.

"I couldn't let them touch me there," Tessa was murmuring, she tucked her knees up to her chin and wrapped her arms around herself as though physically holding herself together. "It was bad enough I had to let them touch me other places. I had cuts and bruises from running through the woods, and a head wound from where Jake hit me. I was dehydrated. I had to force myself to stay there while they examined me. I wanted Anthony to come back but I couldn't make myself call for him. They asked me if someone had hurt me, they said they needed to look for evidence. I knew what they wanted to do, but I couldn't let them do it. I freaked out, became hysterical, and they backed off."

The pain and terror in her eyes as raw as if she was experiencing it this second. Hating to have to push her further. "Some of the blood on your clothes was your own," Parker pressed gently. "From what Jake did to you. Did the police take your clothes?"

"I guess," she squeezed her eyes shut, subconsciously rocking herself backwards and forwards. "I didn't care about those clothes. I never wanted to see my school uniform again. I never wanted to go back to that school. I didn't want to be where Jake had abducted us. I didn't want to be where Ellie and I had met. Where we had spent so much time together. But my grandparents were getting annoyed with me. It had been over four months and I wasn't getting any better. I still wouldn't talk, I wouldn't go out unless they forced me, I hardly ate, barely slept, I wouldn't do anything, I just sat there all day thinking."

Reliving her abduction over and over again in her mind. Punishing herself relentlessly. Because she hadn't saved Eleanor, because she hadn't saved those other girls, because she was alive, because she didn't possess superhuman powers to control the actions of others. Parker hated her parents and grandparents for not ensuring she got the help she needed. Taking her to see a psychiatrist had been pointless because it hadn't been backed up by love and support at home. She had needed both professional help and the unwavering care and devotion of loved ones.

Wondering, not for the first time, how his life would have turned out had it not been for his adoptive parents. Like Tessa, as a child he had known what it was like to be hurt, and sacred, and alone. To have no one to turn to who could take the pain away and make everything better. By the time he'd gone to live with the Bell's he'd been such an angry little boy, but their unconditional love had saved him. He wished Tessa had been as lucky.

"My grandmother said I'd had enough time to get over it," Tessa was rambling, her breath catching in gasps but she didn't seem to notice. "That I had to go back to life as normal. So one morning she brought in my uniform and told me to get ready for school. I couldn't do it. I couldn't put those clothes on again and go back to that place. So I hid. Daniel found me shaking and crying in the back of my closet."

Tentatively reaching out a hand to stroke her face, but Parker pulled it back instantly as her eyes popped open and she flinched away. Kneeling beside her chair, "Daniel was the first person you spoke to after it happened?" he asked gently.

Nodding, "Daniel picked me up, carried me to my bed, and sat me on his lap, holding me while I cried. He was all I had, the only person who'd been there for me, he'd hardly left my side since it happened. I wanted him to promise he'd never leave me."

Parker had never felt so helpless in all his life. He didn't know what to say or do to take Tessa's pain away. Reaching for her hands, which were as cold as ice, he needed his wife to know that he was there for her, "I love you, Tessa. Are you hearing me? I love you." She watched absently as he briskly rubbed her hands to warm them, this time she didn't pull away from him.

"Daniel begged me to tell him what happened to me," Tessa continued to murmur, her eyes eerily blank, he wasn't even sure she knew what she was saying. "He said whatever it was he would be there for me, he said he wanted to help me, he said if I would just tell him then he could make things better. I wanted to. I wanted so badly to tell him but I couldn't. If I had of been able to make myself tell him then maybe those other girls could have been saved. I should have told him. After that day he never asked me again. He knew I couldn't do it. He knew I was never going to tell him. He knew I was a coward."

"No, Tessa." Giving in to the urge to attempt to literally shake some sense into her. "Daniel loves you, he does *not* think that you are a coward, *no one* does."

Wondering guiltily whether he ought to have called Daniel and told him what was going on with Tessa and ask him to come back home. He'd told himself he was just following Tessa's wishes by not contacting her brother, but if he was honest it was more because he didn't like Daniel and was happy to keep him on the fringes of Tessa's life. But this wasn't about him this was about Tessa. And right now she needed all the support she could get. She needed all the people who loved and cared about her by her side. And as much as Parker didn't like Daniel, he knew that the man loved his sister and would do anything for her.

"All those girls," her gaze growing unfocused again. She rose and crossed to the window, staring blankly out it. "All those little girls."

After hearing the horrific story of what little Tessa went through Parker now better understood just what had driven her to go to such lengths later in life to save those she cared about. She was attempting to assuage her guilt over what she believed to be her part in destroying the lives of those other girls.

"Tessa, baby, look at me." Shaking her again until she did, "it was not your fault, do you hear me? What happened to those girls was not your fault." Looking to Beth for support he saw tears glistening in her warm brown eyes.

Coming to them Beth laid a hand on Tessa's shoulder. "Parker's right, sweetie, you were a child . . ."

"She blamed me," Tessa inserted dully.

"Who, honey?" he asked confused.

"Ellie's mom. She blamed me for what happened. And she never forgave me for not telling her how Ellie died, for not letting her bury her only child, for not telling anyone."

"Why didn't you tell anyone? If you had maybe . . ." Parker broke off realizing to Tessa's ears it had sounded like he had just confirmed that she was responsible for the fate of those girls.

"Maybe those other girls could have been saved," Tessa finished for him. "I already told you, because I was a coward. I put myself above them. I was scared that I would get in trouble, I'd just killed a man."

"Maybe you would have been able to get the help you needed," he finished what he'd been about to say. "Tessa," he started once again to tell her that it was self-defense but Beth cut him off with a look.

Guiding Tessa, who was shaky and wobbly on her feet, back to the sofa Beth sat beside her. "Sometimes it's scary to be the only survivor of something traumatic," she said gently. "It's called survivors guilt." Beth took the blanket from Wyatt's outstretched hand and wrapped it around Tessa's trembling form. "I know that you blame yourself, honey," she stroked Tessa's hair soothingly. "You feel guilty because Eleanor died and you didn't. But you were a victim too. Sometimes it's helpful to look at things a different way, to help come to terms with the reality that you are really not to blame."

"How am I not to blame?" Tessa's haunted eyes searched Beth's face imploringly, for an answer she didn't think existed.

Beth kept her tone matter of fact, "you were a child, your captors were bigger and stronger than you, you were scared and hurt, and yet you kept your wits about you. You took note of your surroundings and managed to find a way of escape. Even though you were scared and desperate to get out, you took the time to try to help others, strangers. When you couldn't you took your friend with you. You were willing to sacrifice yourself to save your friend. And when your life was in danger you fought back, defended yourself, and managed to escape. Tessa, you were amazingly brave, and resourceful, and strong. Most adults couldn't have done what you did."

"It sounds like you're putting your own slant on it to make me sound good," Tessa remained unconvinced.

"Isn't that what you've been doing all these years?" Beth asked gently. "Putting a slant on things to make yourself look bad?"

"I . . . I . . . I don't know," Tessa stammered, uncertainty flashing through her greeny-blue eyes.

Crouching in front of Tessa, "was Dino Rollino involved? Is he the man who wants you dead?" Parker asked, not noticing Beth shaking her head until it was too late.

Face clouding over, "is that all you care about?" Tessa demanded. "Names of who was involved?"

Trying to undo it, "no, honey. I just want to know who it is who wants my wife dead, so I can keep you safe. Clara Meyers positively ID'd Dino Rollino as the man who abducted her, so we know he's involved."

"Dino is the man who wants me dead, the one who tried to kill me in the fire and the one who left the spider here the other night."

"I don't understand why if he wants you dead you'd go to him for help," Parker wondered if he was missing something because he still couldn't fathom why Tessa would trust this man.

"I didn't," she snapped.

"But you said that when I was missing you went to the man who tried to kill you for help finding me."

"No," Tessa corrected. "You all said that, I just didn't disagree. There you have all your answers, are you happy now?"

Annoyed that he'd fallen for Tessa's ploy of pretending you were right when you weren't once again. "No, I am not happy. I just found out that when my wife was eleven she was abducted by child traffickers, raped, watched her friend's murder, and was forced to kill a man in self-defense. But I'm a cop, Tess, I can't just sit here, I need to be doing something, and since I can't personally wring Jake's neck I'm going to hunt down Dino Rollino and see that he pays for everything he's done. If I'm going to do that, if I'm going to find the men responsible for Eleanor's death, the men responsible for hurting you, then you need to help me out, you need to give me some names . . ."

"Names," she shrieked, bounding to her feet. "Names, names, names, that's all you care about." Practically throwing herself at the desk where she ripped off a piece of paper and began scribbling furiously.

"Tessa, honey, calm down. Names are not all I care about," Parker struggled to keep his voice gentle and soothing while his insides were churning and fury was bubbling inside him over what his wife had endured. He wanted that tormented look gone from Tessa's eyes now, and had to remind himself that it would take months, maybe years, of therapy for Tessa to be able to move forwards.

"I don't want to calm down." She thrust the list into his hand, "congratulations. You did something in two years that no one else has ever been able to do, find out what happened to Ellie. I hope it was worth it, I hope making me relive the most horrific couple of days of my life was worth it. Well there're your precious names."

"Sweetheart," managing to get a grip on her flailing arms.

Wrenching herself free, "don't touch me." She shuddered violently, "just stay away from me."

"Tessa, sweetie, why don't you take a seat," Beth advised, hovering anxiously at Tessa's side, ready to intervene if she needed medical attention.

"It's not like I don't need these names for a reason," Parker reminded her, trying to calm his wife down with logic. "At least seven little girls that we know of might be with these people right now, along with countless others we don't even know about. These names could help . . ."

"Don't make me responsible for those girls you think Dino has," Tessa started to cry. "I can't do it again. Don't you see that? I'm like poison, everyone who comes into contact with me ends up getting hurt. I can't do it anymore. I can't be responsible for those girls. I won't be."

"Tess, you're not responsible for any of it," he tried to reassure her but knowing he was fighting a losing battle. Tessa's guilt was deep rooted and it was going to take a lot of help, professional help, for her to learn to let it go. "You were only a child, just a little girl," attempting to pull her into an embrace but she moved out of reach.

"Just a little girl," she echoed dismally. "I killed Jake, I left fifteen girls behind to be sold into a life of prostitution and I killed Ellie. I'm a murderer."

Hating hearing his wife call herself that, "no you are not. You are the most loving, caring person I know."

"That's a lie," she shrieked, pressing her hands to her ears. "I *am* a murderer. When we first met I told you that I didn't deserve to be happy, that I was bad luck. Don't you see? I killed a man and my punishment is that everyone I love and care about leaves me." Tears cascading down her pale cheeks, her turbulent eyes were darting around the room in search of some safe haven. She settled on Wyatt and threw herself into his arms.

Momentarily taken aback since things had been so shaky between them lately, Wyatt wrapped his arms around her. "It's alright, Tess," he soothed as he rubbed her back. "Shh, it's going to be okay."

Trying not to be hurt that Tessa had chosen to go to Wyatt for comfort instead of him, her husband. "It'll be okay, honey, I promise." Parker dropped a gentle kiss on the top of her blonde head.

Shrinking away from his touch, Tessa tightened her grip on Wyatt as she continued to sob. Even when her tears finally dried up she refused to release her hold on Wyatt, clinging to him tightly.

Lifting her into his arms, Wyatt started for the stairs, "I'm going to take her up to bed. Beth, can you come up and check her over? Given how she feels about hospitals I don't think a trip there is best for her right now. Parker, are her pain meds up there?"

"Get her settled and I'll be right there," Beth said.

"Yeah, she needs to rest," Parker agreed. "Her meds are probably in the bathroom, she needs to take the antibiotics too. Sweetheart, I'm going to be up soon, okay? I love you." He felt like he was alone in a vast ocean, buffeted from every angle by wave after crushing wave.

Refusing to respond, Tessa kept her eyes closed and her face tucked away against Wyatt's neck.

As they watched Wyatt leave with Tessa, Beth turned to catch Parker in a serious stare. "She didn't say she was scared they'd come after her," she said.

"What?" he asked, too preoccupied with whether or not he had done the right thing pushing Tessa to talk about her abduction to catch the psychiatrist's point.

"When she was telling us why she didn't speak a word for four months after she was found," Beth elaborated. "She didn't say it was because she was scared they would come after her. She said she was scared because she had just killed a man, but she wasn't scared that the people who had abducted her, raped her, and murdered her friend would come after her to stop her telling all to the police." Pausing to let her words sink in, "there's something else, Parker. A reason why she knew they weren't coming after her. Something she didn't tell us."

* * * * *

4:19 P.M.

"Calm down, there's nothing to panic about."

"That's easy for you to say," Dino ranted at John Doe. "I'm the one they're looking for. It's my name the police have. They don't have yours. No one does."

"Tying ourselves into knots isn't going to help the situation," John Doe told him calmly as he took a long drink and stretched back in his chair.

Fuming, "what are we going to do about it? You know that little witch Tessa gave me up. If you had let me kill her then we wouldn't be in this mess."

Eyeing him irritably, with brown eyes that seemed much too mild to belong to such an evil man. "How do you know, Dino, that it wasn't Clara Meyers who gave you up? Or maybe the police managed to link you to some of the girls. You remember don't you that your name came up in two of the girl's cases?"

Summoning every ounce of self-control he possessed to keep from strangling John Doe right here and now with his bare hands.

"We both know it was Tessa. We should have eliminated her the second she got away, nipped it in the bud before she ever had a chance to become a problem."

"She was just a little girl," John Doe reminded him.

"She killed Jake, or have you conveniently forgotten that?" Dino demanded.

"No, Dino," John Doe rose to refresh his drink. "But she was just a child, she was no threat to us."

"Well she's not a child anymore," he snapped. "Now she's all grown up and married to a cop. A cop who's already proved on more than one occasion what lengths he'll go to in order to keep Tessa safe." Catching a ghost of a smile flit across the old man's face at the mention of Tessa. "Just what kind of spell does she have you under?"

"When it comes to Tessa I am under no spell," John Doe told him curtly. "And right now she is not the issue, the police are."

"I think we should hold tight, bring everyone back here to the house, close it down, no one in or out. The police may have my name and they may be looking for me but there's nothing that connects me to this place."

John Doe stared at him, "decisions like that, Dino, are why you'll never be number one in this business."

"What are you talking about?"

"The police have your name," John Doe spoke slowly as though Dino were an idiot. "The police have your picture. The police have Clara Meyers so they know the vicinity of this house. And the police have Tessa so they know exactly what we do."

"Clara was found miles from here," Dino countered angrily. "And as you said before Tessa was only a kid when she was here she couldn't have figured out what we do."

Shaking his head disappointedly, "another mistake, Dino. Tessa is a genius with an IQ of 178, of course she figured out what we do."

"I thought you said she'd never tell, that's why we didn't have to kill her right away," Dino pouted.

"She wouldn't have told, but they would have been relentless, pounding on her and pounding on her until at last she caved," John Doe answered a little sadly and seemed lost in a distant memory.

Hoping to actually get an answer this time. "Just what occurred between the two of you that you know her so well?" he asked softly.

But John Doe bounced back to business, "the police know more about us than is safe, which means it's time to move on. We pack up the girls, we clear out the house, and we move somewhere else, start again."

"But we're all established here," Dino protested. "This is my home. We've only been here a year, I'm sick of moving from city to city. You said this time we were going to stay put," aware he was sounding like a whiny child, but he had been waiting too long to come back here. Now that he was so close to Tessa, so close to his revenge, he couldn't bear to leave without finishing what he'd started.

"What you want is of no value to me," John Doe stood and crossed to his desk. "If the operation is at risk then we must move on. Go and start making arrangements, we must be gone in forty-eight hours."

Skulking from the room, furious at having his opinions dismissed, Dino decided it was now or never, he had a few people to talk to and then he was going to finally complete some unfinished business.

\* \* \* \* \*


10:53 P.M.


"I can't believe you found it."

Beaming at the admiration in her sister's voice. "It was just lucky I guess," Olivia whispered back.

"No it wasn't just luck, *I* never saw it," Cassie contradicted.

Feeling her cheeks heat at her big sister's compliment. Olivia didn't really care whether it was luck or cleverness on her part, all she cared about was that right now she and Cassie were on their way to freedom.

When Dino had been dragging Cassie down to the room the other night, she had noticed a waft of air blowing the coats that hung just by the door. At first she hadn't been sure exactly what that meant but she'd known it meant something. Later when everyone had been sleeping she had snuck from her cell to check it out and found a door leading to a narrow staircase. Olivia didn't know what was at the top of the steps but she knew that it couldn't be any worse than being trapped in the awful basement.

It had taken her a while to convince Cassie that she wasn't dreaming, or imagining, or making things up but that she had really found a way out. She's been trying to explain when Dino had arrived and dragged them to the room. Olivia's insides still burned from that encounter but she didn't want to think about that now, all she wanted to focus on was getting home.

The two girls ascended the stairs quietly. Olivia's heart was beating so loudly she kept expecting it to alert someone to their escape and send one of the guards running up the steps to stop them. They had waited until all was silent before tiptoeing to the hidden door. The TV had been rumbling in the background indicating that their guards were otherwise occupied. Now they'd been climbing up and up for what seemed like hours. Butterflies fluttered wildly in her stomach as she kept checking behind her, wondering when their luck would run out and someone would find them.

Jumping when her sister nudged her, then following Cassie's pointed finger to see that they had reached a door. What was on the other side was anybody's guess but Olivia prayed it was freedom. She could hardly think of anything else other than curling up in the safety of her mom's arms. Brushing away a few stray tears, she nodded and reached a hand to the doorknob.

"Wait," Cassie stopped her. "We don't know if anyone's out there," she whispered.

Hanging back while her sister pressed an ear to the door and listened, then edged it slightly open to peek through. Olivia found herself holding her breath and thinking surely this was too good to be true, but then Cassie was turning around and giving her a thumbs up.

Jittery with excitement Olivia followed Cassie through the door, where the girls found themselves in a small, untidy shed. A rusty lawnmower sat in the corner, old metal tools hung from the walls, several cans of paint sat side by side on a shelf, and a broken rake lay in the middle of the floor. The room looked like it hadn't been used in ages, cobwebs decorated the ceiling and all the corners and a thick layer of dust smothered everything.

Carefully the sisters made their way through the shed, sidestepping the splintered rake, to reach the door on the other side. As Cassie went through Olivia paused and looked back at their smudgy footsteps crossing the floor from the door to hell to the door to freedom.

"Come on, Liv," Cassie tugged on her arm and Olivia followed her big sister out into the dark night.

Breathing in mouthful after mouthful of the cool, fresh air. Drinking in the gentle breeze, her skin tingling, her lungs bursting, tears pricking her eyes as she felt her body coming alive in the clean air after weeks shut up in the damp, stuffy basement.

Throwing back her head, Olivia gazed up at the clear night sky. Millions of stars twinkled merrily as though welcoming her return to the land of the living. The moon, an enormous round circle, seemed to glow as brightly as the sun and seemed so close she was almost tempted to reach out a hand to try to grab it.

"Do you see anyone?" Cassie was surveying the huge open expanse of green grass in which the shed was set, about a hundred yards away from the woods.

Olivia checked too and caught sight of the mansion, imposing and evil in the distance, she couldn't help but shudder as she looked at it, thinking of those other girls still trapped inside. Planting her feet firmly in place and leaning back against her sister's pulling. "Those girls, Cass, we have to do something to help them, we can't leave them there."

"We tried to get them to come," Cassandra reminded her. "They wouldn't listen."

"We can't just leave them there, in that place," Olivia shivered again.

"We won't," Cassie told her fiercely. "We'll go to the police, we'll get help. There's nothing we can do for them on our own, but the police will be able to do something, they'll arrest those men and then all the girls will be able to go home . . . just like us. Now do you see anyone?"

Olivia looked then shook her head. The place was deserted.

"Okay, follow me and stay low to the ground."

As Cassie scuttled across the smooth grass Olivia followed, making sure to keep as close to the ground as possible. They were soon crouching in the safety of the tall trees, checking to make sure they hadn't been noticed. There was no one in sight and after hiding for a while it became apparent that they had not been spotted.

Once again Cassandra tugged on her arm, urging her on, "come on, Livy, they might know that we're gone and be looking for us."

Following Cassie deeper into the thick woods, neither of them could wipe the grins off their faces as they walked in the safety of the shadowy forest. It wasn't until they'd been trudging along in silence for several minutes when Olivia suddenly stopped short. "We don't know where we are. How are we going to get home when we don't know where we are?" panic came flooding back pushing away her joy at being free.

"Don't worry," Cassie told her reassuringly. "We don't have to find our way home. All we have to do is find someone, tell them who we are and what happened to us and let them take us to the police."

Her churning stomach settling Olivia smiled and resumed following Cassandra through the woods, dreaming about what it would like to be back at home.

* * * * *

11:02 P.M.

Enjoying a walk in the moonlight, John Doe was feeling pretty relaxed about things, despite the inconvenience of the police having Dino's name. John Doe didn't care about Dino and he didn't care if the man's world was about to come crashing down. If his second in command was stupid enough to get mixed up in the police's investigation and to let them get his name then that was his problem.

Neither was John Doe concerned that if the police did catch up with Dino Rollino he would spill anything confidential. If Dino was arrested then John Doe would simply use one of his many contacts to shut Dino's mouth. Permanently.

In the morning they would pack up the girls, rid the house of anything that may trace back to him and his business and depart for a new location. Dino wasn't the only one who was sad to be leaving. Of all the places John Doe had lived in the last several decades, this was his favorite. In fact, that was the only reason that he had allowed Dino to pester him into coming back here.

Already a year had passed since their return. Dozens of girls had passed through the place, some taken from hundreds of miles away, others from nearby. Twelve months was usually the longest they remained in any one location, to stay much longer was to tempt fate. If too many little girls started disappearing in one area then the police instantly became suspicious. One of the reasons that he had avoided detection for so long was that no matter where they were based John Doe ensured that the girls were taken from a variety of places both near and far.

This was why John Doe had been so successful in this business and so long lasting. Others had come and gone, some to prison, some to death, some to less risky enterprises, while he still remained. It was also why Dino Rollino would never make it to the top. Dino was too emotional, too temperamental, too stupid. Dino didn't possess the ability to think through all the possible outcomes when faced with a problem, instead he merely jumped to the quickest, easiest, most convenient option.

As he stood enjoying the late summer night, the soft breeze, the winking stars, the glowing moon, he saw two shadowy figures dart from the shed to the thick woods that surrounded the property. Hand hovering above his cell as he readied himself to phone for backup to retrieve the two runaways. Watching the two girls, who were barely fifty yards away from him but seemingly completely oblivious to his presence.

It was the sisters, Cassandra and Olivia Stanton. John Doe liked the girls, thought they had spunk, especially the younger one, Olivia. She was quiet and dreamy, a little in her big sister's shadow, but strong and determined and smart. He had shared his story with her that first day, something he did with only a handful of girls, the ones who reminded him of Tessa.

Dino had asked him what had happened between him and Tessa that made him trust her implicitly. That was a question that even he wasn't quite sure of the answer to. Things between himself and Tessa were complicated, a relationship founded on mutual dependence, but there was more, something he couldn't quite articulate, in a bizarre way they filled a need in the other.

But trust Tessa he did.

He was positive that her Detective husband had coerced an account out of her of the weekend that he and Tessa had met, the weekend Eleanor Matthews had been killed. He was also positive that Tessa had been pressured into naming those involved in the operation. Just as he was positive that while she would have named all the others, there was no way she would have included his own name in her list.

And know his name Tessa did. She was the only person on the face of the planet who knew his real identity.

Now as he watched the Stanton girls rise and disappear deeper into the woods he lowered his hand from his phone. Only once before had a girl managed to escape from his compounds, Clara Meyers didn't count since that had been outside of his control. If Cassandra and Olivia Stanton had managed to achieve something only Tessa Micah Bell had then he was prepared to let them go. He was under no illusion that the girls would keep quiet. In fact, he fully expected them to tell all to the police, but they were miles from anywhere and by the time the girls found help he would be long gone.

With a last look at the forest, John Doe meandered back to the house. Memories of Tessa triggering other, more painful, memories, and he prayed that one day he might find the answers he so desperately sought.

# SEPTEMBER 10<sup>TH</sup>

8:11 A.M.

Tessa wasn't sure she was ready to do this.

She wasn't sure she *could* do this.

Determinedly she continued down the hall, pausing in front of his room.

This was crazy. She didn't do stuff like this. Ever. But then again she'd never thought that she would tell another living soul about what had happened when she and Ellie had been kidnapped. And yet she had. She had spilled all to Parker, Skylar and Elisabeth. Knowing that others knew what she'd done, how she'd left those girls behind, how she'd gotten her best friend killed, how she'd murdered Jake, left her feeling shaky and empty.

She couldn't do this after all.

Turning on her heel to leave when the door suddenly popped open and Charlie Abbott was looming over her.

"Eric warned me you might try to bail," he smiled down at her.

Tessa had met Charlie only once before but he was the spitting image of his younger brother. A little taller than Eric and a little broader across the shoulders but there was no mistaking the family resemblance.

"Are you coming in or not?" Charlie asked, holding the door wide open to reveal his cramped office.

Why oh why had she called him this morning? It had been a stupid idea. She didn't talk to shrinks. She thought they were a waste of time. Talking to Charlie wasn't going to change the fact that Ellie was dead, or that those girls had suffered, or that Jake was dead because she had killed him. What on earth what she doing here? Was her life really spinning this far out of control that she had come to talk to a psychiatrist?

"Tessa . . ." Charlie began and she readied herself for the plethora of platitudes that counselor's were always spouting forth. "Would you please come and sit down because you are making me hurt seeing you stand there," he finished with another easy smile.

Caught off guard she couldn't help but return Charlie's smile. "Fine," she agreed. Entering the room she was unsure where to sit. Charlie had a desk by the window, with a chair on either side, then by the door he had two sofas separated by a small table upon which sat only a box of tissues.

"Do you want anything to drink?" Charlie shut the door and crossed to a small refrigerator in the corner.

"No thanks," she answered, squirming at the thought of putting anything in her already swirling stomach.

"You can sit wherever you want," Charlie told her when he turned around, iced tea in hand, and saw her still standing.

The couch looked the more comfortable option but also the more vulnerable so she limped over to the desk and took the seat closest. Attempting to hide her small moan of relief as she sank down into the chair. She had allowed herself to get too emotional yesterday recounting the story of her abduction and this morning she was paying the price for it with a raging headache.

Charlie took one look at her then returned to his fridge, retrieved a bottle of water, then picked up a small bottle and joined her at his desk. Setting the bottle of pills and the water down in front of her then taking his seat on the other side of the desk and the distance between them made her feel the teensiest bit more relaxed.

"Eric said you checked yourself out of the hospital against his advice," Charlie commented.

"I hate hospitals," she shrugged, as she tipped two painkillers from the bottle into her hand and washed them down with a mouthful of water.

"How are you feeling? You don't look so great, you're not going to pass out on me are you?"

From the probing stare on his face Tessa wondered whether Charlie was itching to check her pulse and take her blood pressure like doctors were always wanting to do. As if they thought they could fix all the problems in the world if they could just get your vitals in perfect order. "I'm fine," she lied, knowing full well that she was pushing her injured body too far.

"Eric told me you always say that," Charlie mused. "He also said that it's not true."

"So much for doctor patient confidentiality," she grumbled.

"Is this your first time seeing a psychiatrist?" Charlie asked, obviously trying to go with her and take things nice and slow.

"No, I'd already gone through five before I was twelve."

"Wow," Charlie's brown eyes widened in surprise. "That's a lot of psychiatrists for such a little girl."

"Yeah well I guess persistence isn't a skill a lot of psychiatrists have." When he raised a questioning eyebrow she elaborated, "I wouldn't talk. They tried all their tricks but I just sat there quietly not saying a word and in the end they just gave up."

Taking this is in, "are you going to talk today?" he asked seriously.

"I don't know," she replied. "To be honest I'm not even sure why I called you."

"How did it make you feel when those psychiatrists gave up on you?"

Rolling her eyes, "don't you think that's kind of a lame question?"

"Do you?" he shot back with a grin.

Smiling, Tessa was definitely starting to like Charlie Abbott. He was different from the other shrinks she'd seen before. "I didn't feel anything," she told him, "I didn't expect them to help. I already knew that I was alone."

"Are you going to tell me what happened to you to make you stop talking?"

"That depends on how much you already know," she scowled. "Or rather how much your big mouth of a brother told you."

"He didn't tell me anything I swear," Charlie held his hands up in mock surrender. "But I do know about what happened to you and your husband a few months ago. And I know that you were just in a car accident and that apparently you found a little girl in the woods covered in blood that wasn't hers. Talk around the hospital is that you were found that way when you were a little girl."

The patient way he sat waiting for her compelled her to tell him, and since she'd already told three other people keeping the secret from him didn't seem to achieve much. She gave Charlie the cliff notes version of the events of that weekend, when she was done she sat anxiously awaiting his reaction.

"Wow, Tessa, I'm really sorry. That's terrible. No child, no person, should ever have to go through something like that."

Charlie looked shocked and horrified but she didn't detect anything judgmental. "Parker thinks that Ellie's and my abduction is related to Clara Meyers," she explained.

"Is it?" Charlie asked.

"Elisabeth, she's a profiler and psychiatrist who works with Parker," she added for Charlie's benefit, "she thinks I'm suffering from survivors guilt."

"What do you think?"

"What do *you* think?" she shot back.

"Do you want to move past this?"

"I'm not sure," she answered truthfully. "I feel guilty about moving on. Ellie died and I didn't, it doesn't seem fair that I get to move on and she has to stay dead."

"I don't think that you're scared of moving on because you have to give Ellie up to do it, I think you're scared of moving on because you've never actually accepted your friend's death."

A little disappointed in the lack of depth of Charlie's answer, she could already have told him that. Tessa was going to bring the session to a close, convinced more than ever of the complete and utter uselessness of psychiatry and wishing she'd spent the morning catching up on some sleep instead when Charlie continued.

"I also don't think that you really feel alone."

"What?" she looked at him in confusement. She must have paled because Charlie rose instantly and came around his desk to stand beside her, his hand gripping her shoulder firmly.

"I think that whatever happened the night that Ellie died, by which I mean the part that you left out of your story, made you feel that for the first time in your life you actually weren't all alone. You mom didn't know you were even missing, your dad never came back from France, your grandparents didn't care, your best friend was dead, but for the first time ever you knew that you weren't alone in the big bad world. And that's what has you feeling guilty. That's why you've spent your whole life pushing everyone away, that's why you're so scared to let Parker really get close to you. Because the night of your friend's death somehow actually gave you the one thing you'd been longing for, and that is eating you alive with guilt."

\* \* \* \* \*

9:42 A.M.

"I'm not going with you," Dino announced as he entered the dining room where John Doe was taking breakfast.

Merely raising an eyebrow his boss continued to eat.

Clinging to patience, after today he would never have to deal with John Doe again. "I think running is the wrong decision."

"Do you now?" drawled John Doe as he took a dainty sip from a glass of orange juice.

"I don't believe the police have a clue as to where we are," he continued a little more confidently than he felt. Dino wasn't exactly afraid of his boss, but this was the first time he had ever openly defied him. "If we just wait things out, in a couple of weeks everything will die down and then we can continue on."

"I'm not staying," John Doe said simply.

Prepared for this, "well I am." Waiting on tender hooks for his boss' reaction.

Eyeing him shrewdly, John Doe stood and crossed to the buffet, helping himself to another serve of bacon and scrambled eggs and French toast. Sauntering back to the table he took several mouthfuls before responding. "Fine."

Thrown off guard, "what?" Dino stammered, sure he must have heard wrong.

"I said that's fine," John Doe repeated.

"Really?" Dino hadn't expected his boss to agree so readily.

"I've never liked you," John Doe said bluntly. "I think you're an idiot. The police know who you are and it won't take them long to find you but if you want to part ways then that's fine with me."

Gaining confidence with his small victory. "I want to take a couple of the men with me."

Narrowing his brown eyes, "how many and who?"

"Three," Dino answered. "Kelvin, Marcus and Jason." Three of John Doe's least favorite employees, but some of Dino's closest confidants. After being dismissed last night Dino had gone straight to the three men and solidified their loyalties by promising them higher positions and more money in his new organization than they had in John Doe's.

Once he'd finalized his new team he had moved on to finishing the final details on his plan for revenge. If it had been up to him he would have liked to take his time with Tessa, play with her for a while, but despite what John Doe thought Dino was not an idiot. He knew that the police had his name, he knew that they knew more about him and John Doe and what they did than he would have liked, and he knew that it was important to finish Tessa off as quickly as possible. Dino also knew that getting to Tessa was going to be a problem. Her cop husband and his buddies would have wrapped her up tightly in their protective cocoon.

"Okay," John Doe agreed, breaking through Dino's thoughts.

"And," Dino decided to risk it since he'd already scored twice today. "I want to take some of the girls with me."

John Doe studied him as if he were a moron. "You want what?"

"I want to take a couple of the girls with me. Look," he reasoned, "we have seventeen girls here at . . ."

"Fifteen," John Doe corrected.

"What are you talking about?"

"The Stanton girls escaped last night. Probably while you were trying to bribe your buddies to jump ship."

"Is someone out looking for them?"

"No."

"No? And you have the gall to call me an idiot," Dino took a menacing step towards his boss but John Doe's two bodyguards reached for their guns.

"How I run my business is none of your business," John Doe pushed away his empty plate. "I thought you were trying to convince me of why I should let you keep some of my girls."

Quashing his outrage at John Doe's hypocrisy. "We have *fifteen* girls, I'm responsible for taking at least ten of them. I've been working for you since I was a teenager. I've been loyal and discreet," ignoring the man's mirthful huff at his mention of the word discreet. "And I think I deserve to walk away with at least five of the girls."

The silence seemed to stretch into eternity but finally John Doe rose, taking his pipe with him. "Fine. You may take Kelvin, Marcus and Jason, and you may have five of the girls, but . . ."

sticking the lit pipe into his mouth, "I choose which girls."

"Okay," Dino agreed, a little reluctantly, knowing that John Doe was going to give him the five least desirable girls. Still, he cheered himself up, he was on the verge of having everything he ever wanted, his own business, money, power, notoriety and revenge. "What about the house?" It was John Doe's usual procedure to sell the mansion they had been using and take the profits to fund the next place.

"You can have it," John Doe said casually, puffing rings of smoke. "I'll be out of here within an hour. I will leave behind your five girls, but every piece of paperwork will be destroyed, you'll have to start from scratch." Pausing by the door, "oh and, Dino," John Doe shot him one of his evil smiles, "enjoy it while it lasts because it won't last long."

As his now ex-boss disappeared down the hall Dino knew that once again John Doe was wrong, he was going to become the greatest this business had ever seen.

*  *  *  *  *

*Sixteen Years Ago*
*Saturday Night*

*Unsure how long she'd been sitting there.*

*Ellie's body was still warm in her arms as Tessa clutched her desperately as though that may be enough to will her own life into her friend's. Jake lay beside her, the pool of blood around him from where she had plunged her knife into his femoral artery seemed to have stopped growing bigger.*

*The sky was darkening, the sun slowly setting, the day was drawing to a close.*

*Tessa kept telling herself to move. There was nothing she could do for Ellie and if she stayed here much longer someone was bound to stumble upon them and drag her back down to that dungeon.*

*Maybe they would punish her for killing Jake. Maybe they would hit her, or cut her, or burn her, or strangle her, mind running away with possibilities of what they might do. Maybe they would do to her what Jake had done. Tessa shivered as she remembered the feel of him pressed down on top of her. Or maybe they would kill her. She deserved it, she had just taken a life, not to mention all those girls she had left behind down in the basement, destined to a life of horror and abuse. Or maybe they would punish her in the worst possible way and let her live to be consumed for all eternity by guilt.*

*Head jerking up as she heard a noise, Tessa surveyed her surroundings but saw nothing so she returned her attentions to Ellie, gently closing her friend's eyes so that they no longer stared accusingly at her own. Beginning to twirl Ellie's dark blonde braids around her fingers, something Ellie always did when she was nervous, when she heard the unmistakable sound of voices. In a panic Tessa's head snapped towards the noise and she could just make out two figures at the top of a small hill several hundred yards in the distance.*

*With a muted squeal she reluctantly set Ellie's body down on the ground beside Jake's and darted for the safety of the woods. Once she started running she couldn't seem to stop. She ran and ran and ran. Completely unaware of the sky turning black, the stars blinking on one by one, the moon rising until it was a glowing orb high in the night.*

*Chest burning, legs aching, so breathless that bright spots danced in front of her eyes, her head spinning wildly, but still she didn't stop. More like she couldn't stop even if she wanted to. Filled to overflowing with the need to be as far away from that place as possible. From Ellie, the friend she had betrayed, from the girls she had abandoned, from Jake the man she had killed, from all of it.*

*Running for miles, for hours, until at last her legs gave out and she collapsed into a gasping heap on the ground. Struggling to catch her breath, she rolled herself up into a tiny ball, as if she could make herself so small she could disappear altogether.*

*Rolling onto her back Tessa gazed up at the stars, twinkling merrily with no care for the horrors they witnessed each night. She and Ellie had loved to stare at the stars, to imagine what it would be like to live in space and they had both decided a year ago that they wanted to be astronauts when they grew up. But now that dream was gone forever, Ellie was dead, and before she knew what was happening tears were streaming down her cheeks, great heaving sobs wracking her body.*

*Once again, Tessa curled herself up into a ball and wept until at last her mind gave out just like her legs had and she fell into an exhausted sleep.*

\* \* \* \* \*

*Little Tessa had been so caught up in Jake and Ellie and her own fears that she hadn't noticed the man who had seen everything. Who had watched silently while Ellie was killed, who had been ready to step in but hung back as Tessa defended herself. He had contemplated stepping in and attempting to console the distraught child but hadn't known what to say or do and in the end had simply stood and watched. As he watched the little girl run for freedom stopping her never even entered his mind. He had more than enough girls here, and this one reminded him of someone important to him.*

*John Doe had never once regretted his decision to let Tessa Micah go.*

\* \* \* \* \*

1:24 P.M.

"Wow this place is really creepy," Maisy shivered as she looked up at the mansion. "I feel like I just walked into a horror movie."

No one disagreed with her.

Parker remembered the first time he had seen this mansion, almost two years ago. A cold wintry night, snowflakes had been fluttering in the air, as he and Wyatt had driven around and around in a frantic search for Tessa. When they'd eventually located her car their trek through the woods had led them to this house, where a body had lain covered in a light blanket of snow. Parker remembered the panic that had coursed through him at the thought of Tessa in danger, even though he'd only known her a few days at the time he had already been in love with her. Now, even though he'd been out to this house several times since,

Parker always felt uneasy here. The feeling had grown even more intense since he'd found out exactly what had happened to Tessa here when she was a little girl.

His wife had been quiet and distant this morning, clearly still angry with him for making her relive those events. Parker felt only partly bad. It hadn't been easy deliberately inflicting pain on her, but in the end it had been for Tessa's own good. Sixteen years was long enough. If she was going to move on then she had to confront those awful days. Tessa may be mad at him now but one day she'd realize that he'd done it to help her and those other girls.

"What is it exactly that you're hoping to find?" Marty asked as he began to unload things from his van, his thin frame looking like it should be squashed by the heavy equipment.

"Anything," he answered, a little helplessly. Parker wasn't sure what he hoped to find here or even if there was anything to find, but he knew he had to do something. "When the place was checked out last time we didn't know about the basement, who knows what could have been left behind when they abandoned this place."

For the time being he was assuming that shortly after Tessa escaped the men who took her had packed up their bags and moved on. Most likely they had continued abducting and selling little girls.

Now for some unknown reason something had drawn them back here where they had picked up their business where they left off, kidnapping seven girls that they knew of so far. They had been running the names Tessa had given them, some of them popping up as petty criminals, a couple with various sexual offences, one had served ten years for sexually abusing two of his little cousins. So far they had been unable to track down any of the men on Tessa's list, and although Parker wasn't entirely sure that his wife didn't know where Dino Rollino was, he had decided to leave her be for the moment.

Thinking about Dino Rollino made him feel physically sick. Knowing that the man was out there and that he was more than likely to go to any length and take any risk in his campaign to rid the world of Tessa left him almost unable to function.

Parker couldn't quite figure out why it was that Dino wanted Tessa dead so badly and that scared him. He didn't like loose ends and Beth's words kept echoing in his head, that there was more to the story than Tessa had shared with them. Beth was right there had to have been a reason that Tessa had never been afraid that the child traffickers would come after her. Unless Dino was the representative sent to take care of her and that was his connection to her. Still Parker had to admit, even to himself that that seemed unlikely, if the child traffickers had wanted Tessa dead then she would never have made it to her twelfth birthday.

"Parker."

"Yeah?" It seemed he had zoned out and missed most of the conversation.

"You okay?" Wyatt asked, concerned. His partner knew better than most the toll that trauma took on a person. A psychopath who had decided that Wyatt was the root of all his problems had decided to make things personal and had killed Wyatt and Casey's daughter when she was only three years old. Following Casey to the gas station one day when she went off to pay he drove off in the car, still containing three-year-old Serena Wyatt. A police chase had ensued and ended when the car the psychopath was driving ploughed straight into a concrete wall killing both him and the child.

"Just tired, didn't get a lot of sleep last night," he replied, rubbing at his itchy eyes. He'd been afraid to go to sleep last night in case Tessa followed her usual pattern and ran off to find the missing girls herself. He was pretty sure that Heather, Carly, Ariyel, Judy, Libby, Cassandra and Olivia were half the reason that Tessa had caved and finally confessed what had happened with Eleanor. "Wyatt, you want to take Marty show him the basement,

I'm going to go check out the stables again. Maisy, you want to come with me?"

"We already did the stables," Marty protested, pushing his thick glasses further up on his beak like nose.

"I know, I just thought we might be able to find where the hidden passage that Tessa told us about comes out."

"I'll go with you, Parker," Maisy smiled.

"We'll meet you in the basement," Parker told Wyatt and Marty, who collected the CSU equipment and headed for the house while he and Maisy veered off to the side to cross the open grassland.

"How's Tessa?" Maisy asked.

Yesterday after Wyatt had sat with Tessa until she finally fell asleep, his partner had then gone to fill J.J. and the others in on what Tess had told them, since Parker hadn't been able to face repeating his wife's story just yet. Instead he'd lain in bed beside Tessa, who, while she hadn't pulled away from him, had simply pretended that he wasn't there. Isolating herself from others and avoiding relationships had been the only way she knew how to survive. And while in the last few years she had gradually been learning to trust others, she was now quickly slipping back into old patterns.

Not wanting to get into all of that now, he was concerned enough as it was about his wife without reanalyzing everything with Maisy. "She's doing okay," he answered vaguely. "How're things going with you?"

A shy smile creeping across her face, "things're going good."

Giving her his full attention, "things with Humphrey heating up?"

Batting at her rapidly reddening cheeks, "you could say so."

"Wedding bells in the air?" he teased. Maisy had been dating a fellow CSU tech on and off since before Christmas, but recently she had been spending more and more time with him. In Parker's opinion Humphrey Jambert was a geek, a sweet guy but definitely a geek. He was tall and impossibly skinny, with shoulder length brown hair, and had a tendency to talk too much about computer games. Still Humphrey made Maisy happy and no one could deny they made a cute couple, albeit a little mismatched. Besides all of that Parker liked Humphrey a whole lot better than Maisy's other long term, on again off again boyfriend Luke.

Blush deepening even further, "maybe."

They both ground to a halt as they reached the stables. Parker recalling finding Tessa here, in a state of shock, after she'd accidentally shot Dylan Riley. Even though the man had been dead for almost two years Parker's hatred still burnt strongly towards him for all the death and pain he'd caused.

"Come on let's get this over with," he muttered heading inside and wondering whether he should have brought Tessa with him after all. He had debated it, but in the end decided against it because he'd already pushed her almost to the point of breaking by dredging up her past and he wasn't sure she could handle coming back here.

"This is where he brought Tessa before he . . .?" Maisy trailed off.

Before he'd planned on whisking her away and forcing her to spend the rest of her life with him, Parker finished silently. "Yeah."

"As much as I hate Dylan Riley he did bring Tessa into our lives, I guess that's one point in his favor. Parker, she's not really okay, is she? We're not going to lose her are we? She can get through this, I mean we can get her through this."

Catching the wobble in Maisy's voice Parker turned to face her, "Tessa is the strongest person I know," he assured Maisy. "And she has all of us who love her to support her. We're going to be there for her, Maisy. We're going to be right beside her every step of the way, and we're going to give her whatever she needs. We'll help her through this."

"I just can't believe what she went through," Maisy blinked

and tears began to trickle down her cheeks. "I hate that she had to deal with that all alone. My heart just breaks for her."

"Mine too," he whispered. Parker wished that he could just take Tessa in his arms and make everything better for her. But that wasn't going to work. So instead he was going to find Dino Rollino and make sure he suffered for what he did to Tessa. "Lets check this place out."

Surveying the empty stables, which remained almost identical to the way it had looked the night Dylan had died, minus the chair and ropes that been used to bind Tessa. The large room was empty save for a few discarded feeding troughs, the huge bloodstain still visible on the clear floor. After a couple of minutes of crisscrossing the area to check for any signs of the trapdoor Tessa had spoken of it became apparent that they were not going to find what they were looking for.

"Maybe it got boarded up," Maisy suggested, brushing back a strand of her red hair that had fallen across her eyes.

"Or maybe it never existed," Parker muttered, thinking of Beth's idea that Tessa was still holding something back.

"You think Tessa made it up?" Maisy queried, clearly confused. "Why would she do that? Why would she lie about how she escaped?"

"Because there's something she doesn't want us to know," he replied, terrified of just what that might be.

\* \* \* \* \*

2:11 P.M.

Maybe she should have stayed home.

Tessa had thought she could handle being here again but now that she was actually here she wasn't so sure. After her talk with Charlie Abbott she'd realized that maybe he was right. Maybe that was why she had strived so hard to make sure she was alone all these years since Ellie died because that was how it was supposed to be. She had been kidnapped, raped, watched her friend die, killed a man and yet she *had* walked away finally no longer alone. Maybe her subconscious had wanted to right that wrong and make sure she ended up just as alone as Ellie had and that's why she pushed everyone away.

Still it had been a shock when Charlie had pointed it out to her. Another thing to add to her already over-burdened mind. Tessa could feel herself starting to crack and wasn't sure how much longer she could hold herself together. Charlie had sensed that and had wanted to take her back downstairs to Eric, but she'd refused. She knew Parker was out here, and now that he had got her feeling responsible for the missing girls she had to follow through until they were home safely. So instead she had allowed Charlie to help her to her car and driven out here to this house.

Tessa hated this house more than any other place on the face of the planet, including her own home. Staring up at the mansion her mind swirled with images of Dylan and Jake and Ellie and John Doe and everything that had happened here . . .

"Hey."

Jumping as a hand rested on her shoulder, turning she saw Parker and Maisy.

"Sorry we startled you," Parker was watching her carefully, clearly concerned about how she would react to finding him here.

Slipping away from him. "That's okay. I knew you were out here," Tessa told him pointedly. Annoyed that he had come back out here and made her feel pressured to join him.

"I had to come back here," instantly defensive. "If there's anything here that can lead me to those little girls then I have to find it."

"That's why I came," she told him, whether she liked it or not she now felt responsible for those kids.

"Hi, Tessa," Maisy too was watching her carefully.

Noting the way Maisy looked at her now, her eyes a mixture of shock and horror and pity, like Tessa was broken. It was a look Tessa was used to seeing. Her brother's eyes had looked at her like that for months afterwards, so had the teachers and other students at her school. She hated that look. It made her feel like a victim. And she wasn't a victim.

"Hi, Maisy."

"Oh, Tessa, you could have told me," Maisy threw her arms around her and squeezed tightly. "I would have been there for you. Wyatt and Beth said that you feel guilty, that you blame yourself for what happened. You silly girl," Maisy's grip tightened, "I wish I could shake some sense into you. I'm so sorry, Tess, I'm so sorry you had to go through that, I'm so sorry you had to deal with it alone. But listen to me, Tessa," Maisy pulled back and held her at arms length, "you are not alone now. I am here for you, and so is Parker, and Wyatt, and Casey, and J.J., and everyone else who loves you. If you need me you call me. Promise me, Tess, promise you'll let me know if you need me."

"I promise," she nodded soberly, hoping that she wasn't lying. She knew that if she was going to move forward with her life then she had to learn to trust people, to let them help her. Unfortunately she couldn't guarantee that she would call Maisy, or any of her other friends, if she needed help.

Pulling her into another hug, "I love you, Tessa, you know that right? What happened to you wasn't your fault, it doesn't change how we feel about you."

"I love you too, Mais," for a moment she allowed her friend to comfort and strengthen her. Then she pulled back, "lets go in." The longer she waited out here the harder it would be to go back into that house.

"Honey, are you sure you're up to this?" Parker asked, ignoring her irritated frown to tilt her chin up and try to force her to meet his gaze.

Steadfastly avoiding meeting his golden eyes, Tessa hated being fussed over, she fixed her sight on the house. "I'm fine," she answered absently.

Wrapping her arms tightly around her middle as though that could ward off the evil that seemed to hover in the air. Once they were inside she found herself overwhelmed with memories, and even though she was still mad at her husband for having her watched and for making her relive Ellie's death, she reached out a hand to grasp Parker's, who squeezed hers back supportively. The warm, firm feel of his hand encircling hers gave her enough strength to keep moving.

"Wyatt's in the basement," Parker announced as he guided her through the maze of halls to the kitchen where the hidden door sat open.

Subconsciously her steps slowed as they descended the stairs to the basement, coming to a complete stop once they reached the large room at the bottom. It looked different than the last time she'd been here, the paint was peeling, it was dirtier, and it had been completely cleared out. The door that led to the rows of tiny cells was open and when Maisy called out Skylar and Marty Jenkins appeared through it.

"Tessa," Marty smiled at her in surprise and crossed to give her a hug.

"Hi, Marty," Tessa smiled back, she really liked Marty and the enthusiastic way he approached his job.

Holding her shoulders as he studied her, "how're you doing? I mean how are you doing really," he added with a raised eyebrow.

In Marty's eyes she saw mirrored the same mixture of emotions she'd just seen in Maisy's. The same emotions she'd seen in Skylar's and Elisabeth's and Charlie's. There was lots of compassion and sympathy, plenty of dismay and revulsion over what had happened to her. But in their eyes she hadn't seen anything judgmental or critical or accusing. Since that weekend everyone had told her that what had happened to Ellie wasn't her fault. She hadn't believed them because they hadn't really known what had happened. But her friends knew and they didn't seem to blame her. She wasn't sure how that made her feel.

"I don't know," she answered Marty's question honestly.

"Hey, Tess," Skylar too came to engulf her in a hug, exchanging glances with Parker above her head.

"Hey, Skylar. Thanks for staying with me yesterday," she squeezed his hand. As much as she loved her husband, sometimes she didn't know what she'd do without Skylar Wyatt. He always seemed to know what to say and do to put her at ease. Yesterday he'd held her while she'd cried, then taken her upstairs, tucked her in, given her some painkillers, then sat beside the bed holding her hand until she'd fallen asleep. When she'd awakened he'd been gone and Parker had been in the bed beside her. She'd wanted to curl up in her husband's arms and let him hold her while memories of that horrible weekend flashed so vividly through her mind. But she'd been scared of what she'd see in his eyes, so instead she had held herself as still as she could to keep from crying and tried to banish the awful images from her mind.

"Anytime, honey, you know that," Skylar squeezed her hand back.

"Did you find anything?" Parker asked Marty.

Shaking his head, "this place has been thoroughly cleaned out."

"Of course it has," Tessa admonished. There was no way that John Doe would allow anything incriminating to be left behind, one sloppy mistake could jeopardize everything that he had worked for. "Let me show you something," resolutely she headed for the passage, trying to close her mind as she went but finding herself stopping in front of the little cell where she and Ellie had been locked away. Unable to tear her eyes away from the small room, she couldn't seem to stop shaking.

Parker's arms came around her, "this is where Jake . . .?"

Nodding, seeing herself and Ellie and Jake as clearly as though they were all standing in the room right now.

Taking her arms and turning her to face him, "you had to do what you did, you know that don't you?" Parker told her, his voice gentle but Tessa could see the boiling rage in his eyes over what she had gone through.

Suddenly too weary to fight it she virtually collapsed against him. Parker's grip tightened, holding her up, and she burrowed her head against his chest, blocking out the rest of the world.

"It's going to be okay, Tess," he assured her, squeezing her firmly and stroking her hair.

"You know I'm still mad at you," voice muffled against his chest.

"I know," he shot back, and she could hear the smile in his voice. "It really *is* going to be okay, I promise."

Pulling back, she knew her husband meant well but Parker didn't know the people who were involved in this, unfortunately she did. Gathering herself, it didn't help the girls that John Doe and Dino were holding prisoner for her to be distracted by her own pain.

"This way." Heading the rest of the way down the passage to the end, she reached up on tiptoes to fiddle briefly with a section of the wall. Seconds later a small compartment sprung open, pressing in the code she had memorized sixteen years ago, a section of what appeared to be solid wall moved sideways.

"How did you know to do that?" Maisy asked, amazed.

Shrugging, "I watched Jake do it once and thought it might come in handy one day so I memorized the pattern he made." Leading the others inside the room where John Doe had taken photos of her and Ellie, the room through which she and Ellie had fled to freedom via the secret tunnel.

The others took in the room. The enormous bed, now just the frame, remained by the wall, upon which an elaborate mural of the ocean had been painted. The thick cream carpet that covered part of the concrete floor, and the glittering chandelier, had been removed, as had the camera and lights. A small table still remained, upon which sat a stack of old photographs.

"Tessa, what happened in this room?" Parker asked her tightly.

Answering even though they both knew he already knew the answer, "they took photos of us in here, to use to show buyers. Then when someone saw something they liked they got to try the girl out in here," she answered, carefully emotionlessly.

"Oh . . ." Maisy gasped as she flicked through the photos.

Parker, Skylar and Marty crossed to see what had caught Maisy's attention. Tessa didn't need to bother. She already knew what the photos contained.

Snatching the stack from Maisy's hand Parker began to rifle quickly through them, then tossed the pile on the floor, where it was retrieved by Marty who went through it at a much slower pace, and started on the next stack. When he was done he turned to her, "is there one of you?"

"There was. I burnt it."

Taking several deep breaths in an effort to remain calm, "who took the photos?" Parker demanded. "Was it Jake?"

Pausing, Tessa didn't really want to answer that particular question. For some inexplicable reason she couldn't bring herself to turn in John Doe, the head of the organization, who she had left off the list she'd given Parker the day before.

Holding up one of the photos of a naked little girl posed suggestively on the bed, Marty jumped in, "we might be able to find some of these girls."

"How?" Skylar asked.

"Well," Marty continued, excitedly, "if we age the girls and then use facial recognition software we may be able to find out who some of them are."

"I wouldn't bother," Tessa told them dully. "They're all dead."

"How do you know that?" Parker asked warily.

"Because I already tried to find them." For a while she had been an expert at locating people.

"They're all dead?" Maisy asked waving a hand at the photos.

"Those are the ones I found."

"What about the girls you couldn't find, or the ones you found that were still alive?" Parker was looking dangerously close to hitting something.

"I found them all. The girls I found alive I burned their photos with mine."

"But some of the girls are still alive?" Skylar confirmed.

"They were when I found them," she replied.

"So you can organize for us to talk to them?"

"I don't think so."

"What do you mean you don't think so?" Parker raised a tiredly irritated eyebrow.

"I mean that it's been a long time since I last saw them, and it's not like we kept in touch, I have no idea where they are now." Just the way Tessa liked it. It had been a terrible idea to find those girls and hear about what had happened to them after John Doe sold them. "Besides you don't need them, you have me, and I've already told you everything that happened."

"Have you?" Parker asked suspiciously.

Narrowing her eyes at him, "what are you talking about?"

"Maisy and I checked the stables, there was no trapdoor there," Parker explained.

"You think I lied about how Ellie and I escaped from this place?" she asked incredulously. "Why would I do that?"

"I don't know and that's what's worrying me." Parker looked like he wanted to grab her and shake the answers he wanted out of her, but she'd already told him all she was prepared to share.

Before she had a chance to respond Skylar stepped in, as always wanting to keep the peace, "these photos aren't going to help us find where Dino Rollino is now . . ."

"Actually . . ." she decided to give them a break and at least point them in the right direction since she was pretty sure that John Doe and Dino already knew the police were onto them and that they would have split up by now. "Dino's real name is Dino Killinger."

"Are you sure? Because we found a complete history on Dino

Rollino. He didn't acquire a new identity by stealing a child's that was born in the same year as him and died," Skylar told her.

"Of course he didn't, he knows how to create a completely new and thorough identity," she scoffed.

"I don't understand why he wants you dead," Parker interjected.

Sighing and deciding he may as well know the truth, "because Jake was Dino's brother. He wants revenge on me for killing his only living family member."

"Why didn't he just kill you back then? Why has he waited sixteen years?"

Hesitating, she didn't really want to answer that question either so instead she decided to help them find the house. "I think I know where Dino might be."

"We checked all the houses close to where Clara was found," Skylar told her, assuming that was what she was going to say.

Shaking her head, "she didn't get away from Dino's." Tessa was positive of this because Clara didn't know about John Doe's history so there was no way he would have let her go. "She must have gotten away when she was being moved. The house where he's staying is probably in Jake's name, at least an anagram of it."

While Skylar phoned that back to the station to get someone to start checking property in the general vicinity, Parker turned to Marty and Maisy, "think you can get anything useful here?"

"Nothing more helpful than what Tessa's already told us," Marty replied. "You're not likely to find this Dino Rollino and the girls through anything we find here, you're more likely to find them through Tess."

"Are you sure about everything you told us?" Parker looked at her doubtfully.

Annoyance sparking back up, she crossed to the far side of the room and opened the door that led to the hidden tunnel. "Still think I'm lying?"

Skylar joined herself, Marty and Maisy at the opening of the tunnel, "why is there a secret passage here?" he asked.

"In case the police ever stumbled onto this place, then they could get away without the police ever knowing," she explained.

"Alright let's go," Skylar started through the door.

Shuddering, "I'm not going through there again." Tessa couldn't face the claustrophobic tunnel right now, not when her head was so full of horrible memories.

Taking her hand again, "Tess and I'll meet you in the stables," Parker told the others as they started down the tunnel. Neither of them spoke as they wound their way back through the mansion and out into the fresh air. "I'm sorry," Parker said at last, turning her to face him. "I should have believed you."

Letting go of her anger, "because I'm always so trustworthy?" she asked sarcastically. Her husband was right to be wary of her since she hadn't told him the whole story. Nor had she told him that she was struggling so much lately that she had actually gone to visit a psychiatrist this morning. It seemed like she'd just replaced one secret with several more.

Bending down to kiss her gently. "I'm so sorry, Tessa," he murmured against her cheek. "I'm so sorry for everything you went through. I'm so sorry that you had to deal with it alone, but I need you to remember that you are not alone now. You have me and I want to help you, but you need to let me. I know it scares you but you have to let me in. I love you and we'll find a way to get through this together . . ."

The air around them came alive as bullets whizzed past and before Tessa knew what had happened Parker had tackled her to the ground and covered her body with his own. As Tessa struggled to draw a breath between the weight of Parker's body against her chest and her rapidly beating heart, she almost wished that Dino's bullet had hit her and ended this nightmare once and for all.

\* \* \* \* \*

3:58 P.M.

Managing to free his gun one handed but realizing it didn't do him much good. He couldn't shoot it from his position on the ground and if he moved it left Tessa unprotected. Still doing nothing wasn't really an option either, they were sitting ducks in the middle of the open field and bullets continued to bounce into the dirt beside them. Parker was just about to decide on his best plan of action when voices shouted behind them.

Bullets began to fly above him from the opposite direction and seconds later Wyatt dropped down beside them. After a few more shots fired from Wyatt it became clear that whoever had been shooting at them had ceased.

"Are you hurt?" Wyatt demanded.

"No," Parker answered shortly. "Tess?"

"I'm fine," came the breathless reply.

Picking himself up and hauling Tessa to her feet beside him, immediately his gaze was drawn to her bloody arm. "You're hit," it came out accusingly as though it were her fault someone had been shooting at them.

"It only skimmed me," she told him, still struggling to catch her breath.

Examining the wound he decided she was right, the bullet had merely skimmed the surface of her skin, leaving a nasty but completely non-life threatening injury. Still the sight of the bloody cut added fuel to the already raging fire that had been burning inside him since Tessa had revealed what had happened that weekend, and he couldn't do nothing about it any longer.

"Stay with her," he ordered Wyatt as he scanned the area where the shots had been coming from. "I'm going after him." There was not a doubt in his mind that the man who had been shooting at them was Dino Rollino.

"Parker, not on your own," Wyatt protested, although he

moved to place himself between Tessa and the tree line where the shots had been fired from, as Marty and Maisy joined them on the lawn.

"We can't leave Tessa alone and unprotected, I need you to stay with her," he called over his shoulder already running in the direction of the shooter's hidey-hole.

"I'm coming with you," Maisy quickly caught up to him with her long legs.

"I don't think . . ." Parker began.

Cutting him off, "you are not going on your own, it's me or Wyatt."

Relenting, he didn't have time to argue, every second he wasted was a second Dino Rollino could use to get away, and Parker was not going to let that happen. Taking off at a gallop he quickly made it to the tree line where a pile of candy bar wrappers and some empty gun casings lay.

"Looks like he was lying in wait," he said when Maisy jogged up beside him.

Catching her breath, "you think he followed her here?"

"Maybe, but he was definitely waiting for us to come out," Parker was scanning the area looking for any indication of which direction Dino had fled. Following a dusty set of footprints as they wound in and out of the trees and ended in a set of tyre treads.

"He's gone," Maisy said softly.

Letting out an angry growl, Parker slammed his fist into the nearest tree, almost enjoying the pain that shot up his arm to his shoulder, he hated the helplessness that seemed to swamp him lately.

"You'll find him, Parker," Maisy consoled.

"Before or after he kills Tessa?"

Maisy said nothing and the two made their way in silence back to the mansion where Wyatt met them, "any sign of him?"

"He was already gone," Maisy replied.

"He was lying in wait for her," Parker added. "Where's Tessa?"

"Marty's cleaning up her arm," Wyatt pointed to the back of the CSU van where Tessa was sitting, Marty wrapping a bandage around her arm.

When Tessa saw him she slid to the ground, wincing as her injured leg bore weight. "Did you find Dino?"

Taking in her pale face, tired eyes, bandaged arm and leg, Parker's fury melted away replaced by fear that that man was still out there, especially when Tessa was clearly in no condition to deal with him. "He got away, honey," he told her. "But he could still be out there somewhere nearby so you do not leave my sight. I mean it," he added when she opened her mouth to protest. "You are not out of my sight for a second. Until Dino's caught you don't go anywhere alone."

Tessa nodded her consent. "I thought you guys were going through the tunnel to the stables," she asked Wyatt, Marty and Maisy.

"We couldn't get out the other end," Wyatt explained, "the door was stuck so we had to come back. Lucky we did or we wouldn't have arrived when we did. Maisy called J.J. when we heard the gunshots, he's sending out some people, and an ambulance," he shot Tessa a pointed look.

"I don't need to go to the hospital," she included them all in her stubborn glare.

Looking like she was half dead on her feet, Parker thought after the accident, Dino's midnight visit, finally talking about her abduction and being shot at, a trip to the hospital was exactly what she needed. "Tessa . . ."

"Really, Parker," she interrupted, "I don't want to go to the hospital."

"Okay," he reluctantly relented. "But I'm taking you home, you need some rest," he told her firmly, ready for a fight but she simply shrugged her acquiescence.

"Marty and Maisy are going to check out every inch of the

basement and then they'll check out where Dino was waiting for you," Wyatt continued. "Maybe we'll get lucky and find something Dino left behind."

Once they were alone, Parker pulled his wife into his arms. Tessa flinched slightly as he squeezed her injured arm but didn't pull away. "When the paramedics get here I want you to let them check you out. Come on, Tess," he wheedled when he felt her stiffen. "You already checked yourself out of the hospital against the doctor's advice. After getting shot I really don't think it's too much to ask that you let them take a look at you."

"Fine," she sighed. "I'll let the EMT's check my arm but under no circumstances am I going to the hospital."

"Deal," a reasonable compromise considering how much Tessa hated hospitals. The churning in his stomach resuming, he began to fiddle with Tessa's silky blonde curls, unable to get Beth's suspicions out of his head. "Was it really Dino who was shooting at you? You're not playing games again are you, leading me on a wild goose chase?"

"It was Dino," she whispered against his chest, too weary to lift her head.

Tightening his grip on her, "but there's something you didn't tell me wasn't there? There was something you left out of your story? Something that you don't want me to know?" Tessa didn't answer. Grabbing hold of her shoulders, he pulled her back so he could look her in the eye. "Did you leave out part of what happened to you when you were kidnapped?"

Instead of answering Tessa merely nestled her head back against his chest, her thin arms encircling his waist and clinging to him.

As sirens whirled in the distance, Parker held his wife and wondered whether she was ever going to learn to completely trust him. It had been close to two years since they had met, two years that he had spent trying to convince her that she could trust him, two years that Tessa had shut him out and continued to deal with things on her own. Unsure whether he was more scared about what the secret Tessa was keeping was, or what the consequences of another secret between them would do to their relationship.

# SEPTEMBER 11<sup>TH</sup>

4:42 A.M.

Luxuriating in the enormous bed, he was still as high as a kite from yesterday's activities.

Dino Rollino was now the proud owner of this hundred plus room mansion. He had his own crew. And he had five little girls tucked safely away in the basement. The only thing he didn't have was any clients. Still he wasn't going to let that bother him, those girls were going to bring him everything he'd ever dreamed of. This, he decided taking in the opulent room, was only the beginning.

When John Doe had left yesterday morning he had taken with him only the most valuable pieces of art, among other things the man was an avid art collector, leaving everything else behind. After he left John Doe had sent in a cleaning crew who had gone over every inch of the mansion, scrubbing and vacuuming and disinfecting absolutely everything.

Immediately after they had gone Dino had begun to make the place his own. He started by moving his things from his old tiny bedroom to the gigantic master suite. Next he'd had some fun with the girls, then taken dinner in the dining room, before retiring to the opulent study where he'd spent the evening enjoying all that was now his.

He had made one little deviation from enjoying his new home. While the house was being sanitized he had gone out to their old house, the place where he had first met Tessa. He'd had to lie in wait for close to an hour before she finally arrived to join her do-gooder husband and his gang of goody two shoes, and then another hour after that before they re-emerged from the mansion. His first shot had been only slightly off, it had hit Tessa but had done little more than skim her arm. Between his first and second shots Parker Bell had managed to throw Tessa to the ground and cover her body with his own. Dino had continued firing knowing that the Detective was in a no win position, he had to get up to shoot back but getting up would leave Tessa vulnerable. In the end help had arrived and Dino had had no choice but to flee.

Still, all in all Dino wasn't too disappointed. Sure he would never be able to rest with Tessa alive but half the fun in getting revenge was torturing the intended victim first. And he intended to make sure Tessa's suffering befitted her crime.

Lying in the dark his thoughts began to turn black as he thought of his brother Jake. Half brother really, they had the same mother but different fathers. Neither that, nor the fact that there was fifteen years between them in age, had stopped them from being close.

Growing up Dino's mother was a drug addict and his father was absent. Until the age of eight he had been in and out of foster care as his mother hovered between jail and rehab. Finally, not long after his eighth birthday, he had a near fatal bike accident, the wake up call his mother needed. For a while life was great, his mother got a job, they had a place to call home and Dino finally began to be happy. That all changed when he was fifteen. He arrived home from school one day to find her dead on their kitchen floor from a drug overdose. He never knew what made her turn back to her addiction after seven good years.

Following his mother's death he went to live with his father. A man who had never spent more than the occasional visit with him in fifteen years. It wasn't that his father was a bad man, he never laid a hand on Dino, didn't drink, or do drugs, it was more that he was too wrapped up in his own life. His father was secretly dating Dino's own fifteen-year-old ex-girlfriend.

Fairly predictably things went quickly down hill. Dino started getting into trouble in school, his grades plummeted, and he started hanging around with the wrong people. Who knows where he would have ended up if his father wasn't killed in a freak boating accident after only three months. With no other family and no where else to go Dino was about to be placed in foster care when his brother arrived to collect him. Fifteen-year-old Dino had come to live with Jake and John Doe in the world of child trafficking.

Perhaps it wasn't surprising that Dino slotted in so well. A drug addict for a mother, a disjointed childhood, and a father dating a teenager. Jake quickly took him under his wing, teaching him the tricks of the trade, and a couple of months after moving in there Dino lost his virginity to the first terrified little girl he abducted.

Never pleased by his presence John Doe reluctantly accepted him into the fold, making it very clear that he thought of Dino as an imbecile. Still, even following Jake's death a year after he'd moved in, John Doe offered him a job and a chance to earn his keep. Over the following sixteen years Dino brought more girls in than any other employee and he quickly worked his way up the ladder to second spot. Now all that loyalty and hard work had paid off and he was finally where he dreamed of being. He had it all money, power, control, the only thing he lacked was the peace that would come with knowing Tessa Micah Bell was no longer in this world.

His brother had been the only constant in his life. Always visiting him and bringing him presents, no matter what foster home he was in at the time, looking out for him and stepping in when he was all alone. In memory of his brother he had gotten a tattoo, Gemini, Castor and Pollux the twins, he and Jake may not have been twins but they were as close as two brothers could be.

He was just dozing off when someone pounded on the bedroom door. "What is it?" he growled, not pleased about being disturbed.

Flinging the door open so forcefully it banged against the crimson walls, Jason's anxious face peered back at him.

"What is it?" Dino repeated.

"The police are on their way here," Jason exclaimed.

"What are you talking about?" There was no way the police could have figured out where they were.

"I just got a call from one of our contacts in the police department. He says they know where we are and they're organizing a team as we speak," Jason's voice was squeaky with panic. "This would never have happened with John Doe."

Ignoring the comment, if the police were really on their way then he didn't have time to waste. "How did they find us? Did the kid, Clara, did she give them directions or something?" Dino demanded as he threw on some clothes.

"They figured out the name," Jason replied.

"Tessa," he spat out. The little witch must have figured out that he was using an anagram of Jake's name.

"We have to leave now," Jason was as jittery as a little girl.

"Yeah, you think," Dino snapped sarcastically, heading for the door and flying through the house to the basement where he met an anxious Kelvin and Marcus standing guard. Catching their resentful scowls, "you two wishing you were with John Doe too?"

"What are we going to do?" Kelvin asked instead.

"We're going to leave," he answered, wondering how things could fall apart so quickly, and vowing that Tessa would pay double for this. Still it wasn't too late to salvage things, he just needed to get out of this house. He could create a new identity, start again in a new town. Once they were settled in a new place he would come back for Tessa. Maybe take her with him and stash her away someplace where they could really spend some quality time together.

"What about the girls?" Marcus's gaze was darting from the passageway that led to the girl's cells to the door to the kitchen. "They're going to slow us down."

"We're not taking them with us," already forming a plan in his head. As much as Dino wanted to keep the girls, Marcus was right, if they needed to make a quick escape the girls would only be a hindrance. And it wasn't as though he'd never be able to get any more, none of these girls was irreplaceable. Therefore there was only one workable solution. "We're going to kill them."

*  *  *  *  *

6:08 A.M.

"We would never have found this place without Tessa," Wyatt commented with one eye on the road as they sped towards the mansion where they were reasonably sure that Dino Rollino was keeping the missing girls.

"To be honest I'm still a little surprised she actually told us what happened at all," Parker told his partner. He was glad that he hadn't left Tessa alone but in Beth's capable hands, when he'd left a couple of hours ago. He was still extremely concerned about her. She had still been asleep when J.J. had rung to say they had found an isolated mansion under a name that was an anagram of Jake Killinger. In fact, she had been asleep ever since they arrived home yesterday. After the paramedics had taken her vitals and checked out her arm and her leg, he had taken her straight home, where she had taken some painkillers and sleeping pills, and collapsed into bed. Exhausted, she had fallen immediately into a deep sleep.

"There is no way we would have figured out that the house was under the name Nellie Jakk Rig," Wyatt continued.

After Tessa had told them she believed the house Dino was using would be in the name of someone who when you rearranged the letters of their name you got Jake Killinger, a team had started processing all houses that fit the criteria. Around two o'clock this morning they had found a large mansion, secluded, surrounded by woods, the owner was a Nellie Jakk Rig, who when they researched her found nothing but a dead paper trail. A team had quickly been assembled and they were now heading out to hopefully arrest Dino Rollino and his cronies, send any little girls still there home, and put an end to this once and for all. All of this should make him happy and yet Parker couldn't shake the feeling that even if they accomplished both the apprehending of the perpetrators and the rescuing of the victims that somehow that would *not* spell the end.

"What's wrong?" Wyatt asked with a sideways glance. "I thought you were desperate to know the answers to your questions about what happened to Tessa and Eleanor."

"It's something Beth said," he rubbed at his eyes. While Tessa may have crashed and slept like a baby last night, he had lain awake holding his wife in his arms and pondering Beth's suspicions.

"Oh yeah?"

"She thinks that Tessa is holding something back," Parker watched his best friend closely for his reaction.

Nodding slowly, "she probably is," Wyatt agreed.

"What?" he had been expecting, more like hoping, that Wyatt would adamantly disagree with a string of logical arguments to back him up.

"Come on, Parker, that's who she is," his partner reasoned. "She only tells us what she thinks we need to know."

"She blames herself, Wyatt. I mean she *really* blames herself. She is one hundred percent convinced that everything that happened was her fault."

"I know she does, Parker," Wyatt nodded somberly.

"I don't know how to get her to believe that it wasn't." Unsure that Tessa would ever be able to believe that everything that happened wasn't because of her. "How am I going to convince her?"

"Now that I don't know."

"I asked J.J. to organize protection for her." Until Dino was found Parker didn't want Tessa left alone, he wanted her watched every second, whether she liked it or not. "And Beth's staying with her today."

Wondering for the hundredth time whether he ought to defy Tessa's wishes and call her brother Daniel. When Matilda had called a couple of days ago to fill him in on everything they'd been doing on their trip he had almost spilled the beans. But he knew if he told his sister what was going on then she, Daniel, and Tessa's niece Winter would be on the first flight home. While be believed that Tessa needed her family around her now he also knew that she was still hurt by them not believing her when he'd been kidnapped. Still Daniel had been around when Jake Killinger abducted Tessa, and he might know something important, something that might be the clue to whatever Tessa was keeping secret. And so his internal argument went.

"Anyway," he sighed tiredly, "I'm hoping that maybe she can get something out of Tessa, because I have a bad feeling that whatever Tess is keeping to herself is going to end badly."

They both lapsed into silence as an imposing Victorian mansion came into view. Set at the end of a winding, tree lined driveway, in the middle of a wide expanse of perfectly manicured lawn. On the gravel in front of the house sat a shiny black car, Parker took that as a sign that they weren't too late.

Everyone assembled on the bright green grass, and with minimal exchanged instructions quickly made their way in small groups to each of the mansion's entry points. With perfectly coordinated timing, they entered the house. Parker and Wyatt heading straight for the kitchen, assuming that would be the entry point for the basement, while the others checked out the rest of the house.

The kitchen was enormous, a huge table in the middle, a variety of pots and pans hanging from the ceiling, the benches stacked with packets of potato chips and candy bars. On the other side of the room was an open door through which a dull light emanated and a staircase was just visible.

With a nod at Wyatt, they moved towards the door, guns out in front, expecting someone to jump out at them, but no one did. Making their way silently down the steps they found themselves in a room eerily familiar to the one at the mansion where Tessa had been taken, the only difference was that this room was full of clutter. A TV sat on a table surrounded by several stacks of DVD's, a table containing more snacks sat in the corner, and a bookshelf stuffed full of books took up most of one wall.

Heading for the closed door next to the TV, when he swung it open it revealed exactly what he expected, a passageway with ten closed doors on each side. Everywhere he looked all Parker could see was a tiny, terrified Tessa, trying to stand up to a man more than twice her size as she fought for her life.

With Wyatt at his side, he threw open the first door on the left and was met by the sight of a small child laying on the floor. Flying to the little girl's side. A sheet of brown hair obscured her face, her neck bent at an unnatural angle. Parker didn't need to feel for a pulse, he already knew the child was dead. And yet still he touched her neck in a vain attempt at denial, nothing moved beneath his fingertips. Easing the little girl onto her back, her head wobbled wildly like one of those bobble headed animals people put on the dashboard of their cars. A pair of chocolate eyes stared lifelessly back at him, and he had to turn away. Holding the child he thought of Tessa who had watched on helplessly as her best friend's neck was snapped.

"She's still warm," he muttered as he heard Wyatt come up behind him. "It's Ariyel Hannock." The nine year old he held in his arms was barely recognizable as the grinning, dimpled, pig-tailed little girl in the photo her parents had used in their appeals to the public.

"There's four others," Wyatt told him.

"That makes five."

"Eleven of the cells were freshly cleaned."

Shaking his head as he closed the child's eyes, no longer able to bear the look of lost innocence haunting them. "They knew we were coming."

"It looks like it," Wyatt agreed.

His heart stopping, "could Tessa have warned them?"

"Parker!" Wyatt exclaimed. "How could you even suggest that?"

"I don't know," he stammered. "But she's keeping something from me and . . ."

"And it's making you lose your mind," Wyatt was staring at him as if he'd suddenly grown two heads. "Tessa said that Dino was not the man she went to for help."

"Then who was it?" he demanded. "Who did she go to for help when I was missing? It had to be someone. You heard her on the phone with him, they found my car, if it wasn't Dino Rollino then who was it?"

"I don't know, Parker," Wyatt said seriously. "But I do know Tessa, and there is no way she would have tipped off Dino that we were on the way here."

"But . . ."

"No," shaking his head, "no buts. Why would Tessa tell us everything that happened to her only to deliberately let the people who hurt her get away?"

"Who knows?" he grumbled, not quite ready to let go of his suspicions. "Who knows what goes on in that curly blonde head of hers . . ." about to continue with pointless ranting about Tessa when they both heard a clunk.

Exchanging glances both he and Wyatt moved to the door of the tiny cell just in time to see a door at the end of the corridor swing closed.

"Stop. Police," Wyatt yelled as they gave chase.

Darting down the hallway Parker cautiously opened the door to reveal a steep, narrow staircase with a pair of feet quickly disappearing from view. In hot pursuit they briskly ascended the steps, calling for whoever was fleeing to stop. The set of feet looked too big to belong to a scared child, but it seemed to good to be true that they might have actually found Dino Rollino.

Something banged above them and they sped up, bursting through another door into an old shed. Three sets of footprints, two smaller and one larger, scattered across the dusty floor. Through the dirty window a head was just visible darting off into the woods. Giving chase they burst out into the slowly lightening world, heading straight for the tree line. Slowing their pace a little to take into account the dense forest, they hadn't gone more than about a hundred yards when Parker spotted something behind a thick tree trunk. Motioning to Wyatt, who circled quietly around to approach from the other direction. Parker's heart was beating so furiously he half expected it to pump itself right out of his chest.

This was it. The end.

Finally he might be able to wake up in the morning without a tense pool of anxiety in the pit of his stomach.

Dino Rollino was going to wish he'd never been born.

* * * * *

10:21 A.M.

Truth be told he felt more than a little sad.

In fact he wasn't quite sure he was ready to go.

It had been a mistake coming back here but he hadn't thought it would affect him so strongly.

Being close to her again.

For some inexplicable reason he couldn't even come close to elaborating on, she was the closest thing to a family he had left. Everything else he had left behind when he made the transformation to John Doe. Everyone he had loved and cared about he had turned his back on. And then he had been given a second chance with Tessa.

He'd done his best to protect her, had helped her on numerous occasions, but their relationship wasn't one sided, she had helped him too. She hadn't wanted to at first, but she'd been scared since he'd seen her kill Jake Killinger, and she had eventually complied. Over the years a fragile trust had been built between them and she had come to lean on him when she had nowhere else to turn. Knowing that she depended on him gave John Doe a warm tingly feeling in his stomach, something he was completely unaccustomed to.

Of course Tessa didn't approve of what he did, hated what he did, had tried on countless occasions to convince him to abandon his life of crime. She's told him that she believed deep down he was a good person. While that may have been true once upon a time he had been forced to squash that part of him in order to survive. He had a mission to complete, and until that was done this was his life.

Still it worried him that he had to leave, that Tessa would now be at the mercy of that maniac Dino Rollino. All he could hope was that Tessa's cop husband was on the ball enough to catch Dino before it was too late.

And to never let Tessa out of his sight.

Poor little Tessa just couldn't help herself. She had to jump in and confront her attacker, she couldn't stand to let herself or anyone else see her as a victim. In fact it was that very characteristic that had drawn him to her in the first place. The defiant way she had eyed him that first night, the fury and hatred in her face when she launched herself at Jake, the pity and understanding in her eyes when he confided in her.

On the outside Tessa was strong, but on the inside she was as broken as he was. Maybe if things had been different he would have taken her in, lavished on her the attention refused her by her parents, and maybe things would have worked out different for both of them.

But things hadn't been different and they weren't different now. He had a plan to focus on and to that end he climbed from the car. John Doe had one last thing to do before he disappeared to start over once again. Everything else been taken care of, the mansion had been cleaned, the girls had been paired up and were stashed away in cars with one of his men who looked the most like their father.

Now all he had to do was sneak inside and leave the letter. His final goodbye. All these years he'd thought he was protecting Tessa, keeping her safe, but he had drawn her into a world that had brought her nothing but pain and heartache. He'd been selfish, back at the beginning when he'd taken advantage of a little girl because he was so desperately lonely, and all the way through the last sixteen years.

Tessa deserved better, she deserved happiness and freedom and the chance to have a normal life. Perhaps the only way for her to do that was for him to back off. She had become overly reliant on knowing that he was there to back her up if she needed it, but she had to learn now to rely on her family and friends. Tessa had a chance to have it all and he was not going to do anything to jeopardize that.

\* \* \* \* \*

1:48 P.M.

"Please tell me you now believe everything I was saying," Parker frowned at his boss.

"There wasn't any evidence," J.J. defended himself. "I didn't know it would end in Tessa getting shot," the big man looked crestfallen.

Rolling his eyes, "clearly that wasn't your fault," Parker snapped, tired, disheartened and irritable about the way things had turned out at the mansion.

"I've organized a security detail for her until Dino is apprehended. How is she?"

"She's fine," Wyatt assured their boss. "The bullet only scratched her arm. I'm more worried about how she's doing emotionally," shooting him a quizzical stare.

Shrugging helplessly. It was easier to get to the crown jewels than to what was going on inside Tessa's head. "When I spoke to her earlier she said that she was *fine*. Did we ID the other missing girls?"

"Yeah we did," J.J.'s eyes drifted to a photo of his granddaughters. "The other four girls were from out of state, their parents are being notified as we speak."

Recalling the look in Ariyel's parent's eyes when he and Wyatt had broken the news to them that their daughter's body had been found. Suppressing a shudder as he thought of little Ariyel's lifeless body lying, discarded, on the cold concrete floor of that house of horrors, it was an image he knew he would never be able to erase from his mind's eye.

"Anyway," J.J. dragged his gaze away from the photograph, "in answer to your question, Parker, yes, I do believe everything you were saying and an official investigation has now been launched to find the other men involved. After this you and Wyatt need to go and talk to him."

Unfortunately the *him* J.J. was referring to was not Dino Rollino.

Parker's bubble had been burst as soon as they had tackled the man to the ground. When he heard them coming he had made another futile attempt at escape but hadn't gotten more than a few feet before they caught up with him. When they'd rolled him over they were met by a black face with grey eyes and a jagged scar across the jaw line.

The man was clearly not Dino Rollino.

He was however one of the men on Tessa's list, a Jason

Mason, who had a wrap sheet as deep as the ocean but had been strangely quiet the last several years. Parker had been so sure that it was the end and when it became clear that Dino Rollino had managed to evade capture it was like a rock of disappointment had come crashing down on top of him.

"We have people going over the house and the bodies hopefully they give us enough to build a strong case against these monsters," J.J. continued.

"What good does that do us while *that* man is still out there," he demanded hopelessly. "I don't care about a court case I just want Dino . . ." trailing off. Parker wanted to say dead because nothing would make him happier than knowing that the man who wanted his wife dead was no longer on the planet, but he settled instead on, ". . . caught."

"Are you sure Tessa doesn't know where he might be?" Wyatt asked.

"She said she didn't but . . ." there was no need to finish the sentence, they all knew what Tessa was like.

"Alright we need to see what we can get out of Jason Mason," J.J. reached for his phone. "I'm going to call Zak and see if he has anything on the bodies."

Medical examiner Zak Fenton was not one of Parker's, or J.J.'s, favorite people. The guy was good at his job but he was also vain and arrogant and a general pain to be around. "We already know cause of death," another flash of Ariyel Hannock's limp body sprung to mind. "Dino snapped their necks, just like his brother did to Eleanor. He has to know Tessa finally turned him in, he probably did it that way on purpose, to torment her."

"But we don't know what else Zak might have found," J.J. dialed the morgue.

Leaving J.J. to make his call, Parker trailed after Wyatt as they headed for the interrogation room where Jason Mason was waiting for then. The one positive for the day he hadn't requested a lawyer, so they were free to ask him whatever they wanted.

Dawdling along, lost in thought, Parker almost walked straight into Wyatt, who had stopped and was studying him intently. "What?"

"Maybe you should go home and check on Tessa."

"I'm fine," Parker quoted Tessa. To be honest he was starting to feel overwhelmed with guilt again, for pushing Tessa too hard, for thinking that she tipped off Dino Rollino so he could get away, for resenting her turning to Wyatt when she needed comfort. The last time he had felt this guilty it had led to some really bad decision making and almost to his and Tessa's deaths. "Beth's with her, she'll be okay."

"Yeah but she needs you," Wyatt said gently.

"If that's true then why was it you that she went to after she told us about what happened?"

"Parker," Wyatt began.

Cutting him off, "look it doesn't matter. I'm fine with it. I just need to *do* something, I just need to get Dino off the streets, and if the only way to do that is by talking to Jason then that's where I need to be. Tessa understands that." At least Parker hoped she did.

Raising a doubtful brow but saying no more Wyatt pushed open the door to the interview room where Jason Mason sat awaiting them. Following his partner in, Parker took a seat beside him, and studied the man across the table. Jason appeared to be in his early forties, a few flecks of grey had begun creeping into his closely cropped black hair. Grey eyes stood out in his brown face and examined him as closely as he was examining them.

"We know exactly what it is you do for a living, Mr. Mason," Parker began.

Shooting him a quizzical look but remaining silent, Jason waited for them to show their hand.

"You kidnap little girls and sell them for men to use as sex slaves."

If Jason was surprised that they did indeed know what was

going on at that house he didn't show it, merely sat calmly waiting for them to say whatever it was they wanted to say.

"We also know that you're not the mastermind behind the operation. You're just a guard, a yes-man, a drone, but the thing is there are five dead little girls . . ."

"I didn't kill a single one of those kids," Jason spoke for the first time since they'd arrested him, his voice was oddly sweet, almost hypnotic.

"Fair enough," Parker nodded agreeably, already positive that Dino had snapped the necks of each of those children. "But you're still going to go down for it because you're the only one we have. Now I understand why you might be hesitant to talk to us," managing to keep his tone light even though the sight of the man who had facilitated such unspeakable acts made him sick. "Your boss must be a pretty evil man to make his living from selling little girls, so it's understandable that you're scared of turning on him. And he has to be doing something right to remain under the radar for so many years so he's obviously very intelligent. There's no way you're getting away from this mess free, but it might help your case at sentencing if we can say that you helped us find and apprehend Dino Rollino . . ."

"Dino?" Jason exclaimed loudly. "You're talking about Dino?" he burst into peals of hysterical laughter.

"Why is that funny?" Wyatt asked, puzzled.

Catching on, "how old is Dino?"

"Thirty-two," Jason managed to get out as he swiped at tears that trickled down his cheeks he was laughing so hard.

Mentally calculating, "so Dino was sixteen when Tessa was abducted." That meant that he was not the mastermind behind the child selling enterprise.

"You thought Dino was in charge because of Tessa?" That sent Jason into fresh waves of giggles. "If Dino was on top of things Tessa Micah would have been dead a long time ago."

"You know about Tessa?" Wyatt frowned.

"Sure. Everyone knows about Tessa," Jason was trying to calm his giggles. "Dino complains about her all the time, hates that he's not allowed to touch one hair on her pretty blonde head."

"And Tessa's protector is . . .?" Parker trailed off, a clearer picture forming in his head of exactly what was going on. This was what Tessa had been holding back. For some reason he couldn't fathom the leader of this gang of child traffickers had become her friend. Parker was willing to bet a year's salary that she had left him off the list she had given them, making Jason their only possibility of finding this man. "You have to tell us who he is," he demanded.

Finally growing serious, "you have got to be kidding," Jason scoffed. "Like you said he's one evil, cold-hearted monster. He's smart, he's got contacts everywhere, and he's willing to do whatever it takes to protect himself. I'd rather rot in jail for the rest of my life than spend it looking over my shoulder waiting for him to take me out in some unimaginably horrible way."

"I don't understand," Parker stammered, "why does he protect Tessa? What happened between them?"

"I don't know. All I do know is that whenever Tessa needs help we all have to drop what we're doing and run to her rescue. And that is the last you're getting out of me, I think I'll have my lawyer now," with that Jason snapped his mouth closed.

Emotions swirled around in his head. For the life of him, Parker couldn't fathom what possible connection Tessa could have to a man who had intended to sell her into a life of prostitution and how that connection, whatever it was, ran so deep that she would do anything to protect him.

\* \* \* \* \*

3:00 P.M.

Opening the front door she was immediately wrapped up in a

hug.

"Hi, Casey," Tessa returned her friend's hug.

"I wish you'd told me, Tess," Casey's arms tightened. "You could have trusted me, you know that right? If I've done anything to make you doubt that I'm sorry."

"No, Casey, I love you, and I know I can trust you," she assured her best friend. "I just couldn't talk about it." Hesitating, debating whether to continue, finally deciding that since she'd already broken down and gone to see a psychiatrist she may as well open up to her friend. "It really messed me up."

Casey pulled back, "of course it did, honey, how could it not? Wyatt said you think what happened was your fault, is there anything I can say to convince you that's not true?"

Shrugging, "probably not," she answered honestly. "Come on in."

"Parker didn't leave you here alone did he?"

"No way," she laughed as she closed the front door. "He doesn't want me alone while Dino's still out there. I have babysitters outside and Elisabeth is here." Tessa wasn't overjoyed about the prospect of someone watching her every move, but it got Parker off her back, and if for any reason she needed to slip away she was confident she could do it without alerting her babysitters. Plus, she reluctantly admitted, it did make her feel a little safer to know that when Dino came back at her there were people who had her back.

"Good," Casey nodded approvingly. "It doesn't seem like Dino's going to stop until you're dead."

"Yeah well he hates me almost as much as I hate him. Hey, Elisabeth, Casey's here," she announced as they entered the living room.

"Hi, Casey," Elisabeth set down the book she was reading and stood.

"Hi, Beth. Tess giving you any trouble?" Casey grinned.

"Nope, she's being a very good little girl," Elisabeth grinned back.

Rolling her eyes, "I'm always good, I just don't always do what you guys think I should."

Still grinning, "I'll let you two talk," Elisabeth grabbed her book.

"You don't have to go," Casey protested.

"Tessa looks like she might actually want to talk, and you have a much better chance of getting her to open up than I do," Elisabeth said matter-of-factly. "I'll be upstairs."

Once they were alone Casey shot her a serious stare, "is Beth right? *Do* you want to talk?"

Shrugging, Tessa sat, she was torn between wanting to block out everything that had happened that weekend and talking about it with Casey.

Sitting beside her, "you must have been so scared, Tess, you were such a little girl."

Twisting her hands in her lap, "at first I was more angry than scared, but that only made things worse. The more I tried to fight back the more Jake liked it."

"Did you see Dino while you were there?"

Nodding, "only once. When we first got there."

"Why hasn't he killed you already? He clearly wants to, he tried to kill you in the fire back when we first met you, he broke into your house, he tried to shoot you. What's stopped him from killing you all these years?"

Tessa continued to twist her hands, John Doe was the reason that Dino hadn't already killed her already. But somehow he'd lost control of Jake's brother because it was clear Dino wasn't going to stop until she was dead.

"It's not a what it's a who isn't it? Wyatt told me that he and Parker and Beth think you're holding something back, is this it?"

Slowly she nodded.

"Okay, I'm not going to push you on that right now because you look like garbage, but be prepared to be grilled on the topic once you're feeling better," Casey warned. "I can't believe you managed to find a way to escape," Casey marveled. "One of the times I guess it pays to be a genius."

"If I were really smart I would never have fallen for Jake's trick in the first place," Tessa contradicted, still clenching her hands tightly together.

Reaching over to pry her hands apart, "don't, Tess, you'll hurt yourself. And you were only eleven, so cut yourself a break."

"Easier said than done," she retorted.

"I know that, honey, but wouldn't Eleanor want you to move on and be happy? Would she blame you?"

Tessa just stared, for some reason it had never occurred to her to consider whether Ellie would have blamed her or not. "I . . . I guess . . . no, she wouldn't have blamed me."

"You two were really close?"

Giving a shaky nod, "yeah we were. We did everything together before she died. I used to wish Ellie's parents would adopt me and I could go and live with them. After Jake killed her every time I thought about her all I could see was how she looked just before he broke her neck. In the hospital I kept seeing it over and over again, I thought it was going to drive me insane. I was so scared, Casey," she whispered forlornly.

"I can't even imagine, Tess."

"Everyone keeps saying that me killing Jake was self defense, and logically I know that's true, but I *hated* him, Casey. I hated him for taking us against our will, I hated him for raping us, I hated him for stopping us from escaping, I hated him for snapping Ellie's neck like she was nothing. I hated him so badly, it seems like it couldn't possibly have been self defense. I still dream about it all the time, the way Jake looked at me makes me as scared now as it did that night. I wish I could forget. I wish I could forget it all like it never happened," she half whimpered.

"Come here," Casey murmured, pulling her into an embrace. "It's over, Tess. Jake can't hurt you anymore."

"He can and he does, every single day. It's never over for me, Casey. And you know what's worse is that Jake would love that he can still torture me all these years later." For several minutes Tessa just clung to Casey, allowing her friend's arms to temporarily make her feel a little safer.

Continuing to stroke her hair, "I'm sorry, honey, I have to go pick up the kids, but I don't want to leave you alone like this, you want me to call Parker?"

"Uh uh," she shook her head against Casey's shoulder. It made her feel uncomfortable to be around Parker now that he knew what had happened to her, and yet at the same time she wanted him here by her side, not out somewhere obsessing over Dino.

"What about Wyatt?"

Wavering, Tessa did want Skylar to come, but he had work and his family and she didn't want to keep getting in the way of that and taking up too much of his time, he'd already done enough for her.

"I'll call him for you," Casey kissed the top of her head. "You know if it were anyone but you I'd be totally jealous of my husband having such a close relationship with a beautiful woman, but I'm really glad he helps you, Tess."

"He's like my big brother, I'm lucky to have him in my life. I'm lucky to have you too, you're a really good friend, Casey. But you don't have to call him, I'll be fine, Elisabeth's here and I want Parker and Skylar to find Dino."

Remaining unconvinced, "okay, if you're sure. I'll call you later."

Once Casey was gone, Tessa squeezed her eyes closed, wishing desperately that she could stop seeing Jake kill Ellie then come towards her. That had been the first time that weekend that fear had really stabbed at her heart. She'd seen in Jake's eyes that he never intended to let her go. He was going to rape her again and then whisk her away someplace where no one could ever find her. From that second on fear had been a steady fixture in her life. At first she's waited desperately for it to ease. She was still waiting.

"Tessa?"

Opening her eyes to find Elisabeth watching her closely from the doorway. Blinking sent tears spilling down her cheeks and Elisabeth crossed immediately to hold her. Tessa couldn't believe how quickly she was falling apart. So many years spent carefully controlling her emotions and now they seemed to be controlling her. "Elisabeth?" hating the needy vulnerability in her voice.

"What is it, Tess?" Elisabeth's calm voice soothed her a little.

"Do you think there'll ever be a day when I'm not afraid anymore?"

\* \* \* \* \*

4:15 P.M.

"I'm so tired, can't we stop for a second?"

Cassandra looked down at her little sister's sweat streaked face and stopped her determined trek through the woods. "Sure we can."

Olivia sunk wearily down, Cassie joining her on the muddy ground. Down here it remained wet, under a canopy of leaves so thick it completely blocked out the sky. Unable to account for the weather since the time she'd been taken but before that it hadn't rained since a huge thunderstorm on the fourth of July. Cassandra remembered the night perfectly. After staying up late to watch fireworks she and Olivia had played tag in the rain with their dad, before curling up at the window to watch the lightening that had put on a more spectacular show than the fireworks.

Fiddling with the dirt, enjoy the cold, wet feel of it on her skin after so long locked away in the dingy basement. They'd been walking for two days. Last night they had sat huddled together in the dark, getting no more than an hour or so of sleep between them. Every noise seemed amplified in the always moving forest.

Creatures scurried about, the wind kept the leaves rustling, and every time anything moved they both expected Dino or John Doe or one of the others to come springing out to drag them back to the mansion.

Not only were they jittery from fear and lack of sleep but they hadn't had anything to eat or drink since escaping from the basement. Cassandra knew that if they didn't find some water soon then neither of them was going to make it.

And it was all her fault.

She was the big sister it was her job to take care of Olivia, instead she had fallen straight into Dino's trap, taking her little sister with her. They'd been on their way back from the bathrooms when he had approached them with a map of the basketball courts. He'd told them that he was there for his niece's game but he was a little confused and couldn't find the right court. Dino had seemed so nice and genuine, with a big smile and twinkling eyes. Cassandra hadn't thought he was a threat. Besides there had been so many people around that nothing bad could happen.

But it had.

When they'd stepped closer to point out the right place on his map he had shown them his gun, and told them that he'd kill everyone in the stadium if they didn't go with him quietly. Once outside he'd bundled them quickly into a waiting van and driven them around for what seemed like hours before finally stopping at the mansion, where they'd been taken straight to the basement and locked away in their cell. They had remained there until John Doe had taken them to the room. Taking their photos before sending her back to their cell and leaving Olivia all alone . . .

"Cass?"

Blinking, her sister's worried face came into view.

"You're crying." Olivia sounded amazed, like she hadn't known her big sister could cry. "What's wrong?"

The more she tried to reign in her sobs the louder they

became.

"Cassie, what's wrong?" Olivia repeated.

"I'm sorry," she wept. "I should have protected you. I shouldn't have left you alone with him. I'm so sorry."

"Sorry about what?" Olivia asked, clearly confused.

"I'm sorry that I let him hurt you."

"Who?"

"John Doe," Cassandra's tears slowing, now it was her turn to look confused.

"John Doe?" Olivia repeated. "He never hurt me."

"What are you talking about? In the room, he . . . he . . ." Cassie couldn't bear to vocalize the word.

"Cass, he never touched me. I swear. He just talked to me." Olivia's cheeks flushed red, "I'm the one who's sorry. I should have told you but he made me promise not to tell anyone what happened in that room. But you have to believe me, he never hurt me."

Hardly daring to hope that was true, "really?"

"Really," Olivia nodded. "He just told me a story, he never laid a hand on me."

Feeling like the weight of the world had been lifted from her shoulders. "He really only talked to you?"

"Uh huh, then he just sent me back to our cell."

Breathing a deep sigh of relief, "I was feeling so guilty that I didn't keep you safe. That I let him do to you . . ."

"What Dino did to us," Olivia finished solemnly.

Both girls shuddered at the memory and Cassie wrapped her arms around her sister, pulling her close. Olivia snuggled her head down against her shoulder, already half asleep.

"We'll rest for a while," Cassandra whispered. "Then we'll find some water and then home. Home to mom and dad, and our dog, our house, our rooms. Home."

Olivia didn't answer, she was already fast asleep. Before Cassandra drifted off she wondered whether being home would change things back to the way they had been before. As much as she hoped that everything would be okay once they got home she had a sinking feeling in her tummy that after everything they had been through things could never go back to normal.

\* \* \* \* \*

*Sixteen Years Ago*
*Sunday Afternoon*

*Tessa didn't know what time it was or how long she'd been walking.*

*Earlier, when she had awakened from her exhausted slumber, it had still been dark. Immediately she had stood and begun to aimlessly wander. Which way she should be heading she wasn't sure, where she was going she wasn't sure, all she knew was that she had to keep moving.*

*She wasn't afraid anymore, at least she didn't think she was, ever since she woke up she had felt empty. A deep, dark emptiness that seemed to consume her. An emptiness that felt so big she wasn't sure she'd ever be able to fill it up. Still at least she wasn't scared anymore.*

*As she weaved her way through the woods Tessa felt like she was stuck in a dream. The endless line of green trees blurred into one, several times she tripped over roots, skinning her hands and knees, yet she hardly noticed.*

*She wondered distractedly whether anyone would be looking for her. Her grandparents were away on vacation, Daniel was away on a class trip, and Emilie would be lucky if she noticed her own clothes on fire let alone that her eleven-year-old daughter was missing. Maybe Ellie's parents would notice. Tessa loved her best friend's mom, she was kind and sweet and attentive, all the things a mom should be. The more she thought about it the more she thought she remembered that Ellie was supposed to be staying at her house this weekend. So her mom would have no reason to think that anything had happened to her little girl.*

*Continuing on and on, Tessa thought she might be crying but wasn't really sure, and didn't have the energy to check. Besides nothing mattered except that she keep moving. If you kept moving them you were safe, it was only when you were still that they could get you. She hardly noticed the blood that stained her school clothes anymore, nor the rips in the arms of her navy blazer, or the huge tear in the skirt of her school dress.*

*She didn't notice anything anymore.*

*It was like every other living being had been transported off the planet and she alone was left. In fact, she was so dazed that she almost choked on a scream when a man suddenly appeared before her.*

*Tessa's first instinct was to run. It was probably one of John Doe's men come to drag her back to that hellhole and punish her for killing Jake.*

*The man's mouth was moving but she couldn't hear what he was saying. She seemed to have gone deaf. Upon closer inspection she saw the man's uniform and realized that he was a police officer. That should have made her feel safe but she still couldn't feel anything.*

*Then her hearing came back with a snap.*

*"Honey, are you hurt?" the policeman was asking, looking at her tenderly with the warmest blue eyes she had ever seen. "Are you hurt, sweetheart?"*

*Not quite sure how to answer that Tessa simply stared back at him.*

*Giving her a reassuring smile, "my name's Anthony, what's yours?"*

*Gulping, Tessa couldn't seem to make her mouth work and decided it was safer anyway to keep it shut. Anthony was a police officer if he found out she had just killed a man then he would have to arrest her and stick her in a little cell just like the one from which she had just escaped.*

*Keeping his smile firmly in place, "that's okay," Anthony told her. "You don't have to talk. I just want to check you over okay, make sure that you're not hurt." When she said nothing he moved slowly closer, taking his time, being careful not to spook her. Reaching her side he knelt down so they were eye to eye, "everything's going to be okay, honey," he assured her as he lightly rested his hands on her shoulders.*

*Flinching involuntarily at his touch. Her mind flashed back to Jake and the feel of his hands roaming her body.*

*Instantly pulling back, his easy smile still in place. "It's alright, sweetheart, I'm not going to hurt you, I just need to know that you're okay." Cautiously he reached for her again, and this time Tessa made herself remain completely still as his hands quickly skimmed the length of her body in search of any injuries that might be the cause of all the blood. When he finished his examination he gently tucked one of her tangled braids behind her ear. "All done," Anthony smiled. "You were really brave. Would it be okay if I took you to the hospital?"*

*Again Tessa found she couldn't speak so she just stared back. Finally aware that it had grown dark again. The moon was visible above the tops of the tall trees, the stars were twinkling merrily without a care in the world, and she and Anthony were illuminated by the stark glow of his headlights. Somehow in her dazed state she had wandered onto a road where this police officer had stumbled upon her.*

*Apparently taking the fact that she hadn't bolted as a sign of assent he slipped out of his jacket, "here you go, sweetheart, you're shaking."*

*Tessa hadn't realized she was cold until Anthony wrapped his jacket firmly around her shoulders, buttoning it up so that she felt like she was snuggled up inside her own soft little cocoon. She didn't protest when he lifted her into his arms and carried her to his police car, sliding her into the back and buckling her in as though she were an infant.*

*"There we go," he smiled again. Tessa had never met such a smiley person in her life. Anthony's smiles were genuine and sunshiny, not like Jake's, which had been dark and malicious.*

*As they sped along the country roads, Anthony babbled away about his own little girls, an eight-year-old named Jilly and a twelve-year-old named Jennifer. He no longer asked her questions, having understood that whatever had happened to her she wasn't ready to talk about, but kept up the chatter to put her at ease.*

*Listening to his soothing voice, Tessa felt her pounding heart slowly start to ease. Her jangled nerves began to untangle and the tight knot in her stomach began to loosen. Before she knew it, she had drifted off to sleep.*

\* \* \* \* \*

8:52 P.M.

She had made the wrong choice.

Before she'd never been sure, now she was.

At the time it had seemed like her only option, she hadn't wanted to do it and yet she had been unable to say no. Tessa hated what John Doe did but she did understand why he did it. She's told him before that it wasn't the way, that he could still achieve what he wanted without having to destroy more lives in the process, but John Doe disagreed. He had long ago convinced himself that this was his one and only option. And so in the end she had agreed to do what he wanted. At first she wasn't sure she'd be able to do it, but it hadn't been as hard as she'd anticipated. In the end it wasn't finding the information that proved to be the problem but what to do with what she'd found. Eventually she made her choice and she had to live with it.

"Tessa?"

Forcing her mind to focus, "yeah?"

"You doing okay?" Elisabeth was inspecting her closely with her guarded psychiatrist eyes.

Normally Tessa would have been annoyed that Parker had sent Elisabeth to babysit her while he went to search the house where John Doe and Dino had been hiding out, but today she had almost enjoyed the company. And talking with Casey earlier had actually made her feel a little better.

Ever since she had recounted the events that took place when she was abducted she had been unable to get it out of her mind. Ellie and Jake and Anthony Higgins. The only good thing to come out of that whole disastrous weekend was meeting Anthony Higgins. He had been so sweet and gentle with her when he found her wandering in the woods covered in Jake's blood and she had stayed in touch with him for several years, until his untimely death. Three years after they met Anthony had been killed in a gunfight with a drug dealer. His death had been hard for her to get over, she had really grown to love his calm, soothing nature.

"Tessa?" Elisabeth prodded anxiously when she didn't answer.

"I'm fine," she assured the psychiatrist. "Do you know what it is?" she asked her gaze dropping to Elisabeth's belly.

Surprised that she had brought up the baby, "uh no, we want to wait and be surprised."

"That's nice." Her mind drifting to her own baby, even though she had only been pregnant for ten weeks she had been sure she was having a girl. "I think I'm going to take a nap," she announced. "Do you have anything to help me sleep?"

Surprised once again, "I think so."

Watching as Elisabeth stood and began to rifle through her bag. On principle, Tessa was against using medications. Ever since Emilie had drugged her and tried to drown her in their bathtub she had veered away from them whenever possible, but since the accident she'd needed the assistance of painkillers and sleeping pills just to function.

"Here you go," Elisabeth held out a bottle.

She took the pills and was at the door when Elisabeth stopped her, "Tessa, are you sure you're okay? If you want to talk I'm here."

Biting her tongue to keep from reminding Elisabeth of her views on the pointlessness of psychiatry, while at the same time contemplating calling Charlie Abbott. "I'm just tired."

"Okay," reluctantly Elisabeth let her go.

Climbing the stairs as quickly as her throbbing leg would let her, in comparison the pain in her arm was mild, but her headache was back. Rubbing blearily at her tired eyes, Tessa wasn't going to bother turning on the light and was about to dry swallow the sleeping pill when she caught sight of something white on her pillow. Switching on the lamp beside the bed she saw it was a plain white envelope. Her mind ticked back in time to the Iceman case and she couldn't quite stop a shiver that trembled through her from head to toe. The envelope wasn't sealed and Tessa slid out a single piece of white card.

*Be Happy*

That was all it said.

Her name wasn't included and neither was it signed but Tessa knew exactly whom it was from. The almost feminine script could only be his and by now he must know that the police were on to Dino, he would be moving on once again.

Without a second thought Tessa knew what she had to do. She also knew that Parker was going to go ballistic when he found out. Still she'd just have to deal with that later. Right now she needed to fix the mistake she had made so many years ago. Who knew how many girls had suffered needlessly because she had lied. She had told him the answer she'd thought would end his campaign, but obviously she'd been wrong. Now she needed to clean up the mess she had created before anyone else got hurt.

A lie hadn't stopped him, maybe the truth would.

# SEPTEMBER 12TH

2:21 A.M.

The station was quiet.

Most of the detectives had retired home for the night a couple of hours ago. Wyatt had left about midnight, and Parker knew he really should go too but every time he made a move to get his keys something held him back. He wanted to go home and check on Tessa but at the same time he felt uncomfortable around her. He'd pushed her to reveal her secrets, pushed her to relive the worst days of her life, and now he didn't know how to make the haunted look in her sad blue eyes go away. He didn't know if he could ever make it go away. He didn't know what to say to her and the only way he knew to make things better was to find Dino Rollino.

With a weary groan he restacked the papers on his desk in a neat pile, and was just collecting his keys when the phone on the desk began to trill.

With a sudden feeling of foreboding he lifted the receiver. "Hello?" he asked a little apprehensively as he answered.

"Don't be mad," were the first words out of Beth's mouth.

"What's wrong?" his wariness growing at the false calmness of her tone.

"Everything was going fine. I mean we had a really nice day and that right there should have tipped me off. Tessa and I never get along this well. She wasn't argumentative or critical, and she didn't give me her usual spiel about the ridiculous pointlessness of psychiatry . . ."

Impatiently cutting her off, "Beth, what's wrong?"

Her voice finally cracking, "she's gone."

"Gone?" he echoed weakly.

"I'm sorry, Parker," she said in a rush. "She said she was tired, and she looked exhausted, she wanted something to help her sleep so I gave her something . . ."

"She was playing you," he muttered. "Eric gave her sleeping pills when she was in the hospital."

"I'm sorry, Parker," Beth said again. "That makes sense but I never even thought of it. I just gave her the pills and when she went upstairs I just sat down for a second, but I must have been tireder than I thought because I fell asleep and when I woke up and went to check on her she was gone."

"I told you not to let Tessa out of your sight," he snapped, he knew his wife was a flight risk and had warned Beth about leaving her alone. The officers that had been assigned to watch her hadn't called in so Tessa had obviously managed to slip out of the house undetected.

"I'm sorry, Parker. I thought she was just going to sleep, I didn't realize how tired I was . . ."

Interrupting, "how long has she been gone?"

"I don't know."

Clenching his free hand into a fist, "when was the last time you saw her?"

"Around nine," Beth answered dismally.

So she could have more than five hours on them, which was more than enough time to get wherever she was going and confront whomever she planned on confronting. It was also plenty of time for whomever Tessa was meeting to kill her and dispose of her body. Forcing himself to stop thinking this way he took a deep, cleansing breath, "okay. I'm going to go and talk to Clara Meyers. She and Tessa talked about something and I have a feeling that she knows something about Tessa's secret."

"It's the middle of the night, Parker," Beth reminded him. "And she's only ten years old."

"I don't care," he muttered tightly. "This is Tessa's life we're talking about and Clara is the only one we have who knows the people involved."

"Alright, I'll call Wyatt and J.J., let them know what's going on."

"Fine," about to hang up when Beth piped up.

"I'm really sorry, Parker, I should have known better, I mean it's not like she's never done this before. I'm really sorry."

"It's not your fault," Parker assured her. In fact it was his own. He should have been the one to stay with Tessa, to remain glued to her side, handcuff himself to her if necessary. "I have to go," he didn't wait for her to reply, just hung up, grabbed his stuff and bolted for the car.

As he sped towards the Meyers' home Parker wondered how much longer he could live his life like this. It wasn't the first, or even the second, but the third time he had gone rushing off to find Tessa after she went off on her own to face a villain. He felt like ever since he'd met Tess his life had become a soap opera. Filled with the kind of things other people only faced in books or movies or TV shows, and he wasn't sure that he could do it much longer.

Pulling to a stop in the driveway he sprinted up the path and began hammering on the door. Inside a light flickered on, then another and another as someone made their way downstairs. A shadowy figure appeared through the frosted glass and he was bathed in light. The door was edged open a crack and one of Robert Meyers brown eyes peeped out. "Yes?" he asked nervously.

"It's Detective Bell," he announced. "I need to talk to your daughter."

"It's very late?" Robert reminded him, pulling the door the rest of the way open.

"I know sir, but it's very important," taking a forceful step forward, the timid man backed up, allowing Parker entry to the house. "I just need to ask Clara a couple of questions."

"She still hasn't said anything?" Robert closed the door behind them.

"Robert? Who was it?" Yvonne Meyers appeared at the top of the stairs, wrapping a blue and green striped robe around herself. "Detective Bell? What are you doing here?"

"I'm sorry to barge in on you at this hour, Mrs. Meyers, but it's an emergency and I need to talk to your daughter."

Frowning, "it's the middle of the night," she stated.

"I'm aware of that," Parker made an effort to retain his composure. "But Tessa's gone missing and I think Clara is the only one with answers as to where she might be."

"Your wife is missing?" Yvonne's creased brow eased.

"She's been gone for over five hours."

Wavering, "and you really think Clara is the only one who can help you find her?"

"When she was eleven Tessa was abducted by the brother of the man who took Clara." The families of the missing girls, including the Meyers, had been filled in on some of what their girls had been destined for. "I think that when they were in the hospital Tessa said something to Clara, I know it's a long shot but at the moment it's all I have," he ended a little desperately.

Nodding her consent, "your wife saved Clara so I guess it's only right that if Clara can help her then she does."

Breathing a sigh of relief, "thank you."

Following the child's mother up the stairs, as they walked down the hall Parker could see a line of light shining underneath Clara's door.

"She insists on keeping the light on all night," Yvonne explained. "I said she could sleep with us in our room but she refused."

Easing the door open Clara Meyers stared back at them from the bed, where she was just visible in a pile of stuffed animals.

"She wanted to get out all her old toys," Yvonne once again

offered an explanation of what she deemed her daughter's strange behavior. "Robert spent all day yesterday bringing them down from the attic." Raising her voice as she addressed her daughter, "sorry to wake you, darling, but Detective Bell needs to talk to you. You remember Detective Bell don't you?"

The girl nodded, studying them all with her haunted brown eyes.

Venturing into the room, Parker retrieved the desk chair and placed it beside the bed, then taking a seat he began to remove the stuffed animals, setting them down on the floor. The child looked uncomfortable at the breaking down of her defenses but she said nothing. Remembering what Beth had said after meeting with Clara, where she too had been unable to make progress with the little girl who was turning out to be every bit as stubborn as Tessa, that she was taking refuge in the past.

"Tessa told you that she was abducted when she was a little girl right?" he began.

Clara hesitated but then bobbed her head in confirmation.

"Did she also tell you that the man who took her was Dino Rollino's brother?" ignoring Yvonne and Robert Meyers who hovered in the doorway as he inspected Clara's expression as she shook her head. When he was satisfied that she was telling the truth he continued, "his name was Jake Killinger and after he murdered Tessa's friend Eleanor she had to kill him to escape." Catching a flash of something in Clara's eyes he stored it away and let it go until she was ready. "After she escaped she wandered alone in the woods for a day before she was found. Dino has watched her these last sixteen years and now he wants to kill her. He's already tried once, shot at us, luckily the bullet only skimmed her arm. Now Tessa's missing and I'm really worried about her. You don't want anything to happen to Tessa do you, Clara?"

The little girl shook her head.

"I need you to talk to me," he said gently. "I need you to tell me everything about Dino that you can. I know you don't want to betray Tessa but she's in trouble, she needs help, and you're the only one who can help her."

Brown eyes stared back at him unblinkingly. Clara remained quiet for so long that Parker was beginning to despair that she would utter a sound when a soft voice spoke, "he said his cell phone was flat."

"Clara . . ." Yvonne Meyers took a step forwards.

Stopping her with a held up hand, "when he took you, Clara?"

Nodding, Clara fixed her gaze on a spot above his head and continued, "after my Mom left he knocked on the door, I thought it was Dad so I answered, but it was Dino. He said that his cell phone had gone dead and his car had broken down, he asked if he could use our phone. I said no because I was home alone and I knew not to let a strange man inside the house. But then he showed me his daughter, she was about my age and he said that she needed to use the bathroom."

So running the ruse with a child in tow was common, Parker thought. It was smart. Put the kids at ease. They knew not to talk to strangers, but when they saw a child their age the man went straight from a stranger to a dad. And dad's were safe. When he found Tessa he'd tell her that she wasn't the only child to have been tricked by this tactic, maybe it would help assuage some of her guilt. *If* he found her, he reminded himself, and focused again on Clara's story.

"He told me that they'd been driving all night to visit his brother who was dying of cancer. He said that was why he needed to use the phone, to call the hospital and tell his Mom that they were going to be late. I didn't know what to do, but he had a kid and I didn't think he would hurt me. As soon as I closed the door behind him he grabbed me. I was kicking and screaming, but he showed me his gun and told me if I didn't go with him then he'd kill the other girl. I didn't know what else to do so I did what he said. He put us both in the car. As we were leaving I saw my Dad come round the corner but I was too scared to call out to him.

Dino drove us around and around till we got to the house."

"We found the house," Parker told her as she gathered herself, leaving out the gruesome find in the basement, no need for the child to know that five of her cell mates had been killed. "How did you get away, Clara?"

Meeting his eye for the first time, "he gave me to a man. We got in his car and drove for ages. I told him I had to go, he got mad but he pulled over, when he went to open the door I pushed it into his face, his nose began to bleed everywhere. Then I got out of the car, I kneed him in the . . ." shifting uncomfortably.

"In the groin?" Parker supplied for her.

Nodding gratefully, "he screamed and bent over and I just ran and ran until I couldn't breathe. Then I hid. After a while, I heard him looking for me. I stayed really still and quiet, and finally he went away and then I ran again. I kept going until I found you . . . Do you really think Dino is going to hurt Tessa?"

Now it was his turn to shift uncomfortably, Parker didn't like misleading the little girl who had already been through so much. "Dino wants Tessa dead as payback for his brother, but . . . I'm not positive that's who has Tessa. We know that Dino isn't the one in control, we have a man named Jason Mason in custody, do you know him?"

Her repulsed shudder confirmed that she did.

"Jason Mason is afraid of this man. So afraid that he won't tell us anything about him, not even his name."

"He doesn't have a name," Clara's gaze shifted once again to a point above his head.

Confused, "what do you mean."

"I mean he doesn't have a proper name," Clara repeated in the exact same annoyed tone Tessa used. "That's what I told Tessa in the hospital."

"What?"

"She asked me who was in charge and I told her."

"What did you tell her?"

"I told her what she wanted to know," the child's gaze had become cold and distant.

"Which was?" he prompted, himself beginning to become annoyed.

"She already knew," Clara said softly, her voice barely above a whisper now, lost in thought. "She already knew his name because she knew him."

Dropping his voice to match Clara's, "what's his name, Clara?"

"His name is John Doe."

"John Doe?" he repeated.

Snapping out of her reverie, "that's what they called him."

"Did you meet him while you were there?"

Clara nodded.

"What was he like?"

"He looked like a grandfather until you got up close," the girl shivered. "Then he was terrifying. Tessa knew him, she wasn't afraid of him."

Deciding he wasn't going to get anymore out of Clara Meyers, Parker began to retrieve the stuffed animals, arranging them back on the bed around the little girl who had lapsed back into silence. When he was done he took her hand, "thank you."

He was at the door when she stopped him, "Detective Bell?"

"Yes?"

"She said something else to me, at the hospital, when she thought I was asleep," Clara paused, once again meeting his eye. "She said she was sorry, and then she said 'I thought I'd stopped him'. I told you Tessa knows John Doe, I think she knows who he really is."

Digesting this information as he climbed back into his car, the chat with Clara had been enlightening but it hadn't been helpful in deciphering where Tessa was or which of the men she'd gone after. Switching his cell phone back on, he'd turned it off earlier to get some uninterrupted work done on the case, intending to call Wyatt to get his partner to locate every available officer and send them out to drive around in search of Tessa, when it beeped at him to inform him he had a missed call. Dialing the message service he sucked in a breath as he was greeted by his wife's voice.

"Hi, Parker, it's me. Don't be mad. I'm not going to do anything stupid. I'm out at the house waiting for you, I'm going to sit right here by the door until you get here so don't freak out on me. I know you have Jason so I'm guessing you know that Dino is not the one in charge. I'm also guessing you talked to Clara, so I suppose you also know that his name is John Doe. Anyway, I think Dino will come out here at some point looking for me so I'm just going to sit here like a good little girl waiting for you. I don't know when you're going to get this message but I hope you aren't too long, it's chilly tonight. Okay well hopefully I'll see you soon, love you."

Letting out a relieved breath, it seemed like at least for once Tessa was actually using that genius brain of hers. Calling Wyatt and explaining the situation to him, then Parker flicked on his lights and sirens and sped towards the mansion where Tessa's life had been destroyed and prayed that Dino Rollino would not be the first to arrive.

* * * * *

*Sixteen Years Ago*
*Sunday Night*

*Someone was touching her.*

*Tessa lashed out with her hands, she was not going down without a fight.*

*"It's alright, honey, it's alright. It's just me, Anthony."*

*The calm voice was familiar, and when Tessa blinked her eyes open the police officer's smooth, smiling face came into view.*

*"We're at the hospital," he told her as he knelt beside the open door, allowing her time to calm down.*

*Tessa gazed past him to the big, bright building full of glowing lights and bustling with people. Overwhelmed she shrunk further back into the safety of the car.*

*Reaching out to take her hand, "it's going to be okay, sweetheart, we'll find your mom and dad and you can go home."*

*Shrinking still further back into the car, Tessa doubted Emilie had even noticed she was gone.*

*Sensing her discomfort and obviously wondering exactly what had happened to her out in the woods. "I'm going to stay right here with you, okay?"*

*Knowing there was no way of avoiding the hospital. There was no way this kind man would simply let her go. So she slowly stretched out her hand and let him grasp it.*

*"There we go," Anthony smiled at her. "Let's go get you checked out."*

*Tessa allowed him to slide her along the backseat and pull her from the car, and the burst of fresh air on her face was like a wake up call. No longer was she a little girl. She had lost everything in the last couple of days. She had been stupid and naïve not to see Jake Killinger as a threat from the beginning, and she vowed she would never make that mistake again. As Anthony took her hand and led her inside the hospital she quickly formulated a plan in her head. Deciding that her initial instincts of self-preservation that she keep her mouth shut and not say a word rather than risk saying the wrong thing were spot on.*

*The only problem with that plan was the other girls she had left behind. Maybe if she told Anthony what had happened to her he could save those girls. But if she told him where she had been and what they had done to her then he would want to know how she got away. Then she would have to tell him about how Jake had snapped Ellie's neck. Then she would have to tell him how she killed Jake. And then he would arrest her and lock her up in a tiny cell like the one from which she'd just escaped.*

*So she was right back where she started.*

*Besides, she consoled herself, she didn't even know if the girls were still there. If John Doe was half as smart as he made himself out to be then the second he realized she was gone he would have moved somewhere far away.*

*"Honey, do you want to come with me and we'll look you over?"*

*A middle-aged doctor was kneeling in front of her, a false smile on his pockmarked face. Tessa stared back at him.*

*"Honey, do you want to come with me?" the doctor repeated a little nervously but his smile still in place. Unlike Anthony's genuine smile that reached all the way to his eyes, the doctor's was forced and anxious. Clearly the police officer had explained the situation to him and he was not pleased with the prospect of dealing with a mute and traumatized child.*

*With a glance at Anthony, who gave her an encouraging nod, she took the doctor's hand and allowed him to pick her up and carry her into a room with pastel colored farm animals stenciled onto the walls. As the doctor set her down on the bed Tessa noticed another doctor and two nurses enter the room. Panic pounded inside her. There were too many people here. She didn't want to be around people. She wanted to be back in the woods. It was quiet there.*

*Before it could strangle her, Tessa imagined her panic as a rock. Then she pictured herself putting it inside a box, locking the box, and throwing the key out a window. And she could breathe a little easier.*

*"Sweetheart, I need to take your clothes, okay?"*

*Tessa jumped. She hadn't noticed the nurse at her side. She was going to have to get better at that. Learn to pay more attention to what was going on around her so she didn't get taken by surprise again. If she'd been paying better attention back at the stables then she would have known Jake was nearby and kept herself and Ellie hidden until they could both escape. She couldn't make that mistake again.*

*The last thing Tessa wanted to do right now was let someone else take her clothes off, but she had to face facts, these doctors and nurses were going to check her out whether she liked it or not. So she chewed on her bottom lip and forced herself to remain completely still while the nurse removed her blood soaked school uniform and dressed her in a hospital gown. As her clothes were placed in evidence bags Tessa caught the glance the nurse shot the others at the sight of her blood stained underwear. She barely contained a shudder as she flashed back to what Jake had done to her.*

*"Did someone hurt you, honey?" one of the doctors was asking her.*

*Of course they did, she wanted to snap, but suppressed the urge.*

*"We need to look down there, okay?" the doctor continued. "Make sure*

*you're alright, and see if the man who hurt you left behind anything that can help us find him."*

*No, she almost screamed, but caught herself. There were too many people in here. One of the nurses was checking her vital signs, the other was cleaning all the scrapes and cuts she'd gotten running through the woods, the other doctor was examining the gash on her head from where Jake had hit her with the knife back at her school. Two more figures suddenly appeared in the doorway, Tessa knew immediately that they were cops. Her panic was rising again. Threatening to break free of the box she'd locked it in.*

*". . . suspected sexual assault," the doctor was explaining to the police officers. "But she won't say anything."*

*"How is she physically?" one of the police officers asked.*

*"Mildly dehydrated but she's stable."*

*"So we can talk to her?"*

*"You can try," the doctor shrugged as all three men came towards her.*

*"Hi," the other police officer crouched down beside her bed, "my name's Detective Holland, can you tell me your name?" He waited for her to say something, when she didn't he reached for her hand, but she snatched it quickly away. "You know you're safe here, no one's going to hurt you again. We all just want to help you. The doctor is going to examine you, look for evidence . . ."*

*Tessa knew exactly what they wanted to do to her. They wanted to do a sexual assault kit on her. They wanted to touch her and poke her and probe her and hurt her all over again. She couldn't let them do that. She couldn't.*

*It was all too much. Her panic was surging. She couldn't catch her breath. There were too many people in the room and they were asking her too many questions. Questions she didn't want to answer. Their voices swirled above her. Mingling with Ellie's sobs. Then suddenly Jake's face flashed into her mind. His black eyes glittering with lust, his slimy voice calling her princess.*

*When the doctor moved to begin his exam she completely lost it. Tessa attempted to flee the room, if she could just get back to the woods then she could get her mind to calm down. The doctors, nurses and cops all grabbed at her and she thrashed wildly, trying to escape.*

*Backing herself into a corner, relieved when they kept their distance, Tessa dropped to the floor, bringing her knees up to her chest and wrapping her arms around then, holding herself tightly together. Rocking subconsciously backwards and forwards, Tessa desperately wanted images of Jake and Ellie to stop flashing through her head. She wanted to stop being afraid, but she didn't know how. She didn't even know if it were possible. The only thing she knew was that she was now completely and utterly on her own.*

\* \* \* \* \*

*Sixteen Years Ago*
*Tuesday Morning*

*"Oh my gosh!"*

*Tessa recognized the voice immediately and curled herself into a tighter ball in the bed. Gluing her eyes to the clouds in the sky outside her hospital window, which was on the opposite wall of the door.*

*"Is this your daughter?" asked Tessa's favorite nurse, Candice Walkman. Candice was in her sixties, with snowy white hair and twinkling silvery blue eyes. She was sweet and nice, and when she wasn't too busy Candice would sit with her and read her stories or make up fanciful tales. She was exactly what Tessa imagined a grandmother to be like and nothing at all like her own grandmother.*

*For two long days she had sat in here. Anthony had come to visit her several times, even bringing his wife and daughters once. The two police detectives that she'd met the day Anthony brought her here had also been back several times, peppering her with questions about who she was and where she had been and what had happened to her. She had resisted the urge to respond to any of their questions and she found that each time they came it got easier and easier to remain silent. She was getting better at controlling her emotions too. Every time she felt panic threatening to engulf her she just kept putting it back in the locked box. Maybe one day she'd learn how to keep it trapped in there.*

*"That's not Eleanor, that's Tessa!" exclaimed Ellie's mother, Elise Matthews.*

"*You know this little girl?*" Detective Hollond had arrived.

"*Tessa, where's Eleanor?*" Mrs. Matthews rushed over to the bed, planting herself in-between the bed and the window. "*Tessa, sweetheart, where's Eleanor?*"

Forcing herself to stare through Mrs. Matthews as though she weren't there, as she heard the nurse and two detectives join them.

"*Mrs. Matthews,*" Detective Kalan began patiently. "*If this is not your daughter then who is she?*"

"*This is Tessa Micah, she's Eleanor's best friend, they go to the same school,*" she explained in a rush then her attention reverted back to Tessa. "*I spoke to the school, they said you and Eleanor never attended any classes on Friday, how long were you gone?*"

"*Your daughter was missing all weekend and you didn't report it?*" Detective Hollond asked.

"*She was supposed to be staying at Tessa's house and going to school with her Monday, it wasn't until last night that I realized something had happened,*" came Mrs. Matthews' flustered reply.

"*What about Tessa's parents? They didn't contact you to say the girls weren't there?*" Detective Hollond forged on, pleased he was finally making progress.

"*Tessa's father walked out on them a year ago, he lives in Paris now with his new wife and their baby son. She lives with her father's parents, but I think they're out of the country at the moment,*" Mrs. Matthews was breathing deeply struggling not to start demanding answers.

"*What about her mother?*" queried Detective Kalan.

Hesitating, "*Tessa's mom has some problems, she might not have even noticed the girls weren't there.*"

"*Then why would you let your daughter stay with her friend if they were going to be unsupervised?*" Detective Kalan asked a little reproachfully.

"*Because Tessa is a genius, she knows how to take care of herself, I thought Eleanor would be safe with her,*" Ellie's mom began to cry. "*Tessa, please, you have to tell me where Eleanor is and if she's okay.*"

Tessa felt all four sets of eyes on her and squeezed her own eyes closed, wishing desperately for someone who could come and make everything better *but knowing that no such person existed.*

*The bed dipped as someone sat beside her, taking her hand. "Your name is Tessa?"*

*Opening her eyes to meet nurse Candice's, their confident silver sparkling made her lose herself for a moment and before Tessa knew what she was doing she was nodding in answer to the nurse's question.*

*Pouncing on this momentary weakness, "what happened to you, Tessa?" Detective Hollond asked.*

*Regaining control she remained steadfastly quiet, meeting his gaze with her unblinking eyes.*

*"Tessa, where's my baby?" Mrs. Matthews demanded shrilly, then turned on the detectives, "where's Eleanor? You have Tessa why don't you know where Eleanor is? What did she tell you? What did Tessa tell you about what happened to my daughter?"*

*"She hasn't told us anything, Mrs. Matthews," Detective Kalan told her. "She hadn't spoken a word since she was found."*

*"Well where was she found? She's only eleven, how far could she have gone by herself?"*

*"The area where she was found was well searched," Detective Kalan assured the terrified mother.*

*"You must have found something," Mrs. Matthews shrieked. "Tessa, tell them, tell them what happened."*

*"Yelling at her isn't going to help," Nurse Candice spoke up quietly. "She's been traumatized enough as it is."*

*"Traumatized?" Ellie's mom repeated. "What do you mean?"*

*Shooting the nurse an irritated frown, "Tessa was found covered in blood," Detective Hollond explained.*

*"Covered in blood?" Mrs. Matthews echoed again before her eyes grew wide. "You think it was Eleanor's blood? Tessa, you tell them right now what happened to my baby? Tell me, tell me where she is, tell me she's okay, tell me . . ."*

*Unable to take it anymore Tessa flung herself around and buried her face in the pillow, desperately attempting to erase pictures of Ellie and Jake from her head. A hand began to rub soothing circles on her back and she had to fight to hold back tears.*

*"I think that's enough," Candice said firmly.*

*"Come on, Mrs. Matthews," Detective Kalan said reluctantly.*

*"No! Make her tell you!" she screamed. "Make her tell you where my baby is!"*

*The detectives must have dragged Mrs. Matthews from the room because it suddenly became deadly quiet.*

*"It's going to be okay, honey," Candice assured her, the woman gently lifted her up and pulled Tessa into her lap. "We're going to get your family here and then you can go home and it will all be okay."*

*But Tessa knew that wasn't true.*

*She was already resigned to the fact that nothing would ever be okay again.*

\* \* \* \* \*

*Sixteen Years Ago*
*Saturday Afternoon*

*"Come along, Tessa."*

*Turning to see her grandmother standing in her hospital room's doorway, a bag of clothes in her hand and her usual stern expression firmly in place. After Elise Matthews' visit the other day the police had managed to track down her grandparents in Egypt. They had also been back several times to try and convince her to tell them what happened to Ellie. She had told them nothing.*

*Her grandparents had taken their time returning home. They didn't like to be rushed. At least they had called last night to say they'd be there in the morning to collect her and that they had picked up Daniel from Italy where he'd been studying on their way back. Tessa couldn't wait to see her big brother, the one person who actually cared about her.*

*"Mrs. Micah, your granddaughter hasn't spoken since she was found, have you considered placing her in a . . ." the doctor cleared his throat nervously, "in a psychiatric facility?"*

*"Tessa will be coming home with us," her grandmother snapped haughtily and crossed the room to hand her the bag of clothes, "get dressed, Tessa."*

*"Mrs. Micah," the doctor tried again, looking no more comfortable with her grandmother than he had with her. "Clearly your granddaughter is traumatized, she needs professional . . ."*

*"I'll decide what my granddaughter needs," Francesca Micah shot the doctor an icy glare. "Hurry up, Tessa, your grandfather is in the car and you know he doesn't like to be kept waiting."*

*Obediently Tessa removed the pajamas Candice had brought for her and donned the white blouse, tartan skirt, stockings and Mary Jane's her grandmother had packed for her. While she changed the doctor discretely took her grandmother outside the room where they continued to argue in hushed voices about what was best for her.*

*Wandering to the window while she waited Tessa stared aimlessly at the grey sky and decided the color matched how she felt about going home. She wanted to see Daniel but not Emilie, and even though it had only been a week since she'd been home it felt like a lifetime.*

*"Let me fix your hair," her grandmother commanded, reappearing in the doorway, the doctor hovering behind her looking half chastised half irritated. Complying with her grandmother's order Tessa crossed the room to her and stood patiently while her wild curls were yanked into a neat ponytail. Then her hand was grasped in her grandmother's firm grip and she was pulled along at such a brisk pace her short legs had to run to keep up with her grandmother's long strides.*

*She wanted to say goodbye to Candice. She also wanted to say goodbye to Anthony, now that she was back with her family he would forget all about her. But she was bundled quickly into the chauffeur driven car. Her grandfather gave her a quick peck on the cheek, then resumed fiddling with his thick silver hair, making sure every piece was in place. They rode in silence back to the estate, not once did either of her grandparents ask her what had happened or where Ellie was.*

*When at last they pulled into the long, winding, tree lined driveway Tessa blinked her heavy eyes open. She hadn't slept much the past week, waking in a cold sweat with her heart thudding and her whole body shaking every time deep sleep brought with it nightmares, and she wondered whether she'd ever sleep through the night again. As the big stone mansion came into view Tessa could just make out her brother's form hovering by the front door.*

*The second the car came to a stop she hurtled out and threw herself at Daniel, who lifted her off the ground and held her tightly.*

*"I'm sorry, Tessie," he rambled. "I should never have gone to Italy, I should have stayed here with you. I'm sorry, Tessie. What happened? What happened to you? Where were you? The police said they found you covered in blood. Did someone hurt you? Tessa? Tessie?" Daniel pulled back and set her down, kneeling in front of her, "Tessie, what happened?"*

*Tessa wanted so badly to tell her big brother what had happened, to believe that he could make things better. And maybe it wasn't too late to save those other girls. She was just about to open her mouth to release the weight of the secret that was crushing her, when through the open front door she caught sight of something moving in the shadows of the house. For a split second she met her mother's eyes. Then Emilie was gone and Tessa knew that she would keep her secret to the grave.*

\* \* \* \* \*

3:58 A.M.

Rubbing her arms against the chill night air and glancing at her watch for about the thousandth time, wondering where he was. Tessa was sure he would have been here by now. Any one of the 'he's' she was waiting for.

Tessa felt a little bad for drugging Elisabeth. Not that it had been hard, when she'd snuck back downstairs Elisabeth had been chatting on the phone with her husband. When the psychiatrist's back had been turned she'd put one of the sleeping pills Elisabeth had given her into the mug of coffee on the table. Then she'd simply waited and once Elisabeth was sleeping soundly she had slipped out, making sure not to alert the officers that had been assigned to watch her.

Once she was in the car she'd called Parker to tell him where she was going, even though she had been pretty positive that he'd have his phone off as he poured over files searching for answers that weren't there. This morning she's managed to wheedle out of Elisabeth what Skylar and Parker had found at Dino's new hideout. Five little girls whose necks Dino had snapped.

She was sure Parker must have heard her message by now and be on his way here. She was also sure that Dino had to turn up soon looking for her. But she was positive that John Doe would have been here by now. Tessa knew his real name but she'd become accustomed to thinking of him by that name. Something must have happened to hold him up, she was sure he would have arrived by now. That was why she had needed to drug Beth, she needed some time before Parker and Dino turned up, some time to undo what she had done, to tell him the truth.

Starting to get annoyed. It was cold, she was tired, she had a headache, and both her arm and leg were stiff and sore from the chilly night. She hadn't taken any painkillers, if Dino was going to have another go at killing her then she needed to keep a clear head.

Standing, she began to pace, hoping to work out some of the pain. Out of the corner of her eye she noticed the slightest of movements at the edge of the woods. Head spinning in that direction she saw two figures in the distance. Taking a few steps forward, she was close enough to see it was two young girls. When they finally spotted her, even in the moonlight Tessa could see their faces grow horrified, as they pointed and then dashed back into the cover of the trees.

"Hey stop," she yelled as she sprinted lopsidedly as fast as she could across the long grass to the woods. "It's okay, I'm not going to hurt you." Quickly catching up to the girls as they scrambled through the forest. "It's okay," she assured them again. "My name's Tessa." Studying them more closely, "you're Cassandra and Olivia Stanton right?" she asked, remembering their photos from the ones Parker had shown her after the accident.

"How do you know that?" the older of the girls asked suspiciously, placing herself between Tessa and her sister.

"Because my husband is a police officer, one of the ones looking for you and the other girls," she explained.

Relaxing a little, "we've been walking for three days," the younger girl said wearily, sinking down to the ground to rest.

"Are you two okay? Are you hurt?" Tessa looked them over carefully, they looked exhausted and dirty but otherwise unharmed. Thankfully, neither was covered in any blood. If the girls had been taken by Dino and kept in the house that Parker and Skylar had found then Cassandra and Olivia Stanton had walked close to fifty miles through the woods to get here.

Chewing on her lip, "we're okay," Cassandra answered shakily.

"It's alright," she comforted the girls. "You're safe now, no one is going to hurt you again. How did you get away?"

Exchanging glances, "Olivia saw this door that led to a staircase, when no one was looking we just ran," Cassandra told her, dropping down beside her sister.

"No one saw you?" Tessa asked, thinking that was unlikely if the girls had really been with Dino and John Doe.

"I don't think so," Olivia shook her head.

"Can you tell me where you've been?"

Shuddering, "they kept us in the basement of this big old house," Cassandra told her.

"Do you know who the people were who took you and kept you there?"

"The man who took us was called Dino . . ." Cassandra started.

"But the man who was in charge everyone called John Doe," Olivia finished.

"Did John Doe talk to either of you? Tell you anything?"

Once again the sister's exchanged glances. "He talked to me," Olivia finally answered.

"Wait, how did you know that?" Cassandra looked suddenly

wary again.

"Did they take you too?" Olivia asked.

"It was a long time ago," Tessa didn't want to get into the details right now, not when she was expecting company at any second. "Look, Parker, my husband, he's on his way here right now, why don't you two go and wait inside," she gestured over to the mansion where she had lived her own tragedy.

"Are we really going home?" Olivia asked a little disbelievingly.

"Yes you are, but I need you to wait quietly inside until Parker gets here," she didn't want Dino stumbling upon the girls if he got here before her husband.

"What are you going to be doing?" Cassandra asked timidly, obviously not liking the prospect of sitting alone in a huge, empty house.

"Waiting with you," she gave them a reassuring smile. "I just need to do something first then I'll meet you there. Off you go."

The girls stood tiredly and took each other's hands then quickly made their way to the house. Once they were safely inside, she quickly scanned the area. About to take a step to join the girls inside when a twig snapped behind her, Tessa didn't need to turn around to know who was there.

"Try anything stupid and I'll kill them," he snarled.

* * * * *

4:20 A.M.

"Stop," he announced suddenly. His driver immediately pulled over to the side of the road.

John Doe sat staring out of the car window for a minute, deciding what he wanted to do. He'd thought he'd made his decision. He'd thought it was best not to see Tessa in person one last time, but now he wasn't so sure. He'd hoped the letter would be enough, a last chance to say goodbye without causing her any more pain, a way to sever the ties so she stopped turning to him for help.

But now he knew he couldn't do it.

He needed to see her before he disappeared once again. He needed to know why she never turned him in al these years. He needed to say his farewells in person.

"We're going back."

Without a word, the driver turned the car around and proceeded back in the direction in which they'd come. Travelling along once again they hadn't been going more than a minute or so when once again John Doe issued an order. "Stop."

Knowing better than to argue with his boss the driver pulled the car over and awaited further instructions. Climbing out into the night John Doe gestured to the drivers of the other cars who had pulled in behind them. Obediently his men also climbed from their cars and gathered around him.

"We're letting the girls go," he declared.

"We're what?"

Shooting the man a disapproving glare, "we're letting them go."

"They know too much, they can turn us in to the police," one of his men protested.

"I don't care," John Doe told him adamantly. "We're letting them go." With that he started for the first car, throwing open the back door and pulling the little girl out, "off you go," he told her, running to the next car and pulling that child out also.

When all ten girls were standing in front of him, he addressed them seriously, "you may all go home, but before I let you go I want to tell you why I'm doing this. I once had the pleasure of meeting a little girl who even though she was scared she cared enough for her fellow man that she helped me even though I didn't deserve it. Even though I didn't deserve her. I'm doing this for her. Go," he finished quietly, turning his back on the children so that they couldn't see the tears that glistened on his cheeks.

Resuming his place in the car, he and his men drove off into the night leaving the little girls behind. Pleased with his decision, and anxious to see Tessa one last time before he created a new identity and disappeared just as he had before.

* * * * *

4:35 A.M.

"Wow, you're looking older than I remember," Tessa said getting her first look at Dino as he started the boat's engine. He'd stayed behind her, with the gun held to the back of her head and his hand gripping her injured arm, as he walked her through the woods and down to the lake.

"You on the other hand are looking as youthful as ever," he smirked at her, his black eyes twinkling with malicious glee.

"You know Parker knows I'm out here," she told him as he maneuvered the boat away from the jetty and out into the vast lake. "He's going to be here soon and I don't think he plans on letting you get away."

"I'm looking forward to meeting your husband in person." Turning to grin at her, "it's a pity you won't be around to see me kill him."

Resisting the urge to massage the arm Dino had shot the other day and taken such pleasure in squeezing on the way here. "You really hate me that much, Dino? That all you can think about is killing me?" she asked him.

"I really do," he brought the boat to a stop in the middle of the lake. "Ever since you killed my brother, killing you is all I think about, and dream about. If it wasn't for your buddy John Doe I'd have killed you a long time ago."

"And Jake's really worth it? Taking my life for his?"

"Jake was the only person who was always there for me," Dino snapped. "If it wasn't for him I don't know where I'd be."

Frowning at him with mock surprise, "you really don't know, do you?"

"Know what?"

"Exactly what your big brother Jake is capable of," she watched confusion scamper across his face.

"You're just trying to throw me off. I know exactly who my brother was," he declared a little disconcertedly.

"Suit yourself," Tessa shrugged and steadfastly began to watch fingers of fog curl themselves out from the woods and settle atop the water.

At last with a frustrated huff Dino spoke, "what are you talking about?"

Turning to face him, "I'm talking about your mom."

"What about her?" his face blackening, obviously unhappy about the conversation veering towards his mother.

"Your mom didn't commit suicide and she didn't die of an accidental overdose," Tessa told him.

"What do you mean? I found her, she'd overdosed," Dino's face blackened further.

"I agree, she did die of an overdose," she nodded.

"Stop talking in circles and tell me what you're talking about," Dino launched towards her.

Staring back at him unblinkingly, keeping her face completely neutral, "Jake killed your mom, Dino. She died of an overdose but he was the one who injected the drugs." It had been John Doe who'd told her about what Jake had done, and she'd filed the information away, hoping it would come in handy one day.

"I don't believe you," Dino stammered.

"Suit yourself," she shrugged again.

After a minute, "why?" Dino snapped. "Why would Jake kill our mom and make it look like an accident or suicide?"

"Because he was jealous. Of you. That your mom changed for you, to give you the life you deserved. That she did it for you but she didn't do it for him."

"He killed her because she didn't go clean for him?"

"And to get you," her voice dropped to a whisper. "So that you didn't succeed. You could have been whatever you wanted, you could have had whatever you wanted, you could have done whatever you wanted, but Jake took that away from you, Dino. He took it away because he knew that could never be him. He knew his life would never be anything more than this, kidnapping little girls, raping them and selling them to pedophiles, but yours can. It's not too late. When Parker gets here you can turn yourself in. You can prove that you're nothing like your brother, you can prove that your mom was right, that she believed in you for a reason."

Dino was silent for a moment then he began to laugh, "nice speech, Tessa. I must admit you almost had me there for a second, but I don't believe you, Jake would never do that to me."

Shrugging indifferently, she hadn't really expected telling Dino the truth to work but it had at least bought her a little time. "You can ask Jake when you join him in hell."

Chuckling, "speaking of hell and family members, you think I don't know my brother, well there's certain things you don't know about your sister."

"Cordelia?" now it was her turn to look bewildered. After a yearlong murder spree her sister had been killed by their brother, but not before Cordelia managed to shoot both her and Daniel. "What do you know about my sister?"

"You ever wonder about your niece's looks? I mean your sister had blonde hair and blue eyes but her daughter has black hair and black eyes. Remind you of anyone?"

The world began to spin. After Cordelia had shot her she had almost died, and the moments before had become nothing but a blur. Now her last conversation with her sister was replaying in her head as clearly as if Cordelia was standing in front of her. She had told Cordelia that she'd already been to hell, referring to Jake and everything he'd done. Her sister had responded that she already knew about her visit to hell and that she wasn't the only one who'd met the devil and lived to tell about it.

Quickly putting things together. "Jake is Winter's father," she murmured weakly.

"My niece too," Dino grinned.

Feeling physically ill, "Cordelia sent Jake to me. She organized everything," pressing a hand to her thumping head. "I thought it was just a dream but she was really there." That first night in the hospital she'd had a dream. In it she'd had to put together the pieces of Cordelia's face like a jigsaw puzzle, and for each second it took her to do it someone was killed. At first she'd wondered why she'd had the dream, at that time she'd never even spoken with her sister face to face. Then during the Iceman murders she had been attacked by Cordelia, tasered and had her arm carved, after that she had had that dream again. Once more she had convinced herself it meant nothing, that Cordelia hadn't been there that weekend with Jake and that she hadn't been the one to leave her bleeding and unconscious in the snow. Apparently she had been wrong both times.

"Indeed she was, in fact she had just found out she was pregnant with our niece, the lovely Winter, while you were there." Pulling a knife from his pocket and moving closer to her, "well as fun as our little chat's been it's time to get things finished off before your pesky husband turns up and ruins things again."

When he got within striking distance Tessa launched herself at him, aiming her shoulder directly into his stomach, and they both tumbled to the ground wrestling for the knife that had flown from Dino's hand. Bigger and stronger it didn't take Dino long to get on top, throwing her up against the side of the boat so violently that her head smacked against the wall making her vision fade in and out.

Struggling to hold onto consciousness, when Dino went at her again Tessa kicked out her feet with all the strength she could muster, and managed to knock him off balance. Clutching at her desperately as he tumbled over the side, she was too dizzy to keep herself in the boat and splashed into the water beside him. As Dino began to sink he kept his hold on her wrist, pulling her down with him. Her eyes locked on Dino's, she held her breath as long as she could until at last her burning lungs forced her to draw a breath sending icy water down her throat.

Dino's face morphed slowly into Emilie's and her last thought was that it was fitting that since it was her mother who brought her into this world and started the chain of events that led to this night it was only fitting that Emilie end it all.

\* \* \* \* \*

5:03 A.M.

Ignoring the cold, Parker wrapped one arm tightly around Tessa's waist and with his other began to swim them both back to the surface. Breathing deeply as his head burst up into the air, then pressing Tessa against his chest he began an awkward one-handed stroke to bring them back to land.

Parker had been almost to the boat when Dino and Tessa had gone tumbling over the side. At first he kept expecting her head to come bobbing back up but it never had. He'd swum as fast as he could but she'd already sunk a fair way down before he reached her.

He had arrived at the house to find Tessa gone. To his surprise, he hadn't been surprised that she had changed her mind and decided to go after Dino on her own. Luckily in the car on the way out here Parker had rung the Meyers and talked to Clara again, getting her to tell him everything she remembered about Dino Rollino. She had mentioned something about how he was always talking about boats, so when he had been unable to find Tessa he had headed straight for the lake.

Feet finding the muddy bottom, Parker stood and swung Tessa

up into his arms, carrying her the rest of the way to shore then laying her down on the grassy bank. Holding his cheek above her mouth, his fingers against her neck, he felt neither a pulse nor the whoosh of air against his skin.

Commencing CPR in a daze.

The cold from the water numbed his brain not just his body, making everything surreal. In the foggy night Parker lost all sense of time. Everything else faded into the white mist but the rhythmic pumping on Tessa's chest. He should feel something, he thought as he covered Tessa's mouth with his own and forced air into her lungs. Anger that Tessa had wandered off on her own again, terror that his wife was lying dead beneath him, fear that this John Doe person was still out there somewhere . . .

Snapping to attention as Tessa began to choke and splutter, then rolling her carefully onto her side when she began to cough up water. Brushing wet, matted hair from his wife's face Parker bounced back into the moment. Fear and guilt and anger and love ran back into his frozen heart.

"Come on, Tessa," he begged as she struggled to suck air into her clogged lungs. "Come on, baby, breathe." When she finished coughing up more water Parker eased her back onto her back. Her glassy eyes found his and she tried to speak but erupted into more coughing. "Don't try to talk," he instructed. "Just concentrate on breathing. Everything's going to be fine, just take it easy, I'm right here."

"Cordelia," Tessa managed to mumble through her gasping.

"Cordelia's dead, honey," he reminded her, confused as to why she was mentioning her deranged sister.

"Cordelia sent . . ." she was shaking so hard her teeth were chattering. "Cordelia sent . . ." she tried again.

"Sweetheart, just rest," Parker urged her, only half listening to what she was saying, he was trying to think of a way to keep her warm before she became hypothermic.

"Cordelia . . ." Tessa's eyes fluttered closed.

"Hey," he shook her until her eyes opened again. "I know you're cold, I'll get you back to the car but you have to stay awake for me." Wondering how many times he would have to say these words to her before she finally started thinking about the consequences of her actions. "Come on," he gathered her up into his arms, pressing her shivering body closely against his chest, attempting to pass on any heat his own wet, cold body could muster.

"Cordelia sent Jake . . ." she whispered against his shoulder.

Stopping short as she finally grabbed his attention. "What did you say?"

"Cordelia sent Jake," she repeated.

Kneeling and setting Tessa down on the ground, propping her up against a fallen tree trunk, "Cordelia sent Jake?"

"Dino said . . . he said Cordelia was the . . . the one who sent . . . Jake . . . that she . . . she . . . she . . ."

"Take it easy," Parker cautioned, taking her face between his hands. "Are you saying that your sister sent Jake to you?"

"Winter," Tessa's dazed eyes darted about.

"What about Winter?" he asked with a sinking feeling. Tessa's niece had come to live with them after her mother's death.

"Jake . . . Cordelia . . . Winter . . ." came Tessa's breathless reply as she broke into more fits of coughing.

"Calm down, calm down," he soothed. "Dino told you that Jake is Winter's father?"

"I knew Cordelia hated me but . . . but how could she . . . how could she do that? How could she send Jake to . . . to kidnap me . . . and rape me . . .?" Tessa started to cry. "And Ellie . . . Cordelia's the reason Ellie's dead. She was there, Parker . . . Cordelia was there . . . I thought I was dreaming but . . . how am I going to tell Winter who her father is?"

"Alright, alright, shh, it's okay, it's okay," Parker pulled Tessa into his arms, holding her tightly and stroking her hair, attempting to calm her down. "Everything's going to be okay. Dino's gone.

I'm going to get you to the hospital. I don't want you to worry about Winter right now, we'll tell her together. Right now you just rest, concentrate on hanging in there." Even in the thin moonlight Tessa's skin had a bluish tinge, she was still trembling violently and she had a sleepy look about her. "Everything's going to be alright," he said again, "okay?"

"Okay," she hiccupped through her tears.

Briskly rubbing her arms, "okay. We'll get you back to the car and out of these wet clothes, then to the hospital to get checked out. Then you can tell me who this John Doe is and we can put an end to this once and for all."

"I found . . ." Tessa was saying as he bent over to pick her up but a crack ripped through the fog, his chest exploded and the whole world turned white.

\* \* \* \* \*

5:48 A.M.

"She's been gone a really long time," Cassandra Stanton whispered, more to herself than her sister.

When Tessa had found them in the woods earlier they had been practically at the end of their rope. Since escaping they had eaten nothing but some berries they had found on some bushes, the only water they had drunk was from an old well they'd stumbled upon behind an abandoned shack. They hadn't slept much because they were both too edgy, every little noise making them jump a mile. If Tessa hadn't found them when she did then Cassie didn't think she and Olivia could have lasted much longer. She had even begun to wonder whether they should have stayed where they were if it came down to dying alone in the woods or living in that basement hell.

"Maybe it hasn't really been that long it just feels like it," Olivia suggested.

"Maybe," Cassie agreed, more to keep her little sister's spirits up than anything else. She was pretty sure something must have happened to Tessa or she would have been here long before now.

As per Tessa's instructions, she and Olivia had dashed across the overgrown lawn to the house. The front door had been unlocked and they'd crept into the first room, closed the door and hunkered down in the corner where they'd been waiting ever since. Most of the time they'd sat in anxious silence, sitting with ears pricked waiting for Tessa or her husband to arrive. But neither ever came.

"Tessa knew them," Olivia said at last. "Dino and John Doe."

"She said it was a long time ago," Cassie agreed.

"Do you think they kidnapped her too, when she was a little girl?"

"I guess so."

"Why do you think she was here?" Olivia asked.

Feeling her sister's eyes on her, "I don't know."

"It couldn't have been because of us," Liv continued. "Because she didn't know we'd be here. Do you think this was the house where they took her?"

They both shivered at the thought of this house where they were hiding having little girls locked in its basement. "Maybe."

"Do you think she's here looking for Dino or John Doe?"

That was what Cassandra had been thinking. The only reason she could think of for the woman to be waiting out here in the middle of the night.

Reading her silence, "do you think he got her?" Olivia asked. "Do you think that's why she hasn't come?"

"I hope not."

"How do you think she got away? When she was little I mean."

"I guess she escaped like we did," Cassie didn't want to think about what had happened to them, she just wanted Tessa to get here and take them home.

"How old do you think Tessa is?"

Shrugging, "maybe in her twenties."

It took a minute before Olivia spoke again, doing the calculations in her head, math was not her best subject. "So it's been like ten or fifteen years since Tessa was kidnapped. It's like she never really escaped. Fifteen years later and she's still here because of them. Where will we be in fifteen years?"

Before Cassie had a chance to reassure her sister that they would be fine a car door slammed shut, the sound coming from just outside the mansion.

"Do you think that's Tessa's husband?" Olivia whispered pressing closer.

"I'll check. You wait here." Leaving the safety of their shadowy corner of the room to tiptoe to the big, glass front door. Peering through she saw a tall blonde man, she wasn't sure if it was Tessa's husband but it definitely wasn't Dino, John Doe, or any of the other men from the house. Easing the door open Cassie couldn't bring herself to speak so she just stared at the man until he turned and caught sight of her.

An easy smile gliding onto his face, "hi there, you must be Cassandra Stanton."

"Are you Parker?" she asked. After weeks of being locked up in that basement it felt odd to be talking to someone.

"No, I'm his partner, my name's Wyatt," he bent over so that his bright green eyes met her hazel ones. "Hey you have got to be Olivia," he looked over her shoulder.

"Who're you?" Liv came up behind her.

"I was just telling your sister that I'm Parker's partner, how do you girls know Parker?"

Exchanging a glance with her sister, she wanted to trust this man who seemed no nice and innocent but if there was one thing she had learnt in her time at John Doe's it was trust no one.

Sensing the reason for their hesitation, "you guys met Tessa huh?"

Reluctantly Cassie nodded, "she told us to wait in the house until her husband got here. She said he would take us home, she said she'd be there with us in a minute but she never came back," the words tumbled out before she could stop them.

"Do you know when that was?" the police officer asked, his eyes anxious, but his face remained calm, smile in place.

"It was ages ago," Olivia piped up beside her.

"Did you guys see anyone else hanging around?"

"You mean like Dino or John Doe?" Liv asked.

"Did Tessa talk to you about them?"

"She said that she knew them a long time ago," Cassie told him.

"Did she say anything else?" Wyatt asked them.

Both girls shook their heads.

"And you didn't see Dino or John Doe hanging around?"

"No, we didn't see anyone," Olivia assured him.

"Okay, I need to go and find Tessa . . ."

"Are you worried about her?" Liv interrupted him.

"Yes I am," Wyatt nodded, the anxiety in his eyes growing.

"Is Dino or John Doe going to hurt her?"

"I hope not, but I think Dino might," Wyatt told her honestly. "I want you two to get into my car, I want you to stay down low and I don't want you to move until I get back or . . ." he looked up as an ambulance emerged from the trees, pulling to a stop beside the police car. "Some other police officers are on their way, I'll let them know where you're hiding. When they get here they'll take you to a hospital to be checked out, they'll also call your mom and dad. They're going to be so excited to have you home."

"You . . . you talked to them?" Cassie asked, she still felt like all of this was just going to turn out to be a wonderful dream and she'd wake back up in that horrible little cell.

"I sure did. They're really great, you're lucky to have such lovely parents," he gave them a kind smile as he ushered them into the back of his car. "And you two must be pretty amazing girls to get away."

They watched as he joined the paramedics who had loaded their arms with equipment and stood ready and waiting.

"Wyatt," she called.

"Yeah?"

"Dino loves boats, there's a lake down that way."

"Thanks, now down out of sight."

Bobbing down, Olivia at her side, they threw their arms around one another and waited to be taken home.

* * * * *

6:15 A.M.

"Well that was worth waiting for," Dino declared happily, stepping closer to admire his handiwork. Tessa lay slumped against a broken tree trunk, still soaking wet from their dip in the icy lake. Her husband's body drooped across hers, pinning her in place, a bright red splodge was steadily growing on Parker's back.

Standing above Tessa, the lure of her smooth, milky skin framed by her damp blonde curls proved too great and he stooped to brush his lips against hers.

The touch made her blue veined lids flutter, her eyes popping open, growing wide and panicked as she saw her husband covered in blood. Tessa hated the sight of blood, had ever since she'd stabbed his brother and stood there watching him bleed to death.

"Wakey, wakey, Tessa," Dino shook her shoulder to focus her attention on him. Enjoying the feel of the narrow bone between his fingers, the knowledge that he could snap it like a twig if he chose.

Dazed greeny-blue eyes focused on him and he wondered if he'd given her a concussion when he'd thumped her head into the side of the boat. "Dino," she began hoarsely, "what an unpleasant surprise." She struggled beneath Parker, trying to maneuver him so that she could see where he was wounded.

"Need some help?" he asked with mocking cordiality, flipping Detective Bell over, pleased to see blood gushing from a hole in his chest. Using every ounce of strength he possessed he lifted the bigger man and tossed him a few feet away, enjoying the lifeless thud the body gave as it connected with the ground.

"How did you get out of the water?" Tessa asked, voice croaky from the water she'd expelled from her lungs. Dino had watched earlier as Parker had performed CPR on her, debating with himself whether he wished she'd revive or stay dead.

"Well," he began, clamping a hand around her wrist as she made a feeble attempt to reach her husband, "after I pulled you down under the water I waited until you'd passed out then I took off. Lucky I left when I did because when I came up for air I saw your husband dragging you back to shore. He was too preoccupied with you to notice me. Then I got back on the boat, dried off, changed, warmed up and came back to finish our little chat. It's a good thing you banged your head or you wouldn't have passed out so quick. It's also lucky that I was a swim champ through middle school, could hold my breath longer than anyone else. I guess you could say it's my lucky day," he grinned, deciding he was pleased to have a second chance with Tessa.

"Skylar'll be on his way here," Tessa glared up at him with the old stubborn glint in her eyes.

"You're probably right," he smiled down at her. "So I guess we better make the most of the time we have." His free hand slid to his belt, wrangling one handed with the buckle, but too wary to release his hold on Tessa because he never knew what she was planning.

Following his hand Tessa deliberately looked away and met his gaze directly. "You don't want to talk about we discussed earlier?"

His excitement slipping slightly, Dino didn't really believe the nonsense Tessa had made up but even if she was telling the truth it only served as another reason to make Tessa pay. If Jake really had killed their mother and taken away Dino's chance to be or do whatever he wanted then he had been denied the chance to exact revenge on his brother. Still Dino couldn't believe Jake would ever do something like that, but he was prepared to play along with Tessa's stall tactics for the time being. "Sure," he nodded enthusiastically, "let's talk."

"Didn't you used to wonder what made your mom turn back to drugs? Didn't you think that it was . . .?"

"Let's talk about Cordelia," he interrupted, "you think Jake was evil, he had nothing on that sister of yours." Fifteen-year-old Dino had been terrified of Cordelia Micah, as had every man who worked there bar John Doe. "I remember how thrilled she was when Jake brought you here, the smile she had on was enough to turn your blood to ice. She hated you so much, her eyes would go dead whenever she talked about you. Then after you killed Jake she just disappeared."

"Did Cordelia love Jake?"

"I don't know," he answered honestly, he'd always been too scared of Cordelia to spend much time with her. "But I don't think she cared about anything except making you as miserable as possible."

"I guess that's something we both have in common," Tessa mused. "My sister and your brother couldn't stand to see us happy, would do literally anything to ensure that we were never at peace."

Not one to dwell too deeply on things Dino merely nodded, got his belt undone and let his pants drop to the ground. As he knelt down, a knee on either side of her hips, Tessa squeezed her eyes tightly shut, and he wondered if she was as good as Jake made her out to be. His brother had even pondered fixing things so that he could keep Tessa himself, considering buying her from John Doe or even kidnapping her from whomever she ended up with. And there had to be some reason that John Doe had gone to great lengths over the years to help and protect her, perhaps this was how Tessa had managed to bewitch him.

One second he was undoing the zip on her jeans and running a hand up under her tee-shirt, then the next there was nothing . . .

* * * * *

6:32 A.M.

"Are you okay?"

Tessa didn't know if she was shaking from her dip in the cold water, her husband being shot and bleeding to death, what Dino was about to do to her, or the fact that his lifeless eyes were now staring into hers, a trickle of blood dribbling down from the bullet hole in his temple.

"Are you okay?" the voice asked again as someone moved Dino's body off her. "Tessa, snap out of it."

So many things were swirling in her head, Jake, Dino, Ellie, Cordelia, Parker.

Dino had shot Parker, she needed to get to him, help him. She didn't even know if he was dead or alive.

"Come on, Tessa."

Someone was slapping lightly at her cheeks.

"Tessa."

The sharp voice finally brought her back to reality.

"Hey, you're okay," a face smiled down at her. "I'm sorry. I should have gotten here sooner."

"Isaac," she breathed deeply, "you have really good timing." She'd known John Doe, a.k.a Isaac Worthington, would have to show up eventually.

"You're soaking wet, are you alright?" Isaac was kneeling at her side and staring down at her tenderly.

"Dino tried to drown me," she explained, sitting up slowly, fighting the nausea that rolled around and around in her stomach. "Then he shot Parker. I need to get to him," she tried to move but Isaac held her in place.

"You're weak, you need to stay put, I checked on your husband, he's still alive," Isaac reassured her. "Besides on my way here I saw Detective Wyatt and some paramedics, they'll be here soon."

"Isaac, I have to go to him," she stared at him imploringly.

Isaac rolled his eyes but helped her to her feet as she wobbled over to her husband. Kneeling at his side Tessa checked for his pulse, relieved to find it thumping rhythmically beneath her fingertips. Parker's skin was ashen, his eyes closed, breathing labored, the gunshot wound in his chest leaking an ever growing puddle of blood. Brushing the back of her hand across his cheek, praying that he would hold on until the EMT's got here, she knew she wouldn't be able to go on if anything happened to Parker.

"Here you go," Isaac handed her his jacket.

"Thanks," she offered him a weak smile as she pressed the jacket to Parker's wound. "Why didn't you come earlier?" she asked a little needily, when it came to Isaac she morphed straight back into the scared little girl she'd been when they'd first met.

Brushing at her hair, "because I wasn't sure I should come at all. I'm sorry, Tessa," Isaac took her hand. "All these years I thought I was protecting you, helping you, but I wasn't, I was only helping myself."

"No, it's my fault, Isaac. I lied to you," she was crying now. "I lied to you. Rebecca isn't dead, she's still alive, I only told you she was dead because I thought it was the only way you'd stop."

"Ah, Tessa, sweet, Tessa," Isaac wiped away her tears. "I always knew that you'd lied, you may be brilliant but you are not a brilliant liar."

"I'm sorry," her tears refused to cease. "I should have told you the truth."

"I knew the truth. You found my little girl, you found Rebecca, you did what I asked. It was my job to find the people who took her. I couldn't stop until I'd found them. I'm sorry, Tessa. I can't ever be who you want me to. To do what I had to for my daughter I knew I had to be ruthless, cold, dead inside. I had to ignore everything but Rebecca. I couldn't think of the innocent children I was hurting. Sweet little girls like you," he paused to stroke her hair lovingly. "I am a monster. I don't deserve happiness after the countless lives I've destroyed, but you, you can be happy. It's too late for me but not for you. Let yourself be happy, Tessa, you deserve it. You have a wonderful life now but you have to trust them, your husband, your friends, you can't keep turning to me for help. I can't be there for you anymore, it's time for me to move away. For good."

"It's not the same with them," she whispered desperately. Tessa didn't know how to live anymore without knowing that Isaac had her back. Charlie Abbott had been right, Isaac had given her the one thing she needed, someone who was unconditionally always there for her.

"I know, but one day it will be different, one day you'll learn how to trust them. I have to go now. Goodbye, Tessa." Isaac had almost disappeared into the foggy woods when he stopped and came back, "I have to know, Tessa, I have to know why you never turned me in. I have to know why you helped me, why you always came to me when you needed help."

Studying him soberly, "because you would have done anything for her."

"For Rebecca?"

Tessa nodded, "you loved Rebecca more than anything. She was your daughter and you did everything you could for her, unlike . . ." she trailed off.

"Unlike your own parents," Isaac finished softly.

"Patrick never came back after Jake, and Emilie never even noticed I was gone, but you . . . you were always there for me when I needed you, you were like the father I always dreamed of having. Besides that's why you let me go that day. You saw me kill Jake and you let me go, knowing that I might tell someone about you, because I reminded you of Rebecca."

"You knew I was there when Jake killed your friend?" Isaac's eyes grew wide with surprise.

"I guess I'm not as bad a liar as you think."

* * * * *

*Sixteen Years Ago*
*Saturday Night*

*She had to be quick, she didn't have a lot of time.*

*To be honest, Tessa thought, it was a miracle she had managed to get away at all. All day Daniel had hardly left her side, and her grandparents had insisted that the nanny not let her out of sight. Tessa had found it more than a little irritating, all she wanted was to be left alone to sort things out. She had played along though, sitting quietly where she was told, watching movies with her brother, picking at her dinner, listening to the stories the nanny read her before bed.*

*Once she'd been left alone in her room she'd thrown on some clothes, crept to the stables and found her horse. Tessa didn't really like riding, she only did it with Ellie because her best friend adored horses, but it was the only way she could think of to get all the way back to the house where she had been held captive.*

*Tessa wasn't sure whether she was ready to be back here or not, but one thing she was sure of was that she had to find out what had happened to Ellie's body. So she had ridden Mercury here and tied him to a tree not far away then walked the rest of the distance to the stables, where the first thing her eyes saw was Ellie's body lying discarded by the door through which she and her best friend had sought freedom.*

*Slowly she approached the body and knelt beside it. Ellie looked just as she had on the day she had died, exactly one week ago today. To Tessa it felt like so much longer than a week. All those days sitting in the hospital made it feel like months had flown past since she escaped, the whole sequence of events seemed like a dream. Maybe Jake had never really kidnapped them, maybe they had never been taken to this house of horrors, maybe they had never really escaped, maybe she had never killed Jake, maybe the whole thing was just a terrible nightmare. Unfortunately all those maybes were wishful thinking. This was all too real.*

*Standing up she crept to the stables, dragging open the heavy door and tiptoeing inside. The room looked just as she had remembered it, only now all the horses were gone, and one of the huge feeding troughs had been moved to cover the trapdoor through which she and Ellie had escaped.*

*Returning to Ellie's body, Tessa reached out a hand to touch her friend but then couldn't bring herself to make contact with the body that looked half dead and half asleep, instead she went to retrieve the shovel from her horse.*

*Scanning the area to decide on the best spot to bury Ellie's body she decided it was fitting to dig the grave where her friend had died. So planting herself next to the stable doors she began to dig. She wasn't sure how long she stood there in the moonlight, shoveling dirt until the pile beside her grew taller than she was, the hole finally deep enough to contain a child's small body. Now there was nothing left to do but put Ellie's corpse into it's final resting place and cover it up, but Tessa found she couldn't do it, couldn't even move.*

*"Here you go," a voice spoke behind her, quietly commanding in the silent night.*

*Tessa realized she wasn't surprised that someone had been watching her. As the man gently eased her to the side, pushing her down to the soft ground to rest, while he lifted Ellie's body, placed it in the grave and began to refill the hole, she found herself feeling like she'd always known him.*

*When at last he was finished he handed her back the shovel and sat beside her, his warm brown eyes studying her. "You're a smart, resourceful little girl," he said at last.*

*Tessa remembered the figure that had watched her run after she'd killed Jake. Watched but done nothing to stop her, and she knew that John Doe was not going to do anything to hurt her.*

*"I'm going to tell you a story," John Doe's usually shuttered eyes had unlocked, revealing a mess of pain and grief and guilt. "I once had a little girl just like you, pretty and smart and lively and everything a father could wish for in a daughter. But one day she was taken from me. Taken away from the people she loved and the life she'd lived. Taken by people who saw her as*

*nothing more than a way to make money. They took her from me and I vowed that I would find her, that I would find the men who took her and make them pay. And so here I am. I left behind everything, my family, friends, job, home, my life, I left it all to find Rebecca. That was ten years ago, ten long years. My little girl is eighteen now but I cannot give up hope. The only thing that keeps me going is knowing that one day, one day, I'll get my baby back."*

*Tessa didn't know what to say, but she did know that this man loved his daughter far more than Patrick and Emilie loved her. And she knew that he had watched her kill a man and yet he hadn't stopped her, he hadn't grabbed her and taken her back to the horrible basement. He had let her escape.*

*Tentatively she slipped her tiny hand into his big one and squeezed. He squeezed it back and smiled down at her, tears glistening in his glowing brown eyes.*

*"Little Tessa, you are a special girl, you need to remember that always, no matter what happens. You have to be strong, and wise, and self-reliant, but if you ever need help you come to me, okay?"*

*Nodding she gripped his hand tighter, feeling for the first time in her life like she had someone to turn to when things got too much. She understood what he did for a living, selling little girls to men who wanted to do despicable things to them, but even though she could never condone what he did she understood why he did it. He did it because he loved his daughter and because he would do whatever it took to get her back.*

*"Come along, child," the man lifted her up and carried her to her horse, setting her up on Mercury's back. "I know it doesn't seem like it right now but one day things will get better, one day you'll be happy."*

*Mercury trotted a few steps before Tessa stopped and turned him around. "What's your real name?" she asked John Doe.*

*Giving her a cheeky smile, his eyes had resumed their hooded look, his emotions once again tucked safely away and Tessa didn't think he was going to answer, but then he tipped his hat, "Isaac Worthington."*

*When Isaac had disappeared into the night she chirped to her horse and headed for home, thinking all the way about Isaac's lost little daughter and how unfair life could be. By the time Tessa reached the stables on her grandparents estate she was exhausted, she just managed to put away Mercury and stumble through the gardens back up to the house.*

*All was quiet in the big mansion, no lights glinted in the windows, and as she crept through the back door nothing stirred inside. Weaving through the halls to her bedroom, a room that looked too neat and orderly to belong to an eleven year old, when she got there she moved around the room collecting each of her teddy bears and dumping them on the bed. Once she'd collected them all she crossed to her desk to retrieve a pair of scissors, taking them with her to the bed she began to chop the teddy bears into pieces.*

*A tangle of emotions was bubbling too strongly inside her and she knew if she didn't do something she was going to explode. When all that was left of her teddy bears was a pile of limbs and heads and stuffing she grabbed a bag and began to put the pieces inside so her grandparents or the nanny or one of the housecleaners didn't stumble upon it. Then she took the bag, dragged her desk chair over to the closet, climbed up on it and tucked the bag safely away in the very back corner.*

*Once everything was back in place, Tessa collected her pillow, left her room and scurried quickly to her brother's room. Tessa couldn't bear spending the night alone anymore. From now on she'd wait for Daniel to fall asleep and then creep into his room, maybe his comforting presence would help her to sleep more than an hour or so at a time. As soon as REM sleep hit it brought with it terrifying nightmares.*

*Placing her pillow at the end of Daniel's bed, Tessa rested her head on it, wondering if she'd ever be able close her eyes again without seeing all those lost girls. Before she drifted off Isaac's words echoed in her head, 'one day you'll be happy', he'd said but Tessa thought she was doomed to spend the rest of her life alone and miserable.*

\* \* \* \* \*

6:46 A.M.

"Come here. Come on, let go. It's going to be okay."

Hands grasped hers and gently but firmly unclamped them and she was pulled to her feet.

261

"Hey it's going to be alright, I'm here now," Skylar kept hold of her hands as he maneuvered her away from Parker so the paramedics could get to him. "You're wet, Tessa, what happened? Are you okay?"

"Dino," she mumbled, her eyes straying to where his body lay just feet away.

Following her gaze, Skylar's grip on her tightened when he saw that Dino's pants were down around his ankles. "Tessa, did he rape you?"

Shuddering involuntarily as she remembered how close Dino had come to raping her. Hands trembling violently as she moved them to re-zip her pants, unable to shake the feeling of Dino's hands on her.

"Tessa? Did Dino rape you?" Skylar's panic-stricken voice repeated.

"He was going to but . . ." she trailed off, not really wanting to bring Isaac onto the police's radar.

"But he was interrupted," Skylar supplied, relief radiating off him. "I saw someone running off and since that jacket," he gestured to Isaac's jacket that the medic's had discarded to examine and bandage Parker's wound, "doesn't belong to you, and that's Dino I'm going to guess it was your friend John Doe."

"Isaac," she whispered. "He said one day I'd be happy but . . ." her eyes riveted to her husband's white face.

Shaking her, Skylar turned her away so that she was looking at him, "but nothing, Parker's going to be fine. Are you hurt?" he asked, running his hands down her arms and legs searching for any injuries, then feeling the back of her head. She hissed as his fingers found the lump at the base of her skull that she'd received on the boat. "This is the size of a golf ball," he admonished.

"It's fine," Tessa murmured, trying to turn back to her husband, "I need to check on Parker."

Refusing to release her, "right now you need to stay here with me. Now tell me what happened."

"I was waiting for Parker just like I told him I would, when I found Cassandra and Olivia Stanton. I left them at the house, did you . . .?"

"I found the girls," Skylar assured her, "they're fine, they're waiting in my car."

Relieved that at least the girls were safe, "after I sent them to wait in the mansion Dino showed up. He had a gun, he said if I didn't go with him he'd kill them. He took me on his boat," she spoke emotionlessly as though these things had happened to a complete stranger. "I told him the truth about his mother and Jake, and he told me that Cordelia was the one who sent Jake after me . . ."

"Cordelia did what?" Skylar repeated incredulously, bending over so he could look her in the eye, horror written all over his face.

"Because she hated me so much," the barrier keeping back her emotions was beginning to falter. "Jake is Winter's father. Dino came at me with a knife. We struggled and fell into the water. Then the next thing I remember I was telling Parker about Cordelia. We were going to come back to the house but Dino came and he," tears began to trickle down her cheeks, "he shot Parker. Then he was going to rape me but Isaac shot him."

"Isaac is John Doe?" Skylar confirmed as a swarm of police officers descended on the area.

Nodding distractedly, Tessa hadn't realized just how exhausted she was. She hadn't slept in forty-eight hours and everything that had happened in the past week had caught up to her all at once. Every inch of her body hurt, her lungs and throat were still rough from the water, her stomach continued to turn somersaults.

"We're ready to move," one of the EMT's called out.

"We're coming," Skylar returned, then eyed her carefully, "hey, you okay? You're looking a little green."

"I'm so tired," she rested against Skylar, letting him hold her up, as she began to shiver. "And I don't feel so good."

"You don't look so good either," Skylar agreed. "How much water did you swallow?"

"I don't know. A lot I think." Tessa didn't really remember much after she and Dino fell into the water, it was basically all a blank until she and Parker were talking about Cordelia.

"Did you pass out?" Skylar pressed.

"I'm not sure," she was shaking so hard it was making it difficult to concentrate. "I think . . . I think I stopped breathing." She had a vague memory of Parker begging her to breathe.

"Alright, I want you to sit here and let someone check you out," Skylar tried to push her down.

"I'm fine," she insisted, beginning to cough. "I just need to know Parker's going to be okay."

"Okay come on," he agreed reluctantly. "Lets get you both to the hospital," keeping a hold of her elbow as they went to follow the paramedics and Parker.

They hadn't gone more than a couple of steps when her stomach protested wildly. "I think I'm going to be sick." Tessa wrenched herself away from Skylar and fell to her knees.

"I need some help here," Skylar yelled as he crouched beside her and held back her hair as she threw up.

Pressing her eyes closed to try and quell the rolling in her stomach, she was starting to get very sleepy.

"Hey, Tessa, I'm Veronica."

Opening her eyes again to see the kind face of one of the paramedics smiling at her. "Is Parker okay?" she asked immediately.

"Your husband's hanging in there," Veronica assured her. "We're just a little worried about you at the moment."

Too tired to do anything but sit patiently while Veronica draped a blanket over her shoulders, took her pulse and checked her blood pressure, felt the bump on the back of her head and shone a light in her eyes.

"Okay can you take a deep breath for me?" the medic's smile

still in place as she positioned the stethoscope against Tessa's back.

Tessa tried to take a deep breath but ended up in another coughing fit. Her ribs, already broken in the accident, had been furthered damaged when Parker performed CPR, and the pressure and pain was now reaching overwhelming.

Wrapping an arm around her Skylar zeroed in on the EMT, "is she okay?"

"She's . . ." Veronica began.

Speaking over the top of her Skylar continued, "she was in a car accident a week ago, and she was shot in the arm a few days after that. I think she hit her head just before she went in the water. She said she stopped breathing . . ."

"She probably has water in her lungs," Veronica jumped in to explain.

"Where's the other ambulance?" Skylar demanded. "There were supposed to be two on their way here."

"They got held up at an accident on the way but another ambulance has been sent," Veronica reassured him soothingly.

"I think I'm going to be sick again," Tessa lifted her weary head from Skylar's shoulder, as both her friend and the medic helped her kneel up. She was shaking again as she threw up, icy cold from the top of her head to the tip of her toes, and so tired that she just wanted to curl up and sleep for a thousand years.

Voices were jabbering above her but Tessa ignored them as a velvety blackness began to wash over her and she started to feel closer to Parker. She was half aware of Skylar picking her up, carrying her, ordering her to stay with him. She tried to do as he instructed but then Parker called her name and she gave in to sleep.

# SEPTEMBER 13<sup>TH</sup>

11:18 A.M.

Isaac was glad he'd gone back to see Tessa one last time.

He was also infinitely glad that he had killed that wretched Dino Rollino. He had never wanted Jake to bring his baby brother to join them all those years ago. He had known even back then that Dino was going to be trouble. At the time he'd gone along with it because he had bigger issues than having an idiot work for him, and it wasn't like any of his other men were intellectually superior, all he cared about was finding Rebecca. In his workers all he needed was tough, scared and under his thumb, he always ensured he had something to hold over their heads as a little extra insurance that they wouldn't go to the police.

To be honest Isaac would have liked a little extra time to punish Dino. Not just for disobeying orders but because of what he had been about to do to Tessa. Isaac found it sickening that any man could lay his hands on a woman without her consent. To do it to a child is beyond despicable. Isaac had never touched a child in his life. He hated that he had to hurt children to accomplish his goals but he had turned off his emotions a long time ago, because as long as he held onto them he would never be able to do what had to be done if he was going to get Rebecca back.

Isaac had left behind everything when his only daughter disappeared. He still remembered that day perfectly. A bright sunny summer's day, he'd taken Rebecca to the park where they had ridden their bikes and eaten ice-cream until he'd met an old friend. His eight year old had quickly become bored while her father talked to his friend and begged to be allowed to play on the playground. Reluctantly he had agreed, and had kept watch as she slid down the slide and swung on the swings. The last time he had seen her she was climbing high atop the jungle gym. He'd only looked away for a second but that was all it had taken for someone to grab her and disappear.

Etched in his mind for all eternity was his frantic search of the playground, the call to the police, their horrible questions when they arrived asking him if he hurt his daughter, if he abused her, if he had killed her. When they had asked him if he had killed his little girl he had lost it, swung at the officer who had the gall to even suggest something so preposterous, anyone who knew him knew that he was devoted to his daughter. The officers had been good about it, not pressed charges or anything, said they understood he was under a lot of pressure and apologized for having to ask him those questions, but that was the second when he knew what he had to do. When his fist connected with the detective's nose sending a squirt of blood down the man's face it was like his daughter's pain and fear became a living entity inside him and Isaac knew that there was nothing in the world he wouldn't do to get Rebecca back.

While the police had floundered around he had begun his own investigation into his baby girl's disappearance. He started skipping work, spending his days mixing with unsavory characters as he chased down leads. In the end he managed to find out that child traffickers had abducted Rebecca and shipped her out of England to America. There had not been a moment's hesitation in his decision to go after her, leaving behind his wife, his elderly parents, two brothers and a sister, seven nieces and nephews, and a job that he loved.

In America he had attached himself to a pedophile ring, talking the talk and playing along, eventually arranging an appointment with a man who had promised to sell him a child. At the meeting he gathered all the information he could from the man before stabbing him in the heart. As Isaac had stood there watching blood fountaining out of the body he realized that he felt nothing. No regret, no remorse, no sense of power. He had just taken a life, the first of many in those first years, and it meant nothing to him, it was merely a necessary step in his quest to find Rebecca.

After that he joined and worked his way up the child selling organization. Quickly building a reputation as a cold hearted, nimble, brainy, ruthless man, feared by all he came into contact with. At last, three years after Rebecca had been kidnapped, he obtained the top position taking over the business and making it more profitable than it had ever been before. Isaac always kept enough money to survive but he donated millions a year to children's charities of all kinds.

Isaac regretted that he had to cause pain to innocent little girls in order to find his own lost little girl. In his room he kept a photo of each and every little girl he had ever abducted. On the ceiling above his bed was a large poster of Rebecca, the photo taken just days before her disappearance and used by the police in their campaign to find his child.

Snapping back to reality as an announcement was made informing passengers of the last boarding call for his flight, he gathered his bag and headed for the plane. Isaac didn't know where he was going and it made little difference, there was nothing left for him here. Tessa had her family and friends, he had slaughtered his men shortly after releasing the girls, and the police here knew too much about him. Besides it was best to keep moving, Rebecca was still out there somewhere and the only thing that would stop him looking for her was death.

With a last look out the airport window he headed onto the plane, focusing on the belief, as he always did, that one day he would be reunited with his daughter.

\* \* \* \* \*

4:41 P.M.

"Hey, how're you doing?"

"I'm okay," Tessa assured Skylar as she curled up in the chair by the window of her hospital room. Both she and Parker had been brought here last night, she had been treated for pulmonary edema, a build up of fluid in her lungs. Her body completely fatigued from everything it had been through, it had been several hours before she finally regained consciousness. By that time Parker was out of surgery and doing as well as could be expected. She hadn't been to see him yet however she had had a constant stream of visitors to keep her occupied, but she had really enjoyed the last hour or so on her own, it had given her time to think.

"Tessa, I'm really sorry," Skylar announced suddenly. "For not believing you when Parker was gone. I really hate how strained things are between us. You're like my baby sister and I want it to be the way it used to between us. I'm really sorry," he said again with guilty desperation.

"I know that you are," she told him, crossing the room to wrap her arms around his waist. "I forgive you, I already had, but I'm sorry I didn't say the words before now."

Squeezing her tightly, "come on, let's get you back in bed, you're still weak, you need to rest."

Allowing Skylar to lead her to the bed, she was still so tired, the experiences of the last week had left her drained.

"We have to talk about Isaac," Skylar told her, once he'd tucked her in.

"On the record or off?"

"Both," Skylar perched on the edge of the bed.

"I'm not going to tell you anything to help you find him," Tessa cautioned, after everything they'd been through together she couldn't bring herself to turn Isaac in.

"It was Isaac that you went to for help when Lachlan abducted Parker, he was the one who found Parker's car, wasn't he?"

"Yes, it was Isaac's men that found the car," she confirmed.

"And I'm going to guess that it was Isaac who kept Dylan Riley busy the weekend Chelsea, Jasper and Tanner fell of the face of the planet," Skylar continued.

Once again affirming this with a nod, "it was the first time I went to Isaac for help. I didn't know what else to do, it was the only way I could think of to safely get them away. Dylan hovered around me all the time, following me everywhere I went, I couldn't let him get his hands on Tanner."

"Why didn't you go to Isaac in the beginning? When Dylan first started abusing you?"

"I though about it," she told him, actually she had laid awake many a night debating whether to ask Isaac to take care of Dylan for her.

"Would he have killed Dylan?"

Tessa nodded, "and he would have made sure he suffered first. I guess I never asked him to kill Dylan because it would make me like him."

"What did you have to do for him in return?"

"I don't know what you mean," she said innocently.

"Come on, Tessa, people like him don't help others without getting something in return," Skylar eyed her seriously. "Isaac took care of Dylan for you, what did you have to do for him?"

Sighing and editing the story in her head so as not to share too much, "Isaac's daughter was abducted twenty-six years ago, she was eight. The police had no leads but Isaac wouldn't give up, he managed to track down the people who took his daughter . . ."

"Let me guess, they dealt in selling little girls to pedophiles," Skylar interrupted.

"Isaac managed to infiltrate a ring of child traffickers, worked his way up to the top. He thought it was the only way he could find and finally rescue Rebecca, but he still hadn't been able to locate her. That's what he wanted me to do, find his daughter."

"Did you?"

Twirling one of her curls around her finger, Tessa had honestly believed that telling Isaac that Rebecca was dead was the only way he would stop hurting more children to find his own. Obviously she had been wrong. Isaac had never stopped because he knew that she had lied, he'd known that Rebecca was still out there somewhere.

"Tessa?" Skylar pressed gently. "Did you find Rebecca?"

"Yes I found her," she replied softly. "She was twenty-two by then, a drug addict and working as a prostitute."

"Did you tell Isaac that?"

"No," she answered even more quietly. "I told him Rebecca was dead. I thought that would make him stop," she continued desperately, needing Skylar to believe her. "I thought that if he thought Rebecca was dead then there would be no need for him to keep doing what he'd been doing."

"But he didn't stop."

"I didn't know," she implored. "I didn't know that he knew I'd lied. You have to believe me, Skylar, I thought he'd stopped. It wasn't until we found Clara that I found out he was still doing it. I thought he'd stopped, if I'd known he was still kidnapping and selling little girls I would have done something. I promise, Skylar, I didn't know . . ."

"Shh," Skylar soothed, pulling her against him. "It's okay, I believe you. What did you have to give him in exchange for his help with Parker?"

"When I went to him for help with Parker I thought he'd stopped with children, I knew he still dealt in drugs and guns, but that was it," catching herself before she became too worked up she took a deep, calming breath. "He wanted me to pose as his wife at some function at his 'legitimate' job."

"What does Isaac do?"

Deciding it was better not to answer that, she'd already told Skylar more than was safe. Tessa was pretty sure that Isaac would have left the country by now but wherever he was he didn't need the police on his tail. "You can't tell anyone else about Isaac," she informed him.

"Tessa, I'm a police officer," he reminded her.

"I won't back you up. I'll say that I was in shock, that I wasn't thinking clearly, that anything I said to you was just shock induced delusions. I won't help you bring him down," she set her jaw determinedly.

"When he's stronger we'll tell Parker . . ."

Cutting him off, "no, Skylar. I mean you can't tell *anyone*, including Parker. I can't explain things between me and Isaac. I abhor what he does but he really loves Rebecca and he has always been there for me, no questions asked."

"You're not going to tell Parker about Isaac?"

"Parker would hunt Isaac down, I can't let that happen."

"What does he have over you?"

"It's hard to explain," she answered vaguely.

"Try," Skylar pushed.

"Isaac was there the night I . . . I killed Jake," it was still hard to say those words aloud. "He saw me run and he let me go. When I went back to look for Ellie's body he was there again. He helped me bury her and then he told me about Rebecca. Isaac loved his daughter so much. He had given up everything to find her, and even though he'd gone about it the wrong way . . . it was the so unlike the way my . . ."

"The way your parents loved you," Skylar supplied. "Tessa, do you love him?"

Many a night she had laid awake trying to sort out her feelings for Isaac, so far she had not come up with an answer. "Maybe," she replied at last. "I don't know how I feel about him. All I know is that Isaac wasn't always an evil man and I guess I always wanted to believe that deep down inside of him that person still existed." What she didn't say was that holding on to that belief was like keeping alive the part of her that existed before Jake.

"Isaac's responsible for the choices that he made," Skylar kissed the top of her head. "You're not responsible for his actions."

"Yeah right," she wiggled free from his grip. "Tell that to the hundreds of people whose lives I ruined by not turning Isaac in. To all the people who's lives are going to be ruined because I still can't bring myself to turn him in." Shrugging indifferently, "Isaac said on the day he told me about Rebecca that one day I would be happy, I didn't believe him then and I don't believe it now."

"Tessa, that's not true, you are happy. You have Winter and Daniel, and me, and so many other friends who care about you, and you have Parker . . ."

"Parker's mad at me because he thinks I went off on my own after I told him I'd wait for him . . ."

"So just tell him that Dino held a gun on you and told you that he'd kill Cassandra and Olivia Stanton if you didn't go with him."

"I'm not going to tell him that," Tessa snapped.

"What?" Skylar's brow creased in confusion.

"I'm not going to pressure him to be with me, Skylar. Even if I did decide to go after Dino myself that is none of his business. Dino was my problem . . ."

"You're just being stubborn," Skylar protested.

"What you hadn't figured that out about me after knowing me like two minutes?" she scoffed, remembering how she had infuriated both Skylar and Parker when they first met by refusing to tell them who wanted her and her friends dead.

"If you're scared to tell him about Isaac I'm sure he'll understand," Skylar reasoned. "You were just a little girl. A little girl who had just been to hell and back. Isaac filled something in you that was missing, he gave you something to hold on to, made you feel safe, Parker will understand that."

"I don't want anyone else to know about Isaac. Promise me, Skylar, promise me you won't tell him," she demanded.

"If you don't tell him he's not going to understand why you let Isaac go."

"He doesn't have to. If he loves me then he should just accept that I know what I'm doing. I told you I won't pressure him to be with me, that's not who I am."

"You're impossible, that's what you are," Skylar complained.

"Promise me, Skylar," she insisted, not about to be sidetracked.

Sighing reluctantly, "I promise."

They sat in silence for a moment, Tessa wanted to ask him something, but she was struggling to gather enough courage to make the words come out of her mouth. "Skylar?" she began at last, catching the timidity in her tone.

"What is it, Tess?"

"Elisabeth said that, that I was brave, when Jake took us." The idea that she had been brave had literally never occurred to her.

"You were, Tessa," Skylar nodded seriously.

"But I got Ellie killed," she reminded him. Confused by everyone's reactions to what had happened to her. Tessa had thought she knew how she felt about her abduction but now she wasn't so sure.

"No, honey," he held her gaze, "a horrible set of circumstances outside your control got your friend killed."

"I left those girls behind." Even if she wasn't responsible for Ellie's death, she was certainly responsible for not trying to get help to those poor little girls.

"Tessa," Skylar took her hands in his, "even if you had told someone right away what had happened to you, there were no guarantees that it would have changed anything. Isaac could have killed them or spirited them away before anyone was able to get to them. I wish that you had had someone there at the time to guide you, support you, get you the help you needed to process this and deal with it, but you have that now, okay?"

"Okay," she nodded her agreement, it seemed somewhere along the way she had actually grown to believe her family and friends would be there for her.

"You need to consider getting yourself some professional help so you can come to terms with what happened to you. I know how you feel about psychiatrists but this is important, you need to deal with this so you can move forward."

"I already talked to Charlie Abbott," she confessed. "I was thinking maybe I might go talk to him again."

Relief washed over Skylar's face, and she thought he looked a little proud of her. "Good. That's a weight off my mind. I worry about you," he added when she raised an eyebrow. "Maybe one day you'll be able to accept that you were not to blame for what happened that weekend."

"Maybe," Tessa wasn't sure she could ever really believe that, but for the first time ever it was an actual possibility. "But I still wish Parker didn't know what happened that weekend with Jake. How is he ever going to look at me the same way again? It was bad enough that he knew what I let Dylan Riley do to me, but to know that I let Jake do it to me too . . ."

"There was no *let*, Tessa," Skylar said sharply. "Dylan Riley sexually abused you, and Jake kidnapped and raped you."

"Jake told me to go and lie down on that mattress, and I did. I knew what he was going to do and I let him do it," she was fighting tears and quickly losing the battle.

"That's not *let*, Tessa. Jake was going to kill Eleanor if you didn't do what he said. You were a victim. Nothing that happened was because you *let* it happen. Oh, Tessa," he pulled her into his arms as she began to cry. "Sometimes you break my heart. I wish I knew what to say to you to help you."

"You do help me," she rested against his chest and let her tears flow and Skylar's arms comfort her. A part of her brain knew that Skylar was right, she hadn't wanted Jake or Dylan to do what they did, and if she had of been able to stop them she would have in a heartbeat. She knew that, just as she knew that most rape victims blamed themselves, but knowing was different than *knowing*. "I don't know what I'd do without you. I just wish I wasn't so messed up, that so many people hadn't played with my life."

"Tessa, did your father . . .?"

Her initial shock at Skylar actually posing that question to her was quickly replaced by a sense of resignation. "No," she took a stab at denial. Skylar said nothing, just waited patiently until she was ready. "He tried," she said at last.

"How old were you?"

"Six."

"How did it happen?"

Unable to suppress a shudder at the memory, Skylar's arms tightened around her. "I woke up one night, he was in my room."

"Did he touch you?" Skylar asked gently.

Head still resting against Skylar's chest she bobbed it up and down. "I told him to stop, we were at my grandparent's house so I yelled for them. They came, said they'd handle it, I told them if he ever did it again I'd go to the police. He never tried anything with me after that, but sometimes when he looked at me I could tell he wanted to. I was so relieved when he left."

"Does Parker know?"

"Yes. He asked me outright a couple of months after we started dating. I'd already been so vague and closed off about everything, I felt bad, Parker had shared so much about his childhood with me, so I told him. Skylar, it wasn't just me, Patrick was sexually abusing Cordelia for years. What he did to her is probably the main reason why she went insane. I think it's why Cordelia hated me so much. She thought that she and Patrick were in love, when Emilie got pregnant with me it was like he'd been cheating on her, and then she saw me as a rival for Patrick's affection. Its all so messed up I can't even believe its real. I can't believe any of this is real."

Before either of them had a chance to say more the door to her room swung open. "What on earth is wrong with you?"

Gathering herself before she faced her brother. "Hi, Daniel."

"Don't give me that butter wouldn't melt in your mouth, innocent little angel smile," Daniel ranted. "You're in the hospital three times in nine days and you don't even call me?"

"Two times," she corrected, assuming that Skylar had been the one to tattle and call her big brother.

"Wyatt said you were in a car accident, then you got shot, and then someone tried to drown you," Daniel frowned, clearly Skylar had filled him in on *everything* that had happened. "That's three times."

"The bullet only skimmed my arm, so I didn't really need to go to the hospital after that," she informed him, "besides I'm fine."

"You always say that," her brother growled.

"I'm going to leave you two to catch up, I'll go check on Parker," Skylar announced, looking pleased to have an escape route from the tense room.

"Remember your promise," she reminded him before he slipped out the door.

"I remember," he told her unhappily.

"And everything we talked about, it's just between us for now."

"Tessa . . ." he began.

"Please, Skylar," right now she didn't want anyone else knowing that she was going to be seeing a psychiatrist.

"Okay." His frown softened a little, "I'll come check on you later."

"What was that all about?" Daniel demanded once they were alone.

"Nothing," she shook her head.

"I know you've been angry at me lately," Daniel gave her his hurt little boy look, the greeny-blue eyes so like her own stared pitifully back at her. "But why wouldn't you call me, Tessie? Wyatt told me this all had something to do with what happened when you were little but he wouldn't tell me any details."

Gazing into her brother's earnest face, the prospect of having to explain once again everything that happened with Ellie and Jake and Isaac brought tears pricking the back of her eyes. Without a word, Daniel was sitting on the bed in front of her, crushing her fiercely against his chest and stroking her hair.

"Why didn't you ever tell me?" Daniel asked.

"I wanted to," she whispered against her brother's shoulder, twisting her hands into his shirt and clinging to him. "I was going to, the day that I came home from the hospital, but then I saw Emilie, and she didn't even know I was gone, and I . . . I just couldn't."

"What happened to you, Tessie?"

Without leaving the safety of her brother's arms she halting repeated the story. This was the third time she had told it and it was still no easier.

Daniel didn't say anything when she was finished, just tightened his grip on her. "You used to come and sleep in my room, after it happened." he said at last. "You'd sneak in once you thought I was asleep, but I always knew you were there. I liked that you knew you could come to me when you were scared, that even though you couldn't speak you knew you were safe with me."

"I didn't know you knew I used to do that," she whispered.

"You were always too stubborn to just ask for help," he whispered back.

Tessa wondered whether Skylar was right, whether she was just being stubborn by not telling Parker about Isaac. Before she had time to make up her mind, there came a small knock on her door.

"Come in," she called, gently extricating herself from Daniel grip.

Three little heads peeped through the open crack.

"Hi, girls," Tessa greeted Cassandra and Olivia Stanton, and Clara Meyers.

"We just wanted to come and say thank you," Cassandra took the lead.

"You saved us," Olivia added, running over and climbing up onto the bed to hug her.

"You girls saved yourself," she reminded them, returning the child's embrace.

"Yeah but if you hadn't found us when you did we might not have made it much further," Olivia countered determinedly.

"You would have made it. Anyone who's strong enough and smart enough to get away from Dino and John Doe would have found a way to survive," Tessa smiled at the sisters. "Besides I hear that I have you two to thank for telling Skylar and the medics where Dino took me. And . . ." she addressed Clara who remained huddled by the door, "I hear that you were the one who told Parker where I'd be. If you hadn't then I wouldn't be here right now."

Looking distinctly unconvinced, Clara wouldn't budge from the doorway.

Climbing from the bed, ignoring a wave of lingering dizziness, and going to the girl, "I mean it, Clara. If you hadn't told Parker about Dino being obsessed with boats and the water then he would have wasted hours looking for me and I would have drowned."

"Really?" Clara asked, still uncertain.

"Really," Tessa assured her, watching a smile light the girl's face. "How did you guys meet up?" she asked changing the subject.

"Detective Wyatt suggested it to our mom's," Cassandra replied. "To help us deal with things. Kind of like a support group," she rolled her eyes as though she thought the idea implied she was a baby, but Tessa caught the haunted gleam in her eyes, the girl had a lot to learn about hiding her emotions.

"You girls should be grateful that you have someone who understands to help you deal with all of this," she told them, wondering whether if she had it would have changed things.

"You didn't?" Cassandra asked, her eyes gone deadly serious.

"No, I didn't," she went wearily back to the bed and sank down onto it, Daniel immediately wrapping an arm around her shoulders.

"You escaped too?" Olivia asked with surprising gentleness, and Tessa turned to study the girl.

"Yes. Dino's brother Jake took me and my friend Ellie from our school when we were eleven. He took us to the house where I found you two. I noticed that the dimensions of the basement didn't add up and realized there had to be a way out. I found it, waited till the guards were busy then took Ellie and we escaped. Only Jake found us. He . . ." she paused to consider her wording, "he wanted me, when I stood up to him he killed Ellie, when he came at me I stabbed him, he died."

"You killed him?" Clara asked in a small voice, crossing to stand beside the bed.

"Yes."

"That's so brave," Cassandra was staring at her in awe.

There was that word again. "Thank you, sweetie, but it was very hard to deal with and I didn't have any family or friends to help me, so you girls should count yourselves extremely lucky to have each other. And you have me too, I'm going to give you my number and you can call me any time."

"Anytime?" Clara's voice trembled.

"Anytime," she confirmed, taking the girl's hand and squeezing it tightly.

"Is that your brother?" Olivia asked pointing at Daniel.

"Yeah this is my older brother Daniel," she informed them, watching as the girls descended on him, within seconds they were giggling at his jokes and hanging off his every word.

Resting her tired head back against the pillows, as Tessa watched them she realized what a strong group of girls they were, especially or maybe because of everything they had been through. Remembering the strong, independent woman she used to be before she met Parker. As awful as it had been confronting Dino, it had been somewhat comforting to deal with him on her own.

That was that way Tessa was used to doing things. She loved Parker, and she adored being married to him, but she felt comfortable dealing with problems on her own, especially problems of her own creating. Tessa also knew that it was very important to Parker that she trust him implicitly, that she turn to him for every little thing. She was beginning to wonder just how she and Parker were going to work things out when they were both so inherently different.

\* \* \* \* \*

10:12 P.M.

"It turns out that one of the original seven girls we thought were related to Tessa's case wasn't abducted by the child trafficking ring."

"What are you talking about?" Parker asked his partner, his brain still a little gooey from the anesthetic and painkillers.

"For some reason John Doe let the other girls go," Wyatt explained. "There were ten of them. Found in a huddle at the side of a road by a passing motorist. All the girls were checked out at the hospital and have been reunited with their families. Libby Marks wasn't among the group found . . ."

"So? He probably just sold her already," Parker spat out, still sickened by the whole thing.

"The girls weren't the only thing we found," Wyatt continued.

"What else?" he shifted irritably trying to find a comfortable position between the tubes and wires that draped from his body to the machines and gadgets beside his bed.

"You want me to come back later?" Wyatt asked.

"No, I want you to tell me what's going on."

"Not far away from where the girls were found there were six cars parked just out of view of the road, the driver of each of the cars had had his throat slashed."

"John Doe killed his men and left them by the side of the road for anyone to find and released the girls who he knows are going to talk?" he clarified.

"Seems so," Wyatt nodded. "And the girls have all relayed the same story as Tessa. They were taken by a man with a child, so none of them thought they were in danger, they were brought to a big house and kept in a small cell in the basement. They all knew Dino and John Doe, and were able to ID the men from the cars, all of the men were on Tessa's list. But that's not all, John Doe also left us a list of the names, accompanied by a picture, of each of the girls he abducted and sold over the last twenty years, Libby Marks wasn't on that list."

"Maybe he left her off by accident?" Parker suggested.

"I don't think so," Wyatt contradicted. "Each of the girls that was found, and the five girls that we found at the house, were on that list. Plus I showed it to Tessa and there were some names she remembered. And the photos we found at the house where Tess was taken, they were all on the list too."

"So Libby Marks . . .?"

"Was killed by her mother," Wyatt filled him in.

"What?" Parker was sure he must have misheard.

"Apparently when she was confronted with the information that her daughter was not among the abducted girls she broke down. Confessed that she was having an affair with her nineteen-year-old next-door neighbor, and that Libby walked in on the two of them together at her birthday party. The mom freaked out and faced with a choice between her lover and her daughter she picked her lover. Killed Libby the next day because she couldn't kill her daughter on her birthday. She and her boyfriend buried the body in a vacant lot a few blocks away, she took us to the site and we dug up the body."

"Have you seen Tessa?" he asked after a few moments of silence, his wife was the only one who hadn't been in to visit him.

"Yeah, I think she's avoiding you because she thinks you're mad at her for being alone with Dino," Wyatt explained.

"I am mad at her." Not so angry though that his first words

upon regaining consciousness weren't asking about how Tessa was doing.

"Parker, there's something you should . . ." Wyatt began.

"Hey, Parker," Tessa appeared in the doorway. "Skylar," she shot his partner a pointed look before crossing to the bed. "Are you okay?"

"Never better," Parker gave her a grim smile, feeling his anger fizzle a little at the sight of her pale cheeks, or maybe it was just the pain kicking back in and dulling everything else.

"So what are you two chatting about?" Tessa continued to stare intently at Wyatt.

"Nothing much," his partner filled her in. "I was just telling Parker about Libby Marks."

"Yeah her mom . . ." Tessa shuddered, probably remembering the time her own mother had attempted to kill her.

"Alright I'm going to let you two talk," Wyatt stood. "I'll come see you in the morning, Parker. You too," he added to Tessa, giving her a pointed look of his own and Parker wondered what exactly was going on between his wife and his best friend.

Once they were alone Tessa lay a hesitant hand on top of his, "I'm really sorry, Parker, I'm sorry you got mixed up in all of this."

"It's not your fault," he replied automatically.

"Of course it is," she told him withdrawing her hand. "You would never have even met Dino if it wasn't for me."

His sluggish mind taking it's time to process what she'd said, "wait, what? Dino? What are you talking about?"

"I'm talking about Dino shooting you."

"Dino drowned in the lake, I saw him fall in," he stuttered.

Shaking her head sadly, "no, he was faking, he just waited until we got ashore then he shot you."

"It wasn't John Doe who shot me?" he asked, sure that the mysterious man had in fact been there.

"No, it was Dino. But you don't have to worry about him

anymore, he's dead now," the glint in her turquoise eyes conveyed she was more than a little joyful about this.

"He was there though wasn't he?" Parker pressed while he still had enough energy to do so.

"Who?" she asked innocently.

Frowning at her, "no games, Tessa. John Doe was there wasn't he?" Her refusal to meet his gaze directly was his answer. "And you let him get away."

She neither confirmed nor denied his accusation.

"You lied to me, Tessa, you told me you'd wait for me but when I got there you were gone, you went after him on your own. When are you going to learn to trust me? I understand that you have this desire to protect people because you think you failed Eleanor. I get that you can't deal with endangering other people even if it's at the expense of your own safety. But we're not talking about some stranger, Tessa, we're talking about me, your husband, when are you going to trust me?"

Eyes suddenly blazing to life, "you want me to trust you, Parker but I told you about Jake and Ellie and then it's like you got the answers you wanted and you just disappeared. Where were you?"

"I was trying to help you by finding Dino Rollino," he reminded her.

"Yeah you were anywhere but actually with me," her voice had dropped to a whisper. "That really helps me."

"I had to *do* something, Tess, you know that I can't just sit back and do nothing." Wondering where this was coming from, Tessa usually pushed him away, but now she was upset that he hadn't been there to comfort her. Remembering guiltily that Wyatt had warned him that all Tessa needed was his presence.

"I wasn't asking you to do nothing," she countered, "but pressuring me to go back to that house . . ."

"I never pressured you, I never even told you where I was going," he reminded her.

Continuing as if he hadn't spoken, "then running off to look for those girls, and hanging around the station rather than coming home. You were avoiding me."

Reaching for her hand, "I'm sorry that you feel that way, honey, but I . . ." trailing off, Parker had been about to say he hadn't been avoiding her on purpose but that wasn't entirely true. "We just need a fresh start," he told her confidently. "When I get out of here we'll move back to our house. We'll try for another baby if you want, I'll take time off from work, we'll travel, whatever you want."

"I'm not going back to that house," she told him solemnly. "The house where Lachlan tried to send me insane. I can't."

"And I can't stay in the house where your mother and Dino tried to kill you," he told her just as solemnly. He had had enough of living in that haunted mansion and he knew Tessa hated the house even more than he did. She was just afraid to move back to their home because she would have to confront her issues of trust, which had taken a battering with the whole Lachlan Mountain drama.

"Then where does that leave us?" Tessa's carefully empty and unrevealing mask was back, the one she had sported when they first met.

Staring at her small, thin hand still resting in his, Parker answered as honestly as he could, "I don't know."

# EPILOGUE

With a bored sigh, she rose with the moonlight, as had been her custom for many years. Each night she dressed and headed out into the night to visit her clients to earn enough money to buy enough drugs to make her life barely bearable.

She had long ago lost track of how long she had lived like this. Once upon a time, very long ago, she had had a real home, a real family, real opportunities. That had all changed when she was eight. Ripped away from her life, she spent the next eight years locked in a tiny apartment in the middle of a bustling city. Never feeling the fresh feel of the sun or the rain or the wind against her skin and never speaking a word to anyone but her captor. It was here that she had learned her trade.

Kicked out at the age of sixteen, half her life spent in those two rooms, with no money and no skills she turned to the only thing she knew how to do. At first it hadn't been so bad, she'd had a few friends, one of whom introduced her to her first high, and ever since she had been hooked. After a while she found her own place, even tried working at a real job for a while, but it hadn't lasted long and she was back to the place where she felt the safest.

For a long time she had dreamed of rescue. Of her knight in shining armor who would come riding in on a white horse to save her, just as the prince's had always saved their princesses in the fairytales she had loved as a little girl. Over time the image of her savior changed, but still he remained fixed firmly in her mind, often entering her dreams at night to take her to a castle and lavish her with extraordinary gifts and wonders. Eventually though, as was the problem with dreams, she began to awake, figuratively as well as physically, and she knew that salvation would never come from anyone but herself.

Now she wanted these dreams to become a reality. She wanted a nice house, and clothes, an expensive car, and most of all someone to love her. She'd been told she was quite pretty, at least when she wasn't doped up on drugs, she could be quite the little actress when the occasion called for it, and she'd certainly learnt how to survive anything. All she needed to do was figure out a plan to use her attributes to her advantage.

Rebecca Worthington stepped out into the starry night. She took a moment to tilt her face to the moon and drink in the feel of air, and then determinedly she set about her business, her decision firmly made.

Jane has loved reading and writing since she can remember. She writes dark and disturbing crime/mystery/suspense with some romance thrown in because, well, who doesn't love romance?! She has several series including the complete Detective Parker Bell series, the Count to Ten series, the Christmas Mysteries series, and the Flashes of Fate series of novelettes.

When she's not writing Jane loves to read, bake, go to the beach, ski, horse ride, and watch Disney movies. She has a black belt in Taekwondo, a 200+ collection of teddy bears, and her favorite color is pink. She has the world's two most sweet and pretty Dalmatians, Ivory and Pearl. Oh, and she also enjoys spending time with family and friends!

For more information please visit any of the following –

Amazon – http://www.amazon.com/author/janeblythe
BookBub – https://www.bookbub.com/authors/jane-blythe
Email – mailto:janeblytheauthor@gmail.com
Facebook – http://www.facebook.com/janeblytheauthor
Goodreads – http://www.goodreads.com/author/show/6574160.Jane_Blythe
Reader Group – http://www.facebook.com/groups/janeskillersweethearts
Twitter – http://www.twitter.com/jblytheauthor
Website – http://www.janeblythe.com.au

*sic enim dilexit Deus mundum ut Filium suum unigenitum daret ut omnis qui credit in eum habeat vitam aeternam*

www.ingramcontent.com/pod-product-compliance
Lightning Source LLC
Chambersburg PA
CBHW070837250626
47159CB00003B/820